A Requiem for the Forsaken

The Kelk Conflict: Implosion

Book 4 of *The Blacksword Regiment*

by

J. L. Doty

TELEMACHUS PRESS

This book or eBook is a work of fiction. Names, characters, places and incidents are either the product of the author's imagination or are used fictitiously. Any resemblance to actual persons, living or dead, or to actual events or locales is entirely coincidental.

A Requiem for the Forsaken, **Book 4 of** ***The Blacksword Regiment***
This book or eBook is licensed for your personal enjoyment only. This book or eBook may not be re-sold or given away to other people. If you're reading this book or eBook and did not purchase it, or it was not purchased for your use only, then you should return it and purchase your own copy. Thank you for respecting the hard work of the author.

The publisher does not have any control over and does not assume any responsibility for author or third-party websites or their content.

Cover designed by J. L. Doty.

Published by Telemachus Press, LLC
http://www.telemachuspress.com

Visit the author's website:
http://www.jldoty.com

ISBN: 978–1–951744–28–1 (eBook)
ISBN: 978–1–951744–18–2 (paperback)
ISBN: 978–1–953757–22–7 (hardback)

Version 2022.12.04

KEpuz!po!KJNEFTLUPQ:
Formatted using eTools for Writers 3.8.8, Dec 4 2022, 09:55:50
Copyright © 2013-2016 by J. L. Doty

Printed in the United States of America

10 9 8 7 6 5 4 3 2 1

A Requiem for the Forsaken

The Kelk Conflict: Implosion

Book 4 of *The Blacksword Regiment*

*Forsaken, damned and dying,
a bad day all around.*

Prologue:

Innocence Shattered

A FRANTIC KNOCK on the door to the apartment drew Mathius's attention away from his homework. Six months ago when the unrest had begun, the Novalis government had tried to keep schools open and busses running. But as the conflict progressed to a shooting war, they relented and closed almost everything. His mother, like many others, had tried to continue his education at home. But at that moment she was out shopping for groceries and he had the apartment to himself for a few hours. He did hope she came home with something decent for dinner. Of late, the selection on the store shelves had been somewhat limited.

The rapid knocking continued, pulling Mathius out of his thoughts of food.

Mathius slid his chair back from the table in their small kitchen and stood. Anything was better than homework, and he hoped that whoever waited in the hall outside their apartment might provide a break from the tedium of his lessons. He left his school reader on the table, and crossed to the apartment door.

On more advanced planets, important people with implants knew instantly who stood out in the hallway, but all their apartment had was the little lensed peephole in the middle of the door. He stood on the tips of his toes and stretched to get his eye level with it. Paulo, his schoolmate and neighbor, stood there pounding on the door. Without hesitation Mathius unlatched the door and swung it open.

When Paulo saw Mathius his eyes widened. "They've captured one of the rebel leaders."

"Really?" Mathius asked. "What's he look like?"

Mathius expected to hear a description of a hardened man with narrow, piercing eyes that constantly darted about with distrust, the way the rebels appeared in the government vid coverage.

Paulo shook his head. "I don't know. I haven't seen him."

That answer disappointed Mathius considerably. "He's not on the vids?"

"Not yet," Paulo said, showing none of the disappointment Mathius felt. "They're holding a public trial in the stadium, and they've invited everyone to attend."

Paulo's eyes widened even farther as he gripped Mathius's shoulders and shook him. "Let's go and see for ourselves."

Mathius's pulse quickened and he desperately wanted to join Paulo on such an adventure, but he looked over his shoulder at the homework spread out on the kitchen table. "But . . . I have homework."

Paulo shook him again, forcing Mathius to look him in the eyes. "We'll only be gone for an hour. You'll have plenty of time to finish your homework."

"I . . ." Mathius glanced once more over his shoulder at his homework, then looked again at Paulo. "Let's go."

After the unrest had begun, the reliability of public transportation had declined steadily, and the two boys had grown accustomed to walking almost everywhere they went. It didn't take long to cross the four kilometers to the stadium, but to their disappointment, a large crowd had queued up at the main entrance. Mathius looked at Paulo, their eyes met, and he saw in the other boy's face that they had the same thought.

Paulo grinned. "The bent gate!"

The outer periphery of the stadium consisted of tall, concrete pillars, each about a meter in diameter and spaced twenty paces apart. Between the pillars a wrought-iron fence prevented unauthorized entry, though the occasional gate in the fence allowed backdoor access to the bowels of the facility for contractors, vendors, employees, and athletes. The gates were kept locked, and opened only when needed. But about a third of the way around the stadium one of the gates had been bent out of shape, probably by collision with a service vehicle of some sort. When closed and locked, the gate's distorted shape produced a thin gap through which two small boys could just barely scrape.

Mathius went first, and that day he found it almost too tight to get through. He realized that, as he continued to grow, that means of entry would soon be barred to him.

Once clear of the gap in the gate, he turned to help Paulo through, and the other boy had even more difficulty, but he made it with only a scrape or two.

"Well now, what do we have here?"

At the sound of the adult male voice, both boys turned and froze. A uniformed security guard stood over them, his hands on his hips, shaking his head sadly. He grinned. "Entrance is free today. Why bother to sneak in?"

Paulo said, "The crowd at the main entrance was too big."

Mathius added, "We didn't think we'd get in."

"Come with me," the guard said. "I'll find you a couple of seats."

Relieved that they weren't going to be booted out, Mathius and Paulo followed the guard as he led them into the stadium. But having entered through one of the back gates, they first needed to cross through a service area deep beneath the massive structure. It was crowded with people who seemed important.

A man in a government uniform stopped them. "What's this?"

A women standing a few feet away with her back to them turned around and took notice. She wore a skirt and jacket that seemed a lot more expensive than the simple garments Mathius's mother could afford.

The guard shrugged. "Caught a couple of kids sneaking in."

The fellow in uniform looked them over. "What are you going to do with them?"

The guard scratched his chin. "It's free today anyway, so I thought I'd find them a couple of seats and get 'em settled."

The government man shrugged it off. "Do what you want." He turned away, dismissing them without further thought.

The woman stepped forward and said, "No, wait."

The uniformed fellow looked at her and frowned.

"We can use them," she said. "All we've got right now is adults. A couple of young kids, that'll be perfect. It'll round it out, look much better in the vids."

The man and the woman lowered their voices and spoke quietly for several seconds. Then the woman took charge of Mathius and Paulo, and to their incredible surprise did not lead them to seats in the stands, but out onto the field. Many times the two boys had watched athletes compete there, and never had they thought they might actually walk upon the hallowed ground of the sports field. The three of them joined a crowd of about two dozen men and women all standing in a group near a long table with empty chairs.

Paulo leaned close to Mathius and hissed, "Wow!"

Nearby Mathius noticed a large, wooden bin filled with rocks and bricks.

At that point the stadium appeared to be almost full. The rumble of thousands of people talking excitedly filled the air with a noisy buzz. But after a half hour of just standing there and waiting, the two boys grew bored. Then, without warning, the crowd went silent and a hush descended over the stadium. Mathius and Paulo were too short to see over the heads and shoulders of the adults standing about them, but that woman in the expensive clothing intervened.

"I want the two boys front and forward," she said, taking them both by the arm and marching them to the front of the group. "It'll make better coverage."

In front of them nine men now sat at the long table, all wearing judge's robes. Their attention was focused on five men marching across the field toward them: four armed government soldiers surrounding a man wearing a uniform nothing like those of his escort. His hands were cuffed in front of him, and manacles on his ankles forced him to take short, choppy steps. To Mathius he looked ordinary, nothing like the hardened, dangerous individuals he'd seen in the government vids. They stopped in front of the table and the nine judges.

The woman who seemed to be in charge of their small group said, "Come on, people. Liven it up a little. Let's hear some noise."

One of the men in their group shouted a crude epithet, and several of them booed. The massive crowd of onlookers seated in the stadium took up the cry, and their jeers turned into a deafening roar. The woman gave both Mathius and Paulo a nudge. "That man is the reason the schools are closed and busses aren't running on time."

"Yah," one of the men standing next to them said. "Because of him and his friends we only had one meal yesterday."

Paulo yelled and booed. Mathius thought of dinner the previous night, just some vegetables and tubers. And when his mother had left that morning to get groceries, she had voiced her fear that there might be little to choose from on the shelves that day.

The woman in charge nudged Mathius again, and he shouted with the rest of them.

The judge sitting in the center of the table stood up and spoke, his voice echoing from the stadium speakers, and easily heard above the roar of the spectators. "The Supreme High Tribunal of Novalis III has found this man guilty of sedition, treason, and murder. We are here today to see justice done."

Two of the guards took the rebel leader by his elbows and hustled him toward the group in which Paulo and Mathius stood. The small crowd parted and spread out, forming a ring of people around an open space, into which the guards dumped the rebel on his hands and knees. As the guards backed away from him, someone threw a rock. It glanced off the man's shoulder and he cried out.

"Hold off," the woman in charge shouted. "Not yet."

The people on the field with Paulo and Mathius gave her angry looks, but nevertheless obeyed, while those in the stands shouted and screamed, a deafening roar that made it impossible to think. The woman handed Mathius a rock about the size of a man's fist and said, "You boys first."

Mathius stared at her, and must have looked rather dumb and stupid at that moment. She asked, "Have you missed any meals lately?"

Paulo shouted, "Yes."

Mathius's heart raced as he said, "Some."

She nodded slowly and carefully. "Have you lost any friends?"

Two of Mathius's classmates had been killed by a stray rocket, and he had cried at their funeral.

Paulo shouted even louder, "Yes," and Mathius's heart raced.

The woman pointed at the rebel. "That man there is responsible for all of this, and he must be punished."

She looked carefully at the rock in Mathius's hand, the rock she had given him earlier.

Paulo understood, shouted again and threw his rock. It struck the man in the back and he cried out. Mathius turned and threw his rock. His aim was better, and it smashed into the man's face, opening a nasty gash. Bright red blood streamed down the rebel leader's cheek and he looked sadly at Mathius. Their eyes met, and there was no hatred in the look he gave Mathius, only pity, and resignation.

The sight of blood inflamed the crowd around Mathius, and they all threw rocks and stones taken from the wooden bin. Mathius watched as the rebel collapsed under a hail of projectiles. Then one of the men next to Paulo ran forward, carrying a large brick. He reached the rebel and smashed the brick into his head. Mathius heard a strange crunch at the impact, and the man collapsed, his eyes rolling about and clearly not focusing on anything. The side of his head seemed misshapen, and what Mathius saw there forced his breakfast to boil up into his throat. He dropped to his hands and knees and spewed the contents of his stomach on the ground.

He didn't move from that position for the longest time as he gagged and choked. The crowd around him screamed and shouted, the people in the stadium seats roared and hollered. On his hands and knees, his eyes closed, trying to ignore the sounds around him, Mathius heard a man say, "Shame the kid puked."

The woman in charge of them said, "Don't worry. We can edit that part out."

••••

John had never before told anyone that story, and when he finished Primatov put a hand on his shoulder. "Don't beat yourself up, John. How old were you, thirteen, fourteen?"

John shrugged. "Yah, something like that. My father saw me on the vids, had a long talk with me, told me that the information on the vids is always shaded by those broadcasting it, that maybe not all of the rebels are as evil as the government makes them out to be."

"Your father was a wise man, John."

The *rebel leader* they had killed that day had apparently been quite high up in their chain of command. With his demise, the rebels had splintered into two factions, and then a short time later one of those had split again. The situation on Novalis III went steadily downhill from there. And while the rebels may have started with honest and sincere intent, they ended up led by men like Cranoch and Mercier.

1

Suspicion

THAT FIRST DAY on Viktorkinde, as John stepped out of the assault boat, intensely bright sunlight forced him to pause and allow his eyes to adjust. The star that illuminated Viktorkinde's sky pumped out a lot of ultraviolet. A blue-white giant, with over two standard solar masses, its spectrum peaked in the UV. Had John come to Viktorkinde a few hundred years earlier, he would have had to shield his skin from its harmful effects. But for several centuries now the Supremacy had made a concerted effort to enhance the ozone layer in the planet's stratosphere, which considerably reduced the UV hazard for common-faces. As it was, John still needed to be careful.

About a hundred meters of carefully manicured lawn separated their landing zone from the Hyvaldsborg Palace. John had expected the structure to loom over them like some monument to Kelk sovereignty, but with the exception of a few towers here and there, it never exceeded more than five stories. It had been constructed more than fifteen hundred years ago, long before plast, transition ships, and modern materials. Its architects had been limited to the materials and techniques available then. Where they couldn't go high, they had gone wide, and the building covered several acres.

As shuttles and assault boats from the diplomatic mission descended toward the lawn, a Kelk male in a business suit approached John. He stood about shoulder high to John with a wire thin build. He had much more pepper than salt in his hair, wore it tied back in a simple, unflattering ponytail, and his cheekbones prominently emphasized the sharp and somewhat unpleasant features of his face. The unfriendly scowl he gave John only added to the harshness of his appearance. "You are John Mathius?" He spoke excellent Lingua with only a hint of accent.

John spoke in Kelk. "Yes, I am. And we can speak Kelk, if you wish."

One of the fellow's eyebrows lifted and his scowl deepened. His upper lip curled with distaste as he continued to speak Lingua in clipped tones. "I wish not."

Only a few seconds ago, just before stepping out of the assault boat, Primatov had admonished John, "Please try not to kill anyone today." It was a private little joke they shared between them, but at that moment, looking at the fellow standing in front of him, John felt like strangling the officious little shit. To one side Kolbeck rolled his eyes, while Matsen shook his head sadly, and Nikaela's brows furrowed with anger.

John decided the little asshole could go fuck himself, so he stayed with Kelk. "And you are?"

The fellow puffed his chest out. "I am Maestra Bekmaan, chief administrative assistant to the Larscom Executive Council."

Standing behind John, Primatov opened a secure link between their implants. *Be careful, John. Kristdokar briefed me on him. He has no real power of his own, but he can influence the thinking of those who wield a fair amount of authority.*

Bekmaan turned his attention to Nikaela and spoke in Kelk. "And you are Mistress Vreekande, are you not?"

From the look on her face, John thought she might strangle the little shit for him. She spoke Lingua. "I am."

Bekmaan didn't like that at all, and John wondered if that would be the tenor of their relationship: the little asshole speaking Kelk to Nikaela while she responded in Lingua, and he speaking Lingua to John while he responded in Kelk. It would make for an interesting day.

Speaking to Nikaela, the fellow pointed to the descending boats and shuttles. "You are to join Brigadier Skalde Kristdokar, and you will sit with your . . . comrades . . . during the ceremonies today."

He had hesitated for a brief instant, as if Nikaela could no longer claim any Kelk as comrades. The insult had been clear and unquestionable, and her eyes flashed with anger. She said nothing, turned, and marched toward the descending boats. That took Stinar by surprise, and she and several Kelk bodyguards hurried to keep up as they followed.

Bekmaan turned his attention back to John and looked at him with lifeless eyes. "As breschkada-sa, people will be watching you closely." In the little shit's mind, the word *people* clearly did not include common-faces. "I'm here to ensure you comport yourself properly." John concluded that, tall or short, fat or thin, officious little shits were the same everywhere.

"Come with me," Bekmaan said. He spun on his heel, and without waiting for John, he marched across the lawn toward the palace. John looked to Primatov for guidance, but she merely shrugged. "I have to join Skalde Kristdokar for the ceremony. I don't think you have anything to worry about with him."

Leeze said, "Fucking right, he don't."

Primatov gave her an unhappy look and Leeze bit her lower lip.

John glanced at Carla, shrugged, and followed Bekmaan. She, May, Matsen, Kolbeck and the rest of his friends stepped into formation behind him, and they too followed.

Bekmaan didn't look back, and had John not followed, the fellow might have marched all the way across the lawn without realizing he was a one-man parade. When he reached the palace, he stopped at the base of some stone steps that led up to an entrance, and turned about. John stopped, and his friends bunched up behind him. Bekmaan's eyes widened as he took in the group following John, and he demanded of May, "Who are you? What are you doing?"

May grinned and gave him a malicious look. "We're here to make sure you don't try to assassinate him."

Carla took a step forward to stand beside John.

Bekmaan spluttered. "Assassinate him!" His eyes glanced for the briefest instant toward the butcher's dagger in the forearm sheath in John's coat. It was the first time any Kelk had lost composure enough to acknowledge the existence of the blade, even if unintentionally and only for a heartbeat.

John reached over and touched the bone handle of the butcher's dagger. He stroked it and gave the little shithead a nasty smile.

Behind John, Kolbeck spoke in Kelk. "Yah, we would all be real upset if you tried that."

"But," Bekmaan said, "I'm not . . . you can't—"

Matsen interrupted him. "He doesn't go anywhere without us."

Carla nodded. "Him and us together, or nobody at all."

Bekmaan frantically shook his head. "But you can't all attend the welcome ceremony. That's only for important people, for dignitaries." He hesitated, then nodded toward John. "And for him too."

John looked over his shoulder at May and Matsen.

May shrugged. "I guess you're not a dignitary."

Matsen cocked his head to one side. "We don't attend, he don't attend."

Before the diplomatic mission had departed Trafalgar, Thealone had taken Professor Dirkson into protective custody, and assigned him to Manifort Gascoigne's retinue. He had been included to advise on Kelk culture and customs, and on the journey he passed the time by offering classes in spoken Kelk, which had been lightly attended. May had been one of the few exceptions, and during their thirty-three day journey from Trafalgar to Viktorkinde, had attended the lessons religiously and crammed hard. She gave Bekmaan an unpleasant look and spoke with a heavy accent. "What he Kelk man said." The look on her face helped get her meaning across.

Bekmaan waved his hands frantically. "But . . . but . . . but . . ."

Kolbeck grinned. "Fuck the ceremony. Let's all go get a beer. That'll be a lot better than trying to stay awake listening to a bunch of shit-of-bull speeches."

Nikaela must have taught him the *shit-of-bull* expression, because John certainly hadn't.

Kolbeck turned serious and looked John in the eyes. "Trust me, Blacksword, you'll like Kelk beer. It's got a lot more kick than that swill your Commonwealth buddies make."

Bekmaan spluttered and grew indignant, but May and Matsen stood their ground. They argued for several minutes, and eventually compromised. May, as the ranking officer, and Carla and Matsen, as the ranking non-coms, would stand at the back of room during the ceremony. The rest of the squad would wait just outside, in constant contact with them via their implants. They would stand ready to make a hard-target assault on the ceremony, guns-a-blazing, if the need arose.

Bekmaan led them to a large auditorium in the palace, and John sat with the Commonwealth dignitaries in a group on one side of the stage. The Kelk Executive Council, plus several high-ranking members of the Larscom General Secretariat, sat with Nikaela in a group on the other side of the stage. The audience seats were filled by the Larscom General Secretariat, and other dignitaries from the Commonwealth and the Supremacy, as well as advisors, minor aids, and news hypes from both sides. John spotted Karya Chemina seated alone. Their eyes met and she gave him a pleasant smile. Not far from her, Primatov sat with Kristdokar, Brynjar, Thordahl and Taugrim. That morning Taugrim had chosen to color her short-cropped, spiky hair coal-black, with streaks of silver. She caught him looking at her, gave him a lascivious grin, ran her tongue across her lips in a provocative way, and winked.

During the ceremony John had no responsibilities other than to sit there, appear unthreatening, and stay awake. His implants helped with that last bit, and while the politicians gave their speeches, he let his mind wander. He recalled how, a few days before landing on Viktorkinde, he told Primatov how he had helped kill the rebel leader during that incident on Novalis III. It occurred to him that back on Miriteen, when they had interrogated him under deep neural probe, they didn't uncover that murder, and that highlighted one of the limits of that technology. One still had to know the right questions to ask to bring the right thoughts to the forefront of the witness's mind.

John also spotted Macus DeLeon in the audience, and he didn't let that ruin his day.

••••

Captain Evaline Miershall had proven herself to be one of Katrine's best assets. The Commonwealth had a standing policy that a yearly quota of foreign nationals could gain the right to citizenship if they fulfilled certain requirements: no criminal record, a basic security check, and five years of unblemished service in any of several government branches. For a young person without advanced training, skillsets, or degrees, enlisting in ComSecCorps was one of the best paths to citizenship. A native of Sarkovie, Miershall had joined the Corps at an early age, and as a young major Katrine had recruited the girl to the Blacksword.

After the welcoming ceremony, the Commonwealth visitors had spent a couple of hours moving into their new quarters in the Hyvaldsborg Palace. While Katrine unpacked in the small bedroom they had assigned to her, her implants came to life. "Colonel, we've just received an urgent message for you from Sarkovie. I've uploaded it to your desk."

Messages like that came in with an unencrypted header that identified only the intended recipient, allowing their Kelk hosts to pass it on to the proper party. Thealone's staff then decrypted a secondary header that might contain additional information, like a flag for urgency, or the sender's identity, or, as in this case, just the sender's location. Only certain individuals could decode the message further and learn more, which provided the necessary anonymity for covert assets. And if the sender and receiver had agreed on a unique, personal encryption key, no one beyond the two of them could decrypt it. Since the message came from Sarkovie, it must have come from Miershall, or one of her subordinates.

With Vagle on her heels, Katrine rushed to her cramped, temporary office. It was larger than a closet, but only just. She left Vagle outside the door as she sat down at her small desk and pulled up the message. After running it through the usual precautionary checks, she uploaded the decrypted message to her implants, and Miershall appeared as if seated across from her at a conference table.

"Colonel," she said, "I wish I could have gotten this to you sooner, but I had to wait for the courier ship to make its next stop here at Sarkovie. I did divert it immediately to the relay chain, which will screw up its normal schedule, but I think this is important."

Miershall had the uncanny ability to look and sound like a flighty young girl in her late teens. But in a heartbeat she might switch to a mature young woman in her mid-thirties. She grimaced as she said, "Anders Eindride has disappeared. As you know, I worked undercover at the same facility as him, and six days ago he simply didn't show up for work. I asked Hohlman what happened to him, using the excuse that Eindride made regular use of my private professional services, and he said Eindride got a better offer from another company. A couple of other employees, whom I suspect of being part of their covert team, told me they heard he'd been sent back to Viktorkinde. They must not have realized their stories didn't match up with Hohlman's."

Miershall paused and brushed a lock of glistening, black hair out of her eyes. "Eindride and I had established a close working relationship, and I'm confident he would have contacted me before leaving, if he could."

Miershall was a Sarkovite through and through; *close working relationship* meant she was probably bedding the fellow. If so, Katrine assumed they had operated on a standard Sarkovian client-server relationship.

Miershall continued. "I must conclude that he left rather hurriedly. Whether that means they killed him and buried him somewhere out in the brush, or hustled him off-planet in a hurry, I have no way of knowing. I don't think he decided to disappear on his own, because I'm confident he would have contacted me in some way to let me know. I think it's safe to assume he's either dead, or on his way back to Viktorkinde, though I did check his apartment and it appears he packed some belongings before leaving, so we can hope it's the latter. And I don't think it's a coincidence that an independent freighter christened *Far Solar Wind* up-transited out of the system shortly after he disappeared. They filed a transition plan with an intermediate stop at a remote Supremacy outpost, and they'll arrive at Viktorkinde about a tenday after you get this message. As a personal matter, I would like to know if he does show up alive, but there's no sign of him here."

Katrine hoped the young woman hadn't gotten too attached to Eindride. But if she had, she would just have to learn from it.

Miershall sat up a little straighter. "On a separate note, we finished interrogating *Caliban*'s crew. There were a couple of men in charge who were downright unpleasant. Their organization is fairly well compartmentalized, so we didn't get much out of them. We learned the names of a few of their contacts on Trafalgar and how they arranged Mr. Mathius's abduction. I've included details on those contacts, but I can't guarantee they won't have gone underground by the time you're able to act upon this information. I've also included details on how badly they mistreated Mr. Mathius on *Caliban*."

She hesitated a moment, a finger toying with a lock of hair. "I know it's not much, but it's all I've got. I'll continue working at Lorenson's company, and if Eindride resurfaces or I learn anything of value, I'll let you know as soon as possible."

Katrine reviewed the additional data Miershall had provided, with pictures of the two men John Mathius had referred to as *calm-voice* and *pissed-off-guy*. She prepared and transmitted a message to a subordinate on Trafalgar. With the relay chain now covering the entire distance between Viktorkinde and Trafalgar, he would receive it within a few hours, and he would act quickly on the names they had acquired from the two assholes. Katrine doubted that information would be of much help.

Miershall had also acquired the names of calm-voice's and pissed-off-guy's Kelk contacts. She would pass that information on to Kristdokar and Brynjar, along with the news that Eindride had disappeared. And she would need to review the whole thing with Thealone.

Katrine trusted Miershall's judgement, and accepted her conclusion that Eindride had not chosen to disappear on his own. So what had they done to him? And why now?

The courier ship had orders to sit tight and wait for any reply from Katrine before resuming its normal rounds of the systems in the neighborhood of Sarkovie. A few years ago Miershall had told Katrine that there were quite a number of Sarkovites running commercial operations independently on Viktorkinde, none of whom were accessible to the local Blacksword head of station, a Norandynian. Miershall had hinted most ran enterprises that skirted the bounds of legal business practices, which probably meant they were smugglers. At the time the young woman suggested that if it ever became necessary, she could tap some of them for information or assistance, but she would have to be physically present on Viktorkinde to do so.

Katrine hastily prepared a reply. She closed her eyes and focused on the virtual image of the young woman seated across the conference table from her. "You once told me you could tap into certain Sarkovite assets on Viktorkinde not normally accessible to the Blacksword. If that's still the case, then drop everything and put your second-in-command in charge of Sarkovie Station. I'm putting this courier ship at your disposal. Get on it, and get here as soon as possible. I assume you can arrange for your own cover. If not, as you get closer to Viktorkinde you can tap into the relay chain. Send me a message and I'll arrange something."

Katrine paused, trying to think of anything she might have missed. "Oh yes, one more thing. There was a female medical doctor on board *Caliban*. She was not there by choice, and she did what she could to help John Mathius. If she's still alive, treat her well, and do what you can to get her back to Trafalgar."

She coded the message, encrypted it, and sent it on its way. She'd have to make arrangements for another courier ship to replace the one she had just commandeered. They would need something making the rounds of the systems around Norandyne and Sarkovie, but at this point, all the action was probably going to happen on Viktorkinde.

Katrine had an uneasy feeling in her gut, and it bothered her that she didn't have anything concrete upon which to act.

2

Followed

AS THE GRAV boat descended toward Capital Airport, Nikaela scanned the other occupants seated in the passenger cabin. She didn't recognize any of them, but her implants identified three as prominent members of the Larscom General Secretariat, two more as high-ranking military officers, and four as aides that accompanied them. Thankfully, Nikaela's face had appeared in the vids only sparingly, so no one recognized her, and none of them paid her the least bit of attention.

Nikaela had never been to Emkeldstadt, and her recollection now of the previous day's events was a blur of ceremonies and tedious, shit-of-bull speeches. Thankfully, the powers-that-be hadn't paraded the two breschkada about like a couple of exotic pets from some far distant planet. It became clear that the politicians, both Supremacy and Commonwealth, were more intent on seeing their own faces splashed across the vids. Nikaela had been content to stand in the background, just another uniform behind all the personages of notoriety. And John had seemed rather subdued. He clearly had not enjoyed himself, though just as clearly his spirits had been buoyed by the presence of his old friends.

For upcoming events Nikaela needed the full gamut of uniforms: full dress, service dress, service casual, fatigues, the works. She also needed some personal items, all of which could be had in short order with a quick trip back to her apartment in Hyerdride. When she made the request to return there, she and her shadow bodyguard, Kyrsten Stinar, had been assigned seats on a special shuttle that departed from a nondescript Capital Guard hangar behind Hyvaldsborg. It serviced dignitaries needing secure transport between the old palace and the airport.

Stinar raised an eyebrow and said, "So now you're a dignitary, huh?"

Nikaela shrugged. "I don't feel like one."

In the domestic terminal at Capital Airport they had some time to kill before their flight. They sat down at a counter that served quick meals, and while they ate a light lunch, they watched people rushing past trying to get to their flights.

Nikaela noticed a woman with chin-length hair walking by. She wore tan pants and a matching jacket, an attractive outfit Nikaela might enjoy owning, if she could afford it. And the woman seemed familiar, though Nikaela didn't know her, couldn't recall having ever met her, but perhaps she had somewhere, sometime. If so, it had been one of those brief encounters with someone she would never meet again, so she hadn't devoted too many neurons to storing the interaction for later recall. She put the woman out of her mind.

She and Stinar finished their meal and headed for the gate. As they waited to begin boarding, a handsome young fellow kept glancing Nikaela's way, eyeing her carefully. It always lifted her spirits a little when she caught the eye of a good-looking man. Thankfully, when she took notice of him he looked away, wasn't rude enough to stare, or to approach her and try some over-used pickup line.

The flight to Hyerdride took three hours. While waiting for their luggage Nikaela noticed that woman again, though she had changed out of the tan pants and matching jacket, opting instead for a gray skirt and white blouse. Nikaela was almost certain the young lady had not been on the flight with her and Stinar, so how had she gotten from Emkeldstadt to Hyerdride? And why change outfits? She probably needed to attend a meeting that required more formal attire. Or perhaps it wasn't the same woman, just someone with similar features, though she could almost be an identical twin to the woman Nikaela had spotted in Capital Airport. Or more likely, Nikaela's fleeting glimpse of her had not been sufficient to instill an accurate recall of her features. Nikaela decided she was being paranoid.

They took a hired car from the airport to Nikaela's apartment building. As Stinar paid the AI, Nikaela stepped out of the car and glanced about. Not far up the street a young man waited at a transit stop. The distance was a little too far to be certain, but he might be the same fellow who had eyed her while they waited to board their flight in Capital Airport. Nikaela's paranoia kicked in big time.

She turned slowly about and looked down the street. She spotted a young woman stepping out of another hired car about a hundred paces behind them. She had chin-length hair and wore an overcoat that covered the rest of her attire. Again, the distance was too great, but it might be the same woman.

As Stinar stepped out of the car, Nikaela leaned close to her and whispered, "I think we're being followed."

Stinar smiled and nodded toward the front of her building. "Don't say anything more until we're inside."

Inside the lobby, Stinar closed the door and turned to Nikaela. "You spotted them too, eh? How many?"

"Two, a man and a woman." As she and Stinar crossed the lobby to the lift, Nikaela described the two people

Stinar nodded. "Good for you, but you missed two."

Nikaela used her implants to call the lift. "I missed two?"

Stinar grinned. "The two you spotted are working with another man. I checked on them. They're working for Kristdokar, and they're supposed to track you inconspicuously, and step in to protect you if need be."

The lift doors opened and they stepped into it. "You said I missed two. What about the fourth?"

Stinar frowned unhappily. "A woman. I'm not getting an ID hit on her, so they're dispatching a team to scoop her up. They'll find out why she's following us."

When the lift reached Nikaela's floor the doors opened. Stinar looked at Nikaela and grinned unpleasantly as she stepped out. "The man and woman you described; they're going to be reprimanded."

As Nikaela followed her, she didn't try to hide her confusion. "Why?"

Stinar shrugged. "Because you spotted them. And all three are going to get a reprimand because they didn't spot the unidentified woman."

Her apartment showed no signs of the assault that had nearly killed her: no broken windows, no splintered doorway, no shattered glass, no bullet holes in the walls. When she stepped into her bedroom her presence triggered a message from Thordahl. "Fire and smoke damage to some of your wardrobe, probably from flashbangs. We left it there so you could go through it. Brigadier Kristdokar said to fill out a voucher for anything that needs repair or replacement."

A pile of damaged clothing and garments lay stacked in the middle of her bed. Nikaela sat down on the edge of the bed to inventory the damage. One of the new pants suits she had purchased lay on top of the pile. It was one of her favorites and it had been badly torn, with a few burn marks. As she worked her way down through the pile she realized that quite a lot of her clothing had been damaged. At the bottom of the pile she found the slinky blue dress she had purchased thinking of John Mathius. Burned, scorched and torn, it was almost unrecognizable. She couldn't vouch that. She would have to explain such an extravagant expense, and that would be embarrassing.

••••

Strikland had been assigned a suite of rooms in the Hyvaldsborg Palace. Thealone, Palmutter, Gascoigne, Catarvin, and Obradour, the five members of the diplomatic mission, had also been assigned suites, but Macus thought it telling that Strikland was the only staffer granted such luxury. And he didn't think Palmutter had gone out of his way to make that happen. With the senator's growing instability, his lack of discretion, and Faith's brilliant strategy of telling Strikland that Palmutter had asked her to seduce and spy on him, Palmutter's relationship with Strikland had been somewhat strained of late. No, Strikland had his own contacts among the Kelk, and quite possibly they were better than Palmutter's.

The suites were equipped as a combination residence and working office facility. They could house a couple of dignitaries in considerable comfort, along with a dozen or so staffers. There were a few larger offices for the dignitaries, and some smaller offices for the more senior staffers. As Macus approached Strikland's suite the door was open, with one of his security people standing outside, a young woman in a somewhat sterile business suit. She nodded at Macus, a neutral look on her face. Macus stepped past her and through the doorway into a reception area that contained a small desk, behind which sat another of Strikland's security people. The fellow wore a business suit almost identical to the young woman's. He smiled, nodded toward a door, and said, "Mr. Strikland is expecting you. Please go right in."

Macus opened the door and stepped into an office. Strikland sat behind a desk, his eyes unfocused, clearly reviewing something visible only to him through his implants.

When Macus stepped into the room, Strikland's eyes focused, he stood, and walked around the desk to greet Macus. As they shook hands, Macus said, "You wanted to see me, sir."

Strikland smiled. "Yes, Macus. Thank you for making time for me."

With a wave of his hand, Strikland indicated a comfortable chair. "Sit down, sit down. Would you like something to drink?"

"I'll have whatever you're having, sir."

"Caff," Strikland said. "I'm having caff."

Macus smiled. "I would enjoy that, sir."

As Macus sat down, Strikland crossed the room to a sideboard, poured two cups of caff, then walked back to Macus and handed him one. He sat down in a chair like Macus's, crossed his legs, and sipped his caff. Macus sipped at his. Again, Macus hoped it was telling that Strikland did not choose to sit behind his desk in the seat of power, and have Macus stand before him like a low-level subordinate.

Strikland paused for a moment and considered Macus carefully. "I'd like to continue that conversation we had on *Lady Victorious*."

Macus liked the sound of that. "I'm at your disposal, sir."

Strikland pursed his lips. "I'm going to be exploring some commercial interests while here on Viktorkinde, and I'm hoping you might assist me."

Yes, this was definitely going the way Macus had hoped. "I'd be most happy to, sir. And the senator's demands on my time, of late, do allow me quite a bit of freedom."

Strikland's features clouded with anger. "Yes, he does spend a lot of time with that . . . woman."

Strikland clearly found it distasteful to refer to Jenine Catarvin by her title of *senator*. When forced to actually say "Senator Catarvin," as when greeting her at the beginning of a meeting, his expression frequently soured, though he took care not to let that happen if anyone but a close associate might see the distaste on his face. Since Macus had been allowed to see that look a few times, he hoped that Strikland now considered him a *close associate*.

Macus decided to test the waters a little. "But I suppose, in politics, as in life, we all must associate with those whose . . . moral and ethical compass is skewed in a different direction than our own. It sometimes requires a great deal of flexibility, don't you think?"

Strikland smiled, and obviously liked what he heard. "It certainly does. And let me caution you, Macus. Moral standards vary widely. An unthinking zealot will react with righteous indignation to something that thoughtful people like you and I might consider trivial."

When they had met in private on *Lady Victorious*, Strikland had recommended that Macus run for supervisor of the forty-third precinct in Trafalgar City. Gaining some experience like that would set Macus up for bigger things, and the man had even hinted Macus might eventually replace Palmutter. A couple of tendays had elapsed since that meeting, and they hadn't met in private like that until now. But during the intervening time the man had repeatedly tested Macus in small ways, just a casual comment here, or a suggestion there, sometimes in lowered voices at the bi-tenday mixer, or in the hallway after a meeting broke up. Nothing overt, but he clearly wanted to know how far Macus would go to advance his career. And now, a private meeting again.

"Your point is well taken, Mr. Strikland. I try to always temper my own thinking with pragmatism. As you pointed out, moral standards vary widely, and I've come to realize that it's not always wise to use my own moral ethic as a boundary condition for a decision. Such narrow thinking might prevent me from taking the most beneficial course of action."

Macus had carefully chosen to use the word *beneficial*. He hadn't used the word *profitable* because Strikland might have found that somewhat crass, but they both knew that's what Macus meant.

Strikland beamed a big smile at Macus, and sipped at his caff. The man clearly wanted to finalize his evaluation of Macus, to know he could trust a new protégé to be discreet. Since that first meeting on *Lady Victorious*, they had used the word *discreet* quite a number of times, and slowly it had evolved into a euphemism for looking the other way when someone's actions pushed the boundaries of lawful conduct, but still benefited them in some way.

Strikland nodded thoughtfully. "That's wise of you Macus, and I'm glad you said that. While assisting me, you're going to meet a number of my contacts here on

Viktorkinde . . ." He paused for effect. ". . . and let's just say you'll probably find some of them unusual." Strikland had used the word *unusual*, but they both knew he meant *disreputable*.

Macus leaned forward to emphasize his words. "I try to be flexible, sir. If one attempts to adhere to an overly rigid set of standards, one can easily become that zealot you mentioned."

Strikland nodded and smiled. Then he put his cup of caff on a small side table next to his chair and stood. Macus had an identical side table next to his own chair. He mimicked Strikland's actions, then stood to face the man.

Strikland shook Macus's hand quite vigorously. "This had been a most profitable meeting."

That word again: profitable, a good word.

When Macus stepped out of Strikland's office into the reception area he spotted that pretty young news hype standing in front of the receptionist's desk. He had run into Karya Chemina a number of times in the lounge on *Lady Victorious*, and he still hadn't made any progress with her, but it was always worth another try. As Macus approached her she said something to the security guy seated behind the desk, and Macus caught the last few words. ". . . have an appointment for an interview with Mr. Strikland."

The fellow nodded. "I'll let him know you're here."

Approaching her from behind, Macus said, "Karya."

She turned to face him. She wore a blouse that exposed a tasteful amount of cleavage, which probably helped her get interviews with men like Strikland and Palmutter. He wondered for a moment if she intended to make a play for Strikland, and considered warning Faith about her. But Faith was in a league way beyond Karya Chemina, so he decided he needn't bother.

Chemina gave him a pleasant smile. "Macus, have you had a chance to unpack yet?"

He pulled his eyes away from her breasts to look her in the face. "Just barely. Why don't you join me this afternoon for a drink?"

Her eyes brightened. "I'd love to, but I can't today."

The damn security guy behind the desk interrupted them. "Miss Chemina. Mr. Strikland will see you now."

"Sorry, Macus," she said. "Gotta run. Perhaps later this tenday."

He watched her walk into Strikland's office. Nah, he didn't need to warn Faith about her. Faith had her way outclassed.

3

Compromise

"I DON'T LIKE it any more than you," Mani Gascoigne said, pacing back and forth in front of Fran. It worried her when he became agitated.

Seated across the conference table from Fran, Primatov had just given the two of them a core-dump on Miershall's report, though Gascoigne did not know either the young Sarkovite or Anders Eindride as anything more than anonymous covert assets.

The senator continued talking as he paced. "Let's don't jump to any conclusions just because one of your people has disappeared."

Neither Fran nor Primatov had told Gascoigne that the missing asset was actually one of Kristdokar's people, nor would they.

Gascoigne stopped pacing and looked squarely at Primatov. "You say he worked undercover in a rogue Kelk operation on Sarkovie?"

Primatov nodded. "I did not specify his or her gender, so you're making an assumption that the asset is male. And it's actually a company with legitimate import-export operations, with only a small number of insiders who handle certain illicit activities."

Gascoigne waved a hand in dismissal. "I don't need to know all the details, and as a matter of course, I assume you're not telling me most of it anyway, but the whole Kelk situation is just too delicate right now. Unless the shit really hits the fan, we have to play it straight. We're guests here. If a problem arises, we let our Kelk hosts handle it. And in any case it doesn't matter, does it?"

He turned and looked at Fran like a distrusting teacher dressing down a disobedient student. "Tell me you did reposition all the firepower as we and our hosts agreed to do."

When the diplomatic mission had arrived the day before, they found that their hosts had stacked the deck. Not counting hunter-killers, there were fifteen Kelk warships in the Viktorkinde system, varying in size and firepower from medium destroyers to heavy cruisers. On any given day there might be one or two warships in the Trafalgar system, and Viktorkinde should be no different.

Behind the scenes Gascoigne had threatened their hosts with cancellation of the diplomatic mission. The Kelk had agreed to sit down to an immediate virtual conference to resolve the situation while the ships containing the mission were still driving in-system. They had come to a compromise agreement only a couple of hours before the welcoming ceremonies.

Fran shook her head. "Mani, I couldn't pull anything sneaky even if I wanted to, and I don't want to."

For all his bluff and bombast, Gascoigne had once again demonstrated his brilliance when negotiating with an opposing party. To ease tensions on both sides, they had all agreed to move any assets with serious firepower to a distance of two lightyears off Viktorkinde, and to separate any Kelk and Commonwealth warships well beyond targeting range of one another. If a hothead wanted to start something, it would take the fastest warship more than four hours to reach the Viktorkinde system. There would be plenty of warning, with a lot of cooler heads ready and able to get in the way. And with *Lady Victorious* in close orbit around the planet, while she didn't have warheads and transition batteries, she did have long range transition scanners, and she provided the monitoring capability necessary to allay the fears of the Commonwealth bigshots.

Fran continued. "Your solution is perfect, and I'm still amazed you got them to agree to it."

Gascoigne grinned. "They need it more than we do, at least on the surface." He turned serious. "But we need it too. If we want to prosper, we can't be the purveyors of interstellar war."

He grimaced. "But it still means if the shooting starts, they may be toast tomorrow, but we're toast today."

Fran carefully shook her head. "No. The shooting's not going to start. Kristdokar and Tiegnordan carefully selected the warships that were in-system. The captains of the Kelk warships, and the commanders of the weapons platforms, are either dovish or moderate, and they recognize that if it comes to interstellar war, we'll overwhelm them ten-to-one. And our captains are under orders that if fired upon, they are to withdraw without returning fire. And the Kelk captains are under orders that if a Kelk ship fires upon a Commonwealth ship, and our ships withdraw without returning fire, then they are to fire upon that Kelk ship to defend the Commonwealth ships, and render aid to said ships, if needed. Katrine and I worked that out with Kristdokar and Nygaard late yesterday, and they got official approval from the Executive Council this morning."

Gascoigne's eyes widened. "That's fucking complicated as all hell."

"Yes," Primatov said, "it is. But that turns it into a kind of twisted stalemate that just might work. And it also means that if something happens, it's going to happen here on the ground."

They needed the politicians to understand that something was up, but it was kind of hard to do that when Fran and Primatov didn't know exactly what was up. At least Gascoigne was the most reasonable and pragmatic of the bunch, and Fran thought a little more information might help. "Katrine, please tell Mani what you heard from Trafalgar this morning."

Primatov sat up a little straighter. "As you know, *Caliban* was in orbit around Sarkovie waiting for repairs, and we captured much of her crew. Our people there extracted from them the names of some of their contacts on Trafalgar."

Gascoigne grimaced. "I'm assuming this is one of those situations where I don't want to know how you extracted that information."

Primatov ignored him. "I immediately used the relay chain to pass that information on to my people on Trafalgar, and in short order we took three individuals there into custody."

Gascoigne demanded. "Did you have proper warrants?"

Again, Primatov ignored him. "Two of the individuals have not been terribly cooperative, though as yet we've only had a little time with them, and I'm certain they will soon soften their stances. The third is a low-level aide making a little illegal income on the side. He is anxious to cooperate in the hope he'll get a lighter sentence, but he really doesn't know much. However, he had heard rumors that something is going on among certain Kelk factions here on Viktorkinde, and whatever that something is, it might break fairly soon."

Gascoigne closed his eyes, waved his hands and shook his head. "Not good enough. Rumor and conjecture from some low-level flunky who doesn't know shit; it's just not good enough."

Gascoigne resumed pacing. "We can't do anything with that, but . . ."

He stopped pacing and looked carefully at Primatov, then at Fran, then he grinned like a young kid. "We can't do anything officially. And we can't do anything unofficially that looks like we're doing something unofficially, but trying to look like we're not doing something. Can you do something sneaky without looking like you're doing something sneaky?"

He held up both hands, palms out as if surrendering to an armed assailant. "Wait. I don't want to know the answer to that. Just be sneaky and underhanded, and make sure it doesn't make problems for the diplomatic mission."

He looked at Fran for an acknowledgment.

She nodded. "We'll do absolutely nothing, Mani."

He looked to Primatov and she merely nodded.

"Good," he said. "And all this nothing you're going to do, please make sure I don't know anything about it."

He turned and walked out of the room.

Fran and Primatov stared at each other for a long moment, then Primatov said, "I'll take care of some nothings that we should do, but I don't think it's time for Plan Z yet."

Fran nodded. "I concur."

••••

Palmutter had offered to assign Faith to a private room in his suite, along with a number of other staffers, but she had turned him down. She couldn't take the chance that if she accepted, he might somehow interpret that as a sign she had relented on her refusal to fuck him. Given his recent penchant for instability, the last thing she needed was him pawing at her again, and her turning him down. A room in his suite might also make it difficult to continue her clandestine relationship with Strikland, and at the same time keep it quiet. Instead, she had requested a small room of her own, and hinted that she'd be bitchy as hell if he didn't make it happen. He made it happen. That was one of the advantages of establishing early-on that she could be the office's bitchiest of bitches, if she wanted to be.

She stepped into the small reception area at the entrance to Palmutter's suite. Four low-level staffers, busy at various tasks, all froze and looked her way. Their faces contained expressions that varied from concern to outright fear.

The young fellow that scheduled Palmutter's calendar grimaced. "He's waiting for you."

She crossed the room to him, leaned close to his ear and lowered her voice. "What's wrong?"

He gritted his teeth. "He got a call this morning from some Kelk mucky-muck, and he's been in a foul mood ever since."

"He hasn't completely lost it again, has he?"

The fellow shrugged, then shook his head. "He's on the edge. He's making some effort to control himself, and at least he's not shouting, but he's in a foul mood."

Like all heterosexual men, the young fellow wanted to get under Faith's skirt. It was a delicate balance keeping him encouraged without going too far. She needed him to continue hoping that if he was nice to her, he might succeed. But if she went too far with that, he might make a pass at her, and she'd have to turn him down. He'd likely turn all pissy on her, which would spoil a moderately valuable asset.

She gave him one of her most pleasant smiles. "Thanks for the warning."

He smiled back. "Any time."

Palmutter sat behind his desk alone in his office. He didn't acknowledge her as she stepped into the room. He sat there with his eyes focused downward just in front of him, but seeing nothing, the opposite of a thousand-yard-stare. His forehead glistened with a fine sheen of sweat, and the skin of his face had taken on a faint flush.

She closed the door, turned to face him, and spoke softly. "Senator."

He started, looked up, and focused on her. In his eyes, she saw a mixture of fear and rage, and he spoke in a growl. "The traitor abandoned us. He's a turncoat, a filthy, fucking turncoat."

If his anxiety had him in a talkative mood, she might learn something valuable. Fearful that she might spook him, and that he would then completely lose control, she took care to avoid any quick movements. His eyes tracked her as she crossed the room slowly and stopped just in front of his desk. "Who are you talking about? Who is a traitor?"

She saw the explosion boiling forth an instant before it happened. He took in a sharp breath of air and shouted at the top of his lungs. "Machtberg! That fucking asswipe told me we're on our own. He accused me of being unstable, said Nvalheim was no better—that fucking piece of shit—and he refuses to work with us anymore."

Faith had not heard the name Machtberg before, though she had heard Palmutter mention Nvalheim once when Strikland tried to calm him down during one of his tirades. She spoke with great care. "Who is Machtberg?"

Palmutter squeezed his eyes shut, then opened them and blinked rapidly. For the first time he seemed to take note of his surroundings. He glanced right, then left, then shot upward out of his chair. He charged around the desk and came at her, his face livid with rage. Faith's heart climbed up into her throat as she gulped and backpeddled. She stopped only when her back slammed against the wall, and he didn't halt until he stood nose to nose with her. He spit words in her face. "You didn't hear that name. You never heard it, do you understand? Neither Machtberg, nor Nvalheim, do you understand? You never heard them, never, never, never."

Faith tried to say something, but all that came out was a tiny squeak.

At that moment, behind Palmutter at the other end of the room, Faith noticed that the door to his office was open a crack, with Jenine Catarvin standing there peering past the door. She floated into the room, oblivious to all the tension in the air. "Silas, my dear, how are you today?"

Palmutter's eyes blinked and he reluctantly turned away from Faith. "Uh . . . Jenine . . ."

Catarvin glanced around the room. "I see your digs are identical to mine." She wrinkled her nose with distaste. "We're going to have to give our Kelk hosts some lessons in interior decoration. This is much too geometric and martial for my tastes."

She looked at Faith and her eyes widened. "Ah, Miss Carlton, I didn't see you standing there."

Palmutter hesitated, looked at Catarvin, then at Faith, then at Catarvin again. "Uh ... Jenine ... uh ..."

Catarvin aimed a vacant smile at Faith, and waved a hand toward the door. "Miss Carlton, why don't you run along? Silas and I are going to have lunch brought in." She approached Palmutter, stopped at an intimate distance, and he couldn't take his eyes off her. "Just you and me, darling. A private little luncheon. It'll be quiet, and fun, and I'll help you calm down."

If Faith hadn't seen it with her own eyes she would never have believed it. If the vacant little airhead kept Palmutter from blowing a one megaton shit-storm, then she certainly had some use. For once, Faith didn't want to strangle the imbecile.

Faith eased her way toward the door, opened it and slipped out of the office. Three of Palmutter's four staffers froze again, standing still like frightened prey. A news hype named Chemina stood at the desk of the fellow that handled Palmutter's calendar. "But I have an appointment for an interview. I arranged it with you this morning."

The fellow grimaced. "I know. I'm sorry. But something unforeseen has come up. I'll personally confirm a new appointment with the senator, and let you know as soon as I have it scheduled."

Chemina sighed unhappily. "Well, I won't say I'm not disappointed, but I do understand. I'm sure he's a busy man."

She glanced Faith's way. "Miss Carlton."

Faith nodded. "Miss Chemina." She was quite good looking, and Faith wondered for a moment if she hoped to seduce Palmutter. If so, Faith certainly wasn't going to stand in her way. She could have the asshole all to herself.

Chemina turned and walked out of the room.

Alone now with the four staffers, an interesting thought occurred to Faith. "Which one of you called Catarvin?"

A young man seated at a tiny desk grimaced and said, "I did."

Faith nodded and smiled. "Good work." It had been a smart move on his part, and Faith would remember him.

She walked out of the reception area thinking of those two names: Machtberg and Nvalheim. She needed to find Macus. Palmutter's reaction had been too over-the-top to take lightly.

If the Kelk had logged their implants into the palace's systems, she could have sent out an informational ping, and known his location instantly. As an alternative, the tech people had set up localized nets in the suites of the five diplomats, and Strikland's people had done the same in his—the more junior staffers referred to them as diplonets. Since she was already there, Faith tried Palmutter's first, sent out a ping for Macus, and got nothing. She wandered down the hall to Catarvin's suite and got nothing there as well, but in Obradour's suite he replied over a secure link.

What's so urgent, Faith?

She took a deep breath and tried to compose herself. *Palmutter almost went off the deep end this morning. We need to talk.*

I'm in a stupid, fucking meeting.

She didn't want to hear that. *Blow the fucking thing off. This is important.*

I can't. Obradour's chairing it.

She closed her eyes and tried again to calm her nerves. *How long?*

Fifteen, twenty minutes.

Then meet me in the lounge.

I'll be there.

The room where they held the mixers also served as the *lounge* at other hours. Faith wasn't a drinker, rarely had more than one at an event, and never during an ordinary day. But that morning she needed something to calm her nerves. She kept seeing the rage in Palmutter's eyes, and couldn't imagine what he might have done if that staffer hadn't called Catarvin.

When she got to the lounge, she realized how bad it would look to sit there alone, before lunch, with a drink in front of her, so she crossed the room to a self-service sideboard and poured a glass of water. During the mixers they cleared most of the tables and chairs out so everyone could mingle, but during the day the place was furnished like a bar in the lobby of a nice hotel. It wasn't terribly crowded so she selected a low table where she could be alone and sat down in a couch facing it. Her hands shook, so she buried them in her lap to hide them. By the time Macus arrived she had achieved some modicum of calm.

He sat down next to her, placed a small access terminal on the table in front of them, opened a secure link between their implants, and pointed at the face of the terminal. *So what the fuck is going on?*

She closed her eyes. *You're not going to believe what just happened.*

After she told him of that morning's events, he closed his eyes and rubbed his temples. *Machtberg and Nvalheim! I heard him mention Nvalheim once. Who the hell are they?*

I have no idea. You think we should tell Strikland?

He frowned and considered that for a long moment, then shook his head. *No. The one time I heard Palmutter mention Nvalheim, Strikland immediately dismissed me, clearly didn't want me to hear that name, and wanted me out of the room before Palmutter said anything else. Let's just keep our eyes and ears open, do a little research on those two names, and see what we learn. This situation is developing rapidly, and we can probably play this to our advantage.*

4

Subterfuge

JOHN HAD BEEN assigned to a fairly Spartan room in a somewhat isolated wing of the Hyvaldsborg Palace. He shared it with Matsen and Kolbeck, and he didn't think it coincidental that anyone who wanted to get to him would have to fight their way through a suite of rooms occupied by May Forrester and her squad of John's Miriteen platoon mates. The suite included toilet and shower facilities, so it was somewhat self-contained. And at all times May and Kristdokar had a team of two armed guards stationed at the entrance to the suite, always one Kelk and one Commonwealth. John didn't ask how the Kelk felt about the presence of armed ComSecCorps soldiers in the hallowed halls of Hyvaldsborg. Everyone needed to make accommodations for the unusual circumstances they all faced.

The day after the welcoming ceremony, he received a call from Colonel Primatov. The signal was encrypted, and encoded with a Commonwealth authentication sequence, so he had no concerns about its validity.

She appeared in his virtual vision and smiled. "John, the principles of the diplomatic mission are meeting as we speak, and you're on their agenda in about an hour. You have yet to meet Mr. Obradour and Senators Catarvin and Palmutter, and they're quite interested in getting to know you a little."

She had warned him that the diplomatic mission would want to meet him sooner rather than later, and that they would most likely ask him to join their meeting for a short time that morning. "I'll be sure to arrive early, ma'am."

"Excellent." She signed off.

After arriving on Viktorkinde, Primatov had been officially assigned to Fran Thealone as her aide-de-camp, and the Kelk had housed the two of them in a suite of rooms and offices elsewhere in the palace. John did not know his way around the massive building, and even though he was still assigned to *Drakan Helgis*'s crew, they had not logged his implants into the building's security, so they couldn't superimpose a virtual map over his vision. Their newfound, mutual trust only went so far.

He asked Kolbeck, "How do I get there?"

The tall unterseergent shrugged. "I'm as lost as you, Blacksword. But they're showing Matsen and me virtual maps, so we'll get you there."

Even if John didn't need the two dregkraag to show him the way, they still accompanied him everywhere. On *Drakan Helgis*, as just another crewman, John had forgotten what it was like to wonder if every new face he encountered might be the next assassin.

Matsen's brow furrowed with thought and he asked Kolbeck, "You think they might lead us astray, maybe to a room full of armed assassins?"

Kolbeck's eyes widened a little. "Could be, but we wouldn't know if they did." He looked at John. "At least not until after he was dead."

Matsen gave Kolbeck a worried look. "We don't have to die with him, do we?"

Kolbeck squinted at John. "I don't know. Do we still hate him?"

Matsen rocked his head from side to side. "Not as much as we used to, but I still ain't dyin' for him."

Kolbeck nodded thoughtfully, still looking at John. "There you have it, Blacksword. Better hope they don't lead us astray."

The first time the two men had gone into their routine in front of John's friends, Carla and Leeze had been ready to pick a fight with the two and kick some serious Kelk ass, but May had seen the banter for what it was. Now, if John's Miriteen friends were present, they usually joined in as well. It was hard to ignore when half a dozen of them ganged up on him that way.

Thealone's suite wasn't far from John's, but was as isolated, and like his, a mixed team of Kelk and Commonwealth soldiers stood guard at its entrance. John, Matsen and Kolbeck provided security authentications through their implants and were admitted.

The suite was identical to John's, with a reception area just off the entrance, and offices, bedrooms and facilities to accommodate guests as well as their security personnel. It hadn't occurred to John until that moment, but of course the Kelk had structured guest quarters in the palace with an eye to housing foreign dignitaries and their staffs. The Supremacy had diplomatic relations with the governments of most of the nearby systems, did a fair amount of trade with them, and common-faces were quite common in the palace, and on the streets of the city. He chided himself for not having realized earlier that the Commonwealth had been the exception to that rule.

As John stepped into the reception area, Matsen and Kolbeck spotted Command Superior Ingrid Vagle, Primatov's personal bodyguard. They peeled off to have a word with her while a ComSecCorps Infantry-Ops Captain approached John. He stood a little shorter than John, had dark brown hair and blue eyes, and when they shook hands, he introduced himself as Edward Fleming. "Nice to meet you, Ensign Mathius."

Primatov had briefed John on Fleming and his nullhead team, and warned him not to be surprised that they weren't wearing Blacksword patches, or the insignia of Zeta Company. She had told him, "With the kind of work they do, we find it's less restrictive if they don't broadcast their Blacksword affiliation. And that's especially true here on Viktorkinde."

Fleming introduced John to a few members of his team, and he got the impression they were evaluating him in some way. One of the female nullheads leaned close to John and lowered her voice. "Maybe sometime you and that young Kelk woman might want to join our team."

She had extended the invitation to Nikaela as well. A Kelk as a Blacksword! In that moment he realized it wasn't just the Kelk going through a lot of change.

Fleming shook his head. "Don't think he's going to be free to do that, not for a while." He gave John a friendly slap on the back. "But later, if you'd like to give it a try, let me know."

John spotted Primatov crossing the room toward them. He noticed Kolbeck watching her as well, his eyes tracking her rather intently. Vagle watched Kolbeck ogling Primatov, rolled her eyes, and shook her head sadly.

Primatov stopped next to Fleming and looked John over carefully. "How are the new uniforms?"

Thealone had brought a complete wardrobe of uniforms properly tailored to John's size, and he no longer needed the uniforms Primatov had cobbled together from *Lightspear*'s crew. He had on his new service khakis, with the butcher's dagger in the elaborate harness strapped to his side. "It's nice to have shoes that fit right, ma'am."

She smiled. "Did you enjoy the welcoming ceremony?"

There must have been something on John's face. Fleming chuckled. "I think he enjoyed it about as much as I did."

Primatov smiled, nodded, leaned slightly toward them and lowered her voice. "It was rather tedious." She straightened. "But that was just the first of many such events. You've got a busy schedule, Mr. Mathius, and it begins right now. Come with me, I've got some people who dearly want to meet you."

••••

The dregkraag held the tall double doors of the Council chamber open as Nikaela followed Kristdokar through them. She tried to calm her racing heart as she walked forward to the stander's podium.

The four councilors sat behind a large curved desk made of a dark and richly stained wood. It accommodated all of them, plus one empty seat previously occupied by Vice Skalde Haugrund. The desk arced in a gentle curve, with the podium placed at its focus, and the desk elevated above the podium so that whoever stood at the center of the councilors' attention must look up to meet their eyes. Kristdokar remained at the back of the room while Nikaela walked forward and took her place standing before the Council.

Nikaela wondered if they had ever made an exception to the rule that one must *stand* before the Executive Council. Supposedly they did so for those hampered by some infirmity, but Skalde Supreme Dornmier, the most senior member, and Skalde of the Supremacy Veskarson, the second most senior member, and the only man on the Council, appeared ancient by any measure. To qualify for such an exception, must one be more infirm than them?

Vice Skalde Nygaard, with whom Nikaela was slightly acquainted, must be as ancient as the other two, and yet she could walk the runway with any model in the fashion feeds. On the other hand, Tiegnordan would be a lot more attractive if she didn't display such a stern and disapproving demeanor.

"Mistress Vreekande," Veskarson said. As the second most senior member of the Council, he chaired their meetings. "We appreciate you standing before us today."

Nikaela nodded, lowered her eyes, and responded with the customary formula. "I am honored to stand before you, Maestra and Mistresses."

The four of them stared at her for the longest, most pregnant moment of Nikaela's life. She recalled Kristdokar telling her, "It is extremely rare for one so junior to stand singly before the Council. Be careful, and beware."

Tiegnordan finally broke the silence, a sour look on her face. "So, you and he are breschkada?"

Nikaela was not prepared for the open hostility she saw in the woman. "I am breschkada only if you four say that I am breschkada."

Tiegnordan leaned forward. "And he is breschkada-sa, not you? You are merely breschkada-se, is that not so?"

From the look on her face, Nikaela thought that, had the vice skalde stood within arm's reach, the woman might have struck Nikaela, and such narrow-mindedness angered her. "Yes, that is so. And I am proud of my actions. Can you even claim breschkada-se?"

Tiegnordan's eyes widened and blinked rapidly. Nygaard raised a hand to cover her mouth, apparently trying to hide a smile. Veskarson's face might have been carved from stone for all the expression he showed.

Dornmier laughed openly. "Young lady, you are impertinent."

Nikaela lowered her eyes. "I most humbly beg your forgiveness." She raised her chin and looked at them squarely, knew she was a fool for speaking out. "My breschkada-sa did something very brave that night on Reisenar. I am proud of what he did, and I am proud of the way I responded."

Any semblance of a smile had disappeared from Nygaard's face. "And that is the crux of the matter, is it not? So tell us the story yourself. Up to this point we have only heard second-hand accounts. I think we would all like to hear in your own words, in detail, exactly what happened that night."

Nikaela had told the story many times, but never before to such an august audience. She started with, "Command Superiors Thordahl and Brynjar had tasked my platoon with a rapid response mission. If the opportunity arose to capture a ComSecCorps soldier to interrogate, we were to move swiftly and deploy to apprehend the target."

Nikaela told the story with few interruptions, just a question or two here and there, though Tiegnordan remained silent throughout the telling, the sour look on her face never changing in the slightest. When Nikaela finished, they focused on her interaction with John on that subway platform, and questioned her thoroughly about it. They made her relate every word she and John traded between them that night, and since the two of them had spoken only in Lingua, she related their words in that language. They found the 'shit-of-bull' part of that conversation humorous and interesting.

When she finished, and there were no more questions, Veskarson said, "And I'm told that until recently your Lingua was rather atrocious. You must have sounded like an ignorant primitive."

At that moment Nikaela realized that their greatest fear was that she had made the Supremacy appear primitive or backward. But her biggest surprise came when they were done with her: Tiegnordan's attitude softened considerably. For the first time Nikaela thought she might understand, just a little, her mother's consternation with *those powerful old women.*

••••

Palmutter's failure to keep the appointment meant Karya had an hour to kill. She decided to wander down to the lounge and do a little networking. Maybe a staffer or two might yield up a decent quote, or she could uncover one of those little tidbits that seemed benign on face value, but eventually led to something nice and juicy, and a great article for the news feeds.

She paused just within the lounge and scanned the room for familiar faces. She spotted Macus DeLeon and Faith Carlton seated on a couch, both intently focused on a small access terminal on the low table in front of them. The two had done something quite similar a number of times, and were apparently a close knit team of considerable value to Palmutter. But of late, Karya had seen little signs that their allegiances had shifted, and she couldn't be sure if they worked for Silas Palmutter's benefit, or Lawrence Strikland's. On the other hand, the one thing she could be certain of with those two, was that whatever they were up to, it would be to their benefit, and probably to someone else's detriment. She was fairly certain Carlton had seduced Strikland, though she and he were exceedingly careful, so Karya couldn't prove anything.

She spotted a couple of Catarvin's staffers lunching on a buffet of finger-food. One of them saw her and waved an invitation for her to join them. She nodded and started across the room. To get there she passed just behind DeLeon and Carlton, and as she did so she noticed some sort of bright image on the screen of the terminal in front of them. DeLeon had extended his hand, pointing a finger at it while the two of them discussed it intently.

She didn't mean to pry, but curiosity got the best of her, and after all, she was a news hype—journalist—so she simply did her job. It was a still picture, taken from orbit, of the sun setting over Viktorkinde. She dare not stop behind them and stare, but she had a couple of solid seconds during which she had a clear view of that screen, then she passed by them and continued on.

At the buffet she poured a cup of caff, then joined Catarvin's staffers. But the image she had seen on that screen bothered her, and to satisfy her curiosity, she positioned herself so that when facing the two staffers, she had a clear view past them of Carlton and DeLeon.

Catarvin's two staffers were quite animated about a recent tour of a Kelk manufacturing facility. Karya didn't have to contribute much to the conversation, which allowed her to focus nicely on her targets. DeLeon and Carlton took turns pointing at the screen in front of them while they spoke. But they both frequently did that thing everyone did when they paused to listen to their implants, or to speak through their implants, the thousand-yard-stare thing. Karya desperately needed to look at that screen again.

"I've got to run," she said to Catarvin's two staffers. "Got an appointment in about ten minutes."

She dropped the cup of caff off at a cleaning station, then made sure her path to the exit took her behind DeLeon and Carlton's couch. The image on the screen hadn't changed, the same image from orbit of the sun setting over Viktorkinde. She paused at the exit, turned around and looked back.

Carlton and DeLeon continued to speak while pointing at the screen. But as she watched them they froze for several seconds, their eyes unfocused. Their clandestine discussion through their implants must have become interesting enough to take precedence over the phony external conversation.

They had something to hide, or they were planning something. But why not simply meet privately? Why not simply retreat to one of their rooms? Of course, if they were seen doing that too frequently, that might start tongues wagging. But what did they care?

Karya walked out of the lounge pondering that, and then it hit her: Strikland. If she was right about Carlton fucking the man, then such rumors could be quite detrimental to that relationship.

So what were Carlton and DeLeon up to?

5

New Alliances

JENINE CATARVIN HAD done an excellent job of keeping Palmutter stable. Seated at a conference table with the rest of the diplomatic mission, Fran Thealone made a mental note to compliment her on a job well done. It must be difficult to be an intelligent woman hiding behind the mask of a vacant imbecile.

Fran watched Palmutter closely as the door to the conference room opened and John Mathius stepped into the room. Palmutter's eyes narrowed with distrust, and she hoped he wouldn't be a problem. The man disliked anything Kelk, and he distrusted anyone who didn't share his dislikes.

John Mathius turned, closed the door, then turned back to face them and paused. Primatov had warned Fran she would not accompany him because she didn't want to appear to be mothering the poor fellow.

Fran recalled the one time she and Mani Gascoigne had met Mr. Mathius in Primatov's office on Trafalgar. Back then he had been somewhat timid, but the young man who had just entered the room stood confidently erect, though without any brashness or bravado. Of course, since Trafalgar he had been gut-shot and abducted, abused and tortured on both *Caliban* and *Sycorax*, and almost executed with a Kelk butcher's dagger. He had killed quite a number of people himself, almost single-handedly destroyed *Sycorax*, and served honorably as a crewmember on a Kelk man-of-war in combat. She glanced down to the sheathed dagger suspended at his side by an elaborate harness.

Their eyes met and he smiled as he said, "Colonel Blacksword."

Mani Gascoigne stood, crossed the room, and shook the young man's hand. "It's good to see you again, Ensign Mathius. But the last time we met it was Cadet Mathius. Congratulations. You're going to make a fine officer."

Gascoigne turned about and threw an arm over Mathius's shoulders. "Let me introduce you to a few people you haven't met."

Gascoigne walked him around the table and one-by-one introduced him to the other three members of the mission.

With Mathius a little taller than most, Obradour's slight stature meant the young fellow might have towered over the man. But Mathius kept himself at arm's length as if he were conscious of that. Fran thought that rather astute of him.

Wearing a surly scowl, Palmutter stood and shook Mathius's hand. "It's a pleasure to meet you, young man." He didn't sound like he meant it, and he added emphasis to that impression by abruptly sitting back down without another word.

Catarvin stood, shook his hand warmly, and beamed like a school girl. While he said something polite, she looked him up and down with a hungry glint in her eye. Fran had seen firsthand that the senator had a keen intellect, even though she kept it hidden from most, but Fran now wondered if the woman's mind took a back seat when her libido reared its horny little head. Fran recalled her first meeting with the woman when she had revealed her true self. She had said something like, "I really do need to find someone besides my husband and Silas for a good hetero fuck." Fran hoped she wasn't setting her sights on young Mr. Mathius, and decided they should keep a close eye on that situation, make sure the poor fellow didn't find himself alone in a room with her.

Gascoigne got John seated in a chair between him and Catarvin.

Palmutter jumped right in. "I'd like to hear about this breshakuda thing with the Kelk."

Catarvin leaned forward. "Yes, we'd all like to know more about your relationship with this young Kelk woman."

John glanced Fran's way, a worried look on his face. Fran tried not to hear a double meaning in Catarvin's words, and kept the look on her own face neutral.

Obradour rescued him. "Yes, Mr. Mathius. Why don't we start with the incident on Reisenar. Please tell us about that."

Again, John glanced Fran's way, a question implicit in the look he gave her. At his hesitation, Palmutter frowned, clearly affronted.

Fran addressed the other members of the mission. "Ensign Mathius has been warned that much of that incident is highly classified, and he's not terribly experienced in such matters."

Fran looked pointedly at the young man. "These people are cleared to hear all the details of your experience on Reisenar. Tell it the way you told it to me and Senator Gascoigne in Colonel Primatov's office on Trafalgar."

The young man started with the assault-boat drop to the planet's surface. He told the story in precise, matter-of-fact wording, didn't embellish anything, and made it clear he wasn't really a storyteller. Catarvin and Palmutter interrupted him occasionally to clarify a point or ask a question, but for the most part they simply listened. And Obradour remained completely silent throughout the entire telling.

When Mr. Mathius finished, Palmutter asked, "So that's what this breshakuda thing is: you saved her life and she saved yours."

He nodded. "That's pretty much it, sir."

For the first time Obradour spoke. "You're a survivor of Novalis III. Tell us about that, please."

Mathius grimaced and spoke carefully. "I'd rather not, sir."

Obradour frowned. "Why not?"

Clearly uneasy, the young man hesitated before speaking. "It's not something I care to discuss."

Palmutter turned indignant. "Well we care to discuss it. What'll you do if I insist?"

Fran thought John held his composure rather nicely. He spoke quietly, but there was a steel-hard edge to his voice. "Then I'll stop being polite when I say no."

Obradour intervened. "I don't think there's any need to press the young man on what must have been a thoroughly unpleasant incident."

Mathius nodded, closed his eyes for a heartbeat, then opened them and smiled. "Interesting that you should say that, Mr. Obradour. I've noticed time and again that people in the Commonwealth refer to Novalis III as an incident, while the Kelk all refer to the murder of twenty million people as a tragedy."

Catarvin laughed. "He's certainly got you there, Tarsik."

Fran had never before seen Obradour appear humbled. "That's a good point, young man, something we should all keep in mind."

Obradour opened a secure link between his implants and Fran's. *Please express my apologies to the young man for putting him in such an untenable position. I should have known Palmutter would be an insufferable ass.*

Fran simply met Obradour's eyes and nodded. The little financier could be just as unreasonable as Palmutter, but he was always far more polite about it.

Obradour perked up and looked around the room. "I believe we have a bi-tenday mixer tonight. I think the young man should attend. That'll give everyone a chance to get to know him a bit."

Fran saw a touch of fear on John's face. Catarvin must have seen it as well, because she leaned forward and patted him gently on the wrist. The hungry look in her eyes had turned just plain horny.

"Don't worry," she said. "You'll do fine. And all the young ladies will be . . . well, I think you'll find them raptly attentive." She looked at Thealone and winked. "Won't he?"

Fran caught Palmutter rolling his eyes.

••••

As John left the meeting of the diplomatic mission, he felt some trepidation at having to attend the bi-tenday mixer that evening. On *Drakan Helgis*, he and his friends had heard of the mixers on *Lady Victorious*, and some of them envied their civilian counterparts. Carla and Leeze thought it would be fun to wear expensive clothing, sip fancy drinks, and rub elbows with beautiful, elegant, and powerful people. As usual, Leeze boiled it down to the least common denominator. "Free booze! I'm all in for that."

John simply thought it unfair that the civilians got to go to a big party every five days, while he and his friends worked hard to overcome the boredom of interstellar travel. They had spent a lot of time on *Drakan Helgis* maintaining their weapons and combat armor, drilling together, exercising, and playing the same old card games. Everyone took their turn winning, and then their turn losing. It seemed like the same old pile of money just kept circulating around the table over and over again.

When John stepped into the reception area of the suite, he spotted Primatov speaking with Edward Fleming. She saw him, said a word or two to Fleming, then turned and headed his way. They met in the middle of the room, she leaned close to him and lowered her voice. "Colonel Blacksword conferenced me in on your meeting with the mission. You handled yourself well with Palmutter, but do be careful of him."

John couldn't hide a grimace, and wasn't sure how to broach the subject foremost on his mind. "I'm more concerned about . . . Senator Catarvin."

John wasn't sure how to take it when Primatov closed her eyes and emitted a quiet laugh. She shook her head. "Don't worry about her. She flirts with everyone. I don't think she was serious."

John had seen in the woman's eyes that she was damn well serious, but he kept that thought to himself. He needed some guidance on that evening's mixer. "What should I wear this evening?"

"Service dress blues," she said. "It's not formal. Most everyone there will be wearing standard business attire. Occasionally, they go full-on formal, but not this evening."

He knew full well he'd be under a microscope. "Why do I have to attend?"

She considered that for a long moment, and he wondered if she was trying to think of a way to give him bad news. "About four or five days before we reached Viktorkinde, there was some talk of transferring you and Miss Vreekande over to *Lady Victorious*. The whole breschkada thing had bubbled to the surface in the rumor mill there, and they were curious about you. Colonel Blacksword had difficulty squashing it. We used the excuse that the Kelk would not allow us to transfer Miss Vreekande to a Commonwealth ship, and we think it best that you attend this one without her."

John thought he understood their reasoning. "Nikaela would be the only Kelk there, right?"

She smiled and nodded. "That's very astute of you, John. We'll orchestrate something in the near future so they'll get a chance to meet her, but it'll be an evenly mixed crowd of Kelk and Commonwealth attendees. And by the way, you're not going to be on your own tonight. Colonel Blacksword and I will be there, and you can count on Senator's Catarvin and Gascoigne, and Mr. Obradour, to help you if a difficult situation arises."

John got the impression that by *difficult situation*, she meant Silas Palmutter.

••••

Karya Chemina had an appointment for an interview with Fran Thealone. Seated alone in the conference room in Thealone's suite, and waiting for the two of them to arrive, Katrine didn't think the young woman would get much interviewing done.

The door to the conference room opened, and a young fellow with sergeant's stripes on his sleeves stepped into the room, one of Thealone's aides. In fact, he was a Zeta Company Blacksword who was good at appearing nonlethal and quite normal. In his case, appearances were deceiving.

"Colonel," he said, all business. "Miss Chemina has arrived, and Colonel Blacksword is on her way. Is there anything you need?"

She shook her head. "We're good."

A few seconds later the door creaked open and Karya Chemina peered around its edge. She saw Katrine and her eyes widened a little. Katrine had met the young woman in the immediate aftermath of John Mathius's abduction from the academy campus. On Trafalgar she had interrogated Chemina and her lover May Forrester, and Katrine had not been terribly concerned with putting a young news hype and a very junior officer at ease. That had been the only time they had met, and it appeared she had left a lasting impression.

Katrine grinned at the young woman. "Come in, Miss Chemina. I could say I don't bite, but that would be a lie."

The young woman stepped fully into the room, but before she closed the door Fran Thealone blew in behind her and dropped into a seat at the table. Chemina closed the door reluctantly, as if she'd like to leave it open for a quick getaway if need be.

Thealone glanced from Chemina to Primatov, a curious expression on her face. Katrine answered the unasked question in the colonel's look. "Miss Chemina and I were just getting reacquainted."

Thealone wrinkled her nose and squinted across the table at Katrine. "Did you scare her? You can be really scary, you know?"

She looked at Chemina. "And if she told you she doesn't bite, don't believe her. Now sit down, young lady. You asked for this meeting, so you've got the floor."

Chemina squared her shoulders, selected a seat and sat down at the table. She took a careful breath. "I don't have anything I can prove, but I have some observations that I'm pretty sure are correct."

Thealone shook her head. "I don't care about proof unless I need to indict someone and put them in prison. So spit it out." Thealone grinned. "And I promise I won't let Katrine bite you, at least not today."

That got a muted smile out of the young woman, and she clearly relaxed a little. She spoke cautiously. "I assume you are familiar with Faith Carlton?"

Both Thealone and Katrine nodded, so she continued. "Faith Carlton and Macus DeLeon are up to something. There's no question the two of them are tight as thieves, in a strange sort of way. They frequently sit in the lounge to work together, just the two of them, a small access terminal in front of them. I happened to be walking behind them one time, heard them saying something about polling results for the next election. DeLeon pointed at the screen, but there was nothing there but an orbital picture of Trafalgar, the kind of thing one might hang on the wall. And in the middle of their verbal conversation they did that thing we all do when we pause to listen to our implants, you know, the thousand-yard-stare thing. And before we got here, DeLeon made a pass at practically every woman on *Lady Victorious*, but not Faith Carlton. They're hiding something, I just don't know what."

The three of them speculated for a bit on what might be going on between Carlton and DeLeon, but everything they came up with had holes in it.

Thealone asked. "What else have you got?"

Any intimidation Chemina had felt earlier had quickly dissipated, and her eyes brightened as she spoke. "There's a big shift in the Palmutter camp. DeLeon and Carlton used to be his right-hand man and woman, his go-to staffers when he needed something important, and he may still think they are. But I suspect they've quietly withdrawn their allegiance from Palmutter and joined Strikland's camp, though I don't think Palmutter's aware of that yet."

Katrine felt obligated to caution the girl. "We've had our suspicions for some time that Strikland is running a game of his own. Stay away from him. We think he might be quite dangerous."

Chemina's eyes blinked as she grimaced. "I'm absolutely certain Faith Carlton has seduced him. Nothing concrete, mind you, just the way the two of them act around each other."

Thealone asked, "Why do you say she seduced him? Why not he seduced her?"

Chemina's eyes hardened and she leaned forward a little to emphasize her words. "No one seduces Faith Carlton."

Chemina sat up straighter. "There's one more thing. The other day I had an appointment for an interview, so I went to Palmutter's office and his staffers were shitting their pants with fear. And while I talked with his receptionist, Senator Catarvin brushes in, and walks right into his office. The door was only open for a second or two, but I heard Palmutter growl something about Nvalheim, and he hissed 'never,

never, never.' It was real tense. Then Carlton walked out of his office and I had to leave."

As Thealone and Chemina discussed that incident back and forth a little, Katrine resolved to check with Catarvin on the matter.

When the three of them finished, Katrine expected Chemina to get up and leave, but she just sat there waiting. She smiled uneasily at Thealone. "I'm supposedly here for an interview with you. Don't you think we should keep up my cover story?"

Thealone threw her head back and laughed. "News hype to the end."

Chemina corrected her. "Journalist, ma'am."

Katrine stood. "I'll leave you two to your interview."

Chemina smiled up at her and asked, "When might I get an interview with you, Colonel?"

Katrine ignored the question. "That was good work, very good work. I'm glad you're on our team."

The young woman smiled. Katrine turned and left.

6

Bird in a Cage

JOHN HAD CONVINCED himself he would not feel like a bird in a cage at the mixer. The event would be attended by classy people who were too sophisticated to gawk and stare like a bunch of bumpkins from some backwater planet, especially since *he* was the bumpkin from a backwater planet, not them. And in any case, he just wasn't interesting enough for them to pay that much attention to him, so he thought he'd skate by without too much attention. He took the extra precaution of not wearing the jacket with the special sheath sewn into the sleeve. The whole purpose of wearing the butcher's blade was to thumb his nose at their Kelk hosts, and wearing it to the mixer would simply raise questions he didn't want to answer.

Matsen and Kolbeck guided him to the event, and as he approached the entrance to the room he heard the buzz of dozens of people speaking in quiet conversation. The two dregkraag peeled off as he stepped into the room.

The place went abruptly silent, and everyone there turned and stared at him like a bunch of bumpkins from backwater planets. John wanted to back out of the room and simply disappear.

"Ensign Mathius."

He turned to find Senator Catarvin at his side. She smiled up at him. "You look like you could use a drink."

The buzz of the crowd picked up again. She wrapped her arm around his and pulled his elbow tightly against her breast. He had no choice but to walk with her as she marched him across the room. The crowd parted before them, and somewhere in the middle of the throng, to John's vast relief, they encountered Gascoigne talking with Primatov.

Catarvin didn't release John's arm. "Mani," she said, "why don't you get us a couple of drinks? Ensign Mathius looks like he could use a little medicinal support." She looked at John and gave him a big inviting smile. "And I could use a good stiff one myself."

John's collar felt really tight at that moment.

Gascoigne gave John a sympathetic look, then smiled at Catarvin. "I'll be happy to, Jenine."

John tried not to sound desperate. "Nothing too strong for me."

Gascoigne nodded and headed for the bar. Primatov leaned close to Catarvin, lowered her voice, and John thought he heard her whisper something about, ". . . a bit thick, aren't you?"

Catarvin didn't lower her voice, and John easily heard what she said. "I'm just having a little fun, dear. It keeps everyone guessing. And someone had to rescue the poor fellow. He froze like one of those Heraclean zealots who had just seen compromising pictures of himself in a Sarkovian bordello, and learned that they were about to be posted on all the major news feeds."

John had heard she was an airhead, but her comment sounded somewhat calculating. He wondered at that.

Catarvin finally released his arm, and she and Primatov put their heads together.

John noticed Macus DeLeon across the room looking his way, and their eyes met. DeLeon didn't react, but he kept his eyes locked on John as he continued to speak with a tall, blond, stunningly beautiful young woman. A few moments later an older gentleman joined them and DeLeon finally looked away from John. The older fellow stood average height, with handsome, distinguished features. He wore a business suit that looked costly and expensive, even to John, who had little experience in such matters.

Gascoigne returned with drinks for all four of them. John sipped at his and was pleased to learn it was nothing more than water, with a fancy garnish that made it look like he was drinking something stronger.

Gascoigne pulled John aside and lowered his voice. "Sorry about Palmutter during the meeting. For various reasons, he's a little unstable at the moment. He's prone to lashing out, so let us handle him."

John nodded, but felt he needed to be cautious about simply agreeing to that, and decided to be candid with the senator. "If he presses me on certain matters, I won't capitulate. And if you don't handle him, then I will, but I'll try to be as tactful as possible about it."

Gascoigne's eyebrows rose. "Colonel Primatov was right."

"About what, sir?"

He grinned. "She told me I'd like you."

To John's surprise, Professor Emmet Dirkson abruptly appeared a Gascoigne's elbow. He hadn't seen the wiry, little fellow since his last Kelk lesson on the academy campus some months ago, and Dirkson hadn't changed in the least. Small of stature, he stood only chest high to John, vibrated with energy, and gestured with short, jerky motions.

"Ensign Mathius," he said. "Are you keeping up with your Kelk studies?"

At that point John spoke Kelk rather well, so he switched to that now. "I did some studying, but most of the time I was simply living among them. I guess I was completely immersed, which helped immensely."

Dirkson scrunched his nose up and leaned forward, as if to help him judge the veracity of John's claim. "You were immersed. How did that happen?"

If Dirkson wanted to quiz John on his experiences with the Kelk, they'd be there for a couple of hours. "I served for a couple of months as a member of the crew of a Kelk warship."

Dirkson turned to Gascoigne, didn't think to shift back to Lingua, and asked in Kelk, "Is he telling the truth?"

At the confused look on Gascoigne's face, John explained, apologized for shifting the conversation to Kelk, and got them all back to Lingua.

"Yah," Gascoigne said. "He's telling the truth." Gascoigne flashed John a big smile. "Our young man here seems to have a knack for making friends among the Kelk."

"Friends," Dirkson said, as if the word held some magical quality to it. He stood up on his tiptoes to get his nose closer to John's, and gripped John's elbow tightly. "You told me you had some Kelk friends, and I heard you're breschkada. This trip has been a gold mine. I've been doing research, digging through their public records and library databases, and it's incredible. But I came across a vague reference that translates to something like, 'right of vendetta,' and I can't find anything about it. It's mentioned a couple of times, and then nothing."

The little man's voice had risen as he spoke, and at that point he was almost shouting. "Just nothing. Strange, eh? Really mysterious."

Gascoigne put a hand on Dirkson's shoulder. "Calm down, Professor."

Dirkson ignored him and continued to shout at John. "Can you help me, ask one of your Kelk friends about it?"

"Yah," John said, "sure, 'right of vendetta,' I'll ask them about it."

That seemed to calm the little fellow somewhat. He lowered his heels back to the floor and let go of John's elbow. "Good. Good. Let me know as soon as you learn anything."

He turned and walked away, mumbling to himself.

Gascoigne shook his head. "That fellow's one odd duck."

Someone behind John drew Gascoigne's attention and the senator frowned unhappily.

"Mathius."

John recognized DeLeon's voice and didn't like having the asshole at his back, so he turned slowly to face him. The older gentleman John had seen him talking to earlier stood sandwiched between DeLeon and the attractive blonde.

Speaking without an unpleasant sneer or snide remark, DeLeon introduced the older fellow: Lawrence Strikland, Palmutter's Commercial Advisor. He introduced Faith Carlton as the senator's Director of Communications. For a moment John considered feigning ignorance regarding Strikland's prior affiliation. But if, as Primatov suspected, Strikland already knew that John had dug up that information in the Transmarin database, he'd know John wanted to hide his actions, and that might be a dangerously telling mistake.

"Mr. Strikland," John said. "Aren't you the executive who took leave from Transmarin to support the mission?"

Strikland didn't miss a beat. "I see you've done your homework."

John shrugged and tried to be the bumpkin from a backwater planet. "There's not much to do on a warship in interstellar space. My squad mates and me, we read everything we could on the diplomatic mission. It's the biggest news in my lifetime."

Strikland leaned forward, and somehow made the move an intimate gesture, as if he spoke with a close colleague. "Biggest news in my lifetime as well. And here you are, the young man who's probably responsible for that. Silas told me what you did on Reisenar."

Most of the details of that incident were highly classified, and John wondered how much Palmutter had revealed to the man. "No, sir. I simply stumbled into it. I was just a grunt. They shot at me and I shot back. Colonel Primatov ran the show."

Strikland smiled and raised a doubtful eyebrow. "You're just being modest. I heard you were badly wounded, and you did that breschkada thing on that subway platform with that young Kelk woman. Now that was thinking outside the box, and giving her that information was a clear and concise strategic move. No, young man, even back then you demonstrated a lot more maturity than just some grunt with a rifle."

John decided to check on Strikland's security status. But even if he were cleared for such information, staffers like Carlton and DeLeon were undoubtedly not, and speaking openly about such details in a crowd definitely violated security protocols.

The young woman beamed a pleasant smile at John. "Macus tells me you and he trained together on Miriteen."

John had been focused on Strikland, and for the first time he took note of Faith Carlton. She had the kind of beauty that effortlessly drew the attention of everyone; heterosexual men looked at her with desire, and women with envy. But in her eyes John thought he saw something cold and detached, as if she measured everyone about her with careful calculation, trying to determine how they might be of benefit to her.

Responding to her remark, Strikland looked to Macus, then back to John. "You trained together? That kind of thing builds relationships that last a lifetime."

DeLeon frowned. "Yes, a lifetime."

John nodded. "We both learned quite a bit from each other."

Strikland gave DeLeon a friendly pat on the shoulder. "There you have it, shared memories to last a lifetime."

Strikland straightened and looked past John. "Ah, Silas just arrived."

Strikland offered his hand, John shook it again, and the conversation ended. As they parted the young woman glanced briefly over her shoulder at John, and again he saw that cold calculation in the look she gave him. And he also saw anger. Something he had done had really upset her.

John recalled the way Strikland had handled him like a pro. The man had a way of making everyone around him feel at ease, as if they were dealing with a congenial gentleman they could trust implicitly. John actually liked the fellow, though if it turned out Strikland did have anything to do with Novalis III, that wouldn't stop John from killing him.

••••

Strikland had wanted to meet John Mathius, and Macus had made it happen. But something bothered him about Faith's reaction to the fellow.

After the three of them worked their way through the crowd a short distance, Strikland stopped abruptly to face Macus and Faith. He did not appear happy as he lowered his voice to a whisper. "That young man is dangerous."

Macus shook his head, but contradicting Strikland might be foolish so he spoke cautiously. "I think you're overestimating him, sir."

"No," Faith said. She looked into Macus's eyes, and what he saw would have frightened him, had it been directed his way. She shook her head. "No, Macus, he's right. That fellow is dangerous, very dangerous."

Strikland focused on Macus. "We need to keep an eye on him." He glanced over his shoulder at Palmutter. "I have to speak privately with Silas. You two enjoy yourselves. We'll talk more about this later."

He turned and eased his way through the crowd toward Palmutter.

Faith's reaction bothered Macus. He turned to face her squarely and lowered his voice. "What is it? What's got you so pissed off?"

She closed her eyes and shook her head as if trying to clear her thoughts. She spoke in a tight-lipped hiss. "I got nothing from him." Her anger bordered on rage.

"Nothing?" Macus asked. "You mean from Mathius? You got nothing from Mathius?"

She opened her eyes. "That man was not in the least attracted to me."

Macus took her by the arm and pulled her to the edge of the room. "When you first met Strikland, you got nothing from him, and that didn't bother you much."

She frowned and her eyes blinked rapidly. "You're right." She hesitated for a long moment. "What I got from Strikland was . . . neutral, like he was gay or something, and that was only because he was faking it, pretending no interest. He's good at acting. What I got from Mathius was . . . true disinterest, dislike actually."

Macus didn't understand. "Surely there've been other men who didn't like you."

She thought about that for a second. "Yes, but they still wanted to fuck me, and he didn't."

She turned away from Macus and scanned the crowd until she spotted John Mathius standing with his back to them. "I'm going to seduce that son-of-a-bitch, fuck his brains out, make him want me, then dump him."

Macus stepped around her to get in front of her and face her squarely. "No."

Her anger boiled to the surface and she sneered. "Are you going all bitchy and jealous on me?"

He leaned close to her and let his own anger show. "No, I'm being rational while you're hysterical. If you fuck Mathius, word will get out, and that'll screw up your relationship with Strikland."

"Fuck!" she hissed, keeping her voice to a whisper. "Fuck, fuck, fuck."

She turned around, turned her back on Macus, and he remained silent, letting her think it through. He watched her shoulders heave with stress and anger for several seconds, then her breathing calmed. He waited, and when she finally turned around, she was once again the Faith he knew.

She grinned unpleasantly. "I'm going to walk out the door and leave this little soiree for a brief time. Wait a couple of minutes, then follow. I'll be waiting down the corridor out of sight."

He tried to ask her what she had in mind, but she ignored him and walked away. She strolled casually around the edge of the room, then disappeared out the entrance. He waited a few minutes, then edged his way through the middle of the crowd and followed. As promised, he found her waiting out of sight about thirty paces down the hall.

As he approached, she said, "Follow me," then turned and marched away.

He followed.

She stopped at a door, tried the handle, but it was locked. She walked to the next door and tried it, and it too was locked. She kept at it until a door finally opened. She looked inside, shook her head, closed the door, and moved on. Eventually, she opened a door, looked in, and said, "This'll do."

She stepped into the room and Macus followed, closing the door behind him.

She had found what appeared to be a supply room for building maintenance. She marched past rows of shelves to a workbench against the far wall. As Macus followed, she bent down, gripped the hem of her skirt and slid it up to her waist, then slid her underwear down to her ankles. With her back to Macus, and her nice ass quite bare beneath her bunched up skirt, she leaned forward and put her hands flat on the workbench. She looked over her shoulder at Macus. "Fuck me. Fuck me hard."

Macus didn't hesitate. He crossed the short distance between them and had his pants down before he got to her.

That night she introduced him to a new side of her. It didn't really last long, though recalling how she always demanded he give as much pleasure as he received, he tried not to finish too quickly. But she demanded he pound away at her while she cursed and spit and swore invectives that would make a dock worker blush, occasionally looking over her shoulder and demanding, "Harder, god damn it. Fuck me harder." Holding back proved to be impossible and he finished long before she achieved any pleasure of her own. Or maybe not.

She straightened, turned around and faced him, a pleasant smile on her face. Reaching out, she gripped his shirt tail and wiped her crotch. Then she bent down and pulled her underwear back up, slid the hem of her skirt down and smoothed it out. Still smiling, she leaned toward him and gave him a gentle peck on the cheek. "I'll return to the party first, darling. You should wait a bit before following."

No, Macus thought, that evening her pleasure stemmed from something other than an orgasm. For Faith Carlton none of it was about the sex; it was all about the control. She had desperately needed to control someone, and she had controlled him completely, leading him around by the head of his dick. No, it was definitely not about the sex.

On the other hand, he had damn-well enjoyed himself, and hadn't been required to waste time trying to please her. Standing there with his pants around his ankles, it occurred to Macus he should look for other opportunities to put Mathius and Faith together, especially if it produced such an enjoyable result.

7

Family Time

IN THE VESTIBULE outside the chambers of the Larscom Executive Council, Nikaela hovered around John, picking at his uniform like a nervous mother. Tall double doors twice the height of a man gave access to the Council's chambers. At that moment they were closed, with four armed dregkraag arrayed in front of them. They stood stiff and formal, their eyes locked forward, as if ignoring the presence of John, Nikaela, Kristdokar, and Primatov.

For some reason John felt only a little stage fright at the prospect of standing before the Council, nothing like the level of anxiety he saw in Nikaela. Standing nearby, Kristdokar and Primatov looked on as Nikaela spotted something on his shoulder, something invisibly small like a piece of lint. She reached out, picked it off, and flicked it away. "You'll do fine. You'll do just fine."

He started to say something like, *Of course, I'll do fine*, but there really wasn't any *of course* about it. He wondered for a moment why he didn't feel more fretful. His life had changed so much since that day more than six years ago when Mercier had murdered his father. He no longer recalled what the young boy Mathius had been like before that, couldn't remember what his hopes and fears had been. He thought of Paulo, and could no longer picture the face of his childhood friend, now long dead and gone. He even had trouble picturing the faces of his mother, father, and sister. Sadly enough, he remembered Cranoch's and Mercier's faces all too well. He especially remembered the look of surprise on Cranoch's face when he put that bullet in the side of his head.

"Now remember," Nikaela said, "you have to *stand* before them, literally. It's traditional, and they only make exceptions for those with infirmities. And you don't salute, no military—"

Kristdokar interrupted her. "Mistress Vreekande, leave the young man alone. He'll do just fine, and stop hovering."

Nikaela pursed her lips. Her lips were normally a little bluer than the pale tint of her skin, and when she pursed them that way they turned an even brighter blue.

John looked into her eyes. He liked looking into her eyes, even though at moments like that they were demonic red. He leaned close to her and whispered, "You sure your tongue isn't splitting and getting forked."

She wrinkled her nose at him. "I'm not going to say. I guess you'll have to personally check to find out." She gave him a shit-eating grin.

He grinned back at her. "I'm looking forward to that."

Without warning the four dregkraag came to life, probably at some signal from the councilors fed directly to their implants. They parted and two of them carefully swung the doors open. A male skalde and two female command eagles walked out of the chamber chatting amiably. John wasn't sure if he was supposed to salute or something, but Nikaela didn't snap to attention, so he followed her lead, though she did stiffen a little with obvious tension.

The three officers approached Kristdokar and she introduced them to Primatov. They exchanged pleasantries, but as was customary among the Kelk, they did not shake hands. Kristdokar craned her neck and looked John and Nikaela's way. "Mistress Vreekande, Maestra Mathius, please join us."

John and Nikaela crossed the short distance to the group of senior officers. Now that his audience before the Council was imminent, John's anxiety had ratcheted up a notch, and while he tried to be polite, he didn't think he'd remember any names. But then one of the female command eagles glanced downward for a heartbeat, and her eyes sharpened with fear. For a moment he thought she had lost control and taken note of the butcher's dagger in the modified sleeve of his service dress blues. But she had diverted her eyes more toward his right side, and the only thing there that might garner such attention for a Kelk was the Blacksword patch on his sleeve.

John paused for a moment, did a little tally in his head, and for the first time realized that only he, Primatov, and Thealone wore their patches. That would certainly make him stand out.

Kristdokar interrupted his thoughts. "The Council is ready for you, young man."

She turned to the other senior officers. "You'll excuse us?"

The male skalde said, "Of course."

The female command eagle whose name John had missed smiled. "Mustn't keep the Council waiting."

The command eagle who had glanced at John's Blacksword patch looked at him and frowned, but didn't say anything.

Kristdokar led John into the Council chamber, and the dregkraag closed the doors behind them.

John thought it interesting the way the desk curved around the podium at its focus. With the desk elevated above the podium, the setting was not designed to put the person who stood before the councilors at ease. John didn't want to admit it, but the intimidation factor worked rather well. Kristdokar remained at the back of the room while he walked forward and took his place at the podium.

Primatov and Kristdokar had thoroughly briefed John on the four people he would face. Skalde Supreme Dornmier, the most senior member, appeared ancient by any measure. Skalde of the Supremacy Veskarson, the second most senior member and the only man on the Council, didn't appear to be any younger. Vice Skalde Nygaard, whom John knew as much as any grunt can know an officer of flag rank, had not a spec of pepper in her hair, and Vice Skalde Tiegnordan appeared to be of a similar age. Of the four of them, Tiegnordan did not seem to be happy that John stood before them. Regardless of their appearances, looking at the flat, emotionless stares they directed toward him, John thought all four of them would do quite well in a card game against any of his friends.

Kristdokar had warned John that it was customary for the second most senior member to chair meetings of the Council. "Maestra Mathius," Veskarson said, speaking Lingua, "thank you for joining us today."

Kristdokar had been kind enough to coach John a little, and he responded in Kelk. "I am honored to stand before you, Maestra and Mistresses."

The looks on Tiegnordan's and Dornmier's faces softened a little, and they both gave a slight nod of approval.

Seated in the center seat of the curved desk, Veskarson glanced right, then left, then looked at John carefully. "Before going any further, I think we'd all like to hear your version of the events that transpired between you and Mistress Vreekande on Reisenar. We would like to hear the story in detail, so please speak plainly, and take as long as you wish."

"Forgive me," John said, still speaking Kelk. "For such an involved story I must speak in Lingua to ensure that I don't accidentally misstate any facts."

Dornmier waved a hand in a dismissive gesture. "That's quite all right, young man. The four of us speak fluent Lingua, and we have professional translators to back us up if any questions arise."

John began his tale with the disastrous drop to the surface of Reisenar. He had told the story so many times it came easily. Interestingly enough, it was the first time anyone let him simply tell it beginning to end without a single interruption. When he finished, they asked several questions to clarify certain aspects of the events of that night. Then the questions shifted to more personal issues about him and his training. They made him relate the events aboard *Caliban* and *Sycorax*, then questioned him about his service as a member of *Drakan Helgis*'s crew. They completely skipped the entire assassination attempt with the butcher's blades, as if it hadn't happened. And at no time did he catch any of them glancing toward the dagger in the sheath sewn into the forearm of his coat. So far, the only Kelk to have lost control enough to glance at the blade had been the officious little shit on the lawn in front of the palace. John had to think for a moment to recall the fellow's name: Berkman. No, Bekmaan.

John thought the questioning was nearly over when Nygaard asked, "Has Mistress Vreekande taken you as a lover yet?"

John managed not to react or flinch at the question, but it surprised him how casually all of them took such a query. He couldn't simply deny that he and Nikaela were lovers, though he was still not sure of the etiquette required in such a relationship among the Kelk. But then, he wasn't Kelk.

"No," he said flatly, and both Nygaard and Veskarson frowned.

John shook his head. "No, she didn't. I took her as a lover."

Nygaard flashed him a look of hard anger, so he softened his tone. "Actually, we took each other as lovers. It was more of a mutual thing."

All four of them frowned, and clearly didn't understand what he meant. Dornmier lifted one eyebrow, as if she might have some inkling that John and Nikaela's relationship didn't conform to the Kelk norm. Veskarson glanced side to side, possibly concerned how the three women might react. Tiegnordan cocked her head to one side and gave John a hard look. Nygaard nodded, almost a gesture of approval. "So she did take you as a lover?"

John decided not to push the matter. "Yes."

Nygaard asked, "Am I correct that you are a survivor of Novalis III?"

Tiegnordan's eyes flashed angrily, and the look on her face could have been cut from stone. John knew that she had considerable interests in Norddansk Interstellar, and sat on its board.

"Yes," John said, "I am."

Nygaard nodded. "Tell us about that." It had been an order from a superior to a subordinate.

John locked eyes with her. "Twenty million people were murdered. There's not much more to tell than that."

Nygaard's face hardened with displeasure.

Tiegnordan leaned forward and snapped words at him. "Do you hold that against us?"

It was almost the same question Falkenberg had asked when he had first joined *Drakan Helgis*'s crew. He decided to give them the same answer. "There are superstitious and greedy Kelk people who are to blame, and there are also superstitious and greedy Commonwealth people who are to blame. And if I ever learn who they are, I'm going to find them and kill them, regardless of their rank, race or nationality."

The room went silent for a long moment. At least none of them called in a squad of kriegers to drag John out to the lawn in front of the Hyvaldsborg Palace and stand him up in front of a firing squad.

Veskarson broke the silence. "Does anyone have any further questions?"

He glanced right and left, and when no one spoke up, he addressed John. "Do you have any questions or observations, Maestra Mathius?"

John couldn't think of any questions, but he did have one observation, the same thought he had shared with the diplomatic mission. "You might find it interesting to know that most of my Commonwealth superiors refer to Novalis III as an incident, while without exception, every Kelk I've spoken with has called it a tragedy."

All four of them sat there staring at him in silence.

••••

Nikaela intended to wait for John in the vestibule outside the Council chamber, but Kristdokar would have none of that. "He might be in there for a couple of hours. And in any case, we have an appointment for lunch."

That sparked Nikaela's curiosity. Kristdokar had told her to keep her schedule open for the next few hours, but not that they would be meeting with someone else. "With whom?"

The older woman gave her a pained smile. "Your mother and grandmother."

Nikaela wasn't sure she wanted to see those two women.

Kristdokar looked at Primatov. "And they'd like to meet the colonel as well, so I've invited her to join us." Kristdokar lowered her voice. "And just in case you're wondering, your attendance is not optional."

Nikaela followed Kristdokar and Primatov out through the front entrance of the Hyvaldsborg Palace. They took a hired grav car to a busy restaurant in the heart of Emkeldstadt, a place frequented by members of the Larscom General Secretariat. The owner hailed from Norandyne, and the menu featured cuisine from a dozen different planets, none of them in the Commonwealth.

As they waited to be taken to their table, Nikaela noticed a lot of people looking her way with furtive, surreptitious glances. That seemed odd, because her superiors had taken care to deemphasize the breschkada relationship. When Nikaela's face had appeared on the vids, more often than not she stood in the background, with the foreground focused on dignitaries and high-ranking officers. But as they followed the manager across the dining room floor, she realized it was not she who drew their attention. Their eyes were drawn to Primatov; tall, beautiful, red-haired, wearing her ComSecCorps uniform, no one like her had ever before come to that restaurant. And the Blacksword patches on her sleeves, while small and non-descript, stood out far more than their size warranted.

Her mother and grandmother waited for them at the table and stood as they approached. Still good-looking, her mother stood taller than Nikaela, with hair that contained only a slight touch of salt. On the other hand, her grandmother, who held a seat on the General Secretariat and the rank of Major Skalde, retired, was a small woman of slight stature, but not of slight demeanor.

Kristdokar introduced them to Primatov.

Nikaela's mother lowered her voice. "You're creating quite a stir here, Colonel." She looked at Kristdokar and at Nikaela's grandmother. "But knowing you two old women, I'm guessing that's by design."

Nikaela thought it interesting that her mother and Kristdokar were of a similar age.

Kristdokar shrugged. "We need to help the general populace adjust to a new reality."

Nikaela's grandmother smiled as she sat down, and she did not lower her voice. "And that starts with the presence of a high-ranking Blacksword officer walking about publicly in Emkeldstadt, the heart of the Supremacy."

Primatov smiled pleasantly and said to Nikaela, "They warned me what to expect."

Her mother nodded toward the butcher's dagger hanging from the belt of Nikaela's uniform. "Nice touch, that. That'll keep everyone off balance. People will wonder why you're wearing that, and they'll ask, and they'll hear the story. So you'll create a stir of your own."

Nikaela's grandmother said, "Like mother, like daughter."

As they sat down, her grandmother leaned forward with a smug grin on her face. "Is he really wearing his in front of the Council this morning?"

There was never any doubt as to who her question referred to. Nikaela nodded. "But his uniform coat won't accommodate a sheath at his belt, so he had a forearm sheath sewn into his left sleeve."

"Oh," her grandmother said, her grin broadening, "then the podium won't hide it."

Nikaela shrugged. "He wouldn't allow it to be hidden regardless, either by accident, or intent."

Her mother didn't seem to share her grandmother's humor. "That is so Kelk of him, I do want to meet this young man."

Nikaela wasn't sure she wanted that meeting to happen.

Nikaela's mother gave her a curious look. "Have you taken him as a lover?"

One of Primatov's eyebrows rose slightly, but she said nothing.

Nikaela's relationship with John was unusual by Kelk standards, even if one disregarded the whole breschkada thing. "Yes and no," she said, and that clearly surprised the three Kelk women seated at the table. "He acts like a Kelk man in many ways, but not in that. In fact, he took me as a lover."

Everyone but Primatov stiffened. Her grandmother's humor disappeared, her mother's eyes flashed with open anger, and Kristdokar merely gave her a curious look, as if wondering what Nikaela hoped to accomplish.

Nikaela fought hard to avoid appearing smug. "He's not Kelk, and as you said, the general populace will have to adjust to a new reality. I think I would say he took me as a lover, just as much as I took him."

Primatov watched the byplay with considerable interest, and Nikaela thought the colonel might have learned something.

They ordered lunch, and while they waited, her mother and grandmother wanted to hear the story of what she and John had done on Reisenar. Nikaela looked at Kristdokar, the skalde nodded her approval, then activated a privacy screen to blur their images and null out their voices to anyone not at their table.

To Nikaela's mother, Kristdokar said, "Much of what she is about to tell you is classified. You are not cleared to hear it, but I have special dispensation from the Executive Council to allow you to do so. And after we leave this table, there is to be no discussion of this."

Nikaela had told the story many times and was now quite certain she sounded rehearsed. She paused when the waiter arrived with their meal, and again several times when she answered questions, but it didn't take long to tell the salient details. Just like everyone else, they were most interested in what happened on that subway platform, and how she and John had become breschkada.

After that they focused on Primatov, and questioned the Blacksword on the differences she had noticed between Kelk and Commonwealth culture. It pleased Nikaela that their attention shifted away from her. She scanned the patrons of the restaurant and noticed a common-face man looking her way. But his gaze passed over her quickly as he looked about the room, and her momentary spate of paranoia passed quickly. After discovering during the trip back to her old apartment that she was under constant surveillance, she had been overly sensitive to such things.

As they left the restaurant, Nikaela noticed the same common-face fellow walking out of the place ahead of them. Kristdokar, Primatov and her grandmother preceded Nikaela and her mother out of the establishment. Just before walking through the door behind them, Nikaela's mother gripped her arm and held her back, and for a moment they were alone. She opened up a secure link between their implants. *The trouble you had during your senior year at the academy, did it have something to do with Novalis III?*

At that moment Nikaela needed to tread carefully. *If I were to confirm your assumption, and someone learned that I discussed that subject with you, we might both suddenly disappear.*

Her mother's eyebrows rose, and it was one of the few times Nikaela had ever taken the woman by surprise. Her mother killed the link between their implants and nodded. "Now I understand." She glanced toward the door of the restaurant, and through its window they saw the other three women waiting outside. "Someday, if the opportunity presents itself, I must thank Kristdokar for you."

She took Nikaela's arm. "Come, daughter."

8

Old Alliances

NIGHTS ON VIKTORKINDE were not unlike nights on Trafalgar. Viktorkinde had one large moon that dominated the night sky when in full aspect. Two smaller moons, when full, were easily visible to the naked eye, but anyone not aware of their existence might simply mistake them for unusually bright stars.

Late that evening Macus met Strikland in the main lobby of the Hyvaldsborg Palace. As they shook hands Strikland smiled, glanced over his shoulder, and lowered his voice. "You're going to meet someone rather interesting tonight, a close associate of mine."

Macus nodded. "I look forward to it, sir."

Strikland was about to say more, but he paused and looked toward the lobby entrance. A Kelk woman wearing the uniform of a senior command superior had just emerged from the night, and she walked straight toward them as she crossed the lobby. Macus had only been on the planet for five days, but during that time had met quite a number of Kelk and had developed a good feel for how to judge Kelk age. The command superior was attractive enough that Macus would be willing to take her on, with no gray whatsoever in her hair, probably mid to late thirties.

She stopped in front of Strikland and smiled pleasantly. "Mr. Strikland, I am Command Superior Torstein."

He nodded and returned her smile. "I was told to expect you, Mistress Torstein." He nodded toward Macus. "This is my associate Macus DeLeon."

She acknowledged Macus with a nod. "My superiors told me Mr. DeLeon will be accompanying you."

Strikland looked at Macus. "She's here to make sure we don't get lost in the city."

A polite pretense, that. All Commonwealth citizens were under strict orders to not leave the grounds of the palace unless accompanied by a Kelk officer in uniform and with a rank of at least command superior. They were also told it was highly advisable they not walk openly on the streets of Emkeldstadt unless accompanied by Kelk armed bodyguards. Their hosts tempered that warning with the qualification that they really had nothing to fear from *most* of the planet's residents, but they would be wise to anticipate the possibility of extremist factions.

Torstein looked at Strikland, then at Macus. "Please follow me, gentlemen."

She turned and headed toward the lobby entrance. Strikland and Macus followed. The woman did not engage them in polite conversation or small talk as they silently marched out the front entrance of the palace.

In front of the palace, a wide turnaround surrounded a large and impressive fountain that depicted some sort of mythical Kelk gods. Torstein led them to a waiting grav car, and as they approached, two palace kriegers opened the vehicle's front and rear passenger doors. Torstein paused. "Mr. DeLeon, you'll ride with me in the front seat. Mr. Strikland, you'll ride with my companion in the rear seat." She spun on her heel and walked around the front of the car to the driver's side.

As Macus climbed into the front passenger seat, he noticed another woman seated in the rear on the driver's side, Torstein's companion. She wore civilian clothing, and had a fair amount of gray in her hair, but the dark interior of the car prevented him from discerning any details beyond that. Strikland sat down next to her as Torstein sat down behind the vehicle's controls next to Macus. Torstein did not introduce Macus or Strikland to her companion.

As soon as they were all seated, and the doors closed, Torstein blanked the windows. Without the right decryption codes, Macus and Strikland now saw only opaque plast panels, but through her implants, Macus knew that Torstein saw just fine through the blanked windows.

At the same moment, Macus's implants went offline. The Kelk had allowed their common-face guests to interface their implants to Emkeldstadt's citynet, and other non-secure communications nodes. Apparently, their hosts wanted to ensure Macus and Strikland didn't know where they went that evening, or how to return there. Macus's curiosity about Strikland's *close associate* grew with each revelation of the extent to which these people wanted to cover their tracks.

Again, no polite conversation or small talk during the drive, which took about an hour. Given the precautions Macus had observed so far, he had to assume Torstein had taken a circuitous route to their destination, so in all likelihood it would be a mistake to assume the place was an hour from the palace by grav car.

When Torstein brought the car to a stop she cleared the blanking from the windows, though Macus's implants remained offline. She had parked the vehicle in what appeared to be a garage of some sort, with plast columns supporting a low concrete ceiling overhead, three other cars parked nearby, and room for several more. It looked like an underground garage, but that was purely a guess.

Two women and two men approached the vehicle. They wore Kelk military uniforms and stopped about five paces from the car on the passenger side. All four wore heavy grav pistols holstered on their hips. A female Kelk officer stood behind them in the background looking on.

Macus looked to Torstein for guidance on his next move.

She glanced at the kriegers outside the car. "Both of you may step out of the car without fear of harm, but you will be searched."

Macus hit the latch on the door and stepped out onto a concrete floor. A male krieger approached him and stopped a pace in front of him. One of his companions stopped a few paces to one side, ensuring a clear line of fire if he needed to draw his weapon and put Macus down. The fellow in front of him held out a small instrument. He positioned it a few inches from Macus's nose, then carefully ran it down the length of him all the way to the toes of his shoes. When he finished, he straightened and said, "Arms out."

Surprised that they would go to the extra trouble of a physical search, Macus extended his arms. The fellow frisked him rather thoroughly, if professionally, and he noticed Strikland got the same treatment. Once satisfied that he and Strikland weren't carrying weapons, the kriegers stepped aside and the officer walked forward. During his basic training Macus hadn't paid much attention during the classes on Kelk rank and insignia. After all, when it came to the Kelk, all one needed to know was how to aim your rifle and pull the trigger. He'd have to brush up on their rank, but he thought she might be a command hawk.

She didn't introduce herself. "Please follow me, Maestras."

Strikland glanced Macus's way, smiled and nodded. The two of them stepped in line behind the officer and followed her as she marched across the concrete floor, the four kriegers in step behind them. To one side Macus noticed a lift that probably ascended up into the building, but the officer didn't lead them to that. Instead, she stopped at a door nearby, opened it, and proceeded through it. Strikland and Macus followed, but the four kriegers remained behind.

Beyond the door they were faced with a featureless hallway. It had a concrete floor and ceiling, plain white walls, with four doors in front of them, two on each side of the corridor. The last door on the right was open. They followed the female officer down the length of the hall to that door. She paused there, and with her hand indicated that they should precede her into the room beyond

They stepped into what appeared to be a Spartan office with a desk, a couple of chairs, and crates of some sort stacked against one wall. The officer did not follow them into the room, but closed the door, leaving the two of them alone.

Macus lowered his voice. "They're not very trusting, are they, sir?"

Strikland grimaced and nodded. "They have good reason not to be."

They were in the heart of the Supremacy, and no one there had any reason to fear Macus or Strikland. Clearly, these Kelk feared discovery by other Kelk. Macus wondered how deep Strikland's involvement with these people went, though the circumstances of this meeting certainly hinted at the answer to that question rather starkly.

The door opened, and a tall, handsome Kelk gentleman stepped into the room. He wore a business suit that differed only slightly from common civilian attire on Trafalgar. The woman who had sat in the back seat of the car with Strikland walked in behind him, followed by the command hawk. Macus had done some homework, and from pictures he had downloaded to his implants, he thought he knew the fellow's identity.

The older man nodded to Strikland with a neutral look on his face. "Lawrence, it's good to see you after all this time."

Strikland smiled. "Aubrecht, how have you been?"

That confirmed Macus's suspicions. Both Faith and Macus had heard Palmutter mention the name Nvalheim to Strikland, and then Palmutter had blown his stack, telling Faith that someone named Machtberg was a traitor to him and Nvalheim. Macus had found nothing in the Commonwealth databases regarding either name, though that could simply be because he didn't have the necessary clearances. But the open media channels and public records on Viktorkinde were another matter. Macus and Faith had had no trouble finding references to Nvalheim and Machtberg.

Both names were associated with influential families, though that didn't narrow either surname down to a specific individual. But among the many given names in the Machtberg clan, *Aubrecht* had been quite prominent. In the highly matriarchal familial structure of the Kelk, men rarely held the reins of a family. But as a member of the Larscom General Secretariat, Aubrecht Machtberg had proven to be an exception. The man standing before them nicely matched the pictures Macus and Faith had acquired.

Machtberg held up a bottle of clear liquid. "I brought some kirva."

Strikland introduced Macus as a close associate. "Mr. DeLeon is going to be a valuable addition to our team."

Machtberg introduced the two women that accompanied him. The civilian was his sister, and now that shadows no longer obscured her face, Macus matched her up to one of the pictures he had downloaded. Macus got the impression the officer was a mid-level lieutenant, more of a hired-hand than a family member.

Machtberg poured shots of the fiery liquor, and they tossed them back. Macus had been cautioned about the stuff, but no warning had prepared him for the burn that worked its way down to his gut.

"Now, Aubrecht," Strikland said. "I heard a rumor you were involved in this *Valhaukr* thing."

Machtberg shook his head sadly as he poured them all another shot of kirva. "Nvalheim lied to me. She and that idiot Palmutter have become a real liability."

Strikland glanced Macus's way, perhaps to gauge his reaction. "Yes, they have, haven't they? But we should be discreet."

At that point the two older men stopped using proper names. Palmutter became simply *him* and *he*, and Nvalheim became *her* and *she*. Between shots of kirva, the two talked about the *tragic incident*, which Macus interpreted to mean Novalis III. Macus got the impression that *he* and *she* were up to their eyeballs in some deep, deep shit, and Machtberg and Strikland thought the two would probably hang for it. Macus also got the impression that the two men in front of him were just as responsible, but were confident they could skate by on this one, especially if they subtly helped the other two hang. Macus wouldn't have been able to put it together as concisely as he did if Palmutter hadn't indiscreetly dropped Nvalheim's name on the journey to Viktorkinde, then blown his stack and made the connection between *her* and Machtberg.

Strikland remained rather quiet on the ride back to the palace, perhaps because Machtberg's sister sat next to him. Macus's head spun a little from the shots of kirva, but it gave him a chance to think carefully about what he had learned that night. Without question, Strikland had brought Macus to that meeting as a test. Strikland could muster resources to which few people had access, and would likely come out on top of just about any situation. Of course, he'd be saddened at the demise of his dear friend Silas Palmutter. Would Macus be willing to work with people who were quite probably responsible for mass-murder on an unprecedented scale? On the return to the palace Macus thought about nothing but that.

When the car pulled up in front of the Hyvaldsborg Palace, Macus and Strikland climbed out. Then the car sped away silently on its grav fields.

Strikland gave Macus an appraising look. "Well, what do you think, young man?"

Macus shrugged. "I get the impression you and the maestra are dealing with a difficult situation. But it appears you have it well in hand. And as the situation develops, if I can be of help in any way, please let me know."

Strikland grinned and threw an arm around Macus's shoulders. "Good lad. Come, let me buy you a nightcap."

••••

Taugrim and Falkenberg had parked *Drakan Helgis* in a repair dock in the Heilbronn Navy Yard, a satellite almost as large as Viktorkinde Prime, but dedicated to outfitting, refitting, and repairing warships. The makeshift repairs they had effected out in the middle of interstellar space had gotten them home, but only a fool would take a ship out again without proper repairs completed in a major facility like the navy yard.

Seated at the pilot's console in one of *Drakan Helgis*'s assault boats, John applied a slight amount of power to the boat's drive and nudged it forward, paying close attention to the docking gantry extended from the destroyer's Hangar Deck. Taugrim had dispatched the boat to the Hyvaldsborg Palace to pick up John, May and her squad, which had become a small platoon since Matsen, Kolbeck, and a number of dregkraag now reported to May. The captain had also given the boat's female pilot orders that John was to fly the boat back up, with the pilot in the co-pilot's couch acting as instructor. During the days in zero-G swinging through the gravity well of the white dwarf, with the three enemy hunter-killers running search patterns trying to locate them, John had spent hours in the simulators on board the destroyer. He had come a long way since hijacking the assault boat from *Sycorax*, could now read the labels on all the controls, and fly the craft as well as any Commonwealth boat.

A loud clang and clatter echoed through the hull as the boat mated with the gantry. John released the controls as the deck crew swung the boat around, then retracted the gantry and backed it into its docking bay. The large doors of the hangar bay dilated shut, and pumps clattered and rattled. When he got the green light indicating proper air pressure in the hangar, he cycled open the large deployment hatch in the side of the boat and May and her platoon spilled out onto the deck. Next to John the pilot nodded, smiled and said, "Good work, Ensign. Perhaps I should take you as a lover."

John now knew the etiquette of properly responding to such an invitation, but he was not Kelk. He decided to switch things up, but first he'd start with a proper Kelk response. "Perhaps not."

She cocked her head slightly to one side in a shrug of indifference at the rejection.

John added, "Perhaps I'll take you as a lover."

She stiffened and her eyes blinked rapidly.

John leaned close to her and said, "If you haven't figured it out yet, I'm not Kelk."

He left her there with her mouth open, walked back to the hatch and jumped down onto the deck.

May's platoon consisted of Carla, Leeze, the four guys from Miriteen, Matsen, Kolbeck and four Kelk dregkraag. They had crowded around six new dregkraag, a mix of men and women, the reason they had made the trip up to *Drakan Helgis*. New recruits to the platoon, they were apparently willing to work with Commonwealth common-faces.

Matsen leaned close to John and lowered his voice. "Taugrim told me she screened 'em pretty good, and Kolbeck and me know 'em well enough. They'll fit in nicely."

He glanced at Kolbeck. "But they ain't gonna die for him any more than we are, right?"

Kolbeck frowned as if to say, *Do you need to even ask?*

Since they stored their combat armor on *Drakan Helgis*, they would spend a couple of days fully suited, drilling with the new people in gravity, in vacuum, in zero-G, the works. Then they'd all return to the palace. Once back on the ground they could drill in light combat armor, and no armor at all.

"Blacksword."

At the sound of Taugrim's voice John turned to face her. She stood half a pace from him and he towered over her. John now had a better understanding of the Kelk etiquette regarding male-female relationships. She had never physically touched him. Had she purposefully done so when not in the line of duty, even just a slight tap on the shoulder, it would have been the most horrific violation of his right to choose, his right to say yes or no. He smiled. "Mistress Taugrim."

She gave him that big, flashy grin of hers. "I knew you couldn't stay away from me for long."

9

To Stand

SKALDE SUPREME DORNMIER leaned forward on the curved desk of the Executive Council Chamber, a wicked grin on her wrinkled face. "Is it true he killed them with a fork?"

Veskarson sat between Nygaard and Dornmier, and Nygaard leaned forward to address her around him. "No. He disarmed the officer, and killed them both with her grav pistol. The whole fork thing is a myth."

Dornmier raised an eyebrow in disapproval. "Lana, I asked the question of Brigadier Skalde Kristdokar, and I'd like to hear her answer."

Kristdokar stood at one of three podiums placed at the focus of the curved desk and tried not to cringe as the old woman turned her head slowly and locked eyes with her. "Please answer the question, Brigadier."

Most Kelk, even those of rank or influence, never in their life *stood* before the Larscom Executive Council. And here Kristdokar was up for her third turn, with Colonel Primatov standing at a podium on her left, and Command Hawk Taugrim standing at one on her right. Kristdokar didn't want to anger Nygaard by contradicting her. "Maestra Mathius took the officer's sidearm, and used it to kill her and her subordinate, both of whom had entered his room to assassinate him. No one died that day of injuries induced by a fork." She sensed that Taugrim wanted to speak up, but wasn't foolish enough to do so.

Veskarson's eyes narrowed. "Tell me, am I correct that this young man had just recovered from serious hypothermia, and brutal beatings at the hands of both Kelk and Commonwealth assailants?" It was a rhetorical question, and he continued without waiting for an answer. "And this young man disarmed two crewmembers and killed them with their own weapons. Tell me how he did that."

Taugrim almost shouted her words. "With a bloody fork." She gave Kristdokar a big, wide grin.

Dornmier grinned as well. "Brigadier Kristdokar, please explain in more detail. How did he come by a fork?"

Nygaard had told Kristdokar she wanted to avoid propagating the myth surrounding young Maestra Mathius and his fork, but at that moment the vice skalde rolled her eyes and cocked her head slightly. Kristdokar took that as a sign she wouldn't hold her testimony against her. "He was alone and eating his first meal after recovering from his injuries. Apparently, he heard what sounded like the report of a grav pistol, muffled by the bulkhead between him and the passageway. So with nothing else at hand that might serve as a weapon, he palmed the fork from his food tray. When they attacked him, he surprised them with it, and was able to take the officer's sidearm. He then shot them both."

Dornmier clearly sensed Taugrim's desire to speak. "Command Hawk Taugrim, would you care to add anything to Brigadier Kristdokar's account?"

Taugrim had dyed her hair copper-brown that morning, and had let it grow a little, which emphasized the spikes even more. "With that fork he ripped out the officer's carotid artery. She would have died rather quickly, even if he hadn't blown her head off."

Dornmier nodded and glanced around Veskarson to Nygaard. "Yes, I too saw the recordings of her injuries. But let's be honest here . . ." She glanced in turn at each of the other councilors, then at Primatov, Kristdokar, and last at Taugrim. The look she gave the captain of *Drakan Helgis* was not a pleasant one. "We don't need some myth about an invincible Blacksword circulating among our people and complicating the situation. Think about it, stories like that will have even more people believing in the Curse of the Blacksword."

Kristdokar thought she might ask John Mathius to forego wearing the pin she had given him, the one with the tiny fork and butcher's dagger. He seemed a nice enough young man. Certainly he would grant such a request.

Primatov spoke. "I agree fully, but we probably can't stop it. The story of the fork certainly made the rounds of *Drakan Helgis*'s crew." She paused and aimed her question at Nygaard. "What of *Konigsborge*'s crew?"

Nygaard closed her eyes tightly and shook her head. "Yes, it made the rounds there too."

Taugrim surprised them all by speaking. "Among my crew the fork is more of a joke now, not some myth blown out of proportion. I don't think it'll be a problem. Just ignore it, give it time, and it'll die away."

"Speaking of your crew," Tiegnordan said. "How did they handle having him among them?"

Taugrim shrugged. "I think they thought it was weird at first, but now they don't think anything of it. He's just another crewman."

"And you," Tiegnordan persisted. "How do you feel?"

She shrugged again. "He's a valued member of my crew, with good marks, hardworking, does the job required of him, does it well, and doesn't complain. And he's smart. He'll make a good Kelk officer."

A common-face as a Kelk officer, and a Blacksword at that! It had never occurred to Kristdokar to consider something so outrageous. And she saw from the looks on the councilor's faces that Taugrim's statement had had the same effect on them.

They adjourned the meeting of the Council and went to closed session. Primatov and Taugrim left, while, by order of the Council, Kristdokar remained. When the Council chamber's doors were once again closed, Veskarson announced, "And now, we must consider the matter of Vice Skalde Haugrund's petition before the General Secretariat. She has requested reinstatement to the Council."

Veskarson slammed his fist down on the desk in front of him. "Well I certainly am not voting in favor of her reinstatement. And since it must be unanimous, there's nothing to discuss."

Nygaard grimaced and shook her head. "But she may have the votes among the General Secretariat, though still, it's a close thing."

Veskarson frowned.

Dornmier pursed her lips, which emphasized the wrinkles around her mouth. "How is she going to get a two-thirds majority, especially after the *Valhaukr* fiasco?"

Nygaard drummed her fingers on the desk in front of her for a moment. "She claims Nvalheim lied to her, and most do believe her. I suppose I believe her too. And no one thinks for a moment that she has any culpability in the Novalis III tragedy."

Tiegnordan made no attempt to hide her anger when she spoke. "Which is more than can be said for Nvalheim."

Dornmier pointed a shaking finger at Tiegnordan. "But we can't prove anything, so we can't act."

Tiegnordan shrugged and feigned indifference. "It doesn't matter. The moderates believe Haugrund, as do I. She's a rational woman, not a flaming maniac like Nvalheim. And with only moderates and doves on this Council, most believe its makeup is not properly balanced at the moment."

Veskarson snarled, "As do you?"

She closed her eyes and gave them a single nod. "As do I." She opened her eyes. "If we councilors held a vote now, I would vote in favor of reinstatement, though I suppose I would be alone in that."

••••

Nikaela had already met the members of the diplomatic mission as a group, and she had stood before the Executive Council, so to some degree she was acquainted with all of them. But Nygaard had decided that the two breschkada should be introduced to everyone under less formal circumstances.

The crew on *Drakan Helgis* had heard of the mixers aboard *Lady Victorious*, and Nikaela knew she would eventually have to attend something of that nature. Thankfully, for her more casual introduction to their Commonwealth guests, her superiors had orchestrated a much smaller event, with only certain Supremacy dignitaries present, plus the mission principles, some of their high-level staffers, her, and John. Kristdokar had said something about having some younger people present other than just her and John, so a few of his friends had been included as well. She and John did not want to lend any credence to the rumors floating around about them, so they agreed that they would arrive and leave separately.

As Nikaela approached the lounge with Stinar in tow, she heard the buzz of many people talking. Stinar peeled off when Nikaela stepped into the room, and it appeared she was one of the last to arrive. She tried to keep her nerves in check. Then every common-face, and some of the Kelk as well, looked her way. The room went silent, and her nerves decided not to cooperate.

She spotted a group of young ComSecCorps soldiers across the room, among them Carla Nigurski and Leeze Caputto. Neither of them had noticed her yet, were instead focused intently on discussing something with their comrades. Nikaela had met both on *Drakan Helgis*, but had never interacted with either beyond a polite nod in passing, or a quick word or two in greeting.

At the onset of the sudden silence, Carla glanced about, saw Nikaela, and their eyes met. She glanced about again, clearly noting the silent people gawking at Nikaela. Then she frowned, elbowed Leeze in the ribs, the two marched toward Nikaela, and stopped a couple paces from her.

"Nikaela," Carla said, but hesitated. She frowned and lowered her voice. "I don't know if I'm violating some long-standing Kelk custom, but I'm not going to call you Mistress Vreekande. We have too much in common, you and I, so you're Nikaela, and I'm Carla, and that's what we'll call each other." She nodded toward Caputto. "And you know Leeze."

Leeze held a drink in one hand. She looked into the glass. "Let's get her a drink. And as long as the booze is free, I need a refill."

The two sandwiched Nikaela between them, Carla on her right, Leeze on her left, and marched her across the room to the bar.

"Hey," Leeze said. "Let's try that kirva stuff."

Carla shook her head. "Shooters? Here? With all the big-shots around? Knowing you, you'll lose a stripe."

Leeze grimaced and wrinkled her nose. She leaned close to Nikaela. "Some night, you gotta introduce us to that kirva stuff. I hear it packs a wallop."

Nikaela found herself smiling, and was actually having fun. "I will, definitely."

Nikaela noticed a common-face man standing at the edge of the room and not mingling with anyone in the crowd. He wore a simple business suit and he seemed familiar, but she couldn't place him.

The bartender delivered their drinks. Nikaela resolved to nurse the one drink and make it last through the evening. But earlier, Carla had roused Nikaela's curiosity. "Carla," she said. "You said we have a lot in common. What did you mean by that?"

Carla stiffened, and she and Leeze shared a look. Gritting her teeth, and clearly uncomfortable, Carla said, "John Mathius."

Nikaela didn't understand. "What do you have in common with John, other than training together on Miriteen?"

Leeze and Carla shared that look again, which spurred Nikaela to replay her question, and Carla's subsequent answer. "No, you meant that John Mathius is someone you and I have in common."

Leeze found the tips of her shoes quite interesting.

Carla took a careful breath. "It was a long time ago, about six months after we returned from Reisenar."

Nikaela shrugged and tried to sound indifferent. "We Kelk women sometimes share a man, if all three parties are comfortable with such an arrangement. Is that what you'd like?" She really didn't want to share John, but she couldn't lie to one of his friends.

Carla smiled wistfully and shook her head. "John's not the sharing type. He's a one-woman guy, and right now you're the only woman he's interested in."

The evening had started out rather poorly, but with that bit of information Nikaela relaxed even more.

She spotted that fellow at the edge of the room again, not talking with anyone or mingling, just standing, watching. Thankfully, he wasn't watching her. She still couldn't recall where she'd seen him before.

Kristdokar approached her, and she pulled her attention away from the fellow at the edge of the room. To Carla and Leeze, the skalde said, "You don't mind if I steal Mistress Vreekande for a bit, do you?"

The older woman's rank obviously intimidated Carla. "Certainly, Mistress."

Kristdokar hooked an arm through Nikaela's elbow, and they walked carefully through the crowd to a small group consisting of Vice Skalde Nygaard, Tarsik Obradour, and Fran Thealone. Nikaela had met Obradour and Thealone briefly the previous day.

Nikaela's brief time with Carla and Leeze had been fun, but she now resigned herself to an evening on display as they paraded her before all the *big-shots*, as Carla had called them. One by one, Kristdokar steered her to every member of the diplomatic mission and the Executive Council, as well as some of the more influential members of the General Secretariat.

Kristdokar had briefed her on all the members of the Commonwealth mission, and while Obradour had a reputation as a wealthy kingmaker, she found him sterile. He probably had no interest in allowing a *youngster* like Nikaela to glimpse anything of the real man beneath the public façade. Nikaela didn't get any insight on Thealone either. The woman seemed observant, and cautious.

When Nikaela met Silas Palmutter, she noticed he kept stealing surreptitious glances at her breasts. But then she realized he was giving her equal treatment, because he stole surreptitious glances at every woman's breasts. Though, when he did so with Nikaela, he seemed torn, as if the thought of doing something about it with a Kelk woman sullied him in some way.

When Kristdokar introduced her to Lawrence Strikland, Nikaela and he shared a few polite, meaningless words, then he and Kristdokar spoke at some length. He expressed enthusiasm about some commercial prospects he would like to develop with certain Kelk companies. While they spoke, the fellow standing at the edge of the room had perked up a bit.

A handsome young couple approached Nikaela and she focused on them, two of Palmutter's senior staffers. Like everyone else present, Nikaela had been briefed on Faith Carlton and Macus DeLeon. Nikaela marveled at Carlton's blond hair, which reminded her of the diversity of natural hair-color among common-faces.

A little later Kristdokar introduced her to Jenine Catarvin and Manifort Gascoigne. While Kristdokar and Gascoigne spoke, Catarvin pulled Nikaela aside and lowered her voice. "I noticed you were a bit uncomfortable when you met good old Silas and he couldn't stop staring at your breasts. Don't worry, he does that with everyone, and he does have good taste. You are quite pretty, you know?"

As the evening wound down, Nikaela ended up with John and Colonel Primatov. And once more she noticed that fellow standing at the edge of the room and not joining in. It was then that she recalled him: He had been at the restaurant the day she had eaten lunch with Primatov, Kristdokar, her mother, and grandmother. "That man," she said, nodding toward the fellow.

Primatov and John both looked his way.

Nikaela continued. "The fellow just standing there, not joining in, do you know who he is?"

Primatov's brow furrowed. "He's one of Lawrence Strikland's security people."

Nikaela recalled her brief introduction to Strikland. "That man was at the restaurant the day we had lunch with my mother and grandmother. He was alone, eating by himself, and then he left just as we did. I think he was following me."

She looked Primatov in the eyes. "Or maybe he's following you."

Primatov slowly looked away from her toward the man at the edge of the room. Nikaela would not want that look aimed at her.

••••

As the mixer wound down, Primatov wandered over to talk with Thealone and Gascoigne, leaving John alone with Nikaela. John would like to get her alone in her room for the entire night, but they had agreed to leave separately, though he still didn't understand why. After all, their relationship was common knowledge, if for no other reason than that most Kelk had no problem asking outright if she had taken him as a lover, and frequently doing so in the middle of a crowd. "Oh, by the way, did you check your assault rifle this morning, and did she take you as a lover?"

"Why so pensive?" she asked him.

Dirkson had nagged him repeatedly about the right-of-vendetta thing since the last mixer. "I have a question for you."

Nikaela leaned close to him and lowered her voice. "If you want to know if my tongue has split and become forked, why don't you come back to my room and find out?"

John frowned. "But we have to leave separately."

She gave him an evil grin. "I'll bet you can find your way to my room without my help."

He returned her grin. "I'll bet I can, but first I have to ask you a question. What does 'right of vendetta' mean to the Kelk?"

Nikaela frowned, the grin disappeared, and all the playfulness left her voice. "Why do you ask that?"

He explained about Dirkson coming across a reference to it, but finding nothing more. "He's kind of frustrated, so I thought you might help me out. What does it mean?"

Her eyes lost focus and went to a thousand-yard stare. "It's an extremely rare means of settling a dispute, and it means someone must die."

She had turned all spooky, which frightened John a little. "What's wrong?"

She ignored that question and continued talking. "If one family has wronged another in a most horrible way, the injured party can claim right of vendetta. And if the Executive Council or the General Secretariat upholds the claim, the lives of the offending family are forfeit."

John wasn't sure what he had just heard. "The entire family?"

Nikaela nodded. "It's up to the claimant, the injured party. They can choose to take just one life, or the lives of all direct ancestors, and all direct descendants, of all family members who were complicit in the offense. It is rare, but vendetta has obliterated entire families."

John shook his head. "Shit! Men, women and children?"

"But," Nikaela continued, "if the claim is not upheld, then the claimant's entire family is forfeit."

Her eyes focused on him. "Does that answer your question?"

Now he understood why his question had shocked her so. "Yes, it does."

She shook her head with a desperate urgency. "John, don't ever claim right of vendetta against a Kelk. You're not Kelk and no Kelk would honor your claim. You could lose your entire family, all your loved ones, everyone you ever . . ."

Her voice trailed off. She must have realized what she had said, and to whom she had said it. John had almost corrected her, had been about to remind her that he no longer had any family to lose, but he saw now that he didn't need to.

Tears welled up in her eyes. "I'm sorry . . . I . . . I'm so sorry."

She didn't excuse herself or say anything, but simply turned and walked out of the room.

That night John walked back to his own room and went to bed alone.

10

Something's Up

WHEN THE DOORS to the lift opened, Faith stepped into it, and by reflex more than anything else, tried to program it through her implants. The lift did not respond, which reminded her again of the Kelk reluctance to allow them access to the systems of the Hyvaldsborg Palace. She reached out and pressed the button for the ground floor.

Two days ago Macus had briefed her on the clandestine meeting Strikland had arranged with Aubrecht Machtberg. She had spent the afternoon of that day digging up what she could on the man, but had learned nothing beyond what she and Macus had uncovered during their initial investigation of the Machtberg name. A wealthy and influential member of the Larscom General Secretariat, he had a reputation as a pragmatic hawk when it came to the Commonwealth. She did find it interesting that his name had been noticeably absent from the news feeds for a couple of tendays. With a man like him, that often meant he'd been off planet.

The lift doors opened and Faith stepped out into the lobby of the palace. She spotted Palmutter standing with a Kelk officer and one of his aides, the same fellow who had been smart enough to call Catarvin when Palmutter had been ready to steam right off the rails. As she crossed the lobby toward them, she noted that the fellow was rather good looking, and she had to think carefully to recall that his name was Andrew Talpano. Maybe she would give young Andrew what he so obviously wanted. It might be fun to fuck him good and hard as a thank-you for thinking quickly that day. But then such a liaison would likely get into the rumor mill and damage her relationship with Strikland, so the poor fellow would just have to stick to dating his right hand.

"Faith," Palmutter said, as she approached. "As always, you look lovely." His eyes focused on her breasts and he gave her a quick look-fuck. She had learned to ignore the lascivious looks, and she pretended not to notice.

To Andrew's credit, he didn't even undress her with his eyes. The young man had manners.

Palmutter introduced the Kelk officer, their mandatory escort when venturing off the grounds of the palace. Faith smiled and acknowledged her with a nod, but didn't bother to register the woman's name. As they followed her to a car waiting at the front of the palace, Palmutter leaned close to Faith and whispered, "We're going to meet some Kelk who are like-minded colleagues of mine."

Andrew sat in the front seat next to the Kelk officer, while Palmutter sat next to Faith in the rear seat. As the woman drove them into the center of the city, Faith carefully considered Palmutter's statement about *like-minded colleagues*. Palmutter feared and hated everything Kelk, but Faith didn't think they would now meet Kelk who feared and hated their own kind. So what did Palmutter consider like-minded—other people who feared and hated the way he did? That just didn't add up.

Their driver pulled the car up to the curb in front of a large restaurant. Palmutter said to Faith and Andrew, "Our hosts have made all the arrangements for the evening."

A fat, common-face man in a business suit stood in front of the restaurant, and as they stepped out of the car he approached Palmutter. "Senator Palmutter," he said, and Faith's implants identified his accent as that of a Sarkovite. He didn't wait for the senator to acknowledge the obvious, nor did he introduce himself. "Please follow me."

The fellow entered the front of the restaurant, and the three of them followed in a line behind him. They walked along the outskirts of a large dining room filled with a healthy mix of Kelk and common-faces, and for the first time Faith grasped the extent to which so many non-Commonwealth governments conducted business with the Supremacy. At the back of the room they stepped through a door into a private dining room.

Two Kelk men and a Kelk woman in civilian attire waited within seated at a large dining table, and they stood as Faith, Andrew and Palmutter entered the room. Their Sarkovite guide didn't follow them in, but closed the door at their backs. The Kelk woman appeared to be middle aged, with a mix of black, white, and gray in her hair. The two men were clearly younger, and the words *thug* and *muscle* came to mind when Faith looked at them. The woman stepped forward, stopped at an uncomfortably close distance to Palmutter, put her fists on her hips, and looked him up and down slowly. She made no attempt to mask the derision in her voice as she asked, "Silas Palmutter?"

Palmutter frowned. "You already know the answer to that, so let's stop wasting time. I was told I would meet someone who spoke with the authority of your superiors. Are you that person?"

The corners of the woman's mouth curled upward in an unpleasant smile. "When my superiors aren't present, yes, I am that person." She turned her head to look at Faith and Andrew. "Who are these two?"

Andrew's eyes widened with fear.

Palmutter shrugged. "The young woman is my Chief Communications Officer, the young man, an aide. It would not have looked right if I had been seen leaving the palace alone."

Faith wanted to kick the asshole in the balls. He'd brought her along, and into what appeared to be a dangerous situation, just so it would look right when he left the fucking palace.

The woman looked Faith over carefully, and Faith's heart pounded with fear. When the woman finished her examination, she turned her attention back to Palmutter. "Well, you're the one who is fucked if they're stupid enough to talk."

Palmutter nodded. "I'll handle the situation."

The woman grinned. "Then I have a surprise for you."

She glanced over her shoulder at one of the men and nodded. Mr. Muscle-Number-One turned and walked to a second door at the back of the room. It was clearly intended to allow wait staff to enter the private dining room without having to traverse the main dining area. Mr. Muscle opened it.

A much older woman in civilian attire stepped through the door and approached Palmutter. She had snow white hair, or as the Kelk would say, her hair had gone completely to salt. A sour look on her face added to the impression of age, making her appear almost ancient, and the look soured further as she regarded Palmutter. Faith recognized her, and tried to flash recall the pictures they had acquired when investigating the Machtberg and Nvalheim names. It didn't take her long to come up with Brigadier Skalde Marta Nvalheim, retired, a member of the Larscom General Secretariat, and a notorious, hardline, anti-Commonwealth hawk.

Nvalheim looked Palmutter up and down as one might examine a piece of shit on the sole of a shoe. "Silas, did you have a nice journey?"

He shrugged. "Boring, though you did liven it up a little with that *Valhaukr* fuckup."

Her eyes darted momentarily to Faith and Andrew, a clear message that he shouldn't have said that in front of them. Faith committed his words to memory, hoping there might be something in them she could use later.

Palmutter noted Nvalheim's reaction, and glanced Faith's way. "Yes, Faith and Andrew." He returned his attention to the old woman. "Why don't you and I adjourn to a more private setting where we can talk openly?"

The old woman glanced over her shoulder at Mr. Muscle-Number-Two. "Make it happen."

The fellow nodded and walked out through the door at the back of the room. During the few seconds it was open Faith got a brief glimpse of wait staff rushing about hurriedly in what appeared to be a large kitchen. When the door closed, Nvalheim and Palmutter stood silently staring daggers at each other, neither of them moving or reacting in any way. After several seconds the thug returned. "The proprietor has given us the room next door."

Palmutter looked again at Faith. "Enjoy your meal. It's one of the better restaurants. But stay away from the Kelk food, if you can. That stuff's all crap."

Thug-Number-Two led Palmutter and Nvalheim through the door. Thug-Number-One said, "Sit down. They'll bring your food shortly."

Faith and Andrew sat down at the dining table. A few minutes later a waiter walked into the room from the rear door carrying a tray laden with food. He didn't offer them menus, didn't say a word, but carefully placed plates of something in front of them both. Thug-Number-One returned to join Thug-Number-Two, and both stood silently over Andrew and Faith as they ate.

During the time they had been on Viktorkinde, Faith had sampled some of the local cuisine. She and Andrew ate in silence, and with one exception she had no difficulty with the stuff on the plate in front of her. About twenty minutes into their silent meal, they heard muffled shouts coming from the room next to theirs. Andrew paused at his meal and looked at Faith with his eyes wide and fearful. Faith managed to hide her own fear. "It'll be all right. Finish the meal." She hoped it hadn't been a lie.

Ten minutes later Palmutter returned without Nvalheim. The two thugs escorted them out to the street where the grav car and the Kelk officer waited for them. They rode back to the palace in silence.

As they stepped out of the car in front of the palace, Palmutter waited a moment for the car to pull away, then turned to Faith and Andrew and lowered his voice. He had an unpleasant look on his face. "If anyone asks, we went out and had a quiet dinner, just the three of us."

Andrew completely failed to hide the fear in his voice. "Yes, sir."

Faith merely nodded, afraid that if she said anything, she'd blow her stack at the asshole and kick him in the balls.

"Good," Palmutter said. He turned and left them standing there.

Once he passed through the doors at the front of the palace, Andrew whispered, "What the hell just happened?"

Faith gave him a hard look. "We went out and had a quiet dinner, just the three of us. That's what happened."

She turned and walked up the steps to the palace entrance.

Palmutter had said they would meet, ". . . some Kelk who are like-minded colleagues . . ."

Yes, they were like-minded, he and Nvalheim; they both hated and feared. Palmutter hated and feared all things Kelk, while Nvalheim hated and feared all things Commonwealth. Faith thought it telling, yet strange and dangerous, that they had found common cause in their mutual dislike of one another. She thought it likely that one or both of them might not survive such a relationship.

••••

Colonel Blacksword, the AI in Fran's implants said, and Fran perked up. *Colonel Primatov requests priority clearance for an urgent link.*

Fran glanced around the room. A mixed crowd of Kelk and Commonwealth citizens had gathered, about forty in total, the subject being economic cooperation and the opening of trade between the two sovereign states.

Fran accepted the call.

Fran, Primatov said, *I just got a message from Miershall, and I think it's important. Can you break away?*

Fran scanned the crowd. The real players were the business people and commercial advisors, all seated front and forward at a large conference table. The members of the Executive Council and the Commonwealth diplomatic mission were seated in the background. Old Dornmier had fallen asleep, and the rest looked as bored as Fran. They were there primarily to make sure the hawks on both sides didn't derail the discussions. Had the main subject been something like the lessening of military tensions between them, Fran would have raised a lot of eyebrows had she walked out during the discussions. As it was, only Gascoigne and Obradour looked her way as she stood and eased her way through the seated observers, then out of the room.

I'm clear, Katrine, where are you?

Your office.

I'm on my way.

With two bodyguards in tow, Fran hurried back to her office and found Katrine there, pacing back and forth. Fran left the bodyguards outside and closed the door. She and Katrine sat down, Katrine transferred the message to Fran's implants, and she keyed the recording.

The pretty young Sarkovite seated in front of her wore a ship's coverall, had her glistening black hair tied back in an unflattering ponytail, and wore no makeup. "Colonel Primatov, we're about four days out, but this has been the first time we've been close enough to the relay chain for me to transmit this. When I sent that last message to you, it took the courier ship about three days to make the round trip to the chain and return with your orders for me to come to Viktorkinde. During that time I learned that Lorenson's import-export company has shut down all their special operations and gone fully legit. It's not much, but I think it's really important. The only reason I can think that they would do that is to avoid endangering a larger or more important operation. But if something big was going to happen here, there'd be rumors of some sort, or hints floating about, something, but there's nothing here, not so much as a squeak."

She paused and leaned back. "I've got no proof, but I think something big is going to happen somewhere, and it's not going to happen here on Sarkovie."

Fran said the word at the same moment Miershall did. "Viktorkinde."

The rest of the transmission contained no new information. Miershall hadn't been able to learn anything more about Eindride's whereabouts, and in the course of her duties she travelled to Viktorkinde on a regular basis, so she had her own cover prearranged.

Fran killed the recording and said, "She's good, isn't she?"

Primatov nodded once. "When the dust settles after this, I think we should bump her up a grade."

"Agreed," Fran said. "But what do we do about the here and now?"

Primatov grimaced. "I think we should go to Plan Z, with extreme prejudice."

Thealone nodded and gave her an unpleasant smile. "Yes, with extreme prejudice."

11

Plan Z

"LIEUTENANT, PLEASE IMMEDIATELY report to the conference room in Colonel Blacksword's suite."

John's implants identified Primatov as the sender of the message. "Acknowledged. On my way."

Because of his experiences, John had been corralled to brief a cadre of the diplomatic aides on some of the more obvious Kelk customs. It was the fourth time he'd given the lecture, and he was getting rather good at it. He focused on the group of bored aides seated in front of him. "Sorry, we're going to have to cut this short. I've just been ordered to report to Colonel Primatov."

One of the fellows in the back row said, "I wouldn't mind taking orders from that red-head."

One of the ladies toward the front looked over her shoulder at him. "You would if she showed you her bitch face."

John had tossed the coat of his dress blues over the back of a chair. He shrugged into it, and noted for a moment the extra stripe on his sleeve. He didn't have enough time in grade for that stripe, but then Nikaela had been promoted just two days before him. He wasn't fooled; they had bent the rules to satisfy the politicians.

For John's briefing they had used a corner of the lounge. As John marched across the room and out the entrance, Matsen and Kolbeck stepped in line behind him.

Kolbeck asked, "We're gonna go see that redhead, eh?"

Matsen grumbled something under his breath.

John left the two dregkraag in the reception area of Thealone's suite and made his way to the conference room. When he stepped into it he immediately knew something was up and hesitated. Captain Edward Fleming and his nullheads sat in a small group at the table, with no one else present. At John's hesitation, one of the female nullheads nodded. "Yah. Something's up, ain't it?" She wore sergeant's stripes, and John noted that the name on the stencil above her left breast pocket read PYKOFF.

Fleming pointed to a chair. "Sit down, Lieutenant. I'm pretty sure we're about to find out what."

John barely got into his seat before the door opened and Primatov marched in carrying a wrapped bundle under one arm. She closed the door, walked to the head of the table, and dropped the bundle on top of it. It made a heavy thud.

She leaned forward and placed her hands flat on the table on either side of the bundle. "We're sealed, this conversation is sealed, and not a word said here goes beyond this room."

One of the men nudged Pykoff, elbowing her in the ribs. "Told you we're gonna have some fun."

Primatov continued. "We've gotten little hints that something's going on beneath the surface here. We don't know what, but we don't want to get caught with our heads up our asses, so we're going to Plan Z, with extreme prejudice."

Pykoff grinned and her eyebrows rose. "Whoopty doopty!"

One of the men said, "So it's party time, big time."

Fleming barked, "Button it, people."

His nullheads went silent.

John didn't have the vaguest idea of what they were talking about.

Primatov smiled. "Thank you, Captain. You once told me you'd be happy to have Mr. Mathius as a nullhead. Well consider it done. We've transferred him to Zeta Company, and he's now officially a member of Assault Team Null, on detached assignment to me."

One of the nullheads seated next to John slapped him on the back. "Welcome aboard, kid."

Pykoff said, "Don't call him kid. He earned his stripes." John was reminded of his old squad mate Sidewinder on *Defiant*, and he wondered if, like Sidewinder, she'd forget herself and call him kid at some point without realizing it.

Fleming said, "I told you people to button it."

As always Primatov remained completely unphased. "Captain Fleming, please explain to Mr. Mathius Plan Z, with extreme prejudice."

Fleming grimaced and pursed his lips. "Outside of Zeta Company it's just a joke, or a myth, and if anyone ever asks you about it, that's what you tell them. But when Colonel Blacksword invokes Plan Z, with extreme prejudice, it means we get to start breaking rules. Don't break any just to break them, and don't be stupid or sloppy about it, because you will be held accountable if you are. Don't kill anyone unless you have to, but if you have to, try to do it quiet-like. You get a whole shit-load of latitude with Plan Z, so be smart about how you use it, and no one will second guess you unless you're stupid or sloppy."

Pykoff said, "He ain't stupid."

Fleming paused and looked at Primatov. "Ma'am, I assume you're Z-Dog."

Primatov nodded.

Fleming turned his focus back to John. "She's Z-Dog, the one in charge of this cluster fuck, and about as alpha as it gets in this pack. When you break some rule, you don't have to clear it with her first, but follow up with her at the first opportunity so she knows what's been broken, and how, and when. And keep a careful tally of any kills you make, and when you can, let her know who, where, when and why."

John hoped they didn't expect him to say anything, because if they did, "Uh" and "Um" were about as articulate as he could be at that moment.

Fleming looked toward Primatov. "Did I miss anything, ma'am?"

She smiled. "Thank you, Captain. I think you summed it up rather nicely. Why don't you brief Mr. Mathius on what we did regarding your armor?"

"Certainly, ma'am," Fleming said.

He nodded and looked John's way grinning. "When we first got here all our powered combat armor was stored on *Hellfire* and *Endurance*, which wouldn't do us much good with those ships parked two lightyears out. A couple of us came up with an idea. Once the diplomatic mission took up quarters in the palace, that left plenty of room on *Lady Victorious*. *Hellfire*'s and *Endurance*'s crews loaded our gear onto a couple of assault boats, and they carried it to *Lady Victorious*, then her shuttles went back to the warships in place of the assault boats. We checked; it's a tight fit, but her hangar bays do accommodate the boats."

Primatov returned Fleming's grin with one of her own. "We also put a few more Blackswords on *Lady Victorious*. If something goes bad down here, they can armor up and be here in a matter of minutes, along with the armor for Mr. Fleming and his people."

The look on her face turned serious. "You need to know this, John, because when it comes to powered combat armor, all we've got close at hand is you, Ed and his people, plus May and her platoon on *Drakan Helgis*. And if they finish the repairs on *Drakan Helgis* and move her two lightyears out with the rest, then all we've got is our nullheads."

John understood Primatov's thinking. If they were isolated and under fire in the palace, a small squad of fully armored combatants stood a much better chance of fighting their way into them, and rescuing them.

Something didn't add up. As far as John knew, Thealone was the only Blacksword not in the room at that moment, and yet Primatov talked about moving Blackswords around like she had an entire company of them at her disposal.

Primatov pushed off the table and aimed her grin at John. "From the look on his face, Mr. Mathius just did the math, and realized it doesn't add up."

John didn't like being that transparent, and at that moment everyone in the room but him grinned as if at some private joke.

"John," Primatov said. "Every member of Fran Thealone's staff is a Zeta Company Blacksword, including those who are supposedly civilians. There are also quite a few interspersed among the diplomatic mission, and a couple among *Lady Victorious*'s crew."

That didn't require a response from John, so he kept his mouth shut.

Primatov put one hand on the bundle in front of her and gave it a shove. It slid across the table and stopped in front of John. He unwrapped it, and found it contained a shoulder harness and an odd looking pistol. He looked at Primatov for an explanation.

Her face went hard and unyielding as she spoke. "I know you trained with old-fashioned chemically-powered slug throwers in basic. That weapon is very much like those, and yet unlike them. It's a mix of high tensile strength ceramics and plast, with high density plast slugs, a chemically powered charge to blast the slugs out of the barrel, and no energy source, very hard to detect. And unlike a grav pistol, the shortened length of the barrel does reduce its accuracy, so it's no good at long range. It doesn't produce the devastating damage of a Mach five fragmentation flechette, but the slug will punch a big hole in someone. It makes a lot of noise and kicks like hell, and you are to wear it whenever possible. Unfortunately, you can't wear it in meetings of the Larscom Executive Council or General Secretariat."

Primatov paused and took a moment to look carefully at Fleming and each of his people, as if she needed to make a point. "I know you nullheads are resourceful, and I wouldn't be surprised if most of you can come up with similar weapons, but please spread the word that I'm giving you a direct order not to. Mr. Mathius is a constant target, so I'm making an exception for him. And if he's caught, our Kelk hosts will take that into consideration, especially since they feel responsible for the fuck-up with the butcher's blades on *Konigsborge*. On the other hand, if one of you people is caught, it could create considerable difficulty for the diplomatic mission. So don't do it. That's an order from me, Colonel Z-Dog."

A couple of Fleming's people looked uncomfortable at that moment, as if they had been mentally making plans to do exactly what she had just prohibited.

She scanned the people in the room. "Any questions?"

John had about a hundred, but since the nullheads didn't start rifling questions at Primatov, he didn't want to stand out so he kept his mouth shut.

"Good," she said. She turned, and walked out of the room.

The nullheads helped John put on the shoulder rig and adjust it to fit comfortably. While doing so, the nullhead who had called John *kid* leaned close to him. "By the way, kid,"—Pykoff gave him a dirty look—"when things get weird like this, carry some extra cash, you know, hard script. If stuff starts happening, you never know when you're going to need to buy something without being traced."

John decided to take that advice to heart.

••••

To protect Jenine Catarvin's status as a covert operative, Katrine, Thealone and Gascoigne did not meet with her as a group. The four of them, without anyone else present, would be an odd mix that might raise eyebrows. The five members of the diplomatic mission met almost daily, with Katrine and other aides usually present. As the meeting broke up, if Catarvin said something negative about Kelk food to one of them, that was their signal to contact her. That morning she had done just that, and Katrine made an appointment through her staff to meet with the senator.

As Katrine stepped into the reception area of Catarvin's suite, the aide who handled her schedule looked up and said, "The senator is expecting you. Please go right in."

Catarvin was alone in her office seated at her desk. She smiled as Katrine stepped into the room. "As always, Colonel, you look absolutely stunning, even in that unflattering uniform."

Katrine returned her smile. "Thank you, Senator."

Katrine placed her briefcase on the senator's desk and used her implants to activate the systems within it. The politicians had extremely good surveillance mitigation systems in place, but nothing beat a Type One Military Security Screen. The AI in the briefcase sent an encrypted message to her implants. *Two monitoring devices detected, possibly benign, but they've been temporarily deactivated anyway.*

Catarvin stood and came around from behind her desk. She pointed to a comfortable chair. "Please, sit down, relax."

Katrine lowered herself into the chair and Catarvin sat in another facing her. The senator seemed excited about something. She leaned forward and lowered her voice. "I think Silas went to see this Nvalheim person."

Catarvin had briefed Katrine on the incident when she'd walked in on Palmutter and Faith Carlton. She had stepped into the room just in time to hear him say, "... neither Machtberg, nor Nvalheim, do you understand? You never heard them, never, never, never." He had been livid, and Faith Carlton had been clearly terrified.

Catarvin's words got Katrine's attention. "Really? Why do you say that?"

Catarvin looked over her shoulder and lowered her voice further, even though, with the security screen in place, there was no need for that. "The other night he went out with an aide named Andrew Talpano and his Communications Director, Faith Carlton. Miss Carlton is the one who refuses to fuck him. It was supposedly just the three of them out for a quiet dinner alone in the city, but Silas came back quite energized."

She grinned and batted her eyelashes. Katrine didn't need her to elaborate on what she meant by *quite energized*.

She continued. "He was most energetic, and during our rather robust time together that night, he said something like, 'Pretty soon we won't have to worry about that traitor anymore.' I asked him why, and he said a Kelk friend of his would take care of it. I must assume that friend was Nvalheim. Just to see what I could learn, the next morning I told Mr. Talpano I wanted to go into the city to try some of the local cuisine, and I asked him if he enjoyed the place where he and Silas and Miss Carlton ate the previous evening. The way he reacted, you would have thought I offered to give him a blow job right then and there. His eyes widened, he spluttered, went completely inarticulate, and couldn't put two words together in a coherent phrase. No, something happened when the three of them went out, and it wasn't just dinner. Something scared the shit out of that poor young man."

Katrine leaned back in her chair and considered Catarvin's story. "It does sound like something did happen, but don't you think it's a bit of a stretch to assume he met with Nvalheim?"

Catarvin shook her head, and she discarded the airhead persona like a warm coat on a hot day. "Silas saw someone that night, and at this point I think Nvalheim is the only real contact he has among the Kelk, or at least the only one that'll still work with him."

Katrine nodded. "That's good input. I'll trust your judgement on that. But let me caution you again to be careful. We know there are some dangerous people involved in this, and it's looking more and more like Senator Palmutter is about as deep into it as one can get. If that's true, and for some reason you're perceived as a threat, he, and any number of people he's working with, will not hesitate to silence you."

Catarvin looked at Katrine for a long moment, as if trying to make up her mind about something. Then without a word she stood and crossed the room to her desk. She reached out and picked up a small clutch purse sitting on top of it, turned and crossed the room back to Katrine. She again sat down in the chair facing Katrine. She opened the clutch purse, reached into it, and with her hand hidden inside it, she said, "I've carried this for years."

When she withdrew her hand from the purse she held a small pistol. It had two barrels that Katrine guessed were a little over two inches long, configured side by side. Catarvin smiled. "It uses a chemical explosive to fire a projectile out of the barrels. It has no energy source, so I'm told it's completely undetectable unless one is physically searched. And who's going to search a vapid little airhead like me?" She hesitated for a moment. "Well . . . Silas does when we're fantasy play-acting, but I don't put the gun in any of the places he searches."

Katrine couldn't believe it. "You know how to use that thing?"

Catarvin rolled her eyes and shook her head sadly. "Of course, I do, dear. In fact, as a young girl, I was quite proficient at competitive target practice, though those were usually grav rifles." She waved the small pistol in front of her. "And once or twice a year I take this thing out and fire it a few times just to remember how nasty it kicks."

In that moment Katrine swore she would never again allow herself to be surprised by anything the little woman revealed.

Catarvin returned the small pistol to the clutch purse and closed it.

Katrine had something she wanted to discuss with the woman, a somewhat delicate matter. "There is something I need to discuss with you. Regarding Lieutenant Mathius, do you think you could . . ." Katrine didn't really know how to broach the subject she had in mind.

Catarvin grinned. "You're going to ask me to back off on the poor young man."

Katrine grimaced. "Well . . . you are coming on a bit strong, aren't you?"

Catarvin raised an eyebrow. "Don't go all prudish on me. That's what is expected of my alternate persona. And who knows, if the young man decides he's interested, I would be remiss if I didn't take steps to preserve my ability to operate covertly on your behalf, and I can't do that if I don't maintain that persona." She flashed a big cheesy grin. "So purely out of a sincere sense of duty, I'll just have to fuck his brains out, though I'll certainly have a good time doing so. And trust me, I'll make sure he does too. There's a good reason old Silas keeps coming back for more."

Katrine didn't want to believe what she had just heard.

Catarvin leaned forward and patted her on the knee. "And in any case, it was kind of fun watching the poor fellow squirm, wasn't it?"

"Yes," Katrine said, recalling the look on John Mathius's face. "I suppose it was."

They didn't have anything more to discuss. When Katrine stood up to leave, the senator stood with her. "One more thing, dear."

She extended her hand with an old-fashioned paper business card pinched between two fingers.

Katrine reached out and took the card. The senator's public contact information was printed on the front of it, all of which Katrine already had, so she flipped it over. An address had been hand-written on the back side.

Katrine looked Catarvin in the eyes and raised an eyebrow in question.

The senator flashed her a big grin. "I got the address of that restaurant from young Mr. Talpano. You should have some of your more sneaky people watch the place. I think you call that a stakeout, don't you? Who knows, you might come across Marta Nvalheim."

It was then that Katrine realized the little woman would always manage to surprise her.

12

Precautions

KRISTDOKAR ASKED KATRINE to meet her in the lobby of the Hyvaldsborg Palace just after midnight. The skalde added, "And be sure to wear civilian clothing, with nothing that is obviously Commonwealth."

Other than that, she had been quite secretive about the purpose of the meeting. Intrigued, and with her interest considerably piqued, Katrine took the lift down to the main floor and stepped into the lobby at exactly midnight. At that time of night the lobby was by no means crowded, but it was still a busy place regardless of the time of day. She saw no sign of the skalde, so she sat down in a comfortable chair to wait.

Ten minutes passed and no Kristdokar. The skalde was not one to ask for a meeting and not show up. But after another ten minutes Katrine wondered how much longer she should wait. Then a woman she recognized walked through the doors at the main entrance. Oberseergent Geltkarl paused just inside the lobby, scanned the room, spotted Katrine and walked toward her. Katrine stood and Geltkarl stopped about a pace away from her.

Geltkarl smiled pleasantly. "Mistress Primatov, Mistress Kristdokar would like you to accompany me."

Katrine returned her smile and nodded. "Lead on."

To her surprise, Geltkarl did not turn toward the main entrance, but instead headed for the bank of elevators. Katrine followed and stopped next to the woman as she called a lift, and when it arrived they stepped into it. Geltkarl must have programmed the lift through her implants, because it took them to the second floor. Katrine followed as Geltkarl stepped out, then walked down the length of the second floor hall to its end, where she turned right and called a service elevator. When it arrived they stepped into it and Geltkarl sent it upward. But it didn't open on an upper floor as Katrine expected. Instead, it opened to the blackness of a night illuminated by a quarter moon. Geltkarl had taken her to the roof of the palace.

As they stepped out of the elevator, Geltkarl said, "We shouldn't have to wait long, mistress."

Katrine heard the whine of grav field generators in the distance, then spotted the dark shape of a small skiff running without lights and descending toward them. It came to a stop hovering about a foot above the roof, and ten paces in front of them. A hatch in its side dilated, displaying an illuminated interior, and she and Geltkarl walked forward. Katrine was not surprised to see Command Superior Brynjar sitting inside the small boat, also wearing civilian clothing.

With his hand he indicated a seat opposite him. "Please join me, Mistress Primatov."

She climbed in and sat down, and Geltkarl sat next to her. The hatch in the side of the boat closed without making a sound, and as the skiff lifted away from the roof, Brynjar said, "Sorry we're late, but I had a few people inside watching you for a bit so we could be sure. Needed to give it a little time before we picked you up, make sure no one is shadowing you."

Katrine asked, "Why all the subterfuge?"

Brynjar shrugged. "You'll see."

She and Brynjar shared a personal level of trust on a different scale from that of the official level between their two organizations, probably the reason he was the one who came to pick her up. They didn't blank the windows of the skiff, nor did they cut her off from citynet, which she took as a sign that some *official* trust still existed between them, a delicate thing at best. She easily tracked their position as they flew above the city, and about five minutes from the palace they descended toward the grounds of a walled estate.

The place appeared to be the residence of a wealthy business person or government official. Bright lights illuminated most of the grounds inside the wall, and a stretch outside as well. The main gates remained open, but a large grav truck parked in the entrance blocked access by all ground vehicles from outside the wall. The wall was thick, with a walkway atop it, much like the parapets in an old, medieval castle. As they descended, Katrine spotted armed guards stationed on the wall at regular intervals.

A two-story residential structure dominated the center of the compound, but in one corner a visual distortion screen completely obscured a large area of the grounds. It was much like the crime scene barrier CIS had erected on the academy campus the night John Mathius had been abducted. From ground level its dome shape shimmered in the lights of the compound, scrambling and blurring any images that passed through it. From up above it would simply appear to be empty ground. They had something they wanted to hide from eyes passing overhead.

The skiff settled to the ground inside the wall and the hatch dilated. Brynjar cocked his head slightly to one side as he looked at Katrine. "Please come with me. We want you to see something."

Katrine followed Brynjar and stepped down onto the grounds of the estate. He turned toward the distortion screen, walked to it and stepped into it. Katrine followed, and when she stepped beneath the dome of the screen, she stood next to two medium sized assault boats, the kind capable of carrying about twenty troops in full combat armor, plus support equipment and weaponry.

Brynjar stood beside her, looking at her, probably trying to gauge her reaction.

She smiled. "Am I correct in assuming Command Superior Thordahl is here?"

Brynjar returned her smile and nodded. "We have Mistress Nygaard's personal guard, plus about thirty actives from First Liaison Company, along with all their equipment, including combat armor. That's about all we could get away with, since we're not supposed to be here in the city, at least not officially."

First Liaison Company, their special operations group. It appeared the Kelk had their own version of Plan Z. Katrine asked, "Rapid response team?"

Again he nodded. "Without warning, we can deploy them anywhere in the city in under an hour."

Katrine turned her attention back to the assault boat. "What about the Hyvaldsborg Palace?"

"Half that," he said. "Maybe a little less."

She looked him in the eyes, and felt that bond of personal trust between them, the bond of comrades in arms. They had first established that bond on Reisenar when John Mathius had done a most unusual thing on a subway platform in the bowels of its capital city.

Brynjar smiled and considered her for a moment. "I've noticed you and I frequently think alike."

He spun on his heels. "Please come with me. Command Superior Thordahl is looking forward to seeing you again."

She followed him out from under the distortion screen. He led her to the two-story residential structure at the center of the compound, where two armed guards stood at the main entrance. They walked between them into the building, then a short distance down a hallway where he stopped and opened a tall set of double doors. They stepped into an elegant library, and waiting for them there were Nygaard, Kristdokar, and Thordahl.

Nygaard stepped forward. "Welcome to my home, Colonel Primatov, well, my home when I'm here in Emkeldstadt."

It had been some time since Katrine had seen Thordahl. He was not a tall man, and when he crossed the room to greet her, it made her uncomfortable to tower over him.

Nygaard served them tea without excess formality, then they passed around a bottle of kirva, and like the other three, Katrine splashed a shot of the liquor into her tea.

The addition of the kirva seemed to indicate that they were among friends, and their meeting would forego the more restrictive formalities.

They sat down in comfortable chairs, the bottle of kirva close at hand on a side table for anyone who wanted another splash. Nygaard had poured a separate shot glass of kirva for herself. She lifted it to her lips and took a delicate sip.

She looked pointedly at Katrine. "No doubt you're wondering why I invited you here under such mysterious circumstances."

Katrine scanned the faces of the four Kelk seated there in the room with her. "You wanted me to see that you're ready for an armed conflict. Are you certain that one is imminent?"

"No," Nygaard said. "We're certain that there's a rift among the anti-Commonwealth hawks. We're certain that there are unstable personalities on both sides of that rift, and that among some of the hawks there is a growing sense of desperation. But beyond that we're certain of nothing. I wanted you to see this so you'll know we're not taking any chances. And we encourage you to do the same, up to, and including—" She leaned forward, as if she wanted Katrine to see the determination in her eyes. "—up to, and including, taking certain risks that could be difficult to explain if discovered by the wrong people."

Katrine nodded, her mind racing. By showing her their preparations, they had demonstrated a great deal of good will, and perhaps it was time to return the favor. "We have already taken similar risks, and are operating under an unusual protocol in which certain highly trusted individuals are allowed a considerable amount of latitude."

At Katrine's words, Brynjar smiled.

Nygaard lifted an eyebrow and gave Katrine a piercing look. "I'm glad to see you recognize the gravity of the situation on your own."

Katrine knew without doubt that Thealone would not second-guess her on this. "I think it time we coordinated our efforts more closely. To that end I'd like you to send the skiff back to the palace to pick up a colleague of mine. I'll call him first to tell him to expect you, and he'll be ready and waiting on the roof. If something does happen, it would be wise if he and Command Superiors Thordahl and Brynjar worked as a command team to coordinate their efforts. The man I'm thinking of is Captain Edward Fleming."

Brynjar grinned. "Blacksword, right?"

Katrine grimaced. "Not just any Blacksword."

Thordahl grinned at Brynjar. "He can probably kill with a thought."

Brynjar shook his head. "But can he kill with a fork?"

Kristdokar intervened. "Maestras, that's enough of that."

••••

Plan Z meant John didn't get to see much of Nikaela. Primatov immediately transferred John, May, and her platoon up to *Drakan Helgis* in the Heilbronn Navy Yard. Primatov confessed to John, "I'm spreading us around so we're not all packaged up nice and tidy here in the Hyvaldsborg Palace. When you're needed down here, Taugrim'll send you down in a boat."

"Come on, people," May shouted. "We've got an assault boat waiting for us. Get the lead out."

Primatov had assigned one of Fleming's nullheads to May's platoon, a female sergeant named Pykoff whom John had met when he'd learned about Plan Z. Fleming and his squad would always be elsewhere, and if something went down Pykoff was there to coordinate with the nullheads. John was the only one there who knew she was Zeta Company and Assault Team Null.

John, May and her platoon of Kelk and Commonwealth soldiers lugged their gear down to the ground floor of the palace and out a back entrance. One of *Drakan Helgis*'s assault boats sat on the lawn, the large deployment hatch in its side open. They climbed aboard, stowed their gear, and strapped in.

John's implants came alive with the pilot's voice. "Lieutenant, please come forward."

John walked forward and found the pilot's couch empty. Strapping herself into the copilot's couch, the woman who had threatened to take him as a lover looked up at him and grinned. "Okay, Maestra not-Kelk, you're driving this boat. Show me again how good you are."

She leaned toward him, a twinkle in her eye. "You sure you don't want to show me anything else you're good at?"

She had clearly recovered from his threat to take her as a lover.

••••

Customs and Identity Control on Viktorkinde Prime was always tight, but with the Commonwealth diplomatic mission on the planet, it had become almost draconian. Evaline Miershall presented her papers under the identity of Racine Damidohl, a wealthy merchant from Sarkovie. She had used that identity on Viktorkinde several times, but never for anything risky or illegal, which meant it remained clean and serviceable. It helped that her father had done business with the Supremacy and still came to Viktorkinde upon occasion, so she knew the commercial aspects of her cover quite well.

A male Kelk security officer questioned her at length. Then he left and a female officer interrogated her, repeating many of the questions the man had asked. They would compare the answers they had received, looking for discrepancies, then review their records of her previous visits. Evaline sometimes had trouble with female Kelk officers. While prostitution was an inalienable right on Sarkovie, which displeased many Kelk women, only male prostitution was allowed in the Supremacy. Among the Kelk, women could be had for a price if one ventured into the right district in a large city, but female prostitution was strictly prohibited. And the penalties were quite harsh, much more so for the woman than the man who hired her, which seemed quite unfair to Evaline.

It took two hours to get through Customs and Identity Control. On Sarkovie she would have simply greased a lot of palms and finished the process in a quarter of that time, even under such heightened security conditions. She collected her luggage then bought a ticket on the next shuttle down to Emkeldstadt. In the city's main airport, as she stepped out of the security gate into the concourse, she spotted a short, bald fellow wearing an archaic tailcoat typical of Norandynian fashion. In his hands he clutched a black hat with a broad, flat brim that helped keep him dry in the torrential rains of Norandyne, and probably also helped shade his face from the intense sunlight on Viktorkinde. Parmak Mandrion, the Blacksword Head of Station on Viktorkinde, saw her and approached her almost hesitantly.

"Mistress Damidohl," he said. "It's so good to see you again. I have a car waiting. I'll let them know you've arrived and it should be at the curb by the time we get there."

She followed him out to the front of the concourse. They only waited a few minutes before an average looking grav car pulled up in front of them. Evaline tossed her luggage into the trunk, Mandrion held the door for her, and she climbed into the back seat. He climbed in and sat next to her.

As they pulled away from the curb he said, "This vehicle is secure. I've arranged for a hotel room for you not far from our office. We'll stop there so you can check in, but we think you should stay in my facility. In the trunk I have an extra suitcase filled with clothing your size, and a small selection of personal items, all of Sarkovie origin and partially used. Take that into the hotel with you when you check in, unpack it and spread the stuff around the room so it appears you are actually staying there. We'll bring your real suitcase with us to my facility."

She grimaced and pursed her lips. "I knew something was up?"

"Yes," he said, nodding carefully. "Something is up. We just don't know what."

Mandrion waited in the car while she checked into the hotel. In her room she unpacked the suitcase he had supplied, noticed that some of the clothing was nicer than her own stuff, wished she could hang onto it, but that probably wasn't going to happen. As she stepped out of the hotel Mandrion jumped out of the car and held the door for her. She wasn't used to that, but being Norandynian, he treated every woman with extreme politeness.

The AI drove them to his facility, a small office building not far from the capital. The building housed half a dozen small companies, one of which was Mandrion's. He managed a lobbying firm organized by the government of Norandyne to advocate its interests with the Supremacy, a function they performed in earnest, though neither government knew that Mandrion and a few of his employees were Blackswords. Because of the paranoia regarding anything Commonwealth among the Kelk, the Blacksword had kept its operations on Viktorkinde quite small. Mandrion showed her to a guestroom in the back of their suite of offices. It was a little larger than a hotel room, but not by much.

Evaline tossed her suitcase on the bed and said, "I can unpack later. Right now I need to see Primatov."

Mandrion smiled. "A gentleman is waiting in my office. He will take you to her."

She followed the Norandynian down a short hallway and into his office. As she entered, Edward Fleming stood to greet her. They were both Zeta Company, and she had worked with him before, but since Mandrion was not Zeta, much of what they needed to say would have to wait until they were alone.

She smiled and nodded. "It's good to see you again, Edward."

"And you," he said. "Sorry to be abrupt, but we're in a hurry."

He started for the door, but she held up a hand. "Just a second or two." She turned to Mandrion. "There's an independent freighter christened *Far Solar Wind* that should arrive shortly at Viktorkinde Prime. By now they should be close enough to have filed an updated transition plan. Can you check on their schedule?"

He smiled. "They're arriving tomorrow afternoon. When I have more accurate data, I'll let you know."

Fleming grinned, turned and marched out through the door. She followed him down the hall, into the lift, then down to a subterranean garage. They climbed into a grav car, and as it pulled out onto the street, she said, "How bad is it?"

Fleming looked at her pointedly. "We don't know. We've just got a lot of hints that something is up on the Kelk side. How big we don't know, but we're being cautious. We've gone to Plan Z, with extreme prejudice."

Evaline closed her eyes and shook her head. "Oh shit!"

13

Accident, Maybe

JOHN TRACKED HIS progress on the display inside the helmet of his armor as he, May and her platoon coasted toward their target six hundred kilometers off. It might be a training exercise, but a live-fire, free-armor assault on a derelict warship in open space would still be dangerous. Their target was an old cruiser in free orbit around Viktorkinde's primary. There were several such aging, abandoned warships parked well out of any regular shipping lanes, all used as training facilities.

Kelk combat armor had a few quirks that John had struggled to get used to back on *Drakan Helgis*, the most obvious being a slightly snugger fit in the waist and hips. Back then he had donned the armor a number of times for training, but only once had he worn it for more than a few hours. That had been when he, Matsen, Kolbeck and Geltkarl had helped Engineering repair some damaged hull plating. He'd worn the armor for over twenty hours that day, and at first the fit had bothered him. But near the end of that shift he realized he was simply being stubborn. It was easy to attribute superior performance to his good, old, familiar Commonwealth armor when he wasn't wearing it, and he chided himself for forgetting it had its quirks as well.

May's voice interrupted John's thoughts. "Ten minutes to target. Let's flip."

Coasting at two kilometers a second, they had a lot of velocity to kill. John tucked his knees up and flipped so his heels were aimed at their target. On the inside of his visor he watched the rest of May's team do likewise. They had done a lot of training together and were now a real team, though a couple of the new dregkraag had a little catching up to do. And John himself was simply excess baggage.

"Slave to me," May said.

Along with the rest of the team, John nav-locked his control systems to May's. When she applied power to her gravity fields, his armor would track her deceleration curve and match it exactly to ensure that they didn't have twenty actives strewn out over several kilometers of space. The techs had needed to do a bit of tweaking to their systems to get the Kelk and Commonwealth armor to work together without any glitches. At two kilometers a second, a glitch could turn them into bug squish.

When Carla had used the term *bug squish*, Kolbeck had wanted her to give him personal instruction on what that meant. John recalled that for an instant a little glint appeared in her eye. After all, the unterseergent was a handsome fellow, and Carla's idea of personal instruction probably included all the extracurricular activities Kolbeck had in mind. But then she mentioned something about Primatov's bitch-face, and would have nothing to do with the handsome dregkraag. Matsen and Kolbeck had needed John to do a careful translation of *bug squish* for them, and Kolbeck was especially interested in the meaning of *bitch-face* since it had somehow thwarted what had almost turned into a very pleasing interstellar relationship.

At a half kilometer out from the target, May said, "Going free," and released their systems from nav-lock. "Remember, Squad One, you've got the bow, Squad Two aft, and Squad Three amidships."

With Carla, Leeze and the four guys from Miriteen, plus twelve dregkraag, not counting John, May, and Pykoff, they had three squads of six. They had interspersed them carefully so each squad was comprised of two ComSecCorps soldiers and four dregkraag. Each had a senior non-com in charge, with Matsen leading one, Carla another, and Pykoff the third. Thealone and Primatov had told John that May's small platoon had become a real test-case for cooperation between the Commonwealth and the Supremacy.

John joined Pykoff's squad as they used their armor's grav fields to aim for the bow. Their job was to blow the fore personnel hatch and go for the bridge, treating every inch of the way as hostile territory, a live-fire training operation.

John hit the hull plating of the derelict travelling at about eight meters a second, the equivalent of a jump from a height of three meters in one G. He reversed the grav fields on his armor so it pushed him against the hull plates, which allowed him to walk along the outside of the hull even though they were not in a gravity well.

Blast marks and weld seams on the fore personnel hatch made it clear it had been blown and repaired a few times before in similar training exercises. Their squad's demolition team of two dregkraag executed a maneuver similar to John's, landing on either side of the hatch. They clamped a grav charge against the hatch just as John walked out of sight around the curve of the ship's structure. A few seconds later the demo team joined him.

"Fire in the hole," one of the demo team said over their squad's command circuit.

John triggered a clear signal. When the demo team got clear signals from the rest of the squad, the hull thumped and vibrated through the souls of his boots as the grav charge blew. It used a combination of a standard demolition charge, with an intense grav field spike aimed in the opposite direction to direct the force of the blast into the hull and keep it from dissipating into open space.

John reversed his grav fields and lifted off the hull of the ship, then reversed them again and came back, landing next to the twisted plating of the blown hatch. Digger, one of his old platoon mates from Miriteen, beat him through it by not first landing on the hull next to it, instead dropping straight through it. He'd always been a bit of a showoff, and a risk taker.

John assembled with Pykoff's squad just inside the blown hatch, and they worked their way forward toward the bridge, using small micro-nukes to blow and clear each compartment as they did so. They used the grav fields from their armor to press them into the deck, which gave them stability, allowed them to walk almost as if they stood in a gravity well, and prevented them from floating around and flailing about.

John and Digger stopped on either side of a stateroom door. John blew the latch with a burst from his assault rifle, Digger elbowed the door open, and tossed a micro-nuke through it.

Since they weren't in a gravity well, the micro-nuke didn't arc, but floated in a straight line through the door and out of sight. John had a glancing view into the stateroom, and in it he saw a small telltale blink. There shouldn't be a telltale blinking in that stateroom, or for that matter, any stateroom in that derelict ship.

Thinking that if he was wrong, his friends would be really pissed at him, he shouted over the command circuit, "Bomb!" and dove for Digger. He keyed his suit's grav fields just as he slammed into his friend, and the bulkhead next to them exploded.

Something slammed into John's legs and he felt an intense stab of pain in his left calf as he and Digger somersaulted and ricocheted off the passageway walls.

Critical armor breach, his armor told him. *Left calf, aft section. Effecting decompression clamp.*

The breach in his suit was too large for the self-healing plates to fix, so his armor resorted to a pressure clamp just below the knee to save his life: sacrifice the limb to save the body. The clamp closed around his calf with crushing force and he screamed as pain blinded him to anything else. Then his suit flooded his system with pain killers designed to augment the pain suppression circuits in his implants.

Everyone screamed at once. He wished they'd all stop that. He heard Carla scream, "What the fuck happened?"

Digger must be okay, because he screamed back, "I don't know. Micro-nuke didn't do that."

May Forrester silenced them all with a parade ground bellow the likes of which would humble any DI. "Everyone shut the fuck up."

John's head swam. From the knee down his leg alternated between throbbing agony and blistering fire. He passed out for a while, woke briefly, then passed out again.

"I've got it," someone shouted. "I've got it sealed. I've got it sealed. It's temporary, but it's good."

His suit released the pressure clamp, and the pain ratcheted up a notch. He screamed again and fluttered near the edge of consciousness. Then his implants and the pain killers took control and the pain receded a little.

They had him grav-clamped to a deck, with May and the platoon's medic leaning over him. "You're lucky," the medic said. "The lower half of your leg was exposed to vacuum for over fifteen minutes before we got the breach sealed. You won't lose the leg. Couple days in the hospital, some nerve regrowth and tissue regeneration, and you'll be good as new."

Carla floated into his field of view. "Did Digger fuck up? If he did, I'm going to kill the son-of-a-bitch."

John tried to shake his head, but the pain in his leg jumbled his thinking, and all he managed to say was, "Booby trap."

••••

Twenty days of utter and complete boredom. Anders had spent his first day on board the *Far Solar Wind* worrying, fearful that his failure to alert Neddaline Macree would prove to be disastrous for them all. He had spent his second day trying to guess what Lorenson's superiors had planned that would be such a game-changer, and got nowhere with that. But by the third day he just didn't have the energy to worry, fret, and fear. He spent the next twenty days reading, sleeping, shitting, eating, working out, and playing cards. The fear and worry didn't start up again until a day before their arrival, and when the small freighter finally docked at Viktorkinde Prime, he was fit to be tied.

Anders grabbed his duffel as the ship's crew maneuvered the vessel into the commercial docks, and he arrived at the personnel hatch ten minutes before they opened it. When they finally got the green light, it took another couple of minutes to properly equalize pressure on both sides of the hatch, then it cycled open with a slight pop.

Anders tossed his duffel over his shoulder and stepped through the hatch onto the dock. As he made his way to Customs and Identity Control, he worried that something might go wrong with the false papers that identified him as Anders Karsten. He had no choice but to use them, because they didn't have any record of Anders Eindride going off planet, and for him to suddenly show up reentering after never leaving; that would get him a quick trip to another cell. He'd spent a lot of time in cells lately. But as it turned out, the false papers worked fine and he stepped out onto the concourse a free man.

Now he needed to get down to Hyerdride, hopefully make contact with Viktra again, his old connection to Kristdokar. Through her he could alert the skalde to the imminent danger, though he didn't really know what imminent danger they should be on the alert for. He bought a ticket for the shuttle down to Hyerdride, then sat down in the departure lounge to wait. He connected his implants to Prime's citynet and scanned the news feeds: no assassinations, no coup d'état, no radical change in the power structure, nothing.

"Excuse me."

At the sound of the voice he focused on the room about him. The departure lounge had begun to fill up and was a little crowded. A young female common-face stood over him, carrying a rather oversized purse. She had glistening black hair that hung past her shoulders in curls and ringlets. She looked quite familiar, and then he realized he was looking at the spitting image of Neddaline Macree, but this woman was about ten years older than the young Sarkovite. She was closer to Anders's own age.

She pointed at the seat next to him. "Is this seat taken?"

He sat up a little straighter. "No . . . I don't think so."

She smiled. "Thank you." She sat down next to him.

She spoke Lingua with a slight Sarkovie accent, much less pronounced than Neddaline Macree's. And beside the age difference, her clothing didn't expose enticing bits of flesh here and there . . . well, on Neddaline Macree it had been almost everywhere. The woman was a little too young to be Macree's mother; perhaps an older sister.

He had to know, so he asked her, "You're from Sarkovie, aren't you?"

She frowned. "Yes, I am. But I thought I'd done a better job of leaving that accent behind."

"Are you any relation to Neddaline Macree?"

She frowned and shook her head. "No, I don't believe I've heard that name before."

"I'm sorry," he said. "I didn't mean to bother you."

She appeared uncomfortable. "That's all right," she said, though it clearly wasn't. She retrieved a small reader from the oversized purse, focused on that, and clearly didn't want some Kelk fellow bothering her.

Anders turned uncomfortably away from her, and that was when she opened up the secure link between their implants. *Anders, it's me, though I'm no longer Neddaline Macree.*

He started and looked her way, but she didn't react in the slightest and continued to stare at the screen of her reader. He averted his eyes. *Who are you now?*

She still didn't look his way. *The name is Racine Damidohl. You left Sarkovie rather abruptly.*

He carefully explained the circumstances of his departure, including the unsuccessful attempt to contact her before leaving. *In the elevator I pressed the button for your floor instead of mine, pretended I didn't realize I was on the wrong floor, and when my key didn't work I grabbed the knob on your door and gave it a shake, but I guess you weren't home. Hohlman stayed with me all the way, so I couldn't even leave a note or message for you.*

Still staring at the screen, she nodded. *That would explain it. So what are they planning?*

He forced himself not to react outwardly, not to shake his head or nod. *I don't know because Lorenson didn't really know. All she knew was that her superiors are moving to an alternate plan, and it's something big. She said it'll really shake things up; those were her words. And they didn't want me around in case the local authorities poked about, didn't think my background could withstand the scrutiny. Said it will take a couple tendays to set up, maybe more. That was twenty-two days ago.*

She took a deep breath and let out a sigh. *I enjoyed our client-server relationship, and wish we could take up where we left off. But I doubt we'll see each other again. From what we can tell the organization you left behind here is still active and in play. Return to them and see what you can learn.*

She stood, stuffed the reader back into her purse, and walked away.

Anders rode the shuttle down to Hyerdride. In the airport he abandoned the false identity and once again became Anders Eindride. He walked to the nearest transit station, and a half hour later stepped through the front door and into his old apartment.

14

Hard Evidence

THE LOOKS ON the faces of the four Executive Council members were not good. As Kristdokar stepped up to the podium she tried to keep her face neutral. Behind her the double doors of the chamber closed with a soft clump as the dregkraag sealed them in the room.

Apparently, the council members were too impatient to put up with the normal formalities. The closing of the doors triggered pent up emotions.

"Five votes," Veskarson said. "Five more yea's and she would have had her two-thirds."

"Yes," Tiegnordan said. "Five more votes and she would have been reinstated by the General Secretariat."

Nygaard shrugged. "She'll probably get them next time."

Veskarson slammed his fist down on the desk in front of him. "There won't be a next time. Haugrund is out, and she stays out."

Dornmier shook her head sadly. "Calm down, Maertin. You know as well as I we can't prevent another vote. The law is quite clear: after the first vote, a tenday wait, then she or one of her stooges can call for another vote, and if we try to dispute it, a vote on having a vote will be carried by a simple majority. She's five votes short of two-thirds. Do you think she'll have a problem getting a simple majority?"

Nygaard leaned back in her chair and steepled her fingers in front of her. "She's got momentum on her side. She'll get the simple majority, and then she'll get the two-thirds. I think we should reinstate her here and now by a vote of the Council. We'll have less contention among the five of us if we act now, and it'll stabilize the Council. It'll also be a sign of good will that might make it easier to work with Haugrund once she's reinstated."

Kristdokar thought it telling that Veskarson did not immediately object. His anger and disappointment had clearly not diminished, but he had never been one to let emotions rule his thoughts. He sat back quietly, his eyes focused at a distant point.

Tiegnordan spoke, her voice calm and measured. "I have a proposal that—"

Veskarson cut her off. "Of course you have a proposal. You've regretted voting her off the Council from the moment you agreed to do so."

"Maertin," Dornmier said. "Let us hear what she has to say."

Veskarson paused and composed himself, then leaned forward to look down the length of the curved desk at Tiegnordan. "My apologies, Mistress Tiegnordan. My outburst was . . . improper."

Tiegnordan acknowledged the apology with a slight nod of her head, the look on her face neutral. "I have an idea that might produce a reasonable compromise for all. I'll propose to her that she openly acknowledge that the *Valhaukr* thing was a mistake. And if she does so, we, the Executive Council, will reinstate her, with no need for a vote of the General Secretariat."

Nygaard shook her head. "She'll never agree to that."

"But she will," Tiegnordan said. "I'll reassure her that she is still free to avow that Nvalheim lied to her. And she'll agree to this compromise because if she doesn't, I will openly withdraw my support from her. So far I've been silent on the matter, and that has probably meant a dozen or more votes in her favor. But if I openly renounce her, she'll lose twice that."

She looked at Nygaard. "And she'll lose all that momentum you spoke of."

Nygaard frowned and shrugged. "If you can convince her, then we'll have an Executive Council that all will agree is again balanced. That would considerably reduce the friction within the General Secretariat."

Nygaard, Tiegnordan and Dornmier all looked to Veskarson. He sat there silently rocking back and forth for a moment, then turned and aimed his words at Tiegnordan. "If she openly acknowledges the mistake without dissembling, then you have my solemn word that I will vote to reinstate. Tell her it must be a simple statement with no qualifications or innuendo. And no, she doesn't have to grovel or debase herself."

Dornmier demanded. "Are we all in agreement?"

Each of them in turn said, "Aye."

Dornmier asked Tiegnordan, "Then is it done?"

Tiegnordan nodded. "I'll speak with her this afternoon."

"Very well," Veskarson said. "Now to the next order of business."

He turned his attention to Kristdokar. "Brigadier Kristdokar, we ordered you to investigate the training accident that almost killed Lieutenant Mathius. Have you done so?"

Kristdokar felt like a small rodent who had just watched the big predators in their cages roaring at each other. "Yes, I have. Someone placed six separate charges in different locations aboard that training derelict, all set to trigger when any power source came near. Thankfully, the one that injured Lieutenant Mathius was triggered by a micro-nuke tossed into the compartment containing the charge, not by direct proximity to his armor reactor pack. The bulkhead enclosing that compartment protected him from more serious injury."

Dornmier shook her head, a frown on her face. "Another assassination attempt?"

"No," Kristdokar said, "we don't believe so. Maestra Mathius is not officially part of Mistress Forrester's platoon, so we think they were simply after anyone from the Commonwealth. We questioned all of the maintenance people who had access to that derelict, and we traced it to a small group who opposes the presence of the diplomatic mission. Their leader is a man who works for Norddansk Weapons Systems, but beyond that is only loosely connected to Marta Nvalheim. He disappeared and we have not been able to question him. We are still looking for him."

Tiegnordan pursed her lips and made no attempt to hide her anger. "Nvalheim again. Her name keeps coming up."

"Yes," Kristdokar said, bracing herself for their reaction to her next piece of news. "Speaking of Marta Nvalheim, I have important new evidence regarding Novalis III."

All four of the councilors froze for an instant, like images in a still picture. The moment ended when Veskarson said, "You have the floor, Brigadier."

Kristdokar took a breath to calm her thinking. "As you know, we recovered a number of survivors from *Sycorax*'s crew. Command Superior Thordahl has been in charge of their interrogation. He uncovered some information that led to other information that led to more information, and we believe we have a solid connection between Nvalheim and the tragedy on Novalis III. We now have hard evidence that she is culpable."

The eyes of all four councilors widened, and as one they leaned back in their seats.

Kristdokar continued. "With your permission, I'll upload the details to the secure nodes in each of your offices."

Tiegnordan leaned forward and pressed the palm of one hand flat on the desk in front of her. "Is Haugrund implicated?"

"No," Kristdokar said. "In fact there is evidence to indicate just the opposite. Nvalheim's people went to some lengths to keep certain information from her. It indirectly clears her of any wrongdoing."

Tiegnordan addressed the other three councilors. "When I meet with Haugrund, may I tell her of this? She has wanted to clear her name, and it would put a butcher's lock on our agreement with her."

"Wait," Veskarson said. "The brigadier will upload the information. We'll all review the details within the hour, then meet remotely. If this is true, you'll have even my enthusiastic endorsement of a reconciliation with her. But you'll have to swear her to secrecy, and she gets none of the hard data until after she is reinstated." He glanced up and down the table at the other councilors. "And none of us reveals any details of what we've learned today to anyone."

The four councilors were in general agreement on that, and it was up to Kristdokar to change their minds. "I beg you to reconsider that last stricture."

In that moment Kristdokar saw in their eyes that her entire career, and perhaps her life as well, were in question. "Lieutenant John Mathius lost his entire family, his mother, father and sister, on Novalis III, and he is breschkada-sa. The right of vendetta dictates that we must tell him."

Tiegnordan pursed her lips and her eyes hardened. "He is not Kelk. He cannot claim the right of vendetta."

Kristdokar fought to keep any note of fear out of her voice. "No, he can't, but vendetta still requires that we must tell him of this."

Each of the four councilors had a different reaction. Veskarson closed his eyes, squeezing them tightly shut. Dornmier put a hand to her breast and blinked her eyes rapidly. Nygaard pursed her lips, quite possibly angry that she could not deny their obligation. Tiegnordan simply spoke in a flat, lifeless tone. "How do you propose to relate the information to him?"

Kristdokar spoke cautiously. "I'll swear Colonel Primatov to secrecy, and pass it on through her."

Nygaard shook her head. "She'll have to tell her superiors."

Kristdokar shrugged. "Of course she'll tell *the* Blacksword, Colonel Thealone. But I've learned a few things about Blackswords: they don't tell their superiors everything. I suppose that means I'll have to brief both of them, but I'll get their promises that it won't go beyond them and young Maestra Mathius until after Haugrund is reinstated."

The four councilors argued the subject for a few minutes, but they could not deny their obligation. Kristdokar received permission to pass the information on to Primatov and Thealone.

Once that was settled, Veskarson asked, "Is there anything else, Brigadier?"

What she was about to reveal frightened even her. "Yes. We may have a hard connection between Nvalheim and a member of the Commonwealth diplomatic mission."

Veskarson asked, "And who would that be?"

Kristdokar spoke carefully. "We believe we've found a trail of financial connections between one of Nvalheim's shell corporations and Senator Jenine Catarvin."

••••

Anders needed to make contact with Viktra, and he also needed to report back to the transit depot to understand the situation there. Did he still have a job there? Were

Thoran and his special friends still gaming the authorities for some purpose Anders had yet to discern? Did Viktra still work at the transit depot? Or had they decided that, with Anders out of the picture, they no longer needed a covert handler for an operative that might never return. Had Viktra taken someone else as a lover? And did she even care one whit about Anders Eindride? If Anders wanted to stay alive, his actions needed to be consistent with his false Anders Eindride persona, an ex SecureMax inmate who had chosen to betray everything and everyone he held dear.

Anders's return from his three-month-long odyssey to Sarkovie had gotten him back to his apartment in the wee hours of the morning. Exhausted after his journey, he slept in, and woke about noon. While he showered, shaved, and ate a late breakfast, he debated what to do. Would the person he pretended to be go to the transit depot first, or to Viktra? He realized he was overthinking the situation. Viktra meant something to him; he would go see her first, if she was still there.

Anders had a couple of hours to kill before Viktra finished her shift and returned to her apartment. He spent the time going through the news feeds, trying to catch up. Almost every article he read had something to do with the diplomatic mission from the Commonwealth. He watched excerpts of the welcoming ceremony. He could have watched a replay of the whole thing, but the excerpts were boring enough. He scanned coverage of meetings between working groups on commerce, trade, and possible tourism—he couldn't imagine going to the Commonwealth as a tourist. There was not a lot of coverage of the groups working to lessen the tensions between the two powers, but reading between the lines it was clear both sides were putting a fair amount of effort into that. He repeatedly saw Nikaela Vreekande in the coverage, and young Maestra Mathius, but interestingly enough, they were always in the background. Someone—probably Kristdokar—had carefully considered their wellbeing, and understood that placing them front and center would just make them targets.

Anders had considered calling Viktra, or leaving her a message, but his encounter with Neddaline Macree in Viktorkinde Prime meant his return was no secret. Late in the afternoon, he left his apartment and walked the short distance to her building. The key she had given him still worked at the main entrance, which was a good sign. He decided that after three months it would not be wise to simply walk into her apartment, so instead of using the key to enter, he knocked on the door.

He waited several seconds, then the door opened and she stood there facing him. She stood shoulder high to him, wore a loose shirt with floppy pants and bare feet, no makeup, and he had missed her very much. Before doing or saying anything, she flashed him a welcoming smile, which meant a lot to him.

"Anders," she said, "when did you get back?"

They had always operated under the assumption that Thoran and his friends had bugged her apartment. The Viktra Kirkdehl who handled a covert operative for

Kristdokar knew full well the answer to that question. The Viktra Kirkdehl who worked as a transit supervisor would not.

"Just last night," he said. "Actually, early this morning."

She stepped back from the open door. "Come in. Come in. I wasn't expecting you. What happened?"

He shrugged as he stepped into her apartment. "The job on Sarkovie turned out to be a temporary thing."

She closed the door, turned and wrapped her arms around him. "I'm glad you're back."

Was it all show for the possible surveillance devices in her apartment?

She opened a secure link between their implants. *I am glad you're back. Me, Viktra Kirkdehl, is glad you're back.*

She looked into his eyes and smiled at him. "You'll stay the night, won't you?"

Together they made dinner and talked of trivial matters. And that night they didn't make wild, passionate love; they made quiet, passionate love.

••••

As Kristdokar laid out the evidence and explained the complexity of the transactions, Fran watched Primatov closely. Katrine had recruited and handled Catarvin, and both she and Fran regarded her as a valuable asset. It was always painful to learn that one's judge of character had been incorrect, that you'd been played. Fran reminded herself that both of them had been played.

Kristdokar showed them a history of interstellar banking transfers from a shell company set up by Nvalheim's lawyers. The money from each transfer had landed in an account on Sarkovie. The funds had then been laundered through an account on Miriteen, which made them available within the Commonwealth. Regular transfers had been taken out of that account and deposited into the corporate accounts of a company owned by Catarvin's husband. Fran didn't really expect Primatov to react to the information, not in front of Kristdokar, especially since the skalde didn't know that Senator Jenine Catarvin was a valued covert asset.

Miershall's people hadn't gotten anything more out of the captured members of *Caliban*'s crew, though they had rescued the doctor who'd been a reluctant participant in John Mathius's repeated torture and healing. The low-level aide they had arrested on Trafalgar had been milked for all he was worth, and as to the other two arrested with him, Primatov's people still hadn't broken them.

Kristdokar's words drew Fran's attention. "I have another piece of information that's troubling. Our agent that handles Anders Eindride at the transit depot, she's not part of the rogue operation there, but thanks to him she knows who is. And recently they appear to have ceased all extracurricular activities. It sounds like they abruptly shut down their illicit operation."

That bothered Fran greatly. The rogues had shut down operations here and on Sarkovie, one hundred and fifty lightyears apart.

Kristdokar looked worried as she spoke. "There is some good news. We have solid evidence that Haugrund was not complicit in the Novalis III tragedy."

Fran was reminded of John Mathius's observation that the Kelk referred to Novalis III as a tragedy, while the Commonwealth used the term incident.

Fran focused on Kristdokar's words. "Her name has been cleared, and by unanimous vote of the Executive Council she was reinstated this morning. And that has considerably calmed the entire General Secretariat. On the other hand, Haugrund is absolutely furious with Nvalheim, who's gone completely underground."

They discussed that briefly, then ended the meeting and Kristdokar left.

As soon as the door closed, Primatov frowned and shook her head. "I don't believe it."

Like Primatov, Fran didn't want to believe the evidence against Catarvin. "Why not?"

Primatov closed her eyes and grimaced. "She's got plenty of wealth to begin with."

Fran shrugged. "It's the old adage: for some, all the money in the universe is just not enough."

Primatov shook her head rapidly. "No, no, no. That's not her. She's not driven by money."

Fran had needed to hear the younger woman's honest opinion, unblemished by their long friendship. "If it makes any difference, I agree with you. So what are we missing?"

Primatov stood. "I'll ask Miershall to have her people look into that account on Sarkovie. And Miriteen is running a courier ship in a straight back-and-forth to the relay chain, so I can now contact them with minimal delay. I'll ask them to look into that laundering account there. And I'll have our people on Trafalgar look into her husband's company."

Primatov faced Fran squarely, the bitch-face in full blossom. "I don't believe it. But if it turns out to be true, when this is done, I'll kill her myself."

15

Therapy

REPAIRING WARSHIPS MEANT the Heilbronn Navy Yard supplied a lot of heavy construction to the vessels parked in its docks. It had its share of accidents ranging from minor to fatal, so it had a fully equipped hospital sector. An hour after the accident on the training derelict, May and company deposited John and Matsen there. Matsen's squad had triggered another booby trap at the other end of the derelict, and he'd lost a good part of his right arm. As they explained the accident to the medical staff, in the background Carla questioned Digger like a DI upbraiding a recruit, and John felt sorry for the fellow.

The medical staff put John into a full body nerve block, the pain went away, and he finally relaxed. He slept well that night and woke the next morning fully rested. They had switched off the full body block and gone to a local so he didn't have to live on a feeding tube. And they had encased the lower half of his leg in some sort of medical apparatus, which limited his movements.

A couple hours after he awoke a male doctor showed up, a common-face. The fellow examined his leg and pronounced it, "Nasty wound on top of decompression damage to a lot of the tissue, and the pressure clamp did some damage too."

For John, boredom had already set in, and he tried not to sound petulant. "How long do I have to stay in here?"

The fellow looked at John's chart. "Two more nights, then I've scheduled you for release. If it had been a hand or arm wound and you were ambulatory, I'd probably only keep you for just one more night."

The doctor looked away from the chart and into John's face. "But a lot of important people are watching your recovery closely. I was ordered to put you in a private room, not a ward, and to make sure there were no complications. So I want to see that leg healed before you leave here, though I do have one question."

The fellow seemed almost angry. "Ask away," John said.

The doctor's eyes hardened. "Why were you using such large charges on a training exercise?"

That was John's first hint that the story was a bit muddled. He pleaded ignorance, and the doctor left. Two more days and two more nights, John wasn't sure he'd survive the boredom. He killed a little time playing cards with Kolbeck, though the handsome dregkraag seemed rather subdued without Matsen present. Getting an arm replaced meant poor Matsen would be bed-ridden for at least a couple of tendays.

After an hour of cards with Kolbeck John's cash reserves had dwindled a little. Then Carla and May showed up. Carla had slung a duffel over one shoulder, and she tossed it on the end of John's bed. "I brought you some clothes."

May turned to Kolbeck and hooked a thumb over her shoulder toward the door. "Would you mind waiting out in the hall?"

That seemed like an odd request, and Kolbeck must have thought the same. He lifted an eyebrow as he shrugged and stood, then walked out of the room.

Both young women seemed unusually reserved, even though the three of them were alone and didn't need to carry any pretense in front of strangers. May stood at the door with her back leaning against it, watching John like a DI who suspected a recruit had something to hide. Carla was upset about something, and as always she was not good at hiding her feelings. John decided to simply call them on it. "You're acting funny. What's wrong?"

Carla ignored him and opened the duffel. She retrieved a khaki tunic and trousers. "Brought you some service khakis." She tossed them on the bed, then retrieved a lightweight deck jacket. "And I brought you a jacket." She tossed the jacket on top of the tunic and trousers. "I made sure to bring the jacket so you can conceal this." She reached into the duffel and retrieved the shoulder harness and old-fashioned slugthrower Primatov had given him when he'd learned about Plan Z. She tossed it onto the bed where it landed on his good leg with a nasty thump. He flinched. "Owe."

May remained at the door, and he now understood she had intentionally blocked it.

Carla demanded, "What the hell is that weapon for?"

When May spoke, her words were a lot calmer that Carla's, but the anger was still there. "Yes, John, we found that in your locker, had no trouble bringing it into the hospital, because nothing short of a physical search is going to detect that thing. Why do you have such a weapon?"

John recalled Fleming's admonition that he was never to acknowledge the existence of Plan Z outside the Blacksword. "I can't tell you."

Carla flashed him an angry look and John thought she might blow her stack at any moment.

May's eyes hardened. "Is it a Blacksword thing?"

John grimaced. "I don't think I can tell you that either."

May and Carla looked at each other and locked eyes. In perfect cadence, they both said, "It's a fucking Blacksword thing."

A knock on the door startled all three of them. From outside someone tried to open the door, the way doctors do when they knock, but don't wait for an answer before entering. The door bumped against May's back, though whoever it was didn't push hard enough to dislodge her.

John tossed the shoulder harness and weapon back to Carla and she quickly stuffed it into the duffel out of sight. May stepped away from the door and opened it, then stepped aside. Primatov walked into the room, hesitated, looked at each of them, and clearly sensed something amiss. She nodded, turned back to the door and closed it carefully, then turned to face them and waited for someone to speak. May and Carla looked daggers at John, waiting for him to say something.

John shook his head. "They found the pistol and the shoulder harness, and they're pissed at me for keeping secrets."

Carla reached into the duffel and retrieved the pistol with the shoulder harness wrapped around it. She placed it carefully on the bed beside the duffel. John was glad she didn't throw it at his leg again.

Primatov looked at John for a moment, nodded once, and her face hardened. Her head turned slowly and she looked at May.

May cringed a little, but stood her ground. "We thought to bring him some clothing, and found that while digging through his locker."

Primatov's look softened and she nodded. "That was kind of you. I gave that weapon to John and told him to wear it. If nothing else, it may be his last line of defense if there's another assassination attempt."

No mention of Plan Z or the Blacksword. Since only a moment ago Carla and May had concluded it was a *Blacksword thing*, John saw in their faces that they both noted the discrepancy. He didn't like keeping secrets from either of them.

Perhaps Primatov saw that as well because she added, "There is, of course, more to it than that, but John is not allowed to discuss that with you."

"Colonel," May said, her face showing obvious strain, "we know there's something going on with the Kelk. Tell us what to do."

Primatov closed her eyes and took a long, slow breath. When she opened her eyes the stern look on her face had considerably softened, but the tightness of her lips testified to a fair amount of strain. "Our hands are a bit tied right now by the political situation. And we can't act decisively because we don't have anything concrete upon which to act, and we don't really know what's going on. Just stay alert, stay diligent, and try to stay armed . . . at all times if possible."

She hesitated for a moment, then smiled at John. "As you know, that derelict was rigged with several charges like the one you triggered."

May nodded. "We figured they tried to assassinate John."

Primatov shook her head. "Too random, a shotgun approach. How could they be sure they'd get John and not someone else? Their other attempts have been more surgical, and John's not officially assigned to your team, so they probably didn't know he was with you. We think they were after common-faces in general, and more specifically, any ComSecCorps soldier they could get. They might also have intended to punish any Kelk who cooperated with us."

Carla closed her eyes and shook her head. "Shit!"

Primatov continued. "There are a lot of big-shots on both sides of the equation that are upset about this. The last thing we need is for this to hit the news feeds as a murder attempt, which would only spawn a lot of conspiracy theories. It was a training accident, nothing more. Do you understand me?"

She looked at each of them in turn and waited for an explicit answer.

Carla said, "Got it."

May said, "Yes, ma'am."

John nodded. "As you wish."

"Good," Primatov said, "because I do wish. And please make sure your platoon mates know that this incident is to be forgotten and never discussed. Tell them I would be unhappy with anyone who leaked this."

John had heard of the bitch-face, but had never seen it full-on before, and to his surprise she didn't show even a hint of it at that moment. But she quite effectively made her point without it.

She turned her attention to John. "I'm also here because I went to your locker to retrieve that weapon and bring it to you, and when I found it missing I decided I wanted to know why." She looked at May for a long moment, then turned her head and looked at Carla for an equally long moment. "It pleases me to know that you two are such intelligent young women."

From the looks on their faces, John thought Carla and May were as uncertain as him about whether or not that was a compliment.

"Now, ladies," Primatov said, "I need to have a word alone with Mr. Mathius."

After entering the room, Primatov had remained at the door, and stepped aside as May and Carla left. When they were gone, she closed the door, then crossed the room to stand beside John's bed.

She hesitated, clearly uncomfortable about something. "I spoke with Brigadier Skalde Kristdokar this morning. They have uncovered evidence that led them to one of the people responsible for the deaths of your family and all your countrymen on Novalis III."

John's heart raced, and he felt a moment of vertigo. He closed his eyes and got himself under control. "I'm listening."

Primatov spoke in flat, lifeless tones. "A woman named Marta Nvalheim. She's the head of a very influential family here on Viktorkinde. She's a retired brigadier skalde and a member of the Larscom General Secretariat. She also sits on the board of Norddansk Interstellar and is a significant shareholder. Forensic analysis of the bio toxins used on Novalis III led to Norddansk, but she didn't do it for profit. She's a notorious, hardline, anti-Commonwealth hawk, and is apparently a bit of a fanatic about it."

John's voice trembled as he spoke. "You have proof?"

Primatov nodded. "Quite a few members of *Sycorax*'s crew survived her breakup. Kristdokar's people interrogated them, and information from them led to hard proof. Nvalheim is culpable."

After John left Novalis III he'd wandered through life in a numb, uncaring haze for about six months. Then he had enlisted, and for a time, caring again had awakened in him intermittent bouts of murderous fury. But that kind of hate only hurt him and left him angry, stressed, and sad, especially when he had no one to aim it at. It had left a black hole in his heart, and now that he knew a name, he didn't want to return to that place, though it took some effort to stay clear of it.

Primatov had remained silent while he thought it through. She had an uncanny ability to know when to keep her mouth shut and let him think. But when she spoke, he realized she hadn't really understood his thoughts. "You can't act on this information, John. She's an influential citizen of the Supremacy, and if you did anything to her, it could spark interstellar war. Kristdokar assures me they will eventually bring her to justice."

John wasn't sure if he had decided to kill Nvalheim or not, but he did trust Kristdokar. "I won't do anything, as long as Kristdokar keeps her promise."

Primatov smiled. "I'll tell her that."

John added. "And tell her I can be patient about it too. I understand that something like that might take a little time."

Primatov placed a friendly hand on John's shoulder. "You've always been smart, and mature, so I'm going to tell you something else, but I don't have permission to tell you this, so you must never repeat it to anyone."

A piece of him wanted to let that fury rule him, but he clamped it down. "I understand."

She pursed her lips for a moment, as if considering how to tell him this new secret. "We know Silas Palmutter is working closely with Marta Nvalheim. We believe, but cannot prove, that he too is culpable in the tragedy on Novalis III."

At that moment John didn't have it in him to say anything, and all he could do was nod.

She continued. "This too, you cannot act upon. But I'll give you a similar promise to Kristdokar's. If we do determine that he, or anyone else, was complicit in that murderous act, you have my promise they will be brought to justice . . . one way or another."

••••

After Primatov left his hospital room, John went through the duffel May and Carla had brought and learned they had also included his butcher's dagger with the complicated harness. He stuffed the old-fashioned slug-thrower under his pillow so it would be close at hand if he needed it. Then he spent a thoroughly tiresome afternoon watching news feeds, practicing his Kelk reading skills, playing cards with Kolbeck, and getting so bored with all of it that he frequently dozed off for short periods, though when he did, he always started awake with that murderous hate pounding at his soul. As the evening progressed a dregkraag from May's platoon relieved Kolbeck. When it was time to kill the lights and get some sleep, the fellow dragged a chair out into the hallway and sat down there to spend the night. With the lights out John lay in the dark and had trouble falling asleep.

He was wide awake when he heard the latch on the door click. The door opened just a crack, splashing a shaft of light that slanted at a sharp angle through the room, but didn't illuminate anything else. Whoever had opened the door stuck their head in just past the edge of it and glanced about. In the shadows John could discern nothing, but the light from the hallway illuminated dark hair with no salt in it: a Kelk.

The intruder slipped into the room, closed the door, and something about her stature gave John the impression it was a woman. He thought it telling that she didn't activate the lights, and as she crossed the room on tiptoe she carried something in one hand in front of her. A stray ray of light glinted off a shiny surface, and he thought he recognized the shape of a blade in her hand, probably another butcher's dagger, if he had to guess. He wondered what had happened to the guard outside the door.

It was awkward doing so, but he edged his hand behind his back and underneath the pillow. He gripped the butt of the pistol, but hesitated. She might be medical staff, carrying some sort of instrument. And she might be tiptoeing in the dark because she didn't want to disturb the sleep of a convalescing patient. If he was wrong about her, he'd kill an innocent woman.

He was a heartbeat away from ripping the weapon out from beneath the pillow and pressing it beneath her chin, hoping she'd immediately recognize he had her outgunned so he wouldn't have to kill her. But at that moment, Nikaela said, "John. Are you awake?"

His heart threatened to hammer its way out of his chest as he stupidly asked, "Nikaela, is that you?"

She whispered, "I thought you might need this."

He reached out and touched the blade she held. It was her butcher's dagger.

"I don't," he said. "I'm armed."

"Oh," she said. "Okay. Well . . . I brought you something else too."

"What?"

She fumbled at her waist, saying only, "This."

He thought she worked to retrieve something, but then the harness for her butcher's dagger dropped to the floor. Then something else dropped to the floor next to it, and a moment later a naked, lithe body slipped under the sheets next to him.

"I brought you me," she said. "It's been a while since you checked to make sure my tongue isn't forked."

They had encased the lower half of his leg in a medical apparatus of some sort, then supported it in a harness, which forced him to lay flat on his back or sit up. He had to stretch a little to run a line of kisses down her neck. "I don't know if I should. I'm wounded, you know."

She shook her head. "I checked your chart, and your wounds don't involve any of the parts I'm interested in."

John's boredom ended rather abruptly, and a short time later they were both having a thoroughly wonderful time. Apparently, they were also making a little too much noise, or maybe some monitor had detected John's rapidly increasing heart rate, because the door opened and the lights came on.

"What's going . . ."

They both froze with Nikaela on top of John. She struggled to stifle a laugh.

John tilted his head up and craned his neck to look past her bare shoulders. A female member of the medical staff stood just inside the door, and the frown on her face slowly morphed into a broad grin. "I'll have to consult your charts, but I don't believe the doctor prescribed that particular therapy for you."

John couldn't think of anything to say, especially with Nikaela desperately choking and spluttering suppressed giggles in his ear.

The woman's grin broadened. "In any case, it does appear to be doing you some good, so I'll ask the doctor to add that to your treatments. But mistress, do be careful about his leg."

The woman killed the lights, stepped out of the room, and closed the door.

Nikaela finally let the laugh escape, and it occurred to John that a Commonwealth doctor would have raised holy hell. But a moment later he was much too busy with other things to devote any further neurons to that thought.

16

Unhappy Alliance

PALMUTTER HAD TRIED to get Faith to join him again for a *quiet dinner in the city*, but after her first experience she would have none of that. She hadn't even been subtle about it. When he asked, she gave him a flat, "No," then joined the crowd in the lounge for the cheap buffet they served there every evening. He finally stopped asking.

Andrew Talpano had been stupid enough to get suckered into it a second time, had even believed Palmutter when he said, "No, really, just a quiet dinner this time." The young man later told Faith that the shouting between Nvalheim and Palmutter had been much less intense the second time around, though the tension had been thick enough to cut with a knife.

Faith spent the afternoon in her room alone, massaging a series of press releases scheduled to be sent back to Trafalgar over the secret relay chain that wasn't much of a secret anymore. Strikland invited her to join him for dinner, and she was looking forward to a pleasant evening with him. They hadn't seen each other for several days, which had given her time to think carefully about whether she would tell Strikland of Palmutter's clandestine meetings with Nvalheim. She still hadn't made up her mind on that matter, and would have to do so before seeing Strikland that evening.

She put on a dress that looked business-like, but one she knew Strikland liked a lot. By keeping the blouse buttoned all the way up, she looked all-business, which was the way she wanted to appear if she ran into anyone on the way to his suite. But just before she got there she'd pop a few buttons at the top and expose a little skin. Lawrence Strikland liked everything tastefully done, so a small, stylish bit of exposed cleavage was just the right thing to excite him.

The knock on the door to her room was unexpected. Since her implants weren't interfaced to the building's localnet, she crossed the room and opened the door. Two men stood in the hallway, both common-faces, one young and thuggish, the other middle-aged, balding, and a bit fat.

The older one seemed oddly familiar from somewhere. "Mistress Carlton," he said, "Senator Palmutter would like you to come with me."

She recognized the accent: Sarkovie. Then she recognized the man: the fellow who had greeted them outside the restaurant the night Palmutter had tricked her into accompanying him to meet Nvalheim. Faith backed up a step and tried to close the door, but the younger one put his shoulder against it and easily overpowered her.

He pushed the door completely open, forcing her to back-step into the room. He stepped through the doorway and advanced on her, a determined look on his face. She tried to broadcast an open call for help through her implants, knowing that without access to localnet her direct link-to-link range was quite limited, but her implants crashed.

The older fellow closed the door while the younger one backed her across the room until the back of her legs encountered a chair, she stumbled, and fell into it. As the young thug loomed over her, panic set in and she cried out, "Please don't hurt me. Please don't hurt me."

She hid her face in her hands, a stupid and useless thing to do, but primal instinct now ruled her actions. "Please don't hurt me. Please, please."

Through the gaps in her fingers she watched the fat, older fellow cross the room, lean down, gently grip her wrists, then pull them apart and away from her face. He had hard, unyielding eyes, and she smelled some sort of cologne wafting off him.

He gave her a cold and heartless smile. The soft tones of his voice contrasted sharply with the look in his eyes. "Young lady, you're going to come with us, and we won't hurt you, as long as you don't resist. On the other hand, should you cry out and attract attention, we will make it unpleasant for you. Do you understand?"

It bothered her to be so helpless, to not be the one in control. She tried to control her composure and nod calmly, but her head bobbed up and down in a series of frantic, spasmodic jerks, and she hiccoughed.

"Good," he said. He released her wrists, straightened, and extended a hand toward her. "May I help you stand?"

She didn't accept his aid, and rose up out of the chair on her own.

He turned and walked toward the door, saying, "Bring her."

The young thug gripped her right elbow and marched her across the room to the door. The older one opened it and stepped out into the hall. Still gripping her elbow, the younger one forced her to follow. The older fellow griped her other elbow, and the three of them walked casually down the hall, as if on their way to some entertaining event for the evening.

Now that the initial panic had subsided, Faith's thoughts cleared. Her one chance was the lobby, which was busy any time of the day or night. There would be plenty of people about, and if she cried out, her two assailants dare not harm her with so many witnesses present. But as they approached the lift, the two men didn't slow down. They walked her past it to the end of the hall where they turned right. They stopped at a service elevator, called it, and when it came, hustled her into it. They didn't relax their grips on her arms as the lift took them down. When it opened they stepped out into a subterranean garage, with row after row of parked cars.

The older man released his grip on her elbow and walked ahead of them. The young thug tightened his grip painfully, and she and he followed. As they walked between rows of cars, they encountered a Kelk woman with very little salt in her hair going in the opposite direction. The young fellow gripping Faith's elbow leaned close to her and whispered in a heavy Sarkovie accent. "If you cry out or cause any trouble, she will die, and later you will regret your stupidity." He tightened his grip on her elbow, and Faith almost cried out at the pain.

Faith managed to keep her mouth shut, her eyes forward.

The three of them climbed into the back seat of a grav car, with Faith sandwiched between the two men. The car's windows blanked and went opaque. It pulled out of its parking space, navigated its way out of the garage, and headed into the night of the city.

Faith's heart threatened to pound its way out of her chest. Were they going to kill her, and dump her body somewhere, and no one would ever find her, and she'd be nothing more than a nameless missing person? But the older fat one had said something about Palmutter. Faith didn't think the senator wanted her dead, but then at that point she wouldn't put anything past the old lecher.

When the car came to a stop and its windows cleared they appeared to be in some sort of alley. The young thug helped Faith out of the car and resumed his grip on her elbow. The fat, older one opened a door in the back of a building, then they marched her through it. They walked through a kitchen with wait staff rushing about, then through a door into a private dining room like the one she remembered, possibly even the same one.

Palmutter and Nvalheim were seated at the dining table, a bottle of kirva and shot glasses between them. The young thug forced Faith into a chair between them, then the two Sarkovites stepped back to the edge of the room.

Faith looked at Palmutter, then at Nvalheim. The old woman reached out to the shot glass in front of her, lifted it to her mouth, and tossed it back. Then she stood and leaned down over Faith. "Silas tells me you don't want to cooperate. He says you were upset by the meeting we had the other night, and you refused to come back. I didn't want you here in the first place, but now that you've seen me, your intransigence worries me. You need to help me understand that I shouldn't be worried."

Nvalheim straightened, and for the first time Faith understood the true danger she faced that night.

Palmutter toyed with the shot glass in front of him. "We're at a critical juncture here, Faith. We can't have any loose ends. You've demonstrated repeatedly that your ethics are flexible. We now need to make sure they're flexible enough."

Nvalheim lifted the bottle of kirva and refilled her glass. "You don't approve of me, so you avoid me."

The old woman clearly wanted to hear something other than silence from Faith. "It's not disapproval. I just think I'm in over my head. You're . . . way out of my league." That was not exactly the truth, but close enough.

Nvalheim gave her an unpleasant grin. "The pretty little girl is frightened."

Faith nodded. "I am, but I'm frightened more of *you*, than of what you're doing, perhaps because I don't know what you're doing."

Nvalheim lifted a questioning eyebrow, so Faith added, "And I don't want to know what you're doing."

Palmutter had a smug smile on his face. "I don't think we have anything to worry about. She'll keep her mouth shut."

Nvalheim gave him a sour look. "Why would she do that?"

His characteristic anger reared up and showed itself. "Because it's in her own interest. Because she's fucking Strikland, and she doesn't want to endanger such a valuable relationship. And because if she doesn't cooperate, I'll tell him she seduced him to spy on him for me."

Nvalheim perked up. "Is that true?"

Palmutter nodded. "She's an ambitious young girl."

It was true, but it wasn't, not in the way Palmutter thought. He didn't know that Faith had long ago revealed his plotting to Strikland, and that she and he were playing Palmutter for a fool. That was her one advantage in this, the secret that might keep her alive.

Looking at Palmutter, Nvalheim waved a finger for him to follow her and walked across the room. Palmutter stood, joined her, and the two of them spoke in whispers. Palmutter seemed to be arguing in Faith's favor, but at one point the discussion grew heated, and Nvalheim snarled something about not being the only one who ". . . gets fucked if this goes bad."

When the two of them finished they called the fat Sarkovite over and spoke quietly with him for a few seconds. Then Palmutter and Nvalheim left the room, leaving her alone with the fat fellow and his young thug. The thug gripped Faith's elbow painfully and forced her to stand. As the two of them marched her out through the kitchen and back to the car in the alley, she wondered if she would live through the night.

They blanked the windows on the car, and again sandwiched her between them in the back seat. As the car wove through the streets of Emkeldstadt, Faith almost vomited with fear, but when they cleared the windows, the car had stopped in front of the

Hyvaldsborg Palace. The thug climbed out of the car and waited while she followed. Then he climbed back into it, and it sped away.

Faith's knees trembled as she walked up the steps to the entrance to the palace. When she stepped through the doors into the lobby, one of Strikland's security people appeared at her elbow. He had clearly been waiting there for her.

"Miss Carlton," he said. "Mr. Strikland was disappointed that you didn't join him for dinner. He hopes there was a good reason for that."

At that moment, Faith had no trouble coming to a decision on what she would tell Strikland. "Yes, I was abducted, against my will."

The fellow lifted an eyebrow and pursed his lips.

Faith wanted to see the look on Strikland's face when he heard her story. "I need to see Mr. Strikland right away. I think he'll be interested in what I have to tell him."

Strikland's security guy paused for a moment and his eyes defocused. When they focused again, he said, "Mr. Strikland will see you right away."

When Faith stepped into Strikland's suite she found him waiting for her. He took her in his arms. "Who abducted you?"

She looked into his eyes. "Two Sarkovites working for Nvalheim and Palmutter."

She told him about the first meeting with the two, and how Palmutter had tricked her into accompanying him. "I thought I would tell you about that this evening when we met for dinner. But that didn't happen."

She told him of her abduction, and the events that followed. As she spoke his face hardened, and she saw in him the kind of cold, determined anger she would never want directed her way.

When she finished, the look on his face softened. "You're not spending another night alone in that room. Go back there and pack your stuff. From now on, you're not leaving the safety of this suite unless you're accompanied by one or more of my people."

He pointed at two of his security people. "You and you, go with her while she packs, and see to it she gets back here unhindered and unharmed."

••••

Anders woke early, and together he and Viktra prepared a simple breakfast. The previous night they had only talked of trivial matters, nothing serious, with no talk of what had happened to him on Sarkovie. But over breakfast Viktra asked, "Is it true what they say about the Sarkovites, that they're all whores, no moral character?"

He frowned, and wasn't sure how to answer that. "It is, and it isn't. They do have moral character."

"But they're all whores?"

"No," he said. "Not all of them."

She leaned forward and ran a finger along the line of his jaw. "Did some Sarkovite woman take you as a lover?"

He didn't know how to answer that either. "Yes and no."

She frowned. "It is, and it isn't. Yes and no. Do you have fond memories of her?"

He did know the answer to that question. "Good memories, but I wouldn't call them fond."

At that, she smiled. "So I don't need to be jealous?"

"No," he said. "No need to be jealous."

She grinned. "I think you might have a strange tale to tell. But I won't press you on it. Tell it when you want to, or don't tell it at all. It's up to you."

He decided not to tell her that Neddaline Macree had come to Viktorkinde. After all, as the young woman had said, they would probably never see each other again.

Using a secure link between their implants, Anders gave her the same information he'd given Macree; that Lorenson and Hohlman had completely shut down their special shipments. She told him what she had passed on to Kristdokar; that Thoran and his friends appeared to have shut down their rogue operation as well. The two of them walked to the transit depot together.

To Anders's surprise, he learned that during the last three months he had reported to work every day without fail. Anders Karsten had left the planet and returned three months later; Anders Eindride had remained there the entire time.

At the end of his shift, as he finished changing out of his transit uniform, a hearty slap on the back startled him. When he turned around, he was not surprised to find tall, bearded Thoran standing there. Nothing about the man had changed: his beard still neatly trimmed, his hair in dreadlocks. "Anders, old friend. It's been a while since we've shared a bottle of kirva."

He hooked a thumb over his shoulder. "I need a drink. Join me."

There it was, their de facto signal to meet privately.

As they walked down the street side by side, Anders asked a question he had voiced a number of times before. "That woman of yours still costs you too much money?" The woman didn't really exist.

The tall fellow shook his head. "As a matter of fact, no. We aren't seeing each other anymore. I gotta admit, not seeing her is doing wonders for my bank account."

That appeared to confirm Viktra's observations. Anders decided to wait for a more private setting before exploring that further.

They went to the bar they'd gone to many times before, found a small table in a dark corner with no one nearby, and ordered a couple of drinks.

"So," Anders said, "you're not seeing that woman anymore?"

Thoran grimaced. "Yah. She ain't costing me as much, which is good." He leaned close to Anders and lowered his voice. "But my moonlighting job dried up, which is hurting my finances a lot."

More change. Anders needed to know what was up. Like Thoran, he kept his voice low. "I take it I'm out of luck too? I mean, financially speaking, no more extra-curricular work, eh?"

"Yah," Thoran said, but he grinned. "But I think I got us a solution to that. We just need to be flexible."

Anders glanced around to make sure no one was close. "What's going on?"

Thoran lowered his voice to a faint whisper. "Don't know the details, but they got something bigger planned, and they'd hate to have some constable stumble on our operation and muck up the picture, so all the special stuff here is shut down until further notice."

Something didn't add up. The big fellow seemed almost pleased at the loss of the extra revenue. Anders shook his head and lowered his voice to match Thoran's. "I don't understand. Why the grin? You sound happy that we're about to take a serious financial hit. Why?"

Thoran's grin broadened further. "They still need people with our special skills. We just gotta go where the action is, so I volunteered you, me, and a couple others."

Anders took the words *special skills* to mean their military training. "And?"

Thoran was clearly pleased with himself. "We're going to go help them with their big plans." He slapped Anders on the back. "We're going to Emkeldstadt, friend."

17

Safe Retreat

AS THE CAR pulled up in front the high-rise, Macus marveled at how Supremacy construction was every bit as advanced as that in the Commonwealth. He had come to Viktorkinde expecting something more primitive or quaint, and he needed to get over that. But he'd grown up thinking of the demon-eyed monsters as primitive and animal-like, and he found it difficult to adjust his thinking, even after more than a tenday living among them.

Strikland had been extremely displeased when he learned that Nvalheim and Pal-mutter had used a couple of Sarkovite thugs to abduct Faith. He had immediately tasked his security people with keeping an eye on her. He no longer made any attempt to keep his relationship with Faith a secret, at least not around Macus. And after Ma-cus's first meeting with Aubrecht Machtberg, it was clear he had passed some sort of test, all of which had helped Macus advance fully into Strikland's inner circle.

Thankfully, Strikland still did not have the slightest inkling of Macus's and Faith's true relationship. Macus had even managed to steer her into the presence of John Mathius a second time, which resulted in another satisfying, fuck-me-hard incident. Sex was so much better when he didn't have to waste time trying to please his partner. He really enjoyed simply hammering away at her and getting the job done without the added distraction.

It was also clear that Machtberg's paranoia had lightened up a bit. This time he sent only Command Superior Torstein to pick them up, and without the presence of his sister, Macus and Strikland rode together in the rear seat. Torstein had also left the vehicle's windows transparent, hadn't blocked their implant's access to citynet, and she pulled up in front of the building where Machtberg owned an expensive suite, not in the bowels of its subterranean parking garage. And their meeting had been scheduled for the middle of the afternoon, in broad daylight.

As Macus and Strikland climbed out of the car, a female command superior ap-proached them. "Maestras Strikland and DeLeon," she said, beaming a pleasant smile at them, "Maestra Machtberg asked me to escort you up to his flat. Please follow me."

Macus and Strikland followed her into the building, then to a lift, and up to the top floor. When the lift doors opened, she said, "This way, gentlemen."

She led them through a penthouse suite furnished in a classical style, then to an outdoor sundeck that occupied half the floor. She left them at the door and didn't follow them out. In the distance they spotted Machtberg standing beneath a trellis that provided shade from the planet's hot, blue-white sun.

"Lawrence, Macus," he called, waving a hand over his head.

They wove their way through a carefully manicured garden. Viktorkinde's sun was quite intense, and Macus sighed with relief as they stepped into the shade.

Machtberg greeted them. "Welcome to my humble abode."

They shared shots of kirva, which Macus had learned was a tradition among quite a few Kelk. He had also heard of the tea ceremony many practiced, but hadn't experienced that yet. Macus sat back and listened carefully as Strikland and Machtberg shared some small-talk, then Strikland asked the question foremost in Macus's thoughts.

"Aubrecht," he said, and casually waved a hand to indicate their surroundings. "You were quite secretive when we last met. What has changed?"

Machtberg lifted a shot glass of kirva, and unlike many Kelk did not toss it back in a gulp, but instead sipped at it. "The Executive Council. With Haugrund's reinstatement, everyone's breathing a sigh of relief."

There must have been something on Macus's face, because Machtberg frowned and added, "Nygaard is dove all the way. Dornmier and Veskarson are moderates with dovish tendencies. Tiegnordan is a moderate with a hawkish bent, and Haugrund is a hardline hawk, though she's pragmatic about it. She and Nygaard balance each other out nicely. And having both of them fighting it out gives everyone confidence the Executive Council won't drift too far one way or the other. And clearing Haugrund's name has indirectly cleared my name as well."

He paused and swirled the kirva in his glass. "Nvalheim's name is on everyone's shit-list." He hesitated. "Well, everyone but her fanatical supporters. Nvalheim and Palmutter are the wild cards."

"How so?" Strikland asked.

Machtberg considered the kirva in his glass, as if he could read the future in the fiery liquid. "We're all wondering where the data came from that cleared Haugrund's name. There's a Brigadier Skalde name of Kristdokar. Rumor has it she's running an operation for Nygaard. Nvalheim's sources are just as good as mine, so I have to believe she knows as much as me. And while healing the Executive Council has stabilized the general situation, I would guess it's made Nvalheim more desperate. She's planning something. So I have to plan something as well."

Again, Strikland asked the question that boiled to the surface in Macus's thoughts. "To thwart her?"

Machtberg raised an eyebrow and rocked his head from side to side. "Perhaps, then again, perhaps not. I have to be prepared to move in any direction. Nvalheim's fanatical zealotry has me worried, so . . ."

Machtberg froze and looked intently at Strikland. "Lawrence, I suggest you have your people tighten up their security as much as possible, and be prepared for anything."

••••

A noisy racket woke John in the dark of his room. It took him a moment to remember he wasn't in his bunk on *Drakan Helgis*, or in the suite in the Hyvaldsborg Palace, was instead still in a hospital room in the Heilbronn Navy Yard. He did recall the previous night, but to his surprise Nikaela was no longer in bed with him. He heard her growl a string of Kelk words, some of which he had trouble translating, but among them he did recognize the Kelk words for shit, fuck and damn.

The stream of epithets continued as he said, "Lights up."

When the room lights came up he saw Nikaela on her butt on the floor, one leg in her pants, the other sprawled out in front of her. She had her tunic half on, and open down to her navel with one breast exposed. She gave him a nasty look.

It seemed rather obvious, but he decided to ask anyway. "Trying to sneak out while I'm asleep?"

She snarled at him, and stumbled to her feet, though with one leg in her pants and one out, she did a funny hop-hop-hop thing across the room trying to get the second leg in, and almost went down a second time.

"Just use me for my body," he said, "then sneak out and dump me like old baggage. Probably tell nasty stories to your girl friends about how easy it was to get me on my back."

From the look on her face, she clearly wasn't enjoying his humor. "Well it was rather easy, and I'll tell them about all the parts of you that are forked."

This was too good to pass up. "I noticed you rather enjoyed those parts last night, forked or not."

Her eyes narrowed as she sealed the front of her tunic. "The medical staff noticed as well."

He shook his head. "Well, you've only got yourself to blame for that. I'm pretty sure it was you making all the noise."

She leaned toward him. "As I recall, you made a fair amount of noise as well." She kissed him on the cheek. "I've got to run."

He reached out and caught her wrist. "I have to spend another day and night in here, and I'm kind of hoping you'll help me pass the time. I guarantee I'll make it worth your while if you stick around, and no forked parts."

She winced and shook her head. "Can't. I wasn't supposed to stay last night anyway, only had permission to check on you."

He couldn't hide a grin. "Well you checked pretty thoroughly. Why don't you hang around and check again?"

She shook her head, sat down in a chair and pulled on her shoes. "I really can't. I've got a meeting with Kristdokar, and if I miss the shuttle down to Viktorkinde, she'll be blistering mad."

She strapped on the harness for her butcher's dagger, leaned over and gave him a quick smack on the lips that wasn't terribly satisfying, then crossed the room to the door and opened it. She hesitated and looked back. "When things calm down, let's find a place to be alone together for a while. We can spend the time making regular checkups on the forked thing."

He liked that idea. "You've got a date, you demon-eyed Kelk monster."

She stepped through the door and was gone.

About an hour after Nikaela left, an orderly brought John a tray of breakfast. The fellow kept glancing at John and grinning.

Late that afternoon John's doctor showed up accompanied by two female medical techs. While the two techs removed the medical contraption from the lower half of John's leg, they kept giving each other surreptitious glances and grinning. The story of the special therapy Nikaela administered to John had clearly made the rounds of the medical staff.

The techs put the apparatus on a grav cart and floated the thing out of the room. The doctor had John walk around, then examined his leg carefully. "It's healed nicely. Try to walk on it as much as you can this evening. That'll be good for it, and you'll be out of here tomorrow."

The second day in the hospital proved to be just as boring as the first. John kept thinking of Nikaela, and how the night would have passed much more quickly had she been there.

••••

Four Kelk military types had joined Strikland's security people guarding the suite. Macus had thoroughly briefed Faith on his meetings with Strikland and Aubrecht Machtberg, so she wasn't surprised when Strikland told her, "A close associate of mine sent them to ensure we're safe."

Supposedly, Faith knew nothing about Machtberg, so she asked, "Close associate?"

He nodded. "Aubrecht Machtberg. We've worked together for years. I suspect you'll get a chance to meet him fairly soon."

She lifted an eyebrow and smiled. "I'm familiar with the name. I do my homework, you know. He's the head of a fairly influential family, is he not?"

Strikland grinned. "That's why I like you. You're intelligent as well as beautiful."

Palmutter had been absent from the palace now for more than a day, which raised concern among the other members of the diplomatic mission. But his staffers assured everyone that he was out of the city on a goodwill tour of Norddansk Weapons Systems. And Obradour had spoken to him personally, so any concern for his safety quickly subsided. Personally, Faith wouldn't mind if some fanatic blew a big, gaping hole in the shithead.

Faith wanted to check the pulse of the mission and their staffers, something Strikland thoroughly understood. With a couple of his security people assigned to each of them, to keep up appearances, they made their separate ways to that evening's mixer. Faith was pleased that young Mr. Mathius was not in attendance. She had heard some minor accident had befallen him and he was spending a few days in the hospital.

The one thing that really stood out that evening was that many of the low-level staffers were somewhat frightened. Faith quizzed a few of them, and they didn't know what to be frightened of, but they were nevertheless fearful of something they couldn't name.

In the middle of the crowd at the mixer, Faith bumped into Strikland, and he had a pleased smile on his face. He leaned close to her and whispered, "I just got some interesting news. I'm going to return to the suite now. Wait a few minutes and follow. I have something to show you, something you're going to like very much."

She ran into Andrew Talpano, and because she had a few minutes to kill, she chatted with him briefly. While some of the other staffers were a little frightened, Talpano was simply scared shitless. He probably had reason to be. But Strikland's hint had piqued her curiosity, so as soon as the required few minutes had elapsed, she quietly left the mixer. In the hall outside, two of his security people fell into step behind her.

Strikland, Macus, and the four Kelk military types were waiting for her when she stepped into his suite. A common-face in a badly rumpled and torn business suit knelt between two of the Kelk, who held his arms completely immobilized and twisted behind his back. His head hung down, his chin resting against his chest. She couldn't see his face, just the back of his head, which was covered with sweaty clumps of hair.

One of the Kelk reached out, gripped the hair, and pulled his head back. His face was a bloody mess of swollen and pulped tissue, one eye so badly inflamed it had closed completely, his nose no longer in the symmetric center of his face. It took a moment to see beyond the blood and injuries, and then Faith recognized the young Sarkovite thug.

One of the Kelk holding him said, "The fat one got away."

Strikland grinned like a kid and nodded toward the Kelk. "I asked two of them to wait in your room in case the Sarkovites were stupid enough to come back."

He straightened and loudly announced. "Change of plans, everyone."

He turned to Faith and Macus. "Both of you pack up your gear. Aubrecht has offered to host us for the time being in a compound he owns on the outskirts of Emkeldstadt. It's defensible, and that's probably going to be important for the next few days."

He turned to Macus, who hadn't moved into Strikland's suite the way Faith had, and would have to return to his room to pack. "I'll send a couple of people with you to make sure you don't run into any difficulty."

Strikland looked down at the battered and beaten thug kneeling between the two Kelk. "And be sure to bring him. I think he still has a lot more he can tell us."

••••

Anders didn't have any information of real value he could pass on to Viktra. Thoran had specified a time the next morning, and told Anders to meet him in the main train station in Hyerdride. Beyond that he knew only that he must resurrect the false identity of Anders Karsten, and they would proceed from there by high-speed grav train to Emkeldstadt. Again, while Anders Karsten moonlighted in Emkeldstadt, Anders Eindride would somehow report to work every day at the transit depot.

The appointed time was late enough that Anders slept in. Viktra got up to report to work and left him still in bed with a kiss on the cheek.

When he met Thoran in the train station, he asked, "What happens when we get there?"

The big man shrugged his shoulders. "They said we'll be contacted."

They spent the better part of the afternoon on the train, and when they arrived in the station in Emkeldstadt, Anders's implants pinged with a message: an address, nothing more.

"See," Thoran said. "I told you they got this stuff all worked out."

Anders learned from Thoran that there were quite a number of them with *special skills* converging on the city, and their employer didn't want them travelling together. Some flew, some came by train, and some by car, and they came in small groups from all over the map. Thoran told Anders a few even came down on the shuttle from Viktorkinde Prime.

As they walked out of the train station, Anders spotted a familiar face. He found it hard to think of her as Neddaline Macree, because the mature young woman standing about twenty paces away on the busy street looked nothing like the flighty young girl he'd known on Sarkovie. She looked his way and didn't react, but their eyes locked together just long enough to confirm that her presence there at that moment was no coincidence. Good, Kristdokar's people were tracking him.

They reached the address just after sunset, a cheap hotel in a district where female prostitutes openly walked the streets, a flagrant violation of the law. The people he saw on the street, both male and female, appeared tough and dangerous. Anders was not a small man, but he would think twice before walking through that district alone in broad daylight, let alone at night. They checked into the hotel and were not given time to settle in, but received another message instructing them to report immediately to an address not far from the hotel.

They took a hired car to the next address, an abandoned warehouse just outside of the red-light district. Next to a couple of large loading docks that had clearly not seen use in a long time, a lone light above a simple door lit the entrance. As they approached it, the door swung open, and neither of them were stupid enough to simply barge forward into the dark interior of the building. They paused just outside the door.

A familiar face stepped out through the door and into the dim light: Erika Kristensen, a hauptseergent they had worked with before when making use of their special skills. She smiled. "Anders, Thoran, welcome to Emkeldstadt. Come with me."

They followed her through the door, then walked across a large open warehouse space. She led them to the back of the building where a small office complex had been carved out of the main floor and closed off behind separate walls and doors. Against the back wall of the open warehouse space, several tables had been piled with equipment.

Kristensen pointed to the tables and said, "Go ahead and equip yourselves. Take what you need."

The equipment turned out to be light combat armor and heavy grav pistols, with a complete absence of heavy assault rifles, explosives, and micro-nukes—they probably didn't trust people like Anders with that kind of stuff. Anders carefully put together a selection of armor that fit comfortably, plus a grav pistol and a couple of extra charge cells and flechette magazines.

A trench knife caught his eye. There were only a few of them, and no one else paid them any attention. He picked one up and unsheathed it, an ugly thing with a razor sharp edge and a vicious point. If he needed to do some quiet killing, it would be just the right weapon.

Thoran looked doubtfully at the blade. "What you doing with that ugly thing?"

Anders needed a good lie. "Always carried one before, though I never had a chance to use it. Just wouldn't feel right if I didn't carry one now." He added the blade and sheath to his small pile of equipment.

They gave him a duffel in which to stuff it all, and as he packed his new gear away, the door to the office structure opened. Two Kelk women and an older common-face man stepped out.

Anders easily recognized the younger of the two women, though she was by no means young. When Thoran had first recommended Anders to his extracurricular superiors, she had interviewed him at gunpoint to determine if they would employ him, or kill him. Later, Thoran had slipped once and called her "Command Eagle."

The other woman was much older, had a sour look on her face, was infamous throughout the Supremacy, and Anders had no trouble recognizing her. But to Anders's great surprise he recognized the older common-face man as well. Anders had only been back on Viktorkinde for a couple of days, but that man's face was one of several that had been splashed across the vids almost continuously during that time.

The old fellow was furious about something, and as they walked by, he snarled at the older woman. "I told you I didn't want to be part of this."

The look on her face soured even further. "Well you've always been part of it before so you're part of it now. You can't . . ."

They walked out of earshot, and Anders could no longer hear their words, but he had easily recognized Silas Palmutter and Marta Nvalheim.

He and Thoran left their duffels in the warehouse and returned to the cheap hotel in the red light district, where Thoran introduced Anders to several colleagues also staying there. They went out together that evening, ate dinner and drank a lot of kirva. Several times one of them toasted the Supremacy with the words, "To the Supremacy. To the *new* Supremacy."

Anders carefully moderated his drinking, but Thoran showed no such restraint. And as the evening ended, the big man nudged Anders in the ribs. "Friend, tomorrow it's all going to change."

18

Confined

A SIGNAL FROM *Drakan Helgis*'s bridge brought Carla fully awake. It always amazed her the way the neural circuitry in her implants, with the right signal, brought her from a sound sleep to full cognizance in an instant. The med techs said it actually took her about three seconds to make the transition, longer for some, shorter for others, but the perceptual change felt instantaneous for everyone. Carla checked her implants; it was just after midnight.

She recognized the XO's voice. "We have a problem, so wake up now. I'll be right down."

May, Leeze and Pykoff stepped out of their bunks only an instant or two behind Carla, all of them in various stages of undress. Because of space requirements on the destroyer, the four of them bunked together.

Carla had reacted an instant before the rest. "You guys get the same message as me? Some sort of problem, Falkenberg'll be down right away?"

She got a general grumbling of agreement from them all and they hurriedly pulled on their uniforms. They were about half dressed when Falkenberg stepped through the open hatch of their bunk room. Someone said, "Attention."

Falkenberg angrily waved that aside. "Belay that. We don't have time. And you shouldn't have gotten dressed."

She turned around and carefully dogged the hatch, then crossed the deck of the small bunk room, stopped in front of May and looked her up and down. She looked Carla up and down the same way, shook her head, and said. "This won't do. Your breasts are too big."

No one had ever complained about Carla's tits before. "Well, there's not much I can do about that, is there? And if there is, I'm not doing it."

Falkenberg shook her head and rolled her eyes. Then she looked Leeze over the same way, an appraising evaluation from head to toe. "You're a little taller than her, but you'll do. Give Forrester one of your uniforms."

Leeze gave Carla a self-satisfied smirk. "See, big boobs aren't always an advantage."

Forrester frowned and shook her head. "What . . . what's going on?"

Falkenberg pointed a finger at her. "Just strip down, put on one of her uniforms, and hide anything that indicates you're an officer."

While Forrester reversed course and stripped out of her uniform, Leeze dug one of hers out of her locker, and Falkenberg gave them a rapid-fire explanation. "They're rounding up all the officers on *Drakan Helgis*, probably going to arrest us and lock us up. We don't have a lot of time."

She focused on Forrester. "Their records on you are probably confusing, so the captain and I think you can slip by. It's not much, but it's all we've got. We don't want to give them an excuse to arrest you."

She didn't say it, but Carla read between the lines, and thought she heard the implication that whoever was doing the arresting, might not be very nice to a ComSec-Corps officer.

Falkenberg waved her hand, indicating all of them. "The rest of you, empty any uniforms and officer insignia out of her locker. Each of you take a little and hide it in your own, and throw a uniform or two in her locker."

While the rest of them went to work obeying Falkenberg, May pulled on the uniform Leeze gave her. After a couple of minutes of frantic activity, Falkenberg stopped to examine her, and shook her head. "Can't do anything about the name stencil on your tunic, but most Kelk who speak Lingua can't read much of it anyway. And I shouldn't be here, so you're on your own. Strip down and get back in your bunks."

Carla wanted some sort of explanation, and decided she could breach the usual prohibition against questioning an officer. "But why are they arresting you, mistress?"

Falkenberg grimaced. "I don't really know, some sort of power-play in the Secretariat."

She didn't say anything more, but marched to the hatch, opened it, stepped out of the bunk room, and walked away leaving the hatch open, as it normally would be when not under alert. Carla and the rest of them stripped down and got back into their bunks, but no one slept.

In the dark, Carla recognized Pykoff's voice when she said, "What the hell is going on?"

Forrester answered her. "I don't know, but I trust Falkenberg, so we play it her way."

Pykoff said, "Yes, ma'am."

Forrester added, "We're dealing with really weird shit here, so that was not an order, but I do think we should stick together."

Carla recognized Leeze's voice. "You're damn right we stick together. We fucking stick together all the way."

Forrester again: "Caputo, shut up. And that is an order."

"Yes, ma'am."

They waited in the dark. Perhaps some of the others returned to sleep, but Carla sure didn't. Then a sharp noise out in the passageway startled her. She heard voices, saw a dark figure step into the room, then the lights came on.

A hard male voice shouted in Lingua. "Everyone out of your bunks and get dressed."

Carla blinked rapidly, feigning grogginess. She killed the grav field in her bunk and stepped out of it.

The male voice belonged to a senior command superior. A female non-com and two kriegers accompanied him, all four of them with heavy grav pistols holstered on their hips.

Leeze, bless her soul, did a good job of not being her usual dumb-shittedness, and put on a good act. She rubbed her eyes and whined, "What's going on?"

"Get up," the command superior barked,

She asked. "Who are you?"

The fellow grinned unpleasantly. "I'm your new commanding officer."

Leeze persisted. "Where's the captain? Where's our officers?"

The command superior dropped the grin and gave her a nasty look. "They're being taken down to Hyvaldsborg to stand trial"

She asked. "Trial for what?"

"Treason," the man said, "and that's enough questions. Get dressed and stand for inspection."

With the command superior and his comrades watching, they all moved quickly, retrieved uniforms—May retrieved the one Leeze had given her—and in short order stood at attention in line in front of their lockers.

The command superior stood quite still for a long moment, then his head swiveled slowly and he looked at each of them. The two kriegers drew their weapons, then stepped forward and to one side of him. He walked slowly down the line of soldiers, stopping and looking at each of them carefully. Carla noticed the two kriegers kept their pistols aimed at the deck, but constantly repositioned themselves so they had a clean line of fire around the officer.

When the fellow stopped in front of Carla, unlike many men he did not take a moment to look at her breasts, and she had to give him credit for having some manners. On the other hand, perhaps he found all common-faces repulsive on general principals, so she decided to withhold the credit, on general principals.

When he stopped in front of Leeze he paused for a long moment. Then he slowly turned his head and looked over his shoulder at Forrester. His head swiveled back to look at Leeze, his eyes hard and untrusting. "You two have the same last name."

Leeze didn't miss a beat and shrugged. "We're sisters. ComSecCorps allows us to serve in the same unit, if we request it."

He looked to his right, then to his left, taking in the entire row of soldiers standing at attention. He focused again on Leeze. "Where's your officer?"

She shrugged again. "They sent her down to Viktorkinde a couple days ago, told her to bring all her gear, so I assume she's down there for a while."

Again, he scanned the row of soldiers, then asked Leeze, "Where's the Blacksword?"

Leeze frowned and squinted at him. "Which Blacksword? There's a couple of them about."

His eyes narrowed. "The one named Mathius."

Leeze rolled her eyes and shook her head. "He spends most of his time down on Viktorkinde with the big shots. We ain't seen him in days."

Carla would never again think of her friend as a dumb shit, though, while Leeze would never admit it, her boobs were still too small.

At that point the officer made them empty their lockers and dump everything on the deck. He checked each locker to make sure they hadn't left anything hidden there. Then he and the non-com wandered through the clothing and items piled on the deck, kicking things about. They were probably focused on looking for weapons, and for that reason didn't notice May's uniforms.

••••

Three grav sedans waited idling inside the wall of Machtberg's compound as Macus and Strikland followed him out the front door of the main building. The lights of Emkeldstadt illuminated the night sky. Macus checked his implants; it was just after midnight.

Strikland's four security people waited along with four of Machtberg's people, and as the three of them stepped into the front courtyard, the security types climbed into the lead and rear sedans. Macus climbed into the front passenger seat of the middle sedan, while Strikland and Machtberg climbed into the rear seat. Next to Macus, a Kelk driver sat behind the controls of the sedan, ready to seize control from the AI should the need arise for emergency maneuvering. If they had to do any emergency maneuvering, it would probably be the kind where one chose to purposefully violate a lot of traffic laws. Armed guards opened the front gates of the compound, and the three sedans sped away into the city.

Faith had been furious when Strikland told her she would not come with them to meet with Nvalheim and Palmutter. "I'm not some demure little girl," she told Strikland. "I'm furious and I want to be there."

Machtberg shook his head, though he seemed sympathetic. "Mistress Carlton, from your description of the way you were treated, Marta Nvalheim has clearly focused on you as an enemy. It will be difficult enough dealing with her in your absence, but impossible if you are there."

Faith was angry enough that Macus thought she might stop fucking Strikland, or maybe cut him off for a night or two. But then if she did that, she couldn't control him, at least to her way of thinking, so she'd probably fuck him all the more. As Macus thought about it, he recalled that sex with Faith was always a lot more fun when she was really pissed off at him, or anyone else, for that matter.

As they drove into the city at a leisurely pace, Macus tracked their position through his implants and his connection to citynet. Not far from the Hyvaldsborg Palace the three sedans pulled up to the curb across the street from a large, busy restaurant. Apparently, the night-life of Emkeldstadt carried on into the wee hours of the morning.

The four security people in the lead car stepped out of it; two of them were Strikland's common-faces, and two were Machtberg's Kelk. They crossed the street, then walked toward the restaurant, but they walked past its entrance. They continued on to the opening of an alley next to the restaurant, where four Kelk in civilian clothing stood trying to pretend they weren't guarding the alley, but clearly were. One of Machtberg's people spoke with them briefly, then Strikland's and Machtberg's people joined the other four, and now eight people guarded the alley.

The four security people from the rear sedan stepped out of it, crossed the street, walked to the alley, then disappeared down it. A few minutes later the driver of their car stiffened for a moment, then looked over his shoulder at Machtberg. "Maestra, it's clear."

Machtberg said, "Then proceed."

The driver pulled the car out into the traffic, drove the short distance to the alley, then pulled down it. He stopped at the end of the alley where two of Machtberg's security people waited. Macus, Strikland and Machtberg stepped out of the sedan, one of the security people opened a door in the back of the building, and they stepped through it. They walked through a kitchen with wait staff rushing about, then through a door into a private dining room. Seated at a large dining table were Palmutter and Nvalheim, a bottle of kirva and shot glasses in front of them.

With a wave of her hand Nvalheim indicated the chairs on the opposite side of the table. "Have a seat, gentlemen."

She grinned, but her face looked more like the death mask on a monster in a cheap horror vid. Macus and Strikland followed Machtberg's lead as he walked around the table, selected a chair and sat down. By pure chance Macus ended up seated directly across from Palmutter. The senator gave Macus a hateful look and mumbled under his breath, "Traitor."

Nvalheim sneered at Palmutter. "Oh, shut up, Silas. He's just placing his bets where the odds are better."

Macus admired the way Machtberg spoke in calm and measured tones. "You requested this meeting, but there had better be more to it than you throwing insults at one of my allies, or we'll leave now."

For a moment it appeared Nvalheim tried to soften the sour look on her face, but if so, she failed miserably. "We need to work together. Together, we can defeat them."

Machtberg shook his head slowly. "We don't need to defeat them. We can work with them and do so quite profitably."

Nvalheim slapped the palm of her hand down on the table. "Profit, that's all you care about. We can never work with them. We have to annihilate them, show them we are not their inferiors."

Machtberg's lips hardened into a thin straight line. "Perhaps I should not have used the term we. It's clear that you can't work with them, but Lawrence, and I, and"—he glanced at Macus—"and our valued colleagues can easily work with them without difficulty."

Nvalheim gritted her teeth, adding to the wrinkles around her mouth, then she abruptly smiled. "Got your name cleared, have you? Aubrecht Machtberg, innocent party, guilty of nothing but listening to my lies." She leaned forward and snarled the next words. "They won't work with you if they learn the truth. And who knows, someone just might decide to tell them the real truth about Aubrecht Machtberg."

Macus had his suspicions, but he would dearly like to know the *real truth* about Aubrecht Machtberg.

Machtberg shook his head sadly. "But no one is going to believe you, because your name is so badly tarnished, you no longer have any credibility."

Nvalheim leaned toward him and snarled, "I don't need—"

Machtberg slammed his fist down on the table. "We have nothing further to discuss here."

He stood, catching Macus by surprise. Strikland and Macus followed his lead and rose out of their chairs beside him. "Good bye, Marta," Machtberg said. "We won't meet like this again."

As he turned and walked toward the door, and Strikland and Macus followed, Nvalheim shot to her feet. "If I burn, you'll burn with me, Aubrecht."

Macus was the last through the door, and just before he closed it, he heard Palmutter hiss, "What are we going to do now, god damn it?"

In the sedan on the way back to the compound, Machtberg and Strikland were both clearly displeased with the situation. They sat quietly for a few minutes, then Machtberg shook his head, his face clouded with concern. "She's a problem. And my contacts in the palace tell me Kristdokar has delivered hard evidence that Nvalheim was complicit in the Novalis III mess, which makes her even more of a problem."

Strikland had a thoughtful look on his face. "Palmutter has me worried as well."

"Yes," Machtberg said. "He's a complete mess."

Macus recalled Nvalheim's last words: "If I burn, you'll burn with me, Aubrecht." That clearly implied Machtberg had something to fear regarding Novalis III. Could Strikland be worried about that as well? Such complicated situations could be of enormous benefit to an innocent party like Macus.

"I have an idea," Macus said, and both men focused their attention on him. "Right now Palmutter is supposedly out of the city touring Norddansk Weapons Systems. Why don't we feed the rumor mill with information he's been seen regularly in the city, and always in the company of Marta Nvalheim. In fact, we know he's staying with Nvalheim at her compound. Let's put that into the rumor mill as well."

Macus had both men's rapt attention. "Though it occurs to me it would be more effective if it weren't rumor."

Macus looked carefully at Machtberg. "Maestra, I assume you have contacts in the intelligence community in the palace. Let's feed it to them as hard truth."

The two men sat motionless for several seconds. Then Machtberg smiled, and a moment later Strikland smiled as well.

19

A Special Target

FOR BREAKFAST, THE Kelk asshole who claimed to be their new commanding officer showed up early and with just one krieger, but this time the krieger had plast manacles draped over his arm. The officer drew his grav pistol, and held it aimed at Carla, May and the others. One by one he called each of them forward and the krieger locked their hands and legs in the manacles. Then Mr. Asshole opened the hatch to their barracks compartment, and he and the krieger marched them out into the passageway. There, they joined a group of a dozen more crew members, all cuffed in hand and leg irons—the manacles weren't really made of iron, but they had been called that for centuries, and would probably be called that for centuries more.

The length of plast between the leg cuffs forced them to walk with short, choppy steps. The asshole command superior didn't slow his pace any to accommodate them, and by the time they reached the main mess hall, Carla gulped for each breath and had broken a sweat. Most of her comrades were no better off.

Another armed guard stood watch over the mess crew as the ComSecCorps soldiers lined up. That morning the mess menu offered no choices. The mess crew simply handed each of them a tray with all items pre-selected, and the asshole command superior directed them to a trio of mess tables.

With a tray in hand, and the manacles limiting the distance between her hands, Carla slowed down and tried to walk more carefully so she didn't spill anything. But the asshole nudged her in the ribs with the barrel of his pistol. "Pick up the pace, bitch, or you don't eat at all."

Carla moved as quickly as she could, and managed to spill only a little.

Once all of them were seated at three tables, asshole bellowed, "You've got ten minutes. You don't finish it in that time, you don't eat it."

Leeze grumbled in a barely audible tone, "Fucking asshole."

Asshole pressed the muzzle of his gun against the side of her head. "No talking, common-face." The term common-face was used quite regularly by everyone and had a simple, benign meaning—it was a label, nothing more. But when spoken in the tone asshole had just used, it carried all sorts of derisive overtones.

As they shoveled food into their mouths, the non-com and krieger who had been present with the asshole the day before, but not that morning, arrived with a line of eighteen crew members in hand and leg irons. The new arrivals each received a tray of food, then sat down, and they too were given ten minutes to eat. Shortly after that another group of eighteen manacled spacers arrived, herded by two kriegers Carla hadn't seen before.

When their jailers had first confined the ComSecCorps soldiers to their bunk room, the asshole, non-com, and two kriegers had worked together, but not that morning. That might indicate that there weren't that many of them guarding *Drakan Helgis*'s crew. For meals, they had obviously split up and were bringing the crew to the mess hall in small groups.

Of their jailers, all Carla had seen were those four, the two new kriegers herding the third group, and the seventh one standing guard over the mess crew. With comp-locks controlled from the bridge or Engineering, those seven, plus a few more, could keep the entirety of the ship's crew nicely confined, though bringing them in small, controllable groups to the mess would take all morning.

That would be a good test of Carla's deductions. If it took them all morning to hustle them in small groups to breakfast, feed them, then hustle them back to their confinement, their jailers wouldn't have time to give crewmembers three meals a day. Their captors would find it necessary to limit them to two, and even doing that much would keep them awfully busy.

Eating in silence, everyone in Carla's group managed to finish their meal within the allotted ten minutes. Mr. Asshole made Leeze and a couple of them carry all their trays to the cleaning station, then he and the krieger marched them back to their barracks. The officer held his weapon aimed at them while one by one the krieger removed the manacles from their wrists and ankles. Then the two of them backed out of the bunk room, sealed the hatch, and it clanked loudly when they engaged the comp lock.

Carla and her friends stood there in silence for a moment, then Leeze said, "Fucking assholes."

May turned to Carla. "Did you see what I saw?"

Carla nodded. "Not sure what you saw, but I noticed they split up."

"Yah," May said. "There aren't that many of them, are there?"

Leeze demanded, "What do you mean?"

As May explained, Carla learned that John's old dorm roommate had come to the same conclusions as her regarding the number of jailers on *Drakan Helgis*.

"Now," Carla said, "let's see how many meals they give us."

May frowned and gave Carla a sidelong look. "I don't understand."

She had missed that part, so Carla explained her reasoning.

May nodded and smiled. "I'll bet we only get two."

••••

Early that morning, Anders, Thoran, and two of their comrades took a hired car from the cheap hotel back to the warehouse where they had selected and stored their armor and arms. A couple of fairly standard assault boats now dominated the floor of the warehouse, with a smaller grav boat, a couple of delivery trucks, and several large sedans parked nearby. A large group of uniformed men and women were busy donning their armor and checking their weapons. Anders noticed it was all light-weight armor, no heavy powered armor, and that seemed odd.

As he and Thoran walked among them, he glanced at their shoulder patches. Dregkraag, those who had qualified for armored combat operations and were fitted with powered armor, were few and far between in the Supremacy. And all dregkraag proudly wore a patch beneath their rank insignia that consisted of an armored gauntlet clutching a lightning bolt. Anders saw no such patches on the uniforms of the people among whom he passed.

At that moment he understood a major weakness of that operation. It took a couple of tendays to properly fit powered combat armor, and months of training to use it effectively. They couldn't just order up a hundred suits of armor, slap them together in a day or two, train for another day or two, then expect to operate with any proficiency. There must be a few dregkraag sympathetic to their cause, but not enough to make a difference. What would they do if they came up against even a platoon of dregkraag? It would be a massacre.

Thoran pulled Anders aside. "Come with me, friend."

He led Anders to the office complex at the back of the warehouse, then through a door and into a room where Hauptseergent Erika Kristensen, also in uniform, waited for them. She handed Anders a uniform. "Put that on."

He shook the uniform out and examined it. It was the right size, and they had granted him his old rank of Command Superior. While he stripped down and put it on, she handed Thoran a uniform, and Anders learned that Thoran had probably been an unterseergent. He still wondered what the man had done to end his career in the military.

Once he had the uniform on, Kristensen pointed to three duffels stuffed in a corner. "Your equipment is in one of those."

The three of them then went to work donning their armor and checking their weapons, though Anders kept wondering why he, Thoran and Kristensen had been separated from the larger group.

It had been a long time since Anders had worn combat armor, and the light armor he donned that morning brought back memories of drilling and practicing with comrades, and the honor that came with serving the Supremacy. He had a lot of good memories, though it brought back a few bad memories as well, but not that many. He had been proud to rise through the ranks, establishing a record of hard work, perseverance, and honest, honorable service, but Novalis III had ended all that. Donning the armor also made him wonder what Thoran and his superiors had planned for that day, and when he thought of that, fear clutched at his gut.

He had sweated over how he might get a warning to Kristdokar. With over a thousand kilometers separating them, Viktra was out of the question, and he didn't know where Brynjar might be. He had no idea how he might contact Neddaline Macree, who now went by the name of Racine Damidohl. She had allowed him to see her as he and Thoran walked out of the train station, which let him know they were tracking him. Since then he had constantly looked over his shoulder, hoping to spot her, hoping she would be within range of a direct implant-to-implant link, even if only for a second or two. But there had been no sign of her. He and Thoran's movements were furtive enough that Mistress Damidohl had probably lost them. And since arriving in Emkeldstadt, they hadn't left Anders alone for more than a few minutes at a time.

As he finished adjusting the light armor and settled the holstered pistol and sheathed trench knife on his hip, a slap on the back brought his thoughts back to the moment. Thoran flashed that big grin of his. "Daydreaming, were you? Thinking of Viktra, I'll bet."

That was partly true. "Thinking a little of Viktra, yah."

Thoran frowned and shrugged. "Sorry to separate you after such a short reunion, but you'll see her again when we finish this. And after today, it's going to be a different Supremacy, a better Supremacy."

Thoran leaned close to him and lowered his voice. "Today, I got a special treat for you."

Anders lifted an eyebrow in question.

Thoran's toothy smile blossomed into a broad grin. He waved a hand toward the larger group of combatants in the warehouse. "All the rest of them, they're going after the Council Chambers and the diplomatic mission, but we're on a special team, you and me, a small team. We're going after the Vreekande bitch, gonna teach her a lesson."

Startled by that news, Anders lost control for a moment and his eyes widened. To keep up appearances, he matched Thoran's grin. "Good. I'm going to enjoy this day more than I thought."

Somehow, he had to thwart them, but if he couldn't stop them altogether, then he'd try to hinder them in small ways. He recalled the way he had started fires and created other diversions when the two breschkada tried to escape from *Sycorax*. If nothing more, he'd look for similar opportunities now.

When they finished armoring up and checking their weapons, Kristensen led them out of the office complex. As they crossed the floor of the warehouse, the much larger group of combatants had split up into squads and boarded the big assault boats, delivery trucks, and large sedans. The three of them climbed into the small grav boat, though there were seats for four passengers. Kristensen sat down in a rearward facing seat immediately behind the pilot. Anders and Thoran sat in two seats facing her. The pilot fired up its engines, but they sat there waiting for something. Next to Kristensen, one seat still remained empty.

One thing didn't add up. If they went after Mistress Vreekande, that meant they planned to penetrate the security of the Hyvaldsborg Palace, and no one simply walked uninvited through the front doors of the palace. They needed the right security clearances and authorizations. Anders pondered that while they sat there, the boat's engines idling. He drifted off into a light doze.

An elbow in his ribs woke him. Seated next to him, Thoran smiled. "It's party time, friend."

The big man nodded toward the open hatch of the small boat. Anders glanced that way and saw the answer to his question: a command eagle striding across the floor of the warehouse in full uniform. It was the same woman who had been in charge of their covert operation in Hyerdride. She climbed up into the boat, took the empty seat next to Kristensen, and strapped in. The stencil on her uniform read DAGBORNE, and Anders thought it telling that she no longer made any attempt to conceal her identity. That frightened him, because that probably meant they were fanatics who had decided they would live openly today as victors, and if not, die openly as martyrs. One way or the other, they had decided to risk everything on that day's venture.

Anders noted that she wasn't armed, which surprised him. But then he realized that he, Thoran, and Kristensen were to act as her bodyguards. And under those circumstances, it would be quite unusual for her to carry a weapon. If they wanted to gain entrance to the palace, everything must appear normal.

Dagborne glanced over her shoulder at the pilot. "We're go. Let's move out."

The whine of the boat's grav generators rose in pitch and it lifted off the warehouse floor. A large portion of the wall of the warehouse split in two, the upper half rising up into the ceiling, and the lower half disappearing into the floor. The pilot eased the boat toward it, then out into daylight, and lifted up into the skies of Emkeldstadt.

As they flew across the city, the command eagle looked each of them in the eyes. "In a few minutes she's got an appointment for a checkup. She'll be alone with a doctor for a while, and that'll be our chance. The rest of the operation is waiting for us. I should have no trouble getting us past security, and once we have her secured, I'll let them know and they'll execute."

She handed each of them a blue armband. "Hide these for now, but once I give that command, put them on. Anyone wearing a blue armband is a friendly."

The command eagle transmitted a picture to their implants: a rather ordinary looking young woman wearing the rank of Command Boss Senior Rank. "This is Kyrsten Stinar, her bodyguard, and the only one assigned to her. She doesn't look terribly dangerous, but she is, so take her out quickly."

"What about the Blacksword?" Kristensen asked. "I heard he wasn't on *Drakan Helgis*."

The command eagle's face hardened with anger. "Minor setback. We've located him. He's in hospital sector on Heilbronn, some sort of training accident. We have a team going after him as we speak."

Until two nights ago Anders had never been to Emkeldstadt, let alone to the hallowed grounds of the Hyvaldsborg Palace. The pilot guided their boat to a Capital Guard hangar behind the palace and set it down nearby. They climbed out of the boat trying to appear casually bored, weapons still holstered. For Anders, Thoran and Kristensen, they needed to look like it was simply another day as the bodyguards of a high-ranking military officer.

A Capital Guard command superior approached the command eagle. She spoke with him briefly, he smiled politely, saluted, and stepped aside. The three of them followed the command eagle as she strolled across the lawn, stopped at a checkpoint at a rear entrance to the palace, had a few words with the guards there, and was admitted without incident. Down a long hall, up a flight of stairs, and they entered a wing of the palace that displayed none of the elegant trappings always so prominent in the news feeds. They passed through an entrance with a sign above it that read MEDICAL WING, and the hallways now appeared sterile and Spartan.

They walked down another hallway, paused outside a door, and there Kristensen and Thoran unholstered their weapons, so Anders did likewise. The command eagle opened the door and the four of them marched into a waiting room. A receptionist sat behind a counter, with a young man—probably another patient—and Stinar seated in chairs.

As they stepped into the room Stinar's eyes widened and she rocketed out of her chair. But with his weapon already drawn, Thoran had the advantage and he shot her in the face. She fell back as Kristensen shot the receptionist in the chest. Thoran shot the other patient in the chest as the command eagle said, "Stay with me."

On the other side of the room she hit another door with her shoulder and slammed it open. Kristensen followed her through as Thoran fired another shot. Anders glanced back. The big man had finished the other patient off with a head shot.

Anders followed the command eagle and Kristensen through the other door, with Thoran close on his heels. They kicked doors open and shot everyone they saw. Then Kristensen called out, "I've got her."

Anders marched down the hall, fearing the worst, fearing that he had failed, and that he would find Nikaela Vreekande dead at Kristensen's feet. But as he stepped into the room Kristensen held her pistol pointed at Nikaela, who stood facing her, very much alive with her eyes wide and frightened. The command eagle stood next to Kristensen, issuing the execute order for the larger operation. The doctor lay face down on the floor, a pool of blood forming around her head.

20

Narrow Escape

AFTER THREE NIGHTS in the hospital, John was anxious to get out of there. He woke early, showered, shaved, then put on the uniform Carla and May had brought him. Guessing the medical people might still do a little prodding and poking before releasing him, he left the pistol, shoulder harness, and deck jacket in the duffel where they'd be out of sight.

An hour later a Kelk orderly brought him breakfast, and John asked, "I'm scheduled to be released today. When do I get out of here?"

The orderly shrugged. "Don't know. Doctor'll probably check on you when he makes his rounds and sign you out then."

John persisted. "When will he make his rounds?"

The fellow didn't try to hide his irritation at John's questions. "I don't know that either. Ask a nurse."

John ate breakfast then played cards with Kolbeck. An hour later his doctor showed up, the same common-face who had treated him since he'd been admitted. He did his poking and prodding, then declared, "You're fit to go. Check in at the nurse's station before you leave."

After the doctor left, John strapped on the shoulder holster and pistol, the butcher's harness and dagger, then pulled on the deck jacket. It concealed the pistol nicely, but not the butcher's dagger.

When Kolbeck opened the door and they stepped out into the hallway, John noticed that next to the door a small panel displayed the number 409 in both Lingua and Kelk. He wondered if the ubiquitous nature of Lingua irritated some Kelk.

No one had given him directions, so he glanced up and down the hall, saw the door to a stairwell and a bank of elevators on the left, and beyond that, what appeared to be the nurse's station. With Kolbeck leading they headed that way, but as they passed the stairwell door the dregkraag stopped and John halted beside him.

Kolbeck pointed at the stairwell. "We'll take the stairwell. That'll be safer than the lift. You check in with the nurse while I check the stairs."

As Kolbeck stepped through the stairwell door, John continued down the hallway. He walked past the elevators, and another thirty paces down the hall he approached a long chest-high counter. Behind it sat the same nurse who had walked in on him and Nikaela while she administered his special therapy.

John immediately felt a little hot under the collar, but the woman was focused on a screen in front of her. She didn't look his way, though she clearly sensed his presence because she held up her hand, indicating he should hold his silence for a moment. Her eyes had that look that one got when listening to something in their implants and trying to take in visual data at the same time.

Off to his left one of the elevators whooshed open, and he heard the words, ". . . Blacksword . . . four-oh-nine . . ."

A female Kelk officer and four Military Constables stepped out of the elevator. They immediately turned away from him and raced down the hall toward the room he'd just vacated, though he caught a fleeting glimpse of their faces in profile. They wore grav pistols holstered on their hips, and when they paused at the door to room 409, each rested a hand on the butt of their pistol. Then they opened the door quickly and rushed into the room.

John glanced up and down the hall. It was empty. He turned and marched away from his room, away from the nurse's station, tried the first door on his right, and it swung inward. He stepped into an empty hospital room and closed the door, but left it open a crack. The angle of his view out the open slit of door limited his sight to about three meters of hallway.

He couldn't see them, but he heard the five Constables come out of his room and rush up the hallway to the nurse's station. "Where's the Blacksword?" a female voice demanded. "Where's the fucking Blacksword?"

He recognized the nurse's voice. "Blacksword? What Blacksword?"

She had never seen him in uniform, hadn't looked his way when he'd stood on the other side of the counter at the nurse's station, had only seen him in the standard issue gown for a hospital patient. She didn't know.

"The fucking Blacksword in room four-oh-nine."

"He's a Blacksword?"

"Yes, he's a fucking Blacksword. Where is he?"

The nurse now sounded terrified. "In his room, maybe."

"We just checked his fucking room."

He heard a scuffle. "Owe, owe, you're hurting me."

John reached into his jacket and pulled the pistol out of the shoulder holster. He would not let them continue hurting the nurse.

"He . . ." the nurse said. "He was . . . supposed to be released today. He must not have checked in here before he left."

"Fuck, fuck, fuck."

John steadied himself and prepared to pull the door open, march down the hall, and start shooting. But then he heard, "Let's move fast. He can't have gotten far."

John heard the elevator doors open, and while he stood there waiting for them to close, a gasp behind him startled him. He spun about and found an older, common-face man standing in the middle of the room. The fellow wore the same type of patient gown John had just changed out of. Behind him the door to the room's private bathroom was open. The sheets on the bed were tossed about, not neatly smoothed, or stripped away, as would be the case in an unoccupied room. The fellow had been in the bathroom when John entered, and during the fear of the moment he had overlooked the evidence of the sheets.

John raised the pistol and pointed it at the man's face. The fellow's eyes widened and he raised his hands as John said, "You'll live and remain unharmed as long as you don't make any noise or raise an alarm. Understand?"

The man nodded, his eyes blinking rapidly.

John decided a good, solid lie wouldn't hurt, and might provide a little insurance. "And don't even think about trying to contact someone quietly through your implants. I'll know, because I'm a Blacksword." He wondered for a moment if that was one of the things about which he should debrief Z-Dog.

John waved the barrel of the pistol toward the bathroom. "Get back into the bathroom."

The fellow backed across the room and John followed him. He backed through the open door and stopped only when he backed against the far wall.

John gripped the bathroom door knob. "Don't come out of the bathroom for anything. Because if and when you do, I'll start shooting."

The fellow's eyes widened further, he nodded again, and John closed the bathroom door.

Even if no one noticed the Blacksword patches, there wouldn't be too many ComSecCorps naval officers wandering around Heilbronn's hospital sector. John needed a change of clothing, then he'd try to catch up with Kolbeck.

The room was identical to the one he had just vacated. He opened a small closet meant for the patient's street attire, and when John saw the archaic tailcoat and black, broad-brimmed hat, he realized the fellow was Norandynian. John yanked off the deck jacket, then pulled on the tailcoat modeled after styles of a far distant past. The fellow had been about John's height, so the coat's length worked fine, but it was a little tight in the shoulders. Nevertheless, it nicely hid the shoulder holster and pistol, as well as the butcher's harness and dagger. The hat was a bit large, but the flat, broad brim would help John hide his face.

He'd stand out like a Norandynian, but they weren't that unusual on Viktorkinde. On the other hand, once the fellow finally emerged from the bathroom, or managed to call help, if he noticed his coat and hat were gone, and reported that to the authorities, John would be an easy target. The outfit would suffice for now, but he'd have to find something a little less conspicuous.

John almost left his deck jacket behind, but feared that might somehow work against him. He decided not to take any chances, rolled up the small jacket, and stuffed it inside the archaic coat on his right where it wouldn't hinder access to the holstered weapon under his left armpit. He'd find some way to dispose of it outside the hospital.

He took his implants offline. They hadn't granted him access to the hospital's systems, but as a precaution he killed all external signals. If someone tried to ping him, he could choose whether or not to respond, but there'd be no automatic reply to an external hand-shake request.

He stepped up to the room's door, opened it just a crack, and peered out into the hall. He thought he heard some sort of commotion at the nurse's station. He stepped out of the room, closed the door, and walked toward the elevators, tried to walk with confidence as if he belonged there. As he passed the nurse's station he saw a couple medical techs leaning over the nurse. She lay slumped forward on the desk in front of her, her face slack, eyes open. John's guess was that the five assholes had snapped her neck.

John walked past the station without stopping, then walked past the bank of elevators. Kolbeck had thought the stairs would be the safest way out, so John slipped through the door into the stairwell, hoping to find his friend. He unholstered the small pistol, and as he started down, he swore that if he somehow managed to identify the five Kelk who had come for him, he'd make them pay for the nurse's death. Killing her had been a Cranoch or a Mercier kind of thing to do, and if he got the chance, he'd make them pay for that needless act of brutality.

••••

Without warning, the hatch to their bunk room popped open and Command Superior Asshole stepped through it. That surprised Carla because they had returned from breakfast only about an hour ago, and she didn't expect another meal until later that afternoon.

Again, Maestra Asshole had arrived accompanied by a male krieger with plast manacles draped over one arm. They both carried heavy grav pistols, but unlike breakfast they left them holstered, and each carried a thin baton about the length of a man's forearm. Asshole slapped his baton against the palm of his hand repeatedly.

Leeze leaned close to Carla and lowered her voice. "Those are fucking neural prods."

Carla hadn't needed Leeze to tell her that. ComSecCorps didn't use prods because it was easy to turn one up too high and hurt someone, but in basic they had all been shown what they looked like. One recruit had been stupid enough to volunteer to be a test subject. He had ended up twitching on the floor, even though the prod used on him had been set to standard shock level. The DIs told them that had they turned it up to maximum, he would have also shit his pants, which would probably have put a twinkle in Sergeant Major Prescott's eye.

"You people stink," Maestra Asshole announced. He looked at his comrade and smirked. "Time to get you cleaned up. We don't want anyone saying we didn't treat you well, so it's shower time. Everyone strip down."

The four women began removing their uniforms.

"Let's go, ladies," Asshole shouted. "Strip down."

Carla moved as slowly as possible, but Asshole demanded, "Come on, ladies, get to it. I wanna see those tits bouncing."

Next to Carla, Leeze hissed, "Fuck him. He can go to hell."

May shook her head, obviously as frightened as the rest of them. "Just do it. We've got no choice."

The four women took their time undressing. Carla stopped while she still had her underwear on, and the others did the same.

Holding the prod down by his side, Asshole marched up to Carla and faced her nose-to-nose like a DI. She couldn't look down, but she felt him slip the business end of the prod between her legs. "All the way, bitch,"—he nudged her crotch with the prod—"or I'll fuck you with this little sweetheart."

He stepped back, but kept the prod between her legs. "I'll make this as hard on you as I have to."

Carla looked at May on her right, then at Leeze and Pykoff on her left. May and Leeze appeared frightened, while Pykoff looked ready to explode like a big warhead. If Carla let that happen, with Asshole and his buddy in possession of all the firepower, one or more of her friends were likely to die, perhaps all of them. To keep them alive she decided to put up with a little humiliation, or possibly even worse.

Carla moved slowly and resumed undressing. At that point she didn't have much left on and it didn't take long before she stood completely naked in front of Asshole. He glanced at his buddy and smirked, then raised the neural prod, and traced the outline of Carla's left breast with its output end. Pykoff stiffened, but Carla shook her head slightly from side to side.

May quickly removed the rest of her clothing. Leeze and Pykoff followed a few seconds later, and all four of them stood naked in front of Asshole and his krieger buddy. The two men grinned luridly at them.

Asshole drew his pistol and made them step forward one by one so the krieger could cuff them in hand and leg irons. When all four of them were fully manacled, Asshole and his buddy marched them out into the passageway. As always, the manacles forced them to move in short choppy steps, and at one point Carla heard the krieger say, "I told you her tits would bounce all over hell."

The Kelk usually spoke to each other in their native language, even when others were present, but he had used Lingua. They wanted the women to hear and understand them. Carla recalled her earlier resolve to put up with the humiliation.

Carla expected them to join other women equally naked and cuffed, but they marched all the way to the showers without encountering another soul. It occurred to her then that the four of them were the only common-face women on *Drakan Helgis*, and she realized it was no coincidence they had the showers to themselves.

The two men herded them into the showers, and Asshole announced, "Take your time, ladies. We got all day."

Under any other circumstances, after days of shipboard water rationing, Carla would have relished the opportunity to ignore the restrictions of life on a ship. But that day she and the others moved quickly to shower, rinse, and be done with it. As they did so, Asshole and his buddy watched them closely, smirking, lowering their voices, and making little comments to each other.

Carla and the others were almost done when a female Kelk command hawk appeared in the passageway behind the two men. Asshole and his buddy didn't notice her at first and she simply stood there frowning. But then the krieger happened to glance over his shoulder, his eyes widened, and he elbowed his companion forcefully in the ribs. Both men spun about to face her and snapped to attention.

Carla and her friends all froze.

The command hawk looked at the four women, frowning with obvious confusion. Then she looked at the two men for a couple seconds, her eyes blinking rapidly. She glanced down, reached out, and touched the neural prod hanging from Asshole's belt. In that moment the automatic timers on the showers shut the water off, and complete silence descended.

The command hawk exploded like a massive warhead. With her nose almost touching Asshole's nose she screamed at the top of her lungs, screamed and bellowed in Kelk, for which Carla had only limited proficiency.

Carla turned to May and had to speak somewhat loudly to be heard over the command hawk's DI-like volume. "You're better at Kelk than me. What's she saying?"

Clearly as bewildered as Carla, May shook her head. "Something about charges, and a courts-tribunal. I think that's their equivalent of a court-martial, though I'm not sure if I translated it right. And I think there was something in there about cutting their balls off and making us eat them."

Pykoff shook her head. "No, she said she's going to make them eat their own balls."

It took the command hawk quite a while to calm down, and when she finished her voice sounded a bit hoarse. She snapped orders at the two men, who handed towels to the four women, and at that point the two jerks would no longer meet their eyes.

The command hawk supervised them as Asshole and his buddy marched them back to their bunkroom. She even made Asshole slow their pace so they didn't have to move with the short, choppy steps. She oversaw them as they removed the manacles, then shouted the two men out of the bunkroom.

Once they were gone she turned to the four women and spoke in Lingua. "You have my apologies. They will be punished most severely."

She turned, stepped through the hatch, closed it, and they heard the comp lock ratchet in place.

21

An Old Friend

WHILE NIKAELA PUT her uniform back on in the examination room, she listened to the doctor drone on with a recitation of all the tests they had performed on her. Kristdokar still insisted that Nikaela endure a full checkup every other tenday, and that frustrated her no end. She had been injury-free now for almost two months, considered it a complete waste of time, and the results the doctor catalogued proved that. But like an overly fearful mother, the skalde refused to listen to her and demanded that until all traces of the stimulated regrowth treatments were out of her system, she would continue with the checkups. In that, she wished Kristdokar were more like her real mother, though unlike her real mother, she did like Kristdokar somewhat.

Nikaela sat down to pull on her shoes, and while doing that she heard what sounded like the report of a grav pistol, but so faint and distant she couldn't be sure. She heard it again, and again, probably just noisy old pipes in a noisy old building. Then she heard it much louder, and now there was no question what that sound must be. She jumped to her feet, scanning the room for some sort of weapon, anything, briefly thought of John and how he had used a fork on *Konigsborge*.

The door burst open and a female hauptseergent stepped into the room, a heavy grav pistol held in a two-handed grip. The woman took one look at the doctor, aimed the pistol and shot her in the face. A spray of bone and blood and brains spattered the wall behind her as she slumped to the floor. The hauptseergent aimed the pistol at Nikaela, then shouted, "I've got her."

Nikaela froze. For a moment she considered lunging for the weapon, but looking down the muzzle of the grav pistol, she knew she'd be dead before she reached the woman.

A command eagle stepped into the room, stopped next to the hauptseergent, and looked Nikaela over carefully. She smiled and said, "Good." Her eyes defocused for a moment. "We've got her. All units move out."

The woman had obviously just issued some sort of command through her implants, and it was then that Nikaela realized this was not just an assassination attempt. Then Anders Eindride stepped into the room. Nikaela started and gasped.

The command eagle's smile broadened into a nasty grin. "Yes, a reunion of old friends. It must gladden your heart to see him again, doesn't it?"

Behind her a tall, broad-shouldered fellow stepped into the room. He wore a neatly trimmed, full beard, and styled his hair in dreadlocks. "So this is the whore who spreads her legs for Blackswords."

Anger boiled up in Nikaela's gut. "So far only one Blacksword. But if I had to pick between them and you, I'd take on every single one of them before I'd fuck you."

His eyes flared with anger, and he gave her no warning as he swung out and hit her in the side of the face with the back of his hand. She bounced off the examination table and hit the floor hard. The big man loomed over her and drew his foot back. With her head spinning Nikaela tried to scramble away.

The command eagle shouted, "Enough, Thoran. Back off."

The bearded fellow hesitated, as if he considered disobeying her. And then Anders Eindride stepped up next to him. "She gave you an order. Obey it. Now."

In that moment, he was very much the officer she remembered.

"Thoran," the command eagle said. "Get out of here. Go cover the front entrance. Anyone tries to enter, let them in, then kill 'em. And put on your armband."

The big man left the room. Nikaela struggled to her hands and knees, but couldn't go further until her head stopped spinning. She looked up and watched Eindride and the two women pull on blue armbands.

The hauptseergent pressed the muzzle of her pistol against the side of Nikaela's head. "On your knees, now."

With the dizziness slowly receding, Nikaela pushed up off the floor to her knees, conscious of the gun that could blow her head off at any moment. The hauptseergent handed her weapon to the command eagle, who took it and aimed it at the center of Nikaela's chest. Then the hauptseergent produced a set of plast manacles, cuffed Nikaela's hands behind her back, gripped her elbows, and crushed them together painfully.

Eindride had so far done nothing to help her, and Nikaela wondered if his bitterness and anger had finally gotten to him. Kneeling there, looking up at him and the command eagle standing over her, Nikaela didn't know what to think.

Eindride turned his head to look at the command eagle. "What next?"

Still pointing the grav pistol at Nikaela's chest, the woman looked at her with cold hatred. She reached into her coat with her left hand, and withdrew a bone handled butcher's dagger. "I'm going to make of her a message that no one will forget, a lesson for all who think to conspire with the enemy."

Standing beside her, Eindride shook his head. "No."

The command eagle's eyes narrowed, and keeping the pistol aimed at Nikaela's chest, she turned her head to look at him.

Eindride said, "No. Let me do it."

Nikaela couldn't believe what she had just heard.

The command eagle's eyebrows rose and she grinned. She lowered the gun to point it at the floor as she casually flipped the butcher's dagger in the air and caught it by the blade. Then she extended the handle toward Eindride.

He grinned and said, "Thank you." Then in a single fluid motion he raised his pistol and shot her in the forehead. The back of her head exploded, and in the same instant Eindride swung the pistol around, aimed it at a point just above Nikaela's head, and fired.

Nikaela dove to one side as the hauptseergent grunted and her hands released Nikaela's elbows. Nikaela landed on her shoulder on the floor. Eindride raised a finger to his lips, telling her to be silent. He quickly crossed to the door, and pressed his back to the wall on the side where he wouldn't be visible when the door opened. A second later it swung around on its hinges and the tall, bearded fellow stepped into the room. "What the hell hap—"

Eindride shot him in the side of his head, and he slumped to the floor in the doorway, blocking it. Eindride grabbed one of the big fellow's legs, dragged him out into the hallway and out of the way of the door, then slammed it shut. He crossed to the crumpled form of the hauptseergent and rifled through her pockets. He came up with a key to the manacles, and a few seconds later Nikaela's hands were free. As Nikaela climbed to her feet, she heard a muffled crump and the building shook.

Eindride leaned over the command eagle, slipped the blue armband off her arm, and retrieved the pistol lying next to her. He handed both to Nikaela. "I'd estimate there're at least fifty armed combatants assaulting the palace right now. Use the blue armband and pretend to be one of them if it helps you stay alive, or don't use it—whatever works. I don't think I need to tell you what to do with the pistol. But first, I have to tell you something."

Eindride then described going to a warehouse the night before where he had been issued armor and weapons. "And while I was there, I saw Marta Nvalheim and Silas Palmutter together, arguing. Whatever they're trying to do, he's in it up to his ears. If I don't make it out of this alive, you need to make sure Kristdokar hears about that."

He walked over to the door, opened it a crack and peered out into the hallway.

"What are you doing?" she asked.

He had a hard, determined look on his face. "My cover's still good so I'm going back to them." He waved his pistol at his two accomplices lying dead on the floor. "I'll make up some story about how they got killed and you escaped."

He hesitated and seemed unsure of himself. "But first I have to make this look right."

The bearded fellow's pistol lay on the floor. Eindride picked it up and said, "Stand back."

He shot the dead command eagle a couple more times, did the same to the hauptseergent and the doctor, then stepped back and fired about twenty rounds into the walls around them, and a few into the floor.

He nodded. "Yah, that looks like the aftermath of a good firefight."

He walked over to the door and opened it, turned back to Nikaela and said, "Do me a favor. Tell some people I'm here, but not part of this. When this is done, if the right side wins, I'd really appreciate it if they didn't stand me up in front of a firing squad."

He stepped through the door and closed it, leaving Nikaela alone in the examination room with a weapon, a blue armband, and three dead bodies.

••••

With Haugrund's reinstatement to the Executive Council, Kristdokar wondered how her presence would affect the tone of the Council. If the woman felt any remorse at her participation in the *Valhaukr* debacle, she had shown no indication of that so far, and Kristdokar doubted she ever would. And if she resented the other four for expelling her, and allowed that to dictate her thinking, that would hinder the Council's ability to steer them through the changes inherent in their new relationship with the Commonwealth. To that end, Nygaard had brokered a special meeting with Haugrund that would not include Veskarson and Dornmier, though it had been arranged with their full knowledge and consent.

Nygaard had scheduled the meeting in a private conference room not far from the Council Chambers. As the most junior member in attendance, Kristdokar took care to show up early and was the first to arrive. When she stepped into the room, she noticed a tray containing an ornate tea set on a table at the back of the room. She crossed to a window in the far wall, and stood there to wait. From the fifth floor of the Hyvaldsborg Palace, the window gave her a magnificent view of Emkeldstadt. The city was one of the oldest on the planet, and by long-standing tradition, with the exception of the palace, no structures stood taller than four floors.

She heard the door open behind her and turned to find that Haugrund had arrived. Kristdokar crossed the distance between them, stopped two paces short of her, nodded and said, "It's good to see you, Vice Skalde."

Haugrund was older than her, but still had quite a bit of pepper in her hair. Kristdokar wasn't sure what to expect from the woman, and was not prepared for the pleasant smile she offered. "I'm told you are the one who uncovered the evidence that cleared my name. I thank you for that."

Kristdokar shrugged. "I only sought the truth."

In that moment, Nygaard and Tiegnordan arrived together. The four of them greeted each other, and Kristdokar got the impression Haugrund resented Nygaard a bit.

Kristdokar, Haugrund and Tiegnordan sat down at the conference table, while Nygaard turned away from them, stepped to the back of the room, and returned carrying the tray containing the ornate tea set. She walked to the head of the table and placed it in front of the seat there. It contained four cups and saucers, and a matching tea pot. She lifted one cup and saucer, carried it around the table, and placed it in front of Haugrund. She returned to the tray, lifted a second cup and saucer, carried it to Tiegnordan, and placed it in front of her. She returned to the tray again, and carried a cup and saucer to Kristdokar. She returned to the tray a third time, retrieved the last cup and saucer and placed it in front of her own seat. Then she lifted the pot, walked around the table, and carefully poured each of them a cup of steaming hot tea.

She walked back to the head of the table and poured tea into her own cup last of all. Then she placed the pot back on the tray, sat down, lifted her cup, and said, "It's a special blend. One of my favorites. I think you'll enjoy it immensely."

Kristdokar lifted her cup, took a sip, and as Nygaard had promised, it was truly delicious tea. Almost as one, all four women placed their cups back on the saucers in front of them, producing a chorus of faint clinks.

"Delicious," Tiegnordan said.

"Yes," Haugrund said. "Very nice tea."

At the faint hint of sarcasm in her voice, Nygaard raised an eyebrow. "But we're not here to discuss tea, are we?"

The look on Haugrund's face remained neutral. "Why are we here?"

Nygaard drummed her fingers on the table for a moment. "During this time of change we need to work together. I hope we can lay old differences aside and—"

Haugrund leaned forward and pointed a finger at Nygaard. "You voted me off the Council."

"Dortea," Tiegnordan said sharply. "I voted you off the Council as well. You and I have been friends for a long time, but the *Valhaukr* thing was ill-timed and ill-thought. And to join forces with a fanatic like Nvalheim, what were you thinking?"

Haugrund closed her eyes and sat silent and still for a long moment. "Nvalheim lied to me."

Nygaard wisely kept her mouth shut and let Tiegnordan continue. "Yes, she lied to Aubrecht as well, and when that came to light, Lana did not hesitate to vote you back in. Even Maertin voted in your favor, and somewhat enthusiastically, I might add, even though you and he have never gotten along. It is time to put aside these old animosities so we can manage the coming changes."

Haugrund craned her neck and turned her head from side to side, as if trying to relieve stressed muscles. "Change! How much change must we suffer?"

Nygaard reached out and lifted her cup of tea, though she didn't drink any. "I recently asked that same question of the brigadier. We were aboard *Konigsborge* and had just stopped chasing you in *Valhaukr*."

She turned her attention to Kristdokar. "Do you recall that?"

Kristdokar nodded.

Nygaard continued. "Her answer was quite eloquent. I recorded it, and I think you'll find it interesting."

Nygaard opened up a direct conference link between her implants and those of the other three. Kristdokar saw herself seated at the conference table in *Konigsborge*. She appeared thoughtful as she spoke. "I don't fear that they will absorb us, and we will cease to exist as an independent race and a sovereign state. I don't fear that our customs and ethos will be lost. We're too strong for that. Don't get me wrong. Unfettered interaction with the Commonwealth will change us, but not in ways that really count. In fact, I think we'll change them more than they change us."

The recording ended, and all four of them sat in silence for several seconds.

Haugrund broke the silence, aiming a question at Kristdokar. "You have evidence that Nvalheim is culpable in the Novalis III tragedy."

Kristdokar didn't like being the focus of their attention, but Haugrund's question was exactly the reason Nygaard had wanted her there. "Yes, and at this point there is no doubt of her guilt."

Nygaard still held the tea cup in her fingers. "And Mistress Kristdokar provided the evidence that indirectly cleared your name, and by implication that of Machtberg as well."

Haugrund's eyes focused intently on Kristdokar. "It was interesting to be there with the two of them together on *Valhaukr*. Look closely at your data, Brigadier. You're assuming that Marta lied to Aubrecht and me, when in fact he lied to me just as much as she did. They've worked together for a long time now, and if she is culpable, so is he."

From the looks on Tiegnordan's and Nygaard's faces, the two women were just as surprised as Kristdokar.

Tiegnordan voiced the thought foremost in Kristdokar's mind. "But Nvalheim is a flaming fanatic, and Machtberg is nothing like that."

Haugrund appeared pleased that she had surprised them all. "If nothing else, Machtberg is pragmatic. Marta's in it to satisfy her paranoid hatreds, while Aubrecht is in it for the money and power. For a time, the same methods satisfied the needs of both, but they have since parted ways."

A thought occurred to Kristdokar. "May I ask a question?"

Tiegnordan raised an eyebrow, Nygaard nodded, and Haugrund shrugged.

Kristdokar aimed her question at Haugrund. "When you were on *Valhaukr* with them, or any other time you were with Nvalheim, did you ever hear mention of Jenine Catarvin?"

"Catarvin?" Haugrund asked. "One of the Commonwealth senators on the diplomatic mission." She shook her head. "No, nothing."

Kristdokar needed proof one way or the other.

Haugrund grinned. "But Marta and Silas Palmutter are as thick as thieves."

They sat in silence for a few seconds as they absorbed that information. Kristdokar needed something better than conjecture and guesswork, she needed—

Her ears popped, accompanied by a loud crump, and the building trembled as a shockwave propagated through its structure.

Tiegnordan's eyes widened. "Was that an explosion?"

22

Some Retribution

JOHN WORKED HIS way slowly down the stairs in hospital sector, taking each step one at a time and listening for anyone else who might have entered the stairwell. Dressed in the archaic tailcoat and black, broad-brimmed hat of a Norandynian, anyone he came across in the stairwell would find his presence there unusual. If he did encounter someone, it might be one of the assholes looking for him, one of the assholes who killed the nurse. But he couldn't discount the possibility that a medical staffer in a hurry might use the stairwell as a quick means of moving up or down one floor, rather than wait for an elevator, so he wasn't going to just start shooting. Unfortunately, if he encountered one of the assholes, that would give the shithead a single instant of advantage.

One floor down he noticed a smear of blood on the concrete of the landing and he slowed his pace to a crawl. A few steps below that he found a grav pistol and picked it up. Continuing downward, he came across another grav pistol, and from there smudges of blood darkened the steps and walls. From several steps above the second floor landing John saw one of the constables sprawled face down on the floor of the landing. And as he slowly approached it he saw Kolbeck and another constable lying there as well. He checked them carefully and learned that all three were dead.

Kolbeck had not drawn his pistol, and his right hand still gripped a plast knife with a five-inch blade. John had never seen Kolbeck carry a knife, and he suspected that if he searched him now he'd find all sorts of weapons hidden away. Kolbeck had died of a gunshot wound to the chest, while both constables were cut up rather badly.

John hadn't realized the officer had sent two of her subordinates down the stairwell. It appeared Kolbeck had encountered them on the landing above, and they had fought a brutal hand-to-hand battle, tumbling down the stairs as they struggled. John's friend had probably finished reconnoitering the stairs and ran into the two constables on his way back up while they were headed down. Either his friend had not had time to draw his sidearm, or he had chosen to use the knife to keep the noise down—probably the latter. Kolbeck had eliminated two of the five, which left three to go. If the chance came John's way, he would avenge Kolbeck as well as the nurse. He continued on and reached the ground floor without further incident.

He opened the stairwell door a crack and carefully checked the hallway beyond, ready to slam it shut and run like hell if someone happened to notice him. A Kelk male in surgical scrubs rushed past. A moment later, a common-face female walked by, going the other direction.

John slid his small pistol back into the shoulder holster, and since he couldn't conceal the grav pistol he left it behind. He opened the door and stepped boldly out into a busy hallway on the ground floor of the medical facility. There was no *ground* on a large space station like Heilbronn. The ground floor was called that simply because somewhere it connected to the main concourse of the station. He didn't have any idea of the direction he needed to go, and he didn't want to stand there looking lost, so he started walking. He tried to look like an innocent person who didn't have anything to fear from three armed Military Constables.

An angry female voice drew his attention, and up ahead he spotted the MC officer leaning on a counter like that of the nurse's station two floors above, though he couldn't be sure that's what it was. The fleeting glimpse he'd seen of her face in profile on the upper floor was enough to identify her. She spit heated words at someone hidden by the counter, and at that moment she looked his way.

He lowered his chin a little, hiding much of his face with the broad brim of the hat. But she only gave him a casual, momentary glance, then returned to haranguing whoever sat behind the counter. John tried to calm his beating heart as he continued walking.

She probably had a picture of him downloaded into her implants, and he readied himself to reach quickly for the pistol in the shoulder holster. But she didn't react, and as he walked past her he heard her say, ". . . Blacksword asshole."

He wasn't sure if that was a threatening accusation aimed his way, or a description of him aimed at someone behind the counter. He continued walking and noticed another stairwell about five paces further down the hallway.

"Hey, Blacksword."

That was an accusation, or a test to see if he'd react. He reached the stairwell door, hit the latch on it and shouldered it open.

"Hey, you, Norandynian."

He pushed the door closed, raced down six steps, reached into the coat, gripped the butt of the pistol and pulled it. Then he turned around and lowered both hands to his sides, keeping the pistol slightly hidden behind his thigh. He walked casually back up the stairs, hoping his timing would be good. Would she follow? Would she come through that door, pistol drawn because she believed she'd found her prey, or empty handed because she wasn't certain and was simply curious?

Two steps before he reached the ground floor landing the door opened and the officer stepped through it. She hadn't drawn her pistol, but as the door swung shut, he had two steps to go.

"I want to talk to you."

Again he lowered his chin to shield much of his face with the brim of the hat, and took one of the steps.

"Yes, officer," he said, trying to imitate a Norandynian accent, and clearly sounding nervous and frightened. "What is it you need?"

Just as the door closed he took the last step and stood on the landing with her.

"Let me see your face."

A single step separated them. He raised his chin, looked her in the eyes, stepped forward, jammed the muzzle of the barrel tightly against her chest, and pulled the trigger. The gun kicked so hard he almost dropped it as blood, bone and muscle tissue splattered the door behind her. The force of the shot slammed her against the door. She stood there for a moment, her eyes wide and blinking rapidly, then she slid down the door and slumped to the floor, leaving a smear of blood behind.

Pressing the barrel tightly against her chest had muffled the blast of the gun, though it had still been fairly loud. But the sound-proofing of the walls would have muffled it further, hopefully enough that no one in the busy hospital corridor had noticed anything more than a faint pop.

John holstered his gun, reached down, grabbed her chin and the back of her head. "This is for Kolbeck and the nurse. Fuck you."

He gave her head a sharp twist and snapped her neck. If nothing more, it was a little payback. But they were in a hospital, and if the medical people got to her quickly enough they could still heal her. He pulled her grav pistol out of her holster, but hesitated. It wouldn't make an explosive report like the old fashioned slug thrower, but it still had a loud, characteristic sound easily recognizable. He'd be pushing his luck if he used it, and it was then he realized he had another weapon. He laid the grav pistol down next to the MC officer, reached across to his left hip and pulled the butcher's dagger.

He looked at it carefully, had never considered using it as a weapon. Until that moment, to him it had been nothing more than a symbol, an act of defiance, a way of thumbing his nose at those who wanted him dead. To them it had also been symbolic, a statement that he was no better than cattle, his fate no better than that of any criminal.

Kolbeck had died as a combatant in a fight, and even though he was a friend, John could be a little philosophical about that. He and they were soldiers, doing a soldier's job, but the nurse had been an innocent bystander. The three MCs were no better than criminals. He gripped her hair and plunged the point of the blade into her right eye.

He wiped the blade off on her tunic then returned it to its sheath.

John picked up the grav pistol and considered keeping it, but the damn thing would show up on detection systems at key points in the big satellite, like the entrance to the hospital. And he didn't look at all like someone who should be carrying a powerful weapon like that. He tossed it aside.

He grabbed the back of the woman's collar and dragged her out of the way of the door. While doing so he noticed blood spatter covered his right arm, and the front of his khaki shirt. Through pure luck the right side of the tailcoat must have flared open as he approached her, because more blood stained the inside of the coat than the outside, and his rolled up deck jacket was soaked with it. He wiped his hand and arm off on the leg of her trousers, removing as much blood as possible. Then he straightened and checked to make sure the blood on the inside of the coat wasn't too visible.

He opened the door and stepped out into the busy hallway. A small sign on the wall pointed the way to the hospital's main entrance. He turned and walked that way, but every time he lifted his right foot it made a squishy sound. He glanced down, saw blood on his shoe, glanced back and saw a trail of red footprints leading back to the stairwell. Thankfully, while the footprints near the stairwell were distinctly well defined, each step had wiped some blood from the sole of his shoe, and the prints slowly faded as they got closer to him. It was too late to do anything about it now. He turned back toward the hospital entrance, marched forward like he knew what he was doing, and continued without looking back.

With blood all over him, John needed to get out of the bright lights of the hospital corridors. If he made it to the main concourse, he might stand a chance. Spacers on leave from different ships would be operating on any number of conflicting day-night schedules. Commercial establishments on big satellites like Heilbronn had learned long ago that those same spacers spent more money at night than during the day, and in the Commonwealth they were quite vocal about that with the satellite's administration. As a result, most big satellites kept *outdoor* lighting perpetually lowered to something like night on the strip near the academy on Trafalgar. John hoped it was the same with Heilbronn.

He was only about twenty paces from the main entrance when a commotion erupted behind him. Like everyone else he paused and looked back. Someone had noticed the bloody footprints, had opened the stairwell door, and a crowd had formed there. A shout echoed up the hallway, "Get a doctor."

Others had turned their attention to the bloody footprints, a trail that led straight toward John, but thankfully dwindled to nothing long before it got to him. As yet, no one had focused on the strangely dressed Norandynian standing in the hallway looking back.

John turned away from the commotion and back toward the hospital entrance. He continued walking, forcing himself not to run or appear to hurry in any way. When he reached the exit and stepped into it, he almost ran into the two MCs, the last of the five. He tensed as they rushed toward him, coming in from Heilbronn's primary concourse, and he almost reached into his coat for the pistol. But one of them growled, "Out of the way, asshole," and elbowed John aside. They ran past him without hesitating, heading for the commotion behind him.

John worked to calm his breathing and slow his racing heart as he continued walking and stepped out into the main concourse, though once outside the hospital he paused. This time he'd gotten a good look at their faces. He quickly retrieved the images from his implants, then resumed walking as he triggered a facial recognition loop to run in the background. As he moved through Heilbronn it would constantly scan the images picked up by his eyes, and if it detected either of those faces, it would alert him immediately.

Luck smiled upon him, for apparently the commercial establishments in the Supremacy were just as vocal about nighttime lighting as those in the Commonwealth. In the dim illumination of the concourse the bloodstains on his clothing lost their vibrant color, and appeared as nothing more than dark stains.

Walking up the concourse he spotted a trash receptacle. As he passed it, he tossed the bloody deck jacket into it, then slipped into the crowd of moving pedestrians, and continued walking.

••••

Seated at the head of the conference table, Gascoigne demanded, "Where's Palmutter? We can't properly hold these meetings without him."

Katrine would like to give him an honest answer to that question, would like to tell him that the senator was probably out conspiring with Marta Nvalheim, and quite possibly committing treason, but she couldn't yet prove that. And she wished they'd damned well end this meeting, because she needed to talk to Thealone in private, needed to talk to her about exactly that.

Catarvin looked Katrine's way and their eyes met. "His staffers told me he's out of the city touring some weapons manufacturer. It sounds rather boring to me."

Obradour grimaced. "I spoke to him myself, personally, on a secure link, and he assured me that nothing is amiss."

Obradour always made some attempt to mask his abhorrence of Catarvin, but frequently did a poor job of it. Since arriving on Viktorkinde, Katrine had had many opportunities to observe the interplay between the two, and she now suspected the woman purposefully pushed the little financier's buttons. Katrine would have missed it completely, had she not known of the real woman hidden behind the mask of Catarvin's assumed persona.

Gascoigne drummed his fingers on the table. "I assume that was over a citynet connection, so how secure could it have been? Are you certain he wasn't coerced?"

For the first time, Fran Thealone spoke up. "Yes, it was over Emkeldstadt's citynet, but I arranged the link myself. The extra software we installed in your implants before leaving Trafalgar allowed me to ensure it was secure. It has its limitations on an open system like this, but if he were coerced, he could have easily made you aware of that without alerting those around him."

Obradour shook his head. "So is he really touring Norddansk, or is he shacked up with some Kelk prostitute?"

That was Obradour's way of pushing Catarvin's buttons, or at least attempting to do so. He didn't realize how little she actually cared for Palmutter.

"My goodness," Catarvin said. "That would be so like Silas. Outwardly he professes disgust for the creatures, but I wouldn't put it past him to harbor a fetish for a little romp in the sheets with one."

"Damn," Obradour said. "Female prostitution is strictly outlawed here. If he is caught, it could spell disaster for us."

Catarvin countered. "But I've heard they're rather lenient with the man, while they're much harsher with the woman, so Silas can probably get away with it. Though that does seem unfair, don't you think?"

Thealone gave Katrine a pleading look, so she intervened. "I have some information that indicates Senator Palmutter is a guest of an influential Kelk colleague if his. All indications are that he's not being coerced, or in danger of any kind."

When the meeting finally broke up, Katrine cornered Thealone. "Do you have a moment?"

Thealone held back as the others filed out of the room. Then Katrine said, "I have some information from Kristdokar. Her people have been monitoring that restaurant in the city."

Katrine had fully briefed Thealone on the address Catarvin had gotten from young Mr. Talpano. And while Catarvin suspected Palmutter had met Nvalheim there, Thealone and Katrine considered that pure conjecture on her part. Katrine had passed the address on to Kristdokar in the hope her people might learn something.

Thealone perked up. "Did they spot Nvalheim?"

Katrine grimaced. "Yes and no. There's an alley running down the side of that restaurant, probably for deliveries and such. And the restaurant is large enough that no other establishment would use that alley. On any given day, the usual gamut of delivery trucks and vans pass in and out of it, but Kristdokar's people noticed certain limousines regularly enter it as well. By the way, the entrance to that alley is heavily guarded day and night."

Thealone smiled and nodded. "You've got my attention."

Katrine continued. "They couldn't get anyone into the alley to check it out, even tried running a micro drone in, but it went dead within a few meters of the alley's entrance. The alley is also shielded from aerial surveillance, so they tried following the cars when they left. One car went to a walled estate in a wealthy district. It's owned by the Nvalheim family. Kristdokar's people have been monitoring it, and they've spotted Palmutter there."

Thealone's smile broadened. "The dots are beginning to connect."

Katrine nodded. "More than might be obvious. In the wee hours of this morning, three sedans arrived at the entrance to that alley. Two parked on the street, and from them eight men and women emerged, a mix of Kelk and common-faces, all wearing civilian clothing. A few of them joined the guards at the entrance to the alley, and the rest disappeared down it. A few minutes later the third sedan then drove down the alley, and was there for about an hour before it reappeared. The eight guards reentered the other two sedans, and all three drove away."

Katrine let Thealone think it through, and after a few seconds the older woman nodded. "A council of war, or a meeting of enemies under truce."

"Probably both," Katrine said. "We identified a couple of the common-face guards: part of Strikland's security team. And we know Strikland, Faith Carlton, and Macus DeLeon have taken up residence as guests of Aubrecht Machtberg in a place he owns on the outskirts of the city. Kristdokar's people followed the three sedans back to that place. It looks more like an armed compound."

Thealone took a deep breath. "Anything else."

"Yes," Katrine said. "Anders Eindride left Hyerdride to come here. They're bringing people in from all over for something big."

Thealone sat for several seconds nodding her head slowly, her eyes pinched with thought. Then she said, "I think we should—"

The sound of a soft crump interrupted her, and a slight tremble propagated through the building's structure. Katrine's implants went off line.

Thealone's eyes widened. "Was that an explosion?"

Katrine wasn't paying attention. She was too busy trying to open up a secure link to Ed Fleming and his nullheads.

23

It Begins

STRIKLAND ASSUMED FAITH would not want to be present during the interrogation of the young Sarkovite thug. But she recalled the fear that had raced through her when the young man had loomed over her, the terror that he would hurt her, would make her cry out, would make her show weakness. He would demonstrate to his fat friend that Faith was his to do with as he pleased, that she was helpless, and he was the one in control. No, Faith would be happy to be there, would even like to have a club so she could personally vent her anger on the fellow. She didn't have the upper body strength of a man, so it would have to be a small cudgel of some kind. But that would only mean she'd have to hit him all the more, hit him again and again. She'd have no problem ignoring the blood that spattered off him, and she'd keep at it until he lost control of his bowels and shit his pants. She'd show him who was in control.

Then she pictured herself with his blood dripping down her face, clots of it stuck in her hair, blotches staining her blouse, coat and skirt. And while that would give her great satisfaction, it would definitely repulse Lawrence Strikland. He didn't like to get his hands dirty, and if she let him see that side of her, she had no doubt that would be the beginning of the end of their relationship. So when Machtberg asked if she'd like to be present, she had shivered with pretended revulsion. "No. It's not something I would be comfortable seeing."

Machtberg seemed disappointed.

Strikland nodded. "Of course you wouldn't."

Machtberg had given Faith a small suite on the fourth floor of his compound. It wasn't grand, just a bedroom, bathroom and small sitting room, but it was more than adequate, and it was comfortable. And she didn't have to worry that a couple of Sarkovite thugs might knock on the door and abduct her again.

Machtberg's compound had been constructed on a low hill on the south side of the city. The sitting room had a pair of doors that opened out onto a balcony, and from it Faith enjoyed looking out over the rooftops of Emkeldstadt. In the center of the city, the Hyvaldsborg Palace dominated the skyline, a truly beautiful structure. She stood there, her hands on the balcony rail, admiring the view.

"We didn't get much out of him."

At the sound of Strikland's voice behind her, Faith turned away from the vista below and faced him. He took her in his arms, and she rested her head against his chest. She sighed with feigned weariness. "You learned nothing from him?"

Strikland shrugged. "Minor stuff. A few addresses in the city. He did know the address Nvalheim is using as her base of operations, and now we know it. But we could have figured that out without him."

Faith chose that moment to make her play. "I have to see him."

Strikland leaned away from her, put a finger under her chin and gently forced her to look up into his eyes. She pulled out the frightened, young heroine look, and played it for all it was worth. Strikland responded with obvious anger. "He terrified you, didn't he?"

"Yes."

"What did he do to you?"

She shook her head. "Nothing physical, though there was the ever-present threat of that." She thought it would be good to embellish the story a little. "He kept touching me in little ways, threatening ways."

Strikland's eyes hardened and he nodded. "And you need closure?"

That was the pitch she had planned on using, but with just a little prompting from her he had come up with it on his own. She gave him a pained smile and said nothing.

His mouth hardened into a thin, flat line. "Very well. Come with me."

He escorted her out of her suite, to the lift, then down to a basement floor. He walked her down a corridor, and as they approached a door, it opened, probably at some signal from Strikland's implants to those within.

Machtberg stepped out into the hallway. "It's done. And we didn't get anything more."

Inside the room the young thug sat in some sort of medical chair covered with instruments. On his head he wore a small harness shaped like a set of earphones, but instead of cupping his ears, two small electrodes the size of the tip of his thumb rested on his temples, the sensors for deep neural probe. The previous day, while his face had been a mess of swollen and pulped tissue, he still had been recognizable. But they had continued to work on him, and his own mother could not have identified him now. And the smell in the room told her he had lost control of his bowels. Good!

A Kelk technician said, "Be careful where you step, mistress, you might slip and hurt yourself."

Faith looked down at the floor. Blood had spattered outward for a radius of about two meters around the thug.

Faith's heart raced. She wanted to cry with tears of joy at what they had done to him. She wanted to cry with tears of sorrow that she hadn't been the one to do it to him. But she had to keep up the show for Strikland.

She raised a hand and touched fingers to her mouth as if the sight the thug's bloody face sickened her, then turned, met Strikland's eyes, and blinked rapidly. She congratulated herself on an excellent performance as he rushed forward, wrapped her in his arms, and hustled her out of the room.

As they rode the elevator up to the fourth floor she kept her eyes downcast. She felt triumph at the thug's demise, and pride at her performance, and didn't want Strikland to see that in her eyes.

By the time they reached her suite, she had managed to come up with a few tears. She stepped into the room with him following behind her, then turned to face him. He opened his mouth to say something, but he froze, looked past her, and frowned at something behind her. Standing with her back to the balcony, she turned around.

Earlier, when they had gone down to the basement room to look at the thug, she had left the balcony doors open. It was a bright, clear sunny day, with no possibility of inclement weather to concern her. But now Faith walked forward and stepped out onto the balcony. In the far distance a column of black smoke rose into the sky from the Hyvaldsborg Palace.

Behind her, Strikland said, "It's begun."

••••

The main concourse on Heilbronn was not as busy as that on Viktorkinde Prime, but there were still enough people moving about that John had no trouble slipping into the flow of foot traffic and hopefully disappearing among the masses. Wearing the broad-brimmed hat and archaic tailcoat, John felt exceedingly conspicuous, and then he saw a Norandynian wearing a similar outfit. The fellow disappeared into a shop.

John had never before paid that much attention to their presence, or absence, for that matter, and now he scanned the people about him carefully. He spotted another Norandynian, but only one. If that was typical, then they were fairly common, but still conspicuous by their limited numbers.

The patient from whom he had stolen the clothing might spend any length of time in the hospital without opening that closet and learning what John had done. Then again, when he reported the maniac with a gun to the authorities, they might search the room and bring it to the fellow's attention. Or they might not. Or—

John's head swam with the possibilities, and he stopped trying to think it through. Regardless of how it played out, he needed a less conspicuous appearance.

He spotted a cheap spacer's hostel, the kind of place where a crewmember off a ship could get a quick shower, a meal, and a bunk in a room with thirty other spacers, all for a dirt-cheap price. Spacers liked script, untraceable cash, and John thought that might be especially true on a world where some forms of prostitution were illegal. Like any soldier he always kept some of the local currency on him. But thanks to the advice the nullheads had given him when Primatov announced she was putting Plan Z into effect, he'd taken care since then to carry a little extra.

He eased his way out of the foot traffic on the concourse, then pushed open the front door of the establishment. He stepped into a cramped lobby that barely had enough elbow room for two people to pass going in opposite directions without bumping into each other. An AI desk clerk embedded in the wall of the lobby greeted him. "Good afternoon, maestra. Would you like a comfortable place to sleep?"

He didn't see any monitors, but there had to be at least one. He kept his chin down, again using the brim of the hat to obscure his face to any pickup monitoring him.

The AI could probably place his accent, or recognize that he wasn't properly imitating Norandynian intonation. And then he thought of Nikaela and her horrible accent when she had spoken Lingua to him on Reisenar. He tried to imitate that. "One bunk, and a shower, one night only."

The AI quoted him a price, he shoved some bills into a receptacle, and a door opened in the opposite wall. The hostel broadcast a virtual map to his implants, and it also sent an identity ping, which he refused to respond to. That didn't seem to bother the AI too much.

He didn't waste any time going to the dorm to check on his assigned bunk, but instead went straight to a toilet. He stepped into a toilet stall and closed the door. No one tolerated pickups in a water closet, but at that point he couldn't take any chances. He leaned his left side into a corner to hide the butcher's harness and blade, and pulled off the Norandynian coat. Assuming there were pickups in the water closet was probably an act of excessive caution, but if there were, it might save his life. He couldn't hide the shoulder harness, but that wouldn't be as telling as the butcher's rig. He kept the broad-brimmed hat on, and his chin down.

The tailcoat extended down to and a little beyond his knees. He pulled the butcher's dagger, estimated where mid-thigh would be on the coat, and a bit below that cut with the dagger into the material. The edges of the dagger weren't that sharp, but after sawing at it for a short time, he had shortened the coat. But most importantly, he had cut the bottom of it off square, removing the obvious aspect of the coat's tails.

Still catering to his paranoia, he draped the coat over his head before pulling off the hat. In the shadows under the coat, he sawed at its brim, removing it almost completely on three sides, and leaving a rather broad bill on one side. He finished with something that looked like a distorted version of the cap an officer might wear on a Commonwealth ship. It made for a rather funny looking hat, but he would no longer look like a Norandynian. However, its appearance was odd enough that it might be easily identifiable, so he needed to keep it hidden until he made his way back to the main concourse.

As a final precaution, he took the pieces of material he'd cut from the coat and draped them over his head and face before lifting the coat off his head. Keeping his new, funny-shaped hat hidden, he pulled the coat on, hid the cap beneath the coat, then walked out of the toilet stall. He returned to the entrance and walked out through the cramped lobby. On his way out the AI said something to him, but he ignored it.

He knew he looked rather odd with the pieces of coat draped over his head and face, but the place was an interstellar space station, so there were plenty of oddballs about. He walked about fifty paces down the concourse, then donned his new hat, and tossed the pieces of material aside. He continued walking, and finally breathed a little easier.

He tried to think his situation through, and briefly considered going to the authorities. He knew from experience that the hardline anti-Commonwealth hawks were a minority, and the murderous fanatics an even smaller number. But he couldn't afford even the slightest miscalculation, and those same fanatics had demonstrated that they could draw on some powerful official resources. He needed to find a friendly face, and in that moment he thought of his friends and crewmates on *Drakan Helgis*. Taugrim would know what to do.

••••

Kristdokar shot to her feet as her implants crashed, and Haugrund and Tiegnordan also stood. Kristdokar damned herself for thinking they'd be safe inside the Hyvaldsborg Palace, damned herself for not carrying a weapon at all times. "Is anyone armed?"

Haugrund shook her head, her eyes wide with fear.

Tiegnordan had a hard, angry look on her face. "Not me."

Nygaard sat calmly as if nothing had happened. "Nor I."

Brynjar was in the building somewhere. Kristdokar tried to reach him as she marched around the conference table to the door, but her implants came back with a null response. "There's no place to hide in here. We need to get out of here before we're trapped."

Nygaard shrugged. "Perhaps Dortea doesn't need to hide. They're probably her friends."

In an instant Haugrund's fear shifted to anger. "I don't have anything to do with whatever is going on here."

"Lana," Tiegnordan snapped, "she may be a hawk, but she's not a fanatical fool. And if we're under assault, that's what we're dealing with here."

With the palace's securenet jammed, they were blind in the conference room and had no idea what awaited them in the hallway beyond. Kristdokar pressed her ear to the door, a piece of her amazed that she must resort to such a primitive means of reconnaissance. She heard nothing, but unfortunately that meant nothing. She turned the latch on the door and eased it open a crack, only to find herself looking down the barrel of a large grav pistol at point-blank range.

She froze and her eyes scanned down the length of the pistol, then the hand holding it, and the arm to which the hand was attached. A blue armband circled the upper arm, which belonged to a young krieger she had seen several times during her days in the palace. She recalled him because he wore his hair in dreadlocks.

His eyes darted right and left. "You're not one of those I'm looking for."

Clearly nervous, he leaned slightly to one side and looked past her. "But I do see two of them behind you." With his left hand he wiped a sheen of sweat off his upper lip.

Behind her she heard Nygaard say, "Don't hurt her."

Tiegnordan said, "Yes, please don't hurt her."

He didn't lower the pistol. "Where are the others?"

Again, Nygaard spoke. "If you mean, 'Where are the other Council members?' I don't know. If we were all meeting together, we'd be in the council chambers. This is a smaller informal meeting of just a few of us."

The fellow pressed the muzzle of the pistol against Kristdokar's forehead. He was clearly frightened and nervous, and young enough to do something stupid. For the first time in a long time she felt true fear, but he merely snarled, "Back away from the door," and pushed the barrel painfully against her forehead, forcing her to take a step back.

Kristdokar backed up another step, and in the corner of her eye glimpsed Haugrund, hidden behind the open door on her left. Kristdokar forced herself not to give the woman away by reacting or looking at her. Given Haugrund's hawkish bent, Kristdokar wondered if she would help them, or help him.

Her implants came back online, and she heard Brynjar's voice. "We're on our way."

Kristdokar flashed him an image of what she saw, the young man standing before her holding a gun.

"Shit!" Brynjar said, echoing her own sentiment.

Nygaard walked slowly around the conference table to her right. "What do you want, young man?"

He swung the pistol toward her, angling it and him away from the door and Haugrund hidden behind it, which was probably what Nygaard hoped for. It was an amateurish mistake, but he appeared quite young and inexperienced.

Tiegnordan followed Nygaard around the right side of the table, walked behind her, past her, and stopped next to her. Tracking her with his weapon, the young man turned a bit more, which put the door and Haugrund squarely at his back, with Kristdokar still in front of him, but angled to one side.

"Yes," Tiegnordan said. "What is it you want, young man?"

He glanced nervously at Kristdokar for an instant, then focused on Tiegnordan. "I'm supposed to—"

In that moment Haugrund stepped out from behind the door and swung out with Nygaard's teapot in her right hand. Kristdokar lunged for the young man's weapon and got her hands around his wrist just as the teapot made contact with the side of his head. She expected the teapot to shatter, but instead it made a dull, metallic thud, the young man grunted, and the weapon fired.

Nygaard cried out and Kristdokar and the young krieger fell to the floor, struggling over the weapon. Then she heard that dull, metallic thud again, and the young man went limp. Kristdokar rolled away from him, taking the weapon with her. She struggled to her feet, gripped the pistol in both hands, and aimed it at him. But he lay on his back, shaking his head, his eyes rolling about wildly. Haugrund stood over him, and still holding the teapot she looked at it oddly then frowned. "It's metal, not ceramic or porcelain."

Nygaard lay on her back, her face contorted with pain. Tiegnordan knelt over her, pressing her hands against a wound in her side, blood pooling on the floor beside her.

Kristdokar keyed her implants. "Brynjar, we need a medic here, now. Nygaard's been shot."

She had barely finished speaking when Brynjar came through the door, pistol in hand, two dregkraag behind him carrying heavy assault rifles. A medic rushed around him as he pointed his pistol at the young krieger lying on the floor. More of Brynjar's dregkraag arrived and they secured the room, while one of them cuffed the young man with the blue armband.

Haugrund demanded, "What about Veskarson and Dornmier."

Brynjar shook his head. "Don't know. I sent a team out to find and protect them, but they ran into a bunch of his friends,"—he nodded toward the young man cuffed on the floor—"and they're deep into a firefight."

24

More Retribution

KRISTDOKAR AND NYGAARD had repeatedly emphasized that John had nothing to fear from the vast majority of Kelk. And if his experience serving on *Drakan Helgis* was any measure of that, he had to believe her. But all it would take was one superstitious fanatic who got lucky, and then no amount of forks would keep John alive. *Don't get confident,* he thought, *play it straight, play it cautious.* As a kid scrounging for food and avoiding the factions on Novalis III, he had chanted that same mantra to himself a hundred times.

Before heading to *Drakan Helgis,* John stopped in a shop that sold simple outdoor clothing to spacers who wanted to go down to the surface of Viktorkinde. He had modified the black, broad-brimmed hat and tailcoat enough to change his appearance significantly from that of a Norandynian, but he didn't want his options limited to that. The intense sun of Viktorkinde made broad-brimmed hats popular for visitors from off-world, so he selected a gray hat with a floppy brim that he could fold up and shove in a pocket. Since he stood a little taller than most, in the crowds on Heilbronn's concourses the black, funny-looking hat he'd carved out of the Norandynian headgear would be the first thing someone spotted. If he needed a quick change, he hoped the gray hat would accomplish that.

While in the store he also bought a simple, light-weight coat several sizes too large. It ended about mid-thigh, and would conceal all but the tip of the butcher's dagger. He shoved the hat in a pocket, folded up the coat, and stuffed it under his arm.

John caught the periphery tube, and as a precaution rode it for one full circuit around the massive satellite, returning to the station where he had boarded it. Then he continued on, but didn't go to the station closest to the repair yards. Listening to his paranoia, he got off a few stations short of that, and walked the rest of the way. The crowds on the concourses there were just as thick as everywhere else on the station, which eased his fears a little.

He'd have to pass a security station to gain access to the docks, and to do that he'd have to link up to localnet and transmit his true identity through his implants. He had purposefully remained offline, and intended to link up only for the few seconds it took to pass through security. It was a calculated risk, because during that brief time anyone with the proper access and clearances could locate him and track his position, but it was a risk he'd have to take. Once past the security station, an easy one hundred meter walk would get him to *Drakan Helgis*'s dock, and he'd be among friends.

He spotted the security station about fifty paces ahead. On the left side a line about ten people long waited to have their credentials checked. They would be temporary-access contractors, or lower echelon civilian employees. Crewmembers like John, with military grade implants, walked straight through the right side where the identity verification was automated and all but instantaneous.

He walked forward and tried to appear confident and unconcerned, scanning his eyes slowly from right to left, trying to take in everyone nearby. He didn't need to examine each face and try to determine if it belonged to one of the MCs hunting him. All he needed to do was make sure his implants got the input from his eyes, and the facial recognition loop running in the background took care of the rest. If it spotted one of them, it would slap a cursor on his face and highlight it in John's vision.

Twenty paces to go and still nothing. He swiveled his neck to scan through a wider angle and include everyone around him: no sign of the two MCs. A few meters short of the security station, he pinged localnet, his implants went online with a quick electronic handshake, established his identity, and without incident he walked past a female guard seated behind a counter in the station. He had made it into the clear, and his comrades weren't far away. He pulled his implants offline.

"Maestra Mathius."

At the sound of the woman's voice behind him, John halted in his tracks. For a nanosecond he considered running, but that would do him no good. He hoped that whatever problem had arisen was minor and he could bluff his way out of it.

He turned around slowly and ran his eyes briefly over the faces following him: no hostile MC holding a weapon aimed at him. He walked back the few paces to the security station, stopped at the counter and smiled at the Kelk non-com seated behind it.

He noted her rank and tried to make the smile pleasant and inviting. "Yes, Unterseergent, what can I do for you?"

She leaned toward him and lowered her voice, a look of uncertainty on her face. "Is it true they tried to kill you with butcher's blades?"

She didn't seem hostile or angry, just curious and a bit sad. He thought he owed her the truth. "Yes, they did."

She squeezed her eyes tightly shut and shook her head. Then she opened her eyes and gave him a pained look. "That was evil of them, and wrong, very wrong. Most of us don't agree with those maniacs." The look on her face shifted to a grin. "And I hear you killed them with a fork. Good for you."

John wanted to correct the misinformation she had received about the fork, but before he could speak, some sort of commotion far down the docks drew his attention. He glanced that way, and his software immediately slapped a cursor on the face of an MC about a hundred paces distant. It was one of the men from the hospital elbowing his way through the people there. The fellow raised a hand and shouted something, but his words were drowned out by distance and the general noises of the repair yard.

John looked at the security guard and spoke rapidly. "I just remembered I forgot something at the hospital. I've gotta go back there."

He spun on his heel and walked as rapidly as he could back the way he'd come.

"Wait, Maestra Mathius," the guard called after him. "You need to log back in, or you won't be signed out of the repair yard."

He ignored her and continued walking. Far back he heard a man shout, and he didn't need to look to confirm it had been the MC chasing him. John didn't dare run, because the fellow would undoubtedly call in his comrades, had probably already done so, and a lone figure racing through the pedestrian traffic would make John stand out and allow them to spot him even faster.

A shout up ahead drew John's attention, and he realized he was almost running. He slowed his pace and hunched over a bit to more closely match the height of the pedestrians around him.

Scanning the faces ahead of him, his implants spotted the second MC and superimposed a cursor over his face. The man created a running commotion by trying to look into everyone's face, probably using implant software similar to John's. If anyone passed by him too quickly, he stopped them for an instant, gripped them by the shoulders, and stared into their face for a fraction of a second, then moved on. John remained slightly hunched, lowered his chin to conceal as much of his face as possible, reached across to his left hip and drew the butcher's dagger.

He angled his path slightly to one side so the MC would have to overtly stop him, and continued walking at a leisurely pace. The MC stopped a person just in front of John for a moment, then shoved the man aside. Then he gripped John's shoulders and they both came to a halt. "Let me see your fucking face."

John rammed the point of the butcher's dagger into the MC's solar plexus, aiming it sharply upward and going for the heart. The fellow grunted as John twisted it to one side, going for maximum damage, then the MC collapsed in his arms. John lowered him carefully to the concourse and at the same time pulled the blade out of his chest. Kneeling beside the man, he hid the blade in the folds of his coat and shouted, "Help. Help. This man's been hurt."

A common-face knelt down on the other side of the dead MC. "What's wrong with him?"

John kept his chin down. "I don't know. He suddenly collapsed and there's blood all over the place."

As more people gathered around, John stood up and eased back away from the dead man, still keeping the blade hidden in his coat. About twenty paces away he spotted the first constable elbowing his way through the gathering crowd. That one had been in the hospital, and like the dead MC lying on the concourse, was one of those responsible for the nurse's death.

John hunched down and stepped back again. He stayed low and backed away until a wall about four people thick separated him from the dead MC lying on the concourse, then he slowly eased his way sideways, keeping the dead man at the center of his movements. He managed to get around the crowd and behind the other MC. He worked his way forward and wasn't kind about elbowing people aside. He approached the MC from behind and reached him just as he knelt down over the dead MC.

John leaned forward, put a hand on the first MC's shoulder and said, "I'm a doctor. Let me help."

At that moment, when he pulled the butcher's dagger out of his coat, his body hid it from the crowd. He leaned closer and whispered, "This is for Kolbeck and the nurse, asshole." Then he jammed the point of the blade into the MC's back at heart level, again cut side to side, and let the fellow fall forward off the blade.

John again hid the blade in his coat and shouted, "They're both hurt. They need help."

Staying slightly hunched so he didn't stand out, he stepped back, and it was easy doing so because everyone in the crowd wanted to move forward. When he reached the edge of the crowd, he turned and headed away from the repair yard. Since John hadn't scrambled the two MC's brains, if the medical people got to them quickly they might live, but he doubted it. He wiped the dagger off on the inside of his coat, then slid it into its sheath.

Heilbronn had vid pickups everywhere, but there were blind spots, some designed for privacy. He stepped into a public toilet and into a water closet where pickups were forbidden. He changed to the oversized coat and floppy gray hat, carefully folded the Norandynian's coat and crumpled his hat, stuffed them inside his new coat, then returned to the concourse. As he passed a trash receptacle, he tossed the carved-up Norandynian hat and coat into it.

He'd have to figure out another way to get to his friends aboard *Drakan Helgis*.

••••

A large transparent plast window allowed anyone passing by to see into the conference room, which made Thealone and Katrine easy targets if an assault came their way. With her implants off line, Katrine stood, reached into her coat and unholstered a pistol similar to the one she'd given John Mathius. Thealone stood and they both put their backs to the wall next to the door. The wall was unlikely to stop a bullet, but the idea was to remain unseen, which was far preferable to attempting to shoot their way out of the conference room.

Katrine received a ping through her implants from one of Thealone's staffers, who must be close enough to establish a direct link. The ping included an authentication sequence that verified his identity. *I'm just outside the door with Command Superior Vagle. We're both armed. Please don't shoot us when we come in.*

Katrine answered him. *Just don't move quickly when you do.*

The door swung inward slowly, and Katrine aimed at it with a two-handed grip. A fellow wearing sergeant's stripes appeared from behind it, his hands up. Katrine tracked him with her weapon as he stepped cautiously into the room. In each hand he held a heavy grav pistol by the barrel, the pistol grips pointed toward the ceiling. Vagle followed, both hands up, a single grav pistol held high by its barrel.

Katrine relaxed and aimed her weapon at the floor. Vagle reversed her pistol, gripped it tightly and stepped back into the doorway to watch the hall. The sergeant smiled and extended one of the grav pistols to Thealone. "Thought you might want this."

Thealone took the weapon and quickly checked it. As she and the sergeant took up defensive positions, with Vagle keeping an eye on the hallway, Katrine's implants came back online. One of Fleming's techs had finally gotten a military network up and running. It would have been nice to set up the damn thing from the beginning, but an encrypted localnet, hardened against intrusion and jamming, would have been a slap in the face to their Kelk hosts.

Katrine immediately connected her implants to Fleming. "Plan Z, magnum protocol, stage green."

Fleming appeared in her virtual vision. "I took the initiative and sent teams out as soon as our systems crashed."

Protocol magnum meant Fleming's people were to find, secure, and protect each member of the diplomatic mission, and if possible, senior staffers like Strikland. Then they were to shelter in place and defend their position until they received orders to the contrary. Stage green meant they were to make it happen, but also make every attempt to minimize loss of life. Had Katrine specified stage red, they would make it happen as fast as possible, with no regard to loss of life. She wasn't ready to go that far yet.

The building's structure trembled again, another explosion somewhere.

Katrine keyed her implants. "Do we know where the explosions are? That's where the heavy fighting is."

"Not yet," Fleming replied. "We're triangulating on the acoustic shocks, but the building's structure distorts them badly. All we've got right now is a general direction, somewhere in the greater vicinity of the Kelk government offices, but nothing close to us."

Katrine's ears popped and the floor shook violently. She looked at Thealone as the older woman said, "Shit!"

25

Alternate Route

JOHN DIDN'T HAVE time to simply wander about on Heilbronn's concourses. The authorities were probably already looking for the homicidal maniac who had just murdered three military constables. And if the assholes hunting him disclosed it was John they were looking for, the implants of every MC, policeman, dock worker, and all military personnel would be running a background facial recognition loop targeting John Mathius, homicidal maniac at large.

He desperately wanted to take a quick look at the news feeds, even briefly entertained the idea of setting his implants to confidential mode and tapping into Heilbronn's localnet. Supposedly they couldn't circumvent the privacy restrictions and locate him, but he thought it best to keep that as a last resort.

While walking briskly along a concourse and pondering all the many ways they might find him and kill him, he received a ping from Heilbronn's localnet emergency services, with an informational push feed. John halted to pay attention, listening carefully to the message in Kelk.

Emergency alert! All Supremacy military personnel and Heilbronn station personnel are ordered to report immediately to their duty stations. All leaves are cancelled. Repeat, all leaves are cancelled. Civilian workers are to remain in place and avoid hindering military and station personnel. This is an emergency.

The emergency response systems repeated the message in Lingua. Everyone on the concourse had come to a halt, standing in place and listening to the alert, many of them looking about uncertainly.

John spotted another public toilet, walked the short distance to it, entered it and stepped into a toilet stall. Kristdokar had kept him on *Drakan Helgis*'s crew roster, and as a crewmember of a Kelk warship, and an officer, he had a fair amount of clearance, especially in an emergency. But he couldn't access those clearances unless fully logged on with an unrestricted identification sequence. He abandoned all caution and logged into localnet for full access.

He took a quick look at the commercial news feeds: no reports of a homicidal maniac indiscriminately murdering military constables on Heilbronn's concourses. The assholes hunting him had probably covered it up, didn't want to explain why they were hunting him. He did find a report of an attack on the Hyvaldsborg Palace by unknown forces suspected of being fanatics.

Had they gone after Nikaela, or Primatov, or both? Of the people who really meant something to John, Carla and his friends were safe on *Drakan Helgis*. Nikaela and Primatov were the only two down in the palace and in danger. He cared about Thealone and Gascoigne and all the rest, but he'd been through so much with the others they meant a lot more to him.

One thing at a time, he thought. Get to *Drakan Helgis*, then Taugrim would help him figure it out from there.

He wasn't sure how deep his clearances would take him into Heilbronn's systems, but unlike Viktorkinde Prime, the navy yard was strictly a military facility, so he went for broke. If he used maintenance and service access ways, he could probably move about more freely. He pulled up a schematic of the satellite, queried it for maintenance depots, and located a large one about four levels above him near the outer skin of the station. In the schematics he also found a maintenance lift to get him there, then took his implants offline, and quickly exited the public toilet. If they had located him while he'd been online, they'd only have a momentary position, and couldn't track him as he moved about.

To get to the lift he needed to reverse course and walk back the way he'd come. About a hundred paces down the concourse a sign above a door read, "Access to station personnel only." In the Supremacy he had noticed time and again how the line between military and government authority was far from clear and distinct. He didn't know if his military status would override the door lock, but that was all he had. He logged on again, keyed the door with his implants, and it opened easily. Inside he found a small room that had no purpose but to provide access to a grav lift. He called the elevator, and a second later its doors opened in front of him. He stepped in, programmed the lift for the maintenance level, then took his implants offline, though even a fraction of a second online was enough for the MCs to get a positional reading on him.

He didn't know what to expect when he got to the maintenance level, so he reached into his coat and rested his hand on the butt of the pistol beneath his left armpit. When the lift doors whooshed open, he stepped out into a wide open staging area for maintenance equipment and personnel. Four small, open-frame, two-man maintenance skiffs were parked in a neat row along one wall, with equipment stacked on shelves nearby. The skiffs were simple rigs without an enclosed cabin. Each had two seats in which a couple of maintenance people in vac suits could strap in. Two women in maintenance coveralls, a Kelk and a common-face, were bent over the engine compartment of one of the skiff's.

A civilian Kelk security guard standing just outside the lift doors turned to him, a bored look on his face. "I'm sorry, maestra, but only station personnel—"

John opened up a secure link between them. The guard's implants were almost rudimentary compared to military grade. John flash-transmitted his identification and his equivalent Kelk grade of Command Boss Senior Rank.

The guard's eyes widened. "I'm sorry, maestra, I didn't realize—"

A direct link to the guard meant he hadn't gone online, so the assholes hunting him didn't get even a momentary reading on his position. But they had enough to get them to the maintenance lift four levels down, and it wouldn't take a genius to figure out where John had gone. If he wanted to stay alive, he needed to keep moving.

"Not a problem," John said. "I'm not in uniform so you couldn't have known." He needed a reason for being there, and thought it best to simply make shit up. "I'm part of the military emergency response team. Where's the maintenance supervisor's office?"

The fellow pointed to a door on the far side of the room. "I don't think he's there right now."

Even better, John thought.

As he walked across the room his attention focused on the skiffs. He might spend hours trying to navigate maintenance passageways, if they even existed. On the other hand, the skiffs reminded him there was a more direct route to *Drakan Helgis*, one to which he might now have access.

He changed direction and headed toward the two women working on the skiff. They saw him coming and straightened up, wiping their hands on greasy rags. As John approached them he flash-transmitted his identification to their implants and hooked a thumb over his shoulder. "Guard says supervisor isn't in. Is that true?"

The common-face woman nodded. "Yah, been out all morning."

John tried to sound authoritative. "Then I need your help. I need a skiff and an all-purpose vac suit."

The Kelk woman frowned. "What for?"

It occurred to John he would have a lot of debriefing to do with Z-Dog. "Can't tell you that. It's classified."

While the Kelk woman pulled a skiff out of line, the common-face led John to a changing room. She opened a large locker in which four all-purpose, one-size-fits-all vac suits were stored. While she was focused on retrieving one of the bulky suits, he pulled off his coat and tossed it aside, then rolled up the butcher's blade harness before she had a chance to see it. Her eyes widened when she saw the shoulder holster and pistol, and the blood staining his service khakis, but she didn't say anything, probably because of the pistol and blood. John popped a few clips on the shoulder harness and shrugged out of it. "I need something I can store this in so I can bring it with me."

She nodded. "We've got small belt packs you can clip to your equipment belt."

She helped him pull the vac suit on and adjust the fit, then jiggle the helmet in place and lock it down. He stuffed the pistol, shoulder holster, and butcher's blade harness into the belt pack she provided and clipped it to his equipment belt.

When they stepped out of the changing room, the other woman had already parked the skiff in a large airlock, and she stood next to it waiting for them. John strapped into one of the skiff's two seats as the two women stepped out of the airlock and sealed it. Pumps chugged in the background as they drained the air out of the lock.

There were a couple of small viewing ports in the airlock hatches. Through one John saw the elevator on the other side of the maintenance depot. As he waited for the pump-down sequence to complete, the lift doors opened, and two MCs stepped out of it. They spoke briefly with the guard and he pointed at the airlock.

A fine mist enveloped John as the airlock's outer door opened to space. John fired up the skiff's grav drive and watched the MCs race across the floor of the depot. He backed the skiff out of the big station and into open space.

They'd track the skiff on the maintenance depot's screens, so John needed to get rid of it. He had asked for it only because it would seem peculiar if he didn't. He eased it to one side and parked it about fifty meters from the hatch against the side of the massive station, left it running with a tenth gravity push against the station so it didn't drift away.

Protrusions, cleats and handholds covered the exterior of the station, put there specifically to aid maintenance crews. He unstrapped from the skiff, gripped a cleat, and through his implants programmed the skiff to accelerate away from the station at its maximum drive of one-tenth G. "Track that, you mother fuckers," he said.

He logged into localnet, pulled up the schematic of the station and got oriented. He'd have to crawl across about a kilometer of the outer skin of the station to get to *Drakan Helgis*. He took his implants offline and began the journey.

••••

In a hardened bunker beneath his estate, Aubrecht Machtberg had installed a combat information center much like that on the bridge of any warship, and he was clearly quite proud of its capabilities. That morning, after disposing of the Sarkovite thug, he had asked Macus, Faith and Strikland to join him there to monitor the developing situation.

As the three of them looked on, he pointed to a bank of technicians sitting at screens. "I have a direct tap into the Viktorkinde defense grid, so we can monitor any ships moving about in the system, and right now there are no warships within two lightyears of heliopause. For information on the situation in the palace, we rely on live assets feeding us data. I've got several people in the building and on the ground nearby."

A large wall screen displayed a live feed of the palace from a distance of about a hundred meters, the plume of black smoke rising from one corner of the structure. The source of the image appeared to be at an elevation about twenty meters above the palace's rooftop and moving slowly around it. Then the image switched to a different perspective, showing the palace from another angle. From that point of view the plume of smoke emerged from two blast holes in the side of the building.

The view impressed Macus considerably. "You've got a swarm of stealthed microdrones out there."

Machtberg gave him an appraising look. "Most civilians wouldn't have deduced that."

Strikland spoke like a proud father. "He's ex-ComSecCorps, knows his stuff, quite valuable to me in many ways."

Machtberg frowned, still evaluating him. "Why did you leave ComSecCorps?"

Macus chose his words carefully. "The opportunities in the Corps were . . . somewhat limited."

Machtberg raised a skeptical eyebrow. "And you found the opportunities with Silas Palmutter better?"

Macus wasn't about to admit that, at the time, his only means of foreshortening his term of enlistment was the aide position he had finagled with Palmutter. "At the time, I wasn't aware of his limitations."

Faith came to his defense. "The senator's public image and reputation are well crafted, and until recently he was rather good at suppressing his basic instabilities."

Machtberg smiled and slapped Macus on the back. "Well, it was a smart move aligning with Lawrence here."

Strikland pointed to the large screen and the plume of smoke rising from the palace. "Are your people involved in the fighting?"

Machtberg shook his head as he turned his attention to the image on the wall. "No, that's Marta playing her hand. I'm staying out of it, at least for the time being."

Faith asked, "What do you think she hopes to accomplish?"

Machtberg did not look away from the image of the palace as he answered her. "It's hard to tell. She's a raving lunatic, probably thinks she'll assassinate the entire Executive Council. I wouldn't be surprised if she has some romantic notion that once they're all dead, a grateful populace will spontaneously rise to support her, and ask her to take the reins of government. Then we'll declare war with the Commonwealth, and since any Kelk is worth two ComSecCorps soldiers, we'll defeat them handily, and she'll rule a Supremacy populated by nothing but admirers."

That description did not fit the woman Macus had met only the day before. "Is she really that foolish?"

Machtberg winced and shook his head. "No, though it would almost be easier if she were. She'd have a lot less support among the hardliners. She is a raving fanatic, but she tempers it with enough reality that they don't dismiss her out of hand. And those that do support her are driven by hate and fear just like her. She feeds them that hate and fear, and somehow that reassures them and offers them hope, and they feed that back to her. It's a never-ending loop of self-deception which I don't really understand, but I can work with it."

Strikland asked the obvious question. "Are you going to intervene?"

Throughout the exchange, Machtberg had not taken his eyes off the image of the palace. "Not yet. Eventually I will, but I have to wait for the right moment."

Machtberg looked at Strikland, Faith and Macus. "I don't want to intervene until at least one member of the Executive Council is dead." He flashed them a big grin. "I've got two assault boats parked in a garage here, and a platoon of dregkraag on standby. In under half an hour they can be in powered combat armor and headed to the palace. And when the time is right, I'll sweep in and shut down this petty little revolt. For public consumption we'll make the attempt to take Marta alive so she can be brought to justice, but of course she'll resist and be killed. It would be quite inconvenient if she survived this and had to go through a public trial and execution. But once one of the council members is dead, that'll create a nice opening for me on the Executive Council."

He looked at Strikland. "You and I, Lawrence, will open up a new era of profitable commerce between the Commonwealth and the Supremacy. And we'll control it completely."

At that moment Macus thought he might be standing in the presence of pure genius. Since no one had as yet connected Machtberg to Novalis III, the man apparently needed to fear only Marta Nvalheim in that respect. It was as if she worked for him. She'd open up a seat on the Executive Council, and he wouldn't have to get his hands dirty. And afterwards, with her dead and gone, he'd be in the clear. Yes, pure genius.

26

Almost There

THE OUTER SKIN of Heilbronn did not have cleats and handholds everywhere. Its architects had probably assumed maintenance personnel would not venture out of the station without a skiff, unless they were really stupid, or desperate like John. Widely spaced hand grips frequently ran in a straight line like a horizontal ladder along the surface of the station, which forced John to follow a zigzag pattern to reach *Drakan Helgis*. If he slipped and became detached from the station, he could use air jets in the wrists and heels of his suit to get back to a grip. The vac suit separated the oxygen out of the air he exhaled and recycled it. It also compressed the waste gasses for use in the jets, but with a freshly charged suit he didn't have much of that, and until he did, if he fired the jets, they'd use a small amount of his breathable oxygen. He didn't want to do that too often.

He let his feet float loose and moved from handhold to handhold, taking care to ensure he had a good grip with one hand before releasing the other. He constantly looked over his shoulder for any pursuit from the maintenance airlock. He had crawled about a hundred meters from it when bright light spilled out of it, telling him the maintenance crew had again opened the outer airlock door.

Gripping handholds with both hands, he pulled his body flat against the surface of the station and froze. A few seconds later a skiff carrying two passengers eased cautiously out of the airlock. There were plenty of protrusions and other features to break up the monotony of Heilbronn's surface, which gave John hope that they wouldn't spot him with a casual glance his way. But if they took the time to carefully scan the surface, they would easily detect him.

At that moment he realized he'd been a damn fool and cursed himself for failing to think ahead and have the small pistol ready at hand. If he moved now to retrieve it from the belt pack, that would surely draw their attention and they'd spot him. He waited and hoped, and watched the two figures on the skiff closely as it drifted away from the airlock. Moving cautiously, they oriented the skiff, aimed it outward, and accelerated away from the station, heading in the direction of the skiff John had abandoned. John breathed a sigh of relief.

Their skiff probably couldn't go any faster than his, and most likely would be slower since theirs carried two passengers, and his carried none. But he assumed that at some point they'd realize even an idiot wouldn't simply accelerate away from the station into open space on the way to nowhere, and they would come back looking for him; time to correct his earlier oversight.

The vac suit included a simple maintenance belt to which he could attach tools. It was empty except for the belt pack and the standard, mandatory reel of wire-thin plast safety line. To anchor himself, John pulled out a meter of line and attached the end of it to a cleat on the station. Floating in zero-G, attached to the station by a short tether, every movement spun him one way or another. But his training helped immensely, and he was thankful for the hours of practice under weightless conditions.

He opened the belt pack, retrieved the wrapped-up shoulder holster, and un-wrapped it carefully to get to the pistol. He clipped the gun by its trigger guard to the suit's belt, returned the shoulder harness to the pack, detached the anchor line from the station, and continued on his way to *Drakan Helgis*.

After another hundred meters of crawling he came to a gap in the grips. Before him stretched a distance of about fifty feet with nothing on the surface of the station he might cling to. He had no choice but to use the jets in his suit, but he'd only built up a small reserve of waste gasses and didn't have much to work with. He considered the situation for a moment, then pushed off from the station at a shallow angle using almost no force. Travelling at about the pace of a person walking slowly, he drifted across the gap, and when above a new series of grips, he fired the jets. To preserve his breathable oxygen, he didn't fire them to kill his forward momentum, merely to push him back toward the station. He caught a grip and killed his motion, then continued crawling from grip to grip. After crossing a couple of gaps that way, he quickly used up his supply of waste gasses and dipped into his breathable oxygen reserves. He moni-tored his oxygen supply closely.

When John crawled into the neighborhood of the repair yard, the situation changed dramatically. Not far away Viktorkinde's sun cast a dark shadow on the back side of a heat dissipation grid about ten meters high. In the vacuum of space, the in-tensity of the bright sunlight made the shadow behind the grid black and deep, with very high contrast at its edges.

John crawled that way and stopped in the shadow. He attached the safety line to a cleat, keeping it a little short. Then he stood up, putting pressure on the line, allowing him to stand and survey the repair yard, while the safety line kept his feet anchored to the surface of the station. A number of ships were docked there. They ranged in size from a large in-system gunboat—small by the standards of an interstellar warship—to

Drakan Helgis, a full-size destroyer. To get to her, John would have to work his way around several smaller ships.

While standing there planning his route, he glanced up at the dark night of space. With no atmosphere to distort the light they emitted, the stars didn't twinkle. He wondered again about Nikaela and Primatov.

John gripped the heat dissipation grid and glanced up and around, looking for any sign of the two constables on the skiff. He didn't really expect to spot them. If they were farther away than about a hundred meters, they'd be just a tiny speck against the star-dotted blackness of space. And he wasn't going to count on them being stupid enough to broadcast their whereabouts with running lights.

He detached his safety line from the cleat and went back to crawling.

••••

On his way out of the doctor's office, Anders put a couple of rounds into Thoran's body, then fired several shots up the hallway so it looked like there had been a firefight there as well. In the hall outside the doctor's office he found a trash receptacle and dumped the extra pistol there.

Anders moved cautiously through the halls of the Hyvaldsborg Palace. Modern government buildings usually demonstrated a more functional use of space, though some frequently had a ceremonial room or two built on a grand scale. And for meetings of the Larscom General Secretariat, the Hall of the Secretariat was primarily a massive meeting chamber that accommodated more than four hundred councilors, plus aides, staffers and functionaries. But everything about the palace had been constructed on a grand scale. Even simple hallways were frequently wide, roomy, and cavernous, with a level of opulence not typically seen in contemporary construction.

Thoran had told Anders that the main body of their attack force was headed for the Council Chambers. Using a map of the building uploaded to his implants, he moved carefully in that direction, and as he did so the sound of gunfire grew louder. Inside the building, his attempts at establishing long-range com contact with Thoran's colleagues had proven wholly ineffective. The attacking force had jammed localnet, and the defenders jammed everything else. But the main attacking force had entered through a large maintenance garage in the side of the building, so he worked his way slowly in that direction.

To review the map in his implants, he took cover behind a statue in a small alcove on the third floor. It placed him two floors directly above the maintenance garage. He followed signs pointing to an exit, and found a bank of elevators, though a blinking sign above each warned that they were out of order. In any case, using one of the lifts would be suicide, but a sign next to them told him he'd find a stairway in a nearby hallway. He peered carefully around a corner into the hallway and saw several kriegers hunkered down behind a barricade protecting the stairwell. They wore blue armbands.

He eased back and keyed his implants to the secure frequency the attackers used, and now that he was physically close to them it worked. He first transmitted an identification sequence Dagborne had given him, then said, "This is Anders Eindride, a comrade. I'm just around the corner from you. I'm going to step out openly with my weapon holstered. I'd really appreciate it if you didn't kill me."

He waited through several seconds of silence, then got a reply. "Proceed, but move real slow."

He holstered the grav pistol, then extended his empty hands before him into the hallway. When no shots were fired, he stepped forward slowly, raised his hands high, and found himself looking down the barrels of several assault rifles. One of the kriegers shouted, "Come forward slowly."

Anders walked forward one step at a time. About five paces short of them, one of the kriegers lowered his assault rifle. "It's him. I know him."

The fellow stood up and waved to Anders. "Come on."

Anders recognized the man. He and Thoran had shared dinner with him and a few others the night before. His comrades, still crouched behind the barricade, lowered their assault rifles as Anders approached. The fellow he had shared dinner with looked past Anders and frowned. "Where's the rest of your team?"

Anders had carefully considered the story he would tell, and decided that the best thing he could do was throw some doubt into their well-made plans. "They're all dead: Thoran, Kristensen and Dagborne. We were double crossed. Somebody tipped them off and they were waiting for us. It was a fucking massacre. I'm only alive because Dagborne had me covering the rear."

A female non-com grimaced and snarled, "Shit, shit, shit! Come with me, Eindride."

Anders followed her into the stairwell. She took the stairs two at a time and Anders kept up with her. When the stairs ended, he followed her through a door into the maintenance garage. A couple of the sedans and delivery trucks he had seen in the warehouse that morning were parked on the concrete floor, along with a few service vehicles, but much of the space remained unused. Crates of equipment and supplies were stacked against one wall near an office complex. Through the large open doors of the garage he saw the two assault boats parked outside on the lawn. Those boats carried a lot of firepower.

The non-com led him across the garage floor to the cluster of offices. She stopped and spoke to an officer, then pointed at Anders and said, "Come here and tell him what you told me."

Anders repeated his story about being ambushed. The officer grimaced and said, "Wait here." He turned and walked through a door into the office cluster. Several seconds passed then the door opened. The officer didn't step out, but stood there and snarled, "Bring him."

Anders followed the non-com as she followed the officer. They walked down a short hall, then into an office where Marta Nvalheim stood with her back to them looking out a window. To one side Silas Palmutter sat in a chair, the strain of anger and fear showing in his face.

The officer pointed a finger at Anders. "Tell them what you just told me."

Nvalheim turned around, and hanging from a chain about her neck, a large metal amulet rested quite prominently between her breasts. It bore the styling of an old fashioned torque, a symbol of tribal rank, and appeared to be quite old, though the crude workmanship displayed the hallmarks of an amateur. The look she gave Anders was far from kind, and as he again told his story, her eyes blinked rapidly and the crow's feet around them grew more pronounced. When he finished, she said, "How do you know you were set up?"

Anders held his hands out in a gesture of supplication. "It was obvious. They were waiting for us, heavily armed. They opened fire immediately. Dagborne had me covering the rear so I didn't get caught in the crossfire, and when she, Thoran and Kristensen went down, I knew I was heavily outnumbered so I ran like hell."

It was a good story, but it might not hold up if they decided to question him at length about the details, or if they sent a team to the doctor's office to investigate.

Palmutter rose up out of his chair and shouted, "I told you from the beginning this whole plan was fucked up."

Nvalheim shouted back at him. "He's assuming they were set up. He doesn't know it."

The officer turned to the non-com and said, "Get out,"—he pointed at Anders—"but keep him close by."

Anders followed her out of the room, glad to leave the two angry old people behind.

As they stepped out into the relative quiet of the garage, the non-com turned to him. "Don't worry. The old woman's no fool. She's got some sort of trick up her sleeve, something she hasn't told anyone about. She's done it before. She's full of surprises, so don't worry."

Anders did not find her words reassuring.

27

Painful Setback

JOHN WORKED HIS way up the dock to the bow of the gunboat. The sight of the boats and ships moored side by side down the length of the dockyard seemed almost surreal in its eerie silence. One or more hatches and mooring beams mated them all to the station, and big cargo hatches connected the larger ships like *Drakan Helgis*. John imagined a lot of activity inside the station and the ships, supplies loaded and unloaded, repair crews coming and going. But none of that was visible or obvious from his vantage.

Each vessel had been carefully nestled into a dock recess in the yard, with about half the boat or ship visible above the station's surface. He briefly considered slipping down into one of the recesses between the hull of a ship and the station, but that might result in an unnecessary detour, perhaps even a dead-end from which he would need to back track, and he didn't have time for that, not with a shooting war in play.

He moved down the dockyard toward *Drakan Helgis*. About half way there he came to a gap in the grips, but he couldn't see any grips in the distance, couldn't see where the gap ended. His present position left him fairly exposed, with no large protuberances nearby, nothing like the heat dissipation grid with a nice shadow in which to hide. About thirty meters to one side the bow of one of the large boats protruded above its dock, but he didn't see any way to take advantage of that.

He had practiced a maneuver in advanced training that would allow him to get a little altitude above the station, reconnoiter his surroundings, then return to the station, all without using the jets in his suit.

He attached the end of his safety line to a grip, then reeled out ten meters of wire-thin plast. Still holding onto the grip, he pulled his feet beneath him into a squatting position. It was important that he not shove off hard, because if he did, he'd rocket out until he reached the end of the tether, snap back hard, and tumble back toward the station out of control. He had learned that lesson the hard way when practicing the maneuver during advanced training.

He pushed off by simply releasing his grip on the handhold, then slowly standing up straight. Once he reached his full height his feet lifted off the surface of the station, and he rose upward at a slow, leisurely pace. Before he reached the ten-meter limit of his safety line, he spotted another horizontal ladder of grips about a hundred paces distant, a doable distance for a slanting jump, if he executed it carefully. Then he reached the end of the safety line, it went taught, and gently snapped him back toward the station.

Since the tether wasn't anchored in line with his center of gravity, the recoil sent him toward the surface of the station with a bit of a tumble and some spin, but he had expected that. The tumble wasn't extreme, the spin was minor, and his velocity back to the station's surface was dead slow. He tumbled completely over into what had become upside down for him, and was headed back toward the handholds. All he needed to do was snag one of the grips with his hand when he got there. But as he extended his hands to do that, his spin brought him around facing the other direction and he saw a skiff with two passengers rocketing toward him.

He succumbed to instinct and cartwheeled his arms and legs, which was a useless thing to do. Drifting weightless toward the station, the laws of physics weren't willing to change their ways for a stupid kid from a dead world. He was completely helpless as the skiff shot toward him. But it missed him, and he felt an instant of relief, which turned out to be premature. A loop of the plast tether had twirled above him, and the skiff plowed into it, snagging it. With the safety line anchored to the station at one end, it looped around the blunt bow of the skiff, then hooked to his belt at the other end. The skiff continued past him and the line when taught, sliding along its bow like a pulley and pulling him toward it. Then he slammed into the skiff, a shock of pain blasting through his hip where the tether met his belt.

He snagged up on something on the underside of the skiff, his left forearm twisted in the tether against its bow. With the tether taught, and the plast line unable to give further, but strong enough to carry the strain without snapping, it pulled the bow of the skiff down and around. The pilot didn't have time to react, and all John could do was ride the damn thing and hope for the best as intense G-forces tossed him about. The bow of the skiff, with his left forearm pinned against it, slammed into the station, crushing his arm.

John screamed as blinding pain hammered through his arm. He tried not to struggle, because any movement brought more pain. The skiff's small grav drive continued to push it against the station, keeping his arm pinned. If he wanted to live he needed to think, but the pain wouldn't allow that. He keyed the pain suppression software in his implants and that helped, allowing him to put together a few thoughts beyond the pain.

A bullet ricocheted off the surface of the station and splattered his helmet with fragments. John scanned the underside of the skiff and saw a hand and a grav pistol, only that. One of the constables had clearly leaned out over the edge of the skiff and extended his hand down, but still strapped into his seat, he couldn't lean down far enough to see beneath the skiff, and was firing blindly. He fired another shot that went way wide, then the hand disappeared. John interpreted that to mean the fellow had decided to unstrap to do the job right.

It had been a simple thing to clip the small pistol to his tool belt by its trigger guard when both hands were free, and would be a simple thing to unclip it under the same circumstances. But pinned between the skiff and the station, his left hand was pretty much out of the picture at that point. And unclipping it with one hand really wouldn't be that difficult either, but add to that the condition that he needed to also keep hold of the pistol and not let it float away proved to be something of an issue.

It was then that John found that strange schizophrenic split in his mind, where a part of him suffered the agony of the pain, and another ignored it completely, functioning like a machine. He used leverage from his left arm to pin the pistol between his hip and the station, keeping it in place while he unfastened the clip with his right hand.

He gripped the butt of the pistol, fumbled it a little, and the heavy gauntlets of the vac suit added to the difficulty of flicking off the safety. But he managed just as the constable stuck his head down below the bottom edge of the skiff to survey the situation.

John aimed the pistol and pulled the trigger. The gun kicked and almost sent him into a tumble. It emitted a blinding flash, and John actually heard the pistol's report, a faint, muffled pop. That part of him that could think clearly realized the expanding gasses from the explosive material had produced a weak, but audible acoustic wave front.

The constable didn't move, as if the sight of John fascinated him. But the asshole's helmet now contained a nice hole in the middle of his visor, with air jetting out of it, and a pattern of fracture lines radiating outward from the hole. Then the fellow tumbled over, and his still body floated away.

The skiff abruptly backed away from the station, and with his safety line still tangled on something on its bow, it dragged him with it, tethered to it by a length of line about two meters long. The pain in his left arm reawoke, reminding that part of him that felt the pain how much he really did feel it. He screamed, the skiff came to a stop, and he slammed into its hull, found himself bent over the front of the skiff and face to face with the pilot.

John brought the pistol around, didn't try to aim carefully, and pulled the trigger. The recoil sent him tumbling head over heels away from the skiff. Two meters in front of it the tether went taught and he snapped back toward it, slammed into the bow and managed to hook his left elbow around a protruding strut.

He struggled to twist around and fire another shot. But when he got oriented and could aim the pistol, the pilot sat motionless strapped in his seat, a jet of escaping gasses pouring out of a hole in the chest of his suit. John had shot the mother fucker in the chest.

Hanging on to the bow of the skiff, John carefully examined his left forearm, expecting to see air pouring out of tears in his suit and heralding his demise. Drops of blood stained the material, and in several places hardened resin had resealed the suit. He'd been lucky; the tears in the fabric of the suit had each been small enough for the self-healing material to work. He thought it ironic that he considered himself lucky, would have preferred to be even luckier and not have his damn arm crushed in the first place.

••••

A medic quickly field-prepped Nygaard's gunshot wound, then Brynjar knelt down next to her. "Mistress, we don't have a grav stretcher here, so with your permission I'll carry you."

"No," Nygaard said, grimacing with pain. "I can walk. I can walk."

Kristdokar wanted to shout at the woman and tell her to put away her near-manic need to be in control, but Haugrund stormed across the conference room and took care of that for her. "By our ancestors, Lana, let him pick you up. We'll live a lot longer if you don't slow us down staggering along like an invalid."

"Yes," Tiegnordan said. "I agree with Dortea. Let him pick you up."

Nygaard closed her eyes and pursed her lips. "All right, young man, you may pick me up."

Brynjar scooped her up as if she weighed nothing. He gave orders to the dregkraag protecting them, then carrying her he carefully eased sideways through the conference room door into the hallway. He walked down the hall, with Kristdokar and the other two councilors following on his heels. His long strides forced them to rush a little to keep up with him.

Brynjar and his people had used Kristdokar's suite as a base of operations. He must have used his implants to call ahead, because he marched through the sitting room in the center of the suite, then into a side room where a medic waited beside an obviously makeshift operating table.

Nygaard demanded, "What are you doing?"

Brynjar placed her gently on the table. "You need surgery now."

She shook her head. "Nonsense. It can wait."

Brynjar looked at the medic and the fellow responded by shaking his head. "A fragment nicked an artery. Right now it's a small problem, but if we don't fix it, in an hour it'll be a big problem."

Again, Tiegnordan intervened. "Lana, if you don't allow him to fix it, Dortea and I will declare you temporarily incompetent because of your wounds, and have it done anyway."

Nygaard rolled her eyes. "You can't do that. And I can't be sedated now. Too much is happening."

Brynjar looked a question at the medic and he said, "We don't need general. I can issue a localized nerve block through her implants, if she grants me access. She'll be conscious and lucid throughout the whole thing, and she won't feel a thing."

Brynjar looked pointedly at Nygaard, and for a moment even she cringed under that gaze. "Councilor Nygaard, when it comes to gunshot wounds and things like that, our medics are as good as the best surgeons in the Supremacy."

She sighed. "Oh, very well. But while he's at it, please brief us all on the situation."

Brynjar appeared quite ill at ease. "Forgive me, mistress, but at the moment there's little I can tell you. There has been a general attack on the palace by Kelk units from within the palace. When the attack began, I sent out squads to find and protect all five councilors, but we're less than a quarter of an hour into the attack and all I've heard from them is that they are encountering well organized armed resistance. And if there's any question in your minds, it is not our guests from the Commonwealth who are the attackers. They too are under assault."

Tiegnordan and Haugrund looked at each other, and they both said, "Nvalheim."

"Perhaps," Nygaard said, "but based on what you told us earlier, Dortea, might it be Machtberg?"

Haugrund shrugged. "That's possible, but I think unlikely. However, I wouldn't be surprised if he shows up to pick up the pieces after Marta propagates as much chaos as she can."

Tiegnordan nodded her agreement. "He is rather adept at seizing an opportunistic moment."

"Yes," Haugrund said, "and quite often he skillfully encourages someone else to create that opportunistic moment. That way he doesn't have to get his hands dirty."

Brynjar flashed Kristdokar a look filled with frustration. It was time for her to intervene. "Mistresses, perhaps it might be best to allow Command Superior Brynjar a little time to gather more information."

Haugrund threw her head back and laughed. "Brigadier Kristdokar is exceedingly polite. I think what she'd like to say is that Maestra Brynjar is the man who is going to keep us alive, and by forcing him to stand here and babysit us, we're not allowing him to do his job right now. I, for one, think we should allow Maestra Brynjar to go out there and keep us alive."

Tiegnordan grinned. "Excellent idea, Dortea. In fact, I think Mistress Kristdokar might be quite helpful at keeping us alive as well. So I say we also relieve her of her babysitting duties."

Lying on the makeshift operating table while the medic worked on her, Nygaard said, "They do have a point. You two may go. Use your own discretion on the matter, but do come back when you have more to tell us."

Kristdokar thought that anything she said at that moment might prompt further discussion, so she nodded politely, kept her mouth shut, turned, and walked out of the room. She heard Brynjar following close on her heels. He too had chosen to say nothing and exit quickly.

As they hurried down the hall Kristdokar said, "Do everything you can to reach Thordahl."

Brynjar acknowledged her order with a sharp shake of his head. "Yes, mistress. But I don't think it will matter. He'll be watching the palace. He will have already scrambled his people."

28

Missing Friends

WITH HIS LEFT elbow hooked around a strut, John clung to the skiff as it floated near the big station. He didn't do anything but hang there and try to catch his breath, try to ignore the throbbing agony in his arm, try to think beyond the pain and come up with his next move. With his left hand useless, and his right hand gripping the pistol, he didn't have a free hand he could use to crawl up over the bow of the small boat. And strapping into a seat would be problematic.

He examined his left arm again, and the gauntlet appeared to be undamaged. He tried moving the fingers and that sent more pain slamming through his arm. But he had moved them, and perhaps he could use that to his advantage. With his left elbow still hooked around the strut and the pistol held tightly in his right hand, he brought the weapon around to his left. Then carefully he transferred the butt of the gun to his left hand and curled his fingers around it, trying to ignore the pain, and not doing a very good job of that. He wasn't going to be doing any handstands and definitely wouldn't be firing the weapon with his left hand, but he had managed to grip it tight enough to park it there and free up his right hand. And with only one useable hand, he also wouldn't be crawling across the surface of Heilbronn to get to *Drakan Helgis*. He now had no choice but to use the skiff.

He felt something tugging at his belt, looked down and noticed the safety line was no longer tangled over the bow of the skiff, but extended straight from the reel on his belt to the grip on the station where he had anchored it. He and the small boat had drifted out to the limit of the ten meters of line he had unreeled. If the boat had been under power he would not have been able to maintain his elbow-lock on the strut. He hated to give up the safety line, but he had no choice. He unbuckled the reel from his belt and tossed it aside.

To climb up over the bow of the skiff he moved carefully, aware that pain muddled his thinking and reactions. He extended his right hand forward and gripped a stanchion, but then paused and carefully considered his next move. He needed to find something he could hook his left elbow around, and that limited his possibilities. And on top of that he needed to maintain his grip on the gun, even if only loosely. If it hadn't been for the pistol, he'd be dead about five times over by then, so he gave that quite a bit of priority. Reach forward with his right hand and grab almost anything, stop and carefully survey his options, bring his left arm forward and wrap his elbow around something that would work, then repeat. In that way he climbed up over the top of the skiff, then pulled himself into the seat vacated by the constable he'd shot in the face. He strapped in next to the constable he'd shot in the chest, and once again clipped the pistol by its trigger guard to the tool belt.

He consulted his implants to check the time. A little more than a half hour had passed since he'd killed the two constables on the concourse. A lot had happened in a short time, much like that night on Reisenar.

He linked up to the skiff through his implants, aimed the small boat down the length of the docks, then gave it a one-second burst of acceleration. It moved forward at about one meter per second, a slow walk. With his thinking jumbled by the confusion of pain, he needed to do everything slowly and carefully, think his next step through then make a deliberate move. He passed the bow of ship after ship, then finally came to *Drakan Helgis*. If he found a way inside that hull, he'd be among friends and Taugrim would know what to do.

A large airlock in the station near the ship's bow was clearly meant to accommodate skiffs like the one he rode. But that would only get him inside the station, probably in another maintenance depot. He had seen the security in the navy yard, and it was tight. They would quickly identify and apprehend him. If they didn't arrest him for being a homicidal maniac, they could rightly claim he had stolen a maintenance skiff. They'd lock him in a cell, and the people who wanted him dead would have no trouble getting to him.

He turned the skiff and guided it slowly down the length of *Drakan Helgis*. The fore personnel hatch was mated to the station, so no access there. The amidships cargo and maintenance hatch was mated as well, but the aft personnel hatch was simply a closed airlock with a viewing port through which he saw bright light. He eased the skiff down and closer until he could see through the port, and per standard operating procedure they kept the inner hatch of the airlock closed and sealed. The inner hatch also had a viewing port, and through the two ports he saw light in the compartment beyond.

He unstrapped from the skiff's seat, pushed off and floated the short distance to the airlock, snagged a grip on the outer hatch and held on. He couldn't create a direct link between implants through the hull of the ship, but the hatch had an intercom relay and he connected to that. "I need help. I'm outside the aft personnel hatch and I'm injured."

He waited several seconds, then repeated the plea for help.

Another short wait, and the reply came. "What do you want? We can't let you in here. We're in lockdown."

Lockdown! That didn't make sense. Why would they be in lockdown? Thinking he was speaking with a fellow crewman, he had been about to identify himself, to say he was John Mathius and he needed help, but at that moment all his paranoia kicked in.

"I'm hurt, badly hurt. Arm is crushed. Can't make it back on my own. Let me in."

"Where's your skiff? Where's your partner?"

It was time to make up shit. "He panicked when the station broadcast that emergency warning, backed the skiff into me, crushed my arm, left me here, that motherfucking asshole."

"Ah shit! Wait there."

As a precaution, John connected to the skiff's controls through his implants and eased it up out of sight of the port. Looking through the port in the outer hatch, John watched the inner hatch open, and a female Kelk stepped into the airlock. She wore the uniform of a non-com military constable, and behind her stood a male Kelk constable. John shouldn't be distrusting of constables in general, but of late his interactions with them had been far from cordial.

The constable stuck her face close to the port. "Show me where you're injured."

John lifted his left arm up and steadied it a couple feet from the port. It was just the admission ticket he needed, because a half-dozen places stood out where the self-healing fabric had resealed tears in the material. No one would mistake his arm for anything but a real mess.

"Shit," she said, "that must've hurt like hell."

"Still does," John said. "I can't make it back to the maintenance lock with no skiff and just one hand."

John was counting on the unwritten code adhered to by everyone who worked in vacuum: No one denied help to someone in trouble.

"Okay, stand back. We've got to pump down the lock."

John didn't have much time. He wasn't about to come out of the airlock shooting, and possibly killing innocent people, but he didn't want them to see the gun and take it away from him. He attached one of the clips on his belt to the grip on the hatch to anchor him there. Then he opened the belt pack, unclipped the pistol from his belt, shoved it into the belt pack, and sealed it. He unclipped his belt from the grip and held onto it with his right hand.

Several seconds passed, and while he waited he felt the vibration of the pumps through the grip on the hatch. The hatch popped open and a small amount of residual air momentarily formed a fine mist, then quickly dissipated.

Throughout his training and his experience as a ComSecCorps soldier, he had switched from floating in zero-G to walking in the gravity field of an airlock a hundred times. But with his thinking clouded by pain, he forgot to brace himself for the sudden change. He stumbled, fell, and instinctively threw both hands out to catch himself. When his left hand hit the deck the shock of pain was so intense he screamed and collapsed, wanted to cry like a baby. Completely blinded by pain, he curled up into a fetal ball and almost lost consciousness.

Somewhere he heard the clunk of a hatch closing, then the rattle of its lock mechanism, followed by the hiss of air jets. His vac suit went lax as pressure returned to the airlock. Voices and a lot of feet moving around him. Someone helped him stand, and they supported him on each side as they walked him out of the airlock. He walked with a bad limp, recalled hurting his hip and leg during his dance with the skiff. He had forgotten about it a moment later when the skiff crushed his arm, and hadn't realize how much it hurt while floating in zero-G.

They eased him into a chair, he looked up and saw a familiar face: a *Drakan Helgis* crewman, a dregkraag medic. It was the medic who had helped him when he had inquired how they had configured the peg-leg gravity fields for Nikaela's foot after he'd blown it off on Reisenar. Since then John's ability to read Kelk had improved considerably. The stencil on the man's uniform read BIRKVAND.

Manacles confined the medic's hands with a short, plast tether between them, making it difficult for him to do his job. Looking at the manacles, John knew his interaction with the constables would continue to be unpleasant, though hopefully he would manage to make it more unpleasant for them than they did for him.

John heard the female constable say, "One of the dock workers. A bad accident. At least it better be bad, because I'm going to be pissed if it ain't. Just prep it enough so we can get him to hospital sector, then let's get him the hell out of here."

The two constables stood a couple paces away on John's left side and slightly forward. The woman had unholstered her grav pistol, but held it casually at her side, aimed at the deck. The man had not drawn his.

Birkvand cut away the damaged material of John's vac suit while someone else popped the seals on his helmet and lifted it off his head. When the medic looked into John's face he froze, clearly recognizing him. John shook his head the slightest amount from side to side, and Birkvand acknowledged that with a nod just as slight.

The medic continued working on John's arm and opened up a link between their implants. *What are you doing here?*

John nodded toward the two constables. *What are they doing here?*

Clearly speaking for the benefit of the constables, Birkvand announced loudly "It's bad. Looks like the forearm is broken in at least four places."

Through their implants he said, *They arrested all of the officers, charged them with treason and took them down to Hyvaldsborg for some sort of tribunal.*

Aloud, he said, "Lot of damage to muscle tissue."

The female constable vented her impatience. "Well hurry up and be done with it. I want him out of here."

Do something for the pain, John said. *And while you're at it open my belt pack so I can get into it, but don't let the constables see you. And be prepared to sedate both constables. I don't want them dead. I don't want their implants going offline.*

Birkvand met John's eyes and nodded. A few seconds later the pain went away, and with it went all feeling in his arm below the elbow. John closed his eyes, sighed and relaxed. "Thank you. I can think clearly again."

He looked into the medic's eyes. The fellow smiled. "I set a nerve block just below the elbow. I did what you asked. A few more seconds and I'll be ready."

John had no doubt of the double meaning in his words. *After I stand, I'll need my right arm free.*

There were at least two other people in the room. They had helped John stagger out of the airlock, but after getting him into the chair they had remained behind him. He didn't know who they were, or if he should worry about them. *Who's behind me?*

The medic kept his eyes focused on John's arm. *A couple other members of my squad. They're friendlies.*

The male constable asked, "Do we have to bring in a grav stretcher for him, or can he walk on his own?"

John shook his head. "No stretcher. I can walk."

"There," the medic said and stepped back. He had encased John's left forearm and hand in some sort of hard, protective shell. He pointed to the people behind John. "You two help him to his feet."

Two dregkraag stepped forward, one on each side of John. With him sandwiched between them, they hoisted him up by his armpits and got him on his feet. They too wore hand and leg irons. John recognized both of them, a medium-height fellow with broad shoulders named Torguard, and a thin wiry fellow named Neibouer.

The medic asked, "Can you stand on your own?"

To hide what he did with his right hand, John lifted his left arm and placed it on Neibouer's shoulders. "I could use a little help." While doing that he slipped his right hand into the belt pack, wrapped his fingers around the butt of the small pistol, and flicked off the safety. John looked to his right and made eye contact with Torguard. The fellow's eyes flicked down to John's belt pack for a brief instant, but he had the presence of mind to not overtly look down.

The medic stepped aside as he and Neibouer walked forward. The leg irons on the dregkraag forced them both to take short, little steps. One step, then another, and John faked a stagger. "I guess I'm not as steady on my feet as I thought."

The constable with the unholstered pistol at her side closed her eyes and shook her head, clearly impatient to be done with the injured dockworker.

John pulled the pistol out of the belt pack, swung it around, and just as she opened her eyes, he aimed it at her face from a distance of a couple feet.

Her eyes widened, and her comrade tensed.

John shook his head. "If you think you're faster than a bullet, then by all means go for it."

He glanced momentarily at the man. "Same goes for you. And I'm a Blacksword, so don't even think about trying to communicate through your implants. I'll know it if you do, and you'll die."

That bit of bullshit had worked once before, and hopefully it worked again.

The three of them stood that way in a frozen tableau while the two dregkraag walked around behind them and disarmed them.

Birkvand stepped up to the disarmed constables, taking care to stay out of John's line of fire. He pressed an injector to the woman's neck. John heard a faint hiss, and she slumped to the deck. The medic repeated that with the man, and he joined her.

Neibouer looked at John. "Can Blackswords really tell when someone uses their implants? Is it like a brain thing?"

29

To the Bridge

NIKAELA QUICKLY CHECKED the grav pistol Eindride had given her. It had been recently charged and contained a full magazine of flechettes. She glanced down at the doctor's body. The female hauptseergent had stepped into the room and murdered the woman without a moment's thought. Then Eindride had killed the hauptseergent, the command eagle, and the tall, bearded unterseergent with no more thought. The sheer brutality of the deaths made it clear there would be no quarter asked or given by those assaulting the palace.

Nikaela stuffed the blue armband in a pocket, then knelt down beside the hauptseergent and checked her holster. It contained a spare power cell and magazine of flechettes for the grav pistol. She might need them, and the holster. The dead weight of the woman's body made removing the holster difficult work, but she managed. She stood up and buckled it on.

The building shook to the crump of an explosion. The sound had been too muffled for it to be nearby in the Medical Wing.

Holding the grav pistol in one hand, she opened the examination room door a crack and peered out into the hallway. Other than her door, the hallway contained three more, all examination rooms with their doors open. The door at the end of the hall that led to the waiting room hung half open, but she couldn't see anything beyond it other than bare floor. Nikaela stepped out into the hallway and closed the door.

She stepped over the dead unterseergent and moved down the hall. As she worked her way toward the waiting room, she stopped at each door and glanced into the room beyond. They had murdered everyone present, and she feared what she would find in the waiting room.

When she reached the half-opened door at the end of the hall, she didn't touch it, but peered past it. A patient lay face down on the floor in a pool of blood. Stinar still sat in her chair. One eye had been cratered by a bullet, while the other stared lifelessly at the opposite wall. A smear of blood and brains covered the wall behind her. Nikaela had come to know Stinar quite well and liked her. She choked back a tear because now was not the time for that, but she would shed that tear later.

At the exit from the waiting room, Nikaela followed the same procedure of first opening the door a crack and peering out into the hallway before stepping out. Earlier that morning when she had walked down that hall on the way to her checkup, it had been busy with people, but now an eerie silence hung over the deserted corridor. She walked down it slowly, listening for any sound that might alert her to some danger.

When she left the Medical Wing she stepped into a cavernous hallway wide enough to drive a couple of large grav cars down its length side by side. She had walked down it a number of times and had never really taken notice of its breadth, but as she stepped into the large open space of the hallway she now felt exposed. Statues of famous military figures were spaced about twenty paces apart along one wall of the hallway. She crossed to one and took cover behind it, though it would only hide her from a casual glance up the hall, and if it came to a serious firefight, she'd be better off running like hell.

Moving from statue to statue she worked her way back to the wing where she, Kristdokar and Brynjar had been housed. As she got closer she heard the sporadic pop of weapons fire, and each time she moved from one statue to the next it grew louder. She came to an intersecting hallway, smaller by comparison, but still fairly wide. She stopped at the intersection and leaned her head slightly past the corner, just enough to see down its length with one eye.

She had come up behind eight kriegers crouched behind a barricade of furniture and equipment about twenty paces down the intersecting hallway. They wore light body armor and carried heavy assault rifles, and as she watched them, bullets chipped away at the barricade, fired by someone out of sight down another hallway. The eight kriegers, all wearing blue armbands, returned fire, but none took notice of Nikaela behind them.

At that moment she recalled Stinar's lifeless body, and the brutality of her execution, and that of the doctor and her office staff. "Fucked them," she whispered.

She stepped out into the corridor in a crouch, raised her pistol in a two-handed grip, took careful aim, and fired six rounds. She would have fired more, but they quickly spun around and returned fired. Nikaela sprinted across the intersecting corridor with bullets hissing past her head, and ran down the large hallway. In the brief exchange of fire she thought she had seen two of them drop to the floor, but hadn't had time to stop and do a careful casualty count. She stayed on the side of the hallway with the statues, and zig-zagged in and out of them as she ran down the hallway, hoping to put some distance between her and them if they chose to pursue her.

A round of automatic rifle fire ripped chips of stone out of one of the statues as she zigged around it, telling her they had chosen to pursue her. She dug her heels in and stopped behind a statue. This time she didn't take careful aim as she swung her pistol out and fired blindly down the hallway, hoping to make them move cautiously rather than charging after her. She didn't wait to learn if that had worked, but turned and sprinted straight at the next statue, then dodged around it at the last instant, her shoulder brushing it lightly as she passed it. Behind her she heard the staccato pop of automatic fire, showering her with more chips of statue.

She reached an intersecting corridor and pulled up just short of it. She peeked around the corner, saw that it was empty, and charged down it.

••••

The two dregkraag knelt beside the unconscious constables and searched them as the medic helped John out of the vac suit.

"What's going on?" the medic asked him.

John shook his head. "I don't know. I was checking out of hospital sector this morning when five constables came for me with guns."

Birkvand pulled the upper half of the vac suit down around John's waist, and when the fellow saw the blood on John's uniform, he frowned and gave John a questioning look. John didn't have time to go into the details of Kolbeck's death, or the way the constables had murdered the nurse. "I killed them. It was kill or be killed."

Kneeling over the constables and searching them, Torguard straightened, held up an electromechanical key and happily announced, "Got it."

John nodded toward the two constables. "How long'll those two be out?"

The medic shook his head. "At least an hour, maybe two. But that's just a guess. It's really dependent on their metabolisms."

They had three weapons: John's small pistol, and the two grav pistols they had taken from the constables. John ordered Birkvand to remain behind and watch the two constables, telling him, "If they come around too soon, dose 'em again."

The two dregkraag took up the grav pistols the constables had carried. John had only fired his weapon three times, and still had nine rounds left in the magazine. But there was one thing that could stop them in their tracks. To the medic and the two dregkraag he said, "Tell me what's gone on here."

He learned how a mix of kriegers and constables had taken over the ship with warrants from the Hall of Justice, arrested the officers, and taken them down to the Hyvaldsborg Palace. The rest of the crew were confined to their quarters under comp lock, shackled in hand and leg irons for each meal, then herded in groups of between eighteen and twenty-four to the mess hall.

John asked, "Are they comp-locking everything, or just barracks and quarters?"

Torguard gave John a confused look. "I don't know. Why?"

"Think," John said. "When they take you to the mess hall or the head, is every hatch and door locked, or just those needed to lock up the crew in their sleeping quarters?"

The medic nodded. "He's got a point." He paused and thought for a moment. "I'm pretty sure everything's wide open." He nodded his head. "Yah, they're only locking crew in their quarters. I'm sure of it."

John let out a sigh of relief. "I don't want to use the lift, don't know what we'll face when the doors open. And I don't know what we would have done if every hatch between here and the bridge was comp-locked."

All three of them gave John a funny look, and Birkvand said, "But you're an officer, and a member of this crew."

John knew he sounded rather stupid at that moment. "Yah, so?"

John had been given a lot of key codes to upload to his implants, and he learned that as an officer and member of the crew, he had the codes to unlock every lock on the ship. He could even override a comp-lock sequence issued from the bridge, though he could only do so manually and while physically at each lock. "You're an officer," the medic said. "You have to command the ship if the need arises."

Torguard asked, "What are you going to do?"

At that question John hesitated. In his mind it had been a foregone conclusion that they would try to take back control of *Drakan Helgis*, and he had assumed her crew felt the same. But assumptions could get him killed. "What do you think I should do?" John immediately regretted his words.

The medic shook his head. "You're the officer. You decide what we do, then you tell us, and we do it."

The medic wore the insignia of an unterseergent, the lowest rank of NCO. John had noticed that without an officer present Kelk NCOs operated with far less independence than a ComSecCorps non-com under similar circumstances. "I'm going to do what I think Captain Taugrim would want us to do. We're going to take back this ship."

All three Kelk soldiers gave him big, flashy grins.

John decided to go for the bridge, and Neibouer suggested opening every comp-locked hatch or door they came across on their way there. John rejected that. "None of the crewmembers are armed, so they can't really support us, and the bridge will get a notification for every comp-lock I clear. We take the bridge now, while we've got the element of surprise."

The biggest issue they faced would be at the entrance to the bridge. If whoever presently commanded the bridge learned that three armed crewman were headed their way, they could seal up a lot of the ship and make it difficult or impossible for them to regain control. They stripped the tunics off the two constables, and thin, wiry

Neibouer donned the woman's. It clearly didn't fit him, but the deception would probably survive a cursory glance from anyone they encountered in a passageway.

While the two dregkraag pulled on the constables' tunics, John rifled through several lockers. The small compartment adjacent to the airlock functioned as the staging area for extra-vehicular vacuum work. He found a half-dozen all-purpose vac suits, but he needed something to cover up the blood stains and officers' insignia on his uniform. He found a one-piece coverall a couple sizes too small and stained in several places by some sort of dark, greasy gunk. It was no time to be picky, so he pulled it on over his uniform. The coverall hid the blood stains, with the added benefit that he didn't have to discard the butcher's harness and dagger because it hid that as well.

Torguard came up with the idea that since John was a common-face, they should manacle him in hand and leg irons. The two dregkraag now wearing constable's insignia could *escort* him. John didn't like that idea.

"Don't worry," the fellow said. "We'll give you the key, and we won't really lock the manacles."

Neibouer said, "Anyone got a fork handy. I heard he can fight his way out of anything with a fork."

John gave the fellow an unhappy look. "If there's humor there, I'm not seeing it."

The man grinned. "Sorry, maestra."

The dregkraag strapped on the constables' holsters and holstered their grav pistols. John shoved his ugly little gun in the thigh pocket of the coveralls, and they tried cuffing him in the manacles without locking them. They learned the manacles wouldn't actually stay on his ankles unless they closed and locked them, but John came up with the idea of cutting a hole in the material of each coverall ankle and threading the cuff through that. Anyone who glanced down would see the plast tether connecting his ankles. But if John needed freedom of movement, he could simply jerk one leg to the side and tear the manacle cuffs out of the material. They did the same with the manacles on his wrists and John hid the protective casing on his left hand by covering it with his right.

"One thing to keep in mind," the medic said. "I haven't done anything to properly treat your arm, just field prepped it, and without proper treatment, the nerve-block's effectiveness will diminish with time."

John shrugged. "I don't have much choice in the matter, do I?"

The medic didn't answer.

With Torguard in front of him, and Neibouer behind him, John and the two dregkraag stepped out of the airlock's staging compartment and into the passageway beyond.

30

Taking it Back

"COLONEL, THIS IS Team Obradour. Mr. Obradour is alive and well and un-harmed."

Seated at a small console in Ed Fleming's makeshift Combat Information Center, Katrine keyed her implants. "Did he cooperate?"

She could imagine the smile on the face of the young lieutenant in charge of Team Obradour. "He did insist that his own security personnel were more than adequate to protect him, ma'am, and that we were unnecessary. But per your instructions, I politely didn't hear him because we were moving quickly, and we hustled him out of there. We're now inside the perimeter so he's safe, but he's not happy."

"Well done, lieutenant. If there's any more difficulty just tell him you're following orders."

"Yes, ma'am."

Seated nearby and listening to the conversation, Fran Thealone grinned and whis-pered, "I'll handle Obradour."

Ed Fleming had established a secure perimeter that extended about fifty feet be-yond the confines of Thealone's suite, and it included one floor above and below them. They had positioned gun emplacements at the intersections of all the nearest hallways so that any hostiles who wanted to come at them would have to charge down a long, cavernous corridor into the face of withering fire. The oversized nature of the hallways in the palace would prove to be a considerable disadvantage to an attacking force.

Jamming still limited the range of their hardened localnet, but as they got more da-ta on the interference signature of the signals hampering their communications, their error correction grew more robust and their range and bandwidth increased steadily. Individual squad members communicating with their teammates over shorter distances had much more bandwidth to work with, but over longer ranges in the palace, most of their communications were still limited to low-bandwidth vocal information.

Mani Gascoigne walked into the room and sat down at an empty console. He held up his hands as if surrendering to an armed enemy. "I know, don't touch anything. You don't have to tell the civilian to keep his fucking hands off the warhead buttons."

Katrine ignored him. "Obradour's fine, and they're bringing him in now."

Gascoigne started to say something, but her implants beat him to it and Katrine held up a hand to silence him.

"Colonel, Team Catarvin here. The senator is with us now, and unharmed. But we're under fire. We've established a temporary perimeter, but are pinned down and cannot move. We need assistance."

Katrine opened up the communications to the general command frequency so everyone heard her, including Team Catarvin. "Sortie teams Charlie and Foxtrot, Team Catarvin is under fire and needs assistance. Move out on the double. Plan Z, magnum protocol, stage red. And keep me informed."

She spun her seat to face Fleming. "Anything from *Lady Victorious* yet?"

While carrying on another conversation through his implants, Fleming shook his head. Like Katrine he was juggling a lot of balls.

In the distance Katrine heard several bursts of automatic weapons fire mixed with the staccato pops from assault rifles. She waited through a long span of silence, then her implants came to life.

"This is Team Catarvin. The senator's fine. We're coming in. Two casualties: one critical, one dead. Thanks for the backup."

Katrine had a moment's respite and took a long, deep breath.

Gascoigne simply asked, "Anything on Palmutter yet?"

Thealone shook her head. "He wasn't in his suite and hasn't been there for a couple of days now, which we already knew."

A thought struck Katrine and she looked over her shoulder at Fleming. "Any contact with our Kelk colleagues?"

He shook his head. "No, but at this point we're pretty sure that's where the fighting is heaviest."

Katrine looked at Gascoigne. "They want the Executive Council."

He grimaced. "Yup."

"Colonel," Fleming shouted, and Katrine looked his way. "I just got through to one of my people on *Lady Victorious*. Supremacy Operations Command has grounded all air traffic over the city and issued a no-fly order in the vicinity of the palace. And there are two large gunboats sitting off *Lady Victorious*'s bow standing by to enforce that order if we think to ignore it. We can still go for it anyway. With the element of surprise they might make it down here with our combat armor, and heavy armor would go a long way toward keeping us alive."

Katrine considered it for a moment. Heavy combat armor could make the difference, but while assault boats carried a lot of firepower, those gunboats had more of the kind of firepower needed in a ship-to-ship confrontation. And under the circumstances it was perfectly reasonable for Supremacy Operations Command to issue a no-fly order. "No. Tell them to sit tight but be ready to move in a nanosecond. We need to get hold of Kristdokar and see if we can get that no-fly order lifted."

Gascoigne shook his head. "This stinks of a double cross. But it doesn't sound like the Executive Council. They wouldn't fuck us that way. This is being done by someone who wants war."

••••

Drakan Helgis's passageways were eerily silent. John had walked or rushed up or down them any number of times, and under normal circumstances, even on first watch he usually ran into someone. He and the two dregkraag worked their way up two levels without encountering anyone, though to reach the bridge they still needed to climb three more. But after they climbed up to the next level, they ran into a female command superior going in the opposite direction. She was not wearing a constable's insignia, and John didn't recognize her as a member of the crew.

She stopped in the passageway in front of them, put her hands on her hips, and looked them over carefully. "What's this?"

Torguard stammered a little. "Well he ah . . . he busted his arm, really bad, and we have to get him down to a medic."

John wanted to kick the idiot for not coming up with a better lie than that. If she decided to examine his arm, she'd most likely slide the cuff of his coverall up and see that he wasn't properly manacled.

Her frown deepened. "Why'd you do that? You had standing orders to keep them locked up no matter what."

Torguard shook his head. "I didn't get them orders."

Her eyes hardened with distrust. "I don't know you. Where'd you come from?"

At least the fellow did a good job of sounding like a recalcitrant enlisted man. "I only came aboard about twenty minutes ago. I gotta say, this is a shit detail. It's unorganized, and no one seems to know who's in command."

She shook her head. "I don't care what you think about it. Step aside. Let me see his arm."

She didn't wait for Torguard to obey, but elbowed him aside and stepped past him.

John kept his eyes focused downward as she reached out for his hands. But she glanced down and paused. "What's wrong with your leg irons? Something's wrong there."

She bent forward to get a better look at John's ankles, lowering her head as she did so. At the same time she placed her hand on the butt of the pistol holstered on her hip. She had clearly intended it to be a casual move that wouldn't spook them, but there was nothing casual about it.

Behind her Torguard reached for the grav pistol holstered at his hip. John looked him in the eyes and shook his head. He lifted both hands upward, ripped them apart, tearing the manacles out of the cuffs of his coverall, and brought his right fist down on the back of her head. He purposefully avoided hitting her in the brain stem, didn't want to kill her immediately because her implants would go off line and that might alert someone. She grunted and crumpled into a heap at his feet. Torguard stepped forward, pulling his grav pistol and aiming it at her.

"No," John said, and the fellow hesitated. "If you kill her now her implants go offline, and somebody might get a warning she's dead."

John crouched down, took her grav pistol, and checked her pulse. "She's still got a pulse, but I hit her hard enough she may not last long. We have to get to the bridge now. If we run into anyone, shoot first, ask questions later. And try not to kill—gut shoot 'em, or something like that."

John lifted his right leg and kicked it to one side, tearing the leg irons out of the material of his coveralls. He ripped the hand and leg manacles out of the material and tossed them aside, then he sprinted down the passageway, the two dregkraag behind him. They climbed up one more level, but paused before going further. Once they climbed the next ladder they would be faced with a short, narrow passageway with one stateroom door on each side, and a hatch at the end. The staterooms were the living quarters of the captain and the XO, and the hatch opened directly onto the bridge. For all intents and purposes, the ladder in front of them was the entrance to the bridge, and the most likely place they would face resistance.

John climbed up a step, but Neibouer put a hand on his shoulder. "No, maestra. You're the only officer we got. We take point. You cover our rear."

John felt a little shame that he hadn't issued that order himself. He'd been about to make the worst mistake an inexperienced officer could make. One of his academy instructors had told them, "Sometimes you have to lead by following."

He stepped aside. "Go, but I'm right behind you."

Neibouer and Torguard faced each other and holstered their weapons. Neibouer said, "My match." Then he quickly counted, "One, two, three," and they both extended their hands. On one hand Neibouer held out three fingers, and on the other only one. Torguard's hands had five fingers extended on one, and three on the other.

Neibouer grinned and pulled his grav pistol. "I win." He charged up the ladder.

Torguard drew his pistol and followed, and John followed on his heels. Before Torguard got to the top of the ladder John heard the report of a grav pistol, followed by several more shots in rapid succession. Above him Torguard stopped just short of the top of the ladder and fired several rounds. Then he continued up to the next level.

John followed, and when he stepped into the short passageway he saw Torguard charging down it toward the bridge, jumping over a lifeless body about half way down the passageway and firing his weapon. Neibouer lay face down on the deck at John's feet. Just as Torguard reached the hatch at the end of the corridor it thudded shut with a loud clunk. Torguard slammed into it, but it didn't budge.

John bent, gripped one of Neibouer's shoulders and lifted him slightly, uncovering a large puddle of blood that had come from a hole in his chest. The dregkraag's eyes stared lifelessly at the deck.

John moved carefully down the corridor, stopped just short of the two stateroom doors where the body of an unknown female krieger lay. Both stateroom doors hung open. Torguard looked back his way, John quickly pointed to the two staterooms and the dregkraag nodded.

John glanced quickly into the XO's quarters: nothing. He stepped across to the other side of the passageway and glanced into the captain's quarters: nothing. He easily pieced together what had happened. The unknown female krieger had waited in one of the staterooms, had ambushed Neibouer, and Torguard had shot her.

John walked quickly down the corridor to join Torguard. The dregkraag leaned close to him and whispered. "I'm guessing they don't know there's an officer on board. They probably think they can sit tight, take all the time they need, and wait for reinforcements."

John nodded. "And that means we don't have much time. I'll go in low aiming right, you go in high aiming left."

Torguard glanced down the passageway at Neibouer's body. "That works for me."

John pulled up the access code for the hatch blocking their way, keyed his implants to transmit it, and the hatch popped open. John threw his shoulder against it, it creaked loudly as it opened, and he dove for the deck, landing on his left shoulder and looking for a target. Torguard dove over him, landed in a shoulder roll and came up firing. John didn't have a target, and since Torguard was shooting at something, he did have one.

John rolled over, but lying on the deck he couldn't see anything above the instrument clusters and duty stations. He got his feet beneath him in a crouch, rose up to peek over the command console, and saw a command hawk firing at Torguard. John couldn't grip with his left hand, but he lifted his left arm and rested his right hand and the butt of the pistol on the protective shell the medic had installed. The command hawk spotted John and swung her weapon toward him, but he had had that fraction of a second to take aim while she was forced to go for a quick, wild shot. He pulled the trigger, the gun kicked, the command hawk jerked and her weapon fired. A sledge hammer of pain slammed into John's thigh and he almost fell.

The command hawk stood statue still, staring at John with a confused look on her face, her eyes blinking, a red stain blossoming on her tunic just below her left breast. John aimed again, but he heard Torguard's weapon fire. The command hawk's head jerked to one side, and she crumbled to the deck.

Torguard staggered across the deck to stand over her, clutching his side where a blood stain discolored his tunic. He kicked her weapon aside, then bent down and checked her pulse. He looked John's way and nodded. "She ain't going to bother us no more."

John checked his thigh. The dirty coverall had both an entrance and an exit wound. The bullet had only gone through a few inches of flesh, though the wound had already soaked his leg with blood.

John had one thing he must do above all else. He limped to the command console, sat down, logged into it, and through his implants issued a general command to lock down the ship. The hatch to the passageway slammed shut along with every other door and hatch in the ship. Then he issued a general command to seal every comp-lock on the ship.

Torguard leaned against the command console and looked at John's thigh wound. John reached down and checked it one more time. The bleeding appeared to have slowed, but to be safe, he pressed his hand against it to apply pressure, though that hurt like hell.

He nodded at Torguard's bloody hand clutching his side. "How bad?"

The dregkraag grimaced and shook his head. "Hurts like hell, but not a bad wound. Took a ricochet off a console, bullet fragmented and got me with several small pieces. Just a bunch of small puncture wounds. Birkvand'll have to dig 'em out of me, but I can function, and I can fight. What's next?"

John looked at the command console. "I've got the ship locked up tight, so the bad guys can't move around any more than the good guys. Gather up all the grav pistols. I think we've got five." John pulled the little pistol out of the thigh pocket of his coveralls. "I've got this so I don't need one. Take them down to May Forrester and her people. I'll clear a way for you hatch by hatch down to their quarters, but keep an eye out for bad guys all the way. Then I'll clear a way for all of you to their combat armor. Once they're armored up, we'll have this ship locked up tight, and anyone who wants to take it away from us is going to have a real hard time doing so."

Torguard nodded, a thoughtful look on his face. "What are we gonna do after that?"

John had expected to find Taugrim so she could tell them what to do. He shook his head. "I have no fucking idea."

31

The Best Laid Plans

A NEARBY EXPLOSION rocked the building and Kristdokar shielded her head as dust settled out of the old structure. The pop and crack of weapons was an almost constant din as the attackers closed in on them. Where was Thordahl? Why had he not come?

Hunkered down behind a barricade in the hallway outside her suite, Kristdokar checked her implants. Just over a half hour had elapsed since the first explosion shook the building. A bullet zinged off the wall overhead as she did the math. To don powered combat armor, board the assault boats, then cross the distance from Nygaard's compound; under the best of circumstances Thordahl might do that in a half hour. They would just have to hold out a little longer, and hope. She dearly hoped it would only be a little longer.

Brynjar pinged her implants. "I just reached Thordahl. You're not going to believe it."

Kristdokar shook dust out of her hair. "I'll be right there."

She holstered her grav pistol, backed away from the barricade on her hands and knees, then stood up and jogged down the hallway. Like many walls in the palace, the main walls of corridors and her suite were built of blocks of stone thick enough to stop even a Mach five flechette from an assault rifle. But interior walls added during the last few hundred years were a death sentence if one tried to use them as cover.

When she reached her suite she hurried across the central sitting room to the small room Brynjar had set up as his base of operations. Inside Brynjar sat at a small console, with Haugrund and Tiegnordan standing behind him and looking over his shoulder.

As she approached them, Haugrund glanced Kristdokar's way and asked, "How close are they?"

Kristdokar shook her head and made no effort to hide a grimace. "We control the hallway outside the suite, and a couple of branching hallways. Beyond that, they've regrouped at an intersecting corridor. What about Thordahl?"

Brynjar glanced over his shoulder. "I'll let him tell you."

Her implants came to life with Thordahl's voice. "Mistress Kristdokar, Supremacy Operations Command has declared martial law and issued a no-fly order for the city, even for authorized military craft. Just a few minutes ago we tried to lift anyway, but were immediately confronted by a flight of eight gunboats patrolling the airspace above the city. I've been arguing with Operations Command, but they won't budge. But if your situation is critical, give me the order and we'll make a run for it regardless."

Under any other circumstances, issuing the no-fly order had been the right thing to do. Either Operations Command was working for Nvalheim, or they simply didn't understand that they were hampering Kristdokar's clandestine efforts to keep them alive.

"No," Kristdokar said. "Not yet. But stay in constant contact with Brynjar. We may issue that order yet."

Nygaard's image appeared in Kristdokar's virtual vision. "We have to meet. Unfortunately, I can't come to you, so I must ask you to come to me."

From the looks on Tiegnordan's and Haugrund's faces, they had just received the same summons. Without saying anything, Kristdokar headed for the room where Nygaard was recuperating from her surgery, Haugrund and Tiegnordan on her heels.

They found Nygaard seated in a chair, bandages encircling her midsection. The three of them stopped in front of her, facing her. She smiled pleasantly. "Mistress Kristdokar, please ask Maestra Brynjar to give my compliments to his medic."

Kristdokar nodded. "I shall, mistress."

Nygaard raised an eyebrow. "And what is our situation?"

It took Kristdokar a moment to realize that Tiegnordan and Haugrund expected her to answer that question. She outlined the situation with Thordahl, and with the attacking force surrounding them, then concluded with, "I think it's safe to assume Nvalheim is behind this, and it's possible she's got her claws into Operations Command at a fairly high level. If so, they won't lift the no-fly order, and that doesn't bode well for our chances."

When she finished, Nygaard sat silent and still, staring in the distance for several seconds. Then her eyes brightened. "Well, what do you think? Do we surrender?"

"No," Tiegnordan said. "If Nvalheim wanted us dead, they could simply plant charges beneath this suite, then take out this wing of the palace, and us along with it."

Haugrund sucked air through her teeth and shook her head. "No, you don't know Marta. She wants us dead, but she'll want to gloat first, then kill us, which does give us a certain advantage. She can't gloat if she kills us first. She wants to take us alive, but that doesn't mean she'll keep us alive."

Kristdokar had assumed from the beginning that she was on Nvalheim's shit list along with the councilors. She had done too much to thwart the woman's ambitions.

Realizing that she might soon die, her first thought was of all the other people that would have to die with them.

Apparently, the same thought occurred to Nygaard. "If it comes to that, we must surrender. Yes, if it's Marta, she'll probably kill us anyway, but if we don't surrender, she'll overrun us and kill everyone with us as well. We're dead either way, but personally, I'd prefer to die without the deaths of innocent subordinates haunting my soul."

The four of them remained silent for several long, uncomfortable seconds. Then Nygaard said, "I suppose—"

Brynjar's voice interrupted her, speaking through their implants. "Mistresses, we've just managed to reestablish contact with Colonel Primatov and the Commonwealth diplomatic mission. All of the mission principles are alive and accounted for except Senator Palmutter, but as you know he's been off premises for a couple of days. We're going to coordinate our forces, which should give us a better chance."

Nygaard sat up straighter. "Let's see if we can get hold of someone reasonable at Operations Command and get that no-fly order lifted."

For the first time that day Kristdokar felt it in her heart, and she saw it in the faces of the other three women: hope.

••••

John cleared the comp-lock on the hatch to the bridge so Torguard could leave, but as the dregkraag ducked to step through it, John had an idea. "Wait a minute."

Torguard had already stepped through the hatch, so he stuck his head back through it. "What do you need, maestra?"

John hoped Torguard wouldn't ask him to explain. "Who on this ship right now knows the people on her, knows their skill sets, knows what they can and can't do."

Torguard's eyes narrowed. "What are you looking for exactly?"

John wasn't sure how to answer that. "To start with, I need someone who knows how to operate the main com on this boat a lot better than I do. With that operational we can get some information, and then we might have an idea where we stand. And I'd like to get Scan operating too, give us some eyes as well as ears."

Torguard smiled and nodded. "Seergentmeister Kelbacher. She can help you."

"Okay," John said, "change of plans. When you get to Forrester's bunk compartment, give them four of the pistols, and I'll get them to their armor without you. You then head for Kelbacher so you can make sure she gets here alive."

To John's surprise Torguard saluted him in the Kelk fashion. "Yes, Maestra." A moment later the hatch closed with a clunk. John comp-locked it again.

John cleared a couple of comp-locks in front of Torguard, and as the dregkraag passed through each, he closed them off again. His main worry was that officers among their opposition might have the same codes he had, and a few moments later he received confirmation that his fears were justified. A comp-lock cleared down in the security section, and John immediately relocked it. Someone down there had at least some of the codes, and since John was the only officer from *Drakan Helgis*'s crew on board the ship, it must be one of the bad guys. Whoever it was tried again, and John immediately reengaged the lock. Interestingly enough, John now knew the location of one of the enemy leaders.

By locking everything up, he had done to them what he had feared they would do to him if they learned too soon that one of *Drakan Helgis*'s officers had boarded the ship. With John clearing locks ahead of Torguard, the dregkraag moved slowly but steadily through the ship, while John made the bad-guy officer clear each lock four or five times before he or she finally got through it. John also killed localnet in that area, cutting whoever it was off from any subordinates not within shouting distance.

John was so preoccupied with the comp-locks he almost forgot to warn May and Carla that Torguard was headed their way. Communicating through localnet, John pinged their implants and got an immediate response.

"John," May and Carla said in unison, "is that you?"

"Yah," he replied, seeing an indicator on his console that the bad-guy officer had just cleared another comp-lock. While the two women threw a dozen questions at him, he reset the comp-lock, and Leeze, Pykoff and a couple of Kelk non-coms conferenced in.

John didn't have time to answer their questions. "Shut up and listen to me. I don't have time to explain. I've taken control of *Drakan Helgis*'s bridge and locked her down. There's a dregkraag named Torguard headed your way. He's carrying five heavy grav pistols. Do what he says, and I'll get you and your squad to your combat armor, then we're going to seal this ship up and no fucking constables are going to be giving any more orders here."

Carla wasn't satisfied with that. "When the dust settles, you're going to do some explaining."

As always, Leeze was Leeze. "Johnny-boy, if we get out of this alive, I'm going to give you a thank-you fuck that'll leave your dick limp for a month."

Leave it to Leeze, John thought.

••••

Standing in the background of the combat information center in the bunker beneath Machtberg's compound, Macus watched the man orchestrate the developing situation. The large screen on the wall now showed several plumes of smoke rising from the Hyvaldsborg Palace. At that point it had become clear Machtberg had connections into just about every aspect of Emkeldstadt's government. Machtberg glanced over his shoulder at Macus and smiled pleasantly. "If you want to rule a nation, young man, simply take control of the city from which its rulers rule."

Strikland nodded, clearly enjoying himself. "Yes, Macus, that's something both Aubrecht and I learned long ago."

Both men were brilliant, truly brilliant.

Standing next to Macus, Faith opened up a secure link between their implants. *They're cut from the same cloth, aren't they: brilliant, ruthless, powerful, and wealthy.*

Macus glanced briefly her way, and realized that he actually felt something for her beyond simple carnal desire. *You're brilliant and ruthless, you know.*

She glanced up at him and gave him a wistful smile. *You're brilliant and ruthless too. And if we're smart, someday we'll both add powerful and wealthy to that.*

Yes, he said. *We do share brilliant and ruthless, and I can't think of anyone else I'd rather share powerful and wealthy with.*

She lifted an eyebrow, but didn't look his way. *And you can't think of anyone else who is as well-equipped as I am to make sure you and I get to powerful and wealthy.*

His attention remained on Faith, but for appearances he focused his gaze on Strikland and Machtberg. *That's what we have in common.*

Yes, Macus, we do.

"Did you hear that, Lawrence?"

Machtberg's triumphant shout brought Macus's attention back to him and Strikland. Machtberg looked at Macus and Faith. "Dornmier's dead. I just got it confirmed." He looked at Strikland. "Time to add a new player to the board."

Both men grinned like children.

For a moment the look on Machtberg's face was that of a man concentrating on his implants, then he announced, "They'll be airborne in about five minutes."

Strikland waved for Faith and Macus to join them. "Come and look at this."

Three paces put the two of them standing beside the two older men looking down at a console screen. There was no mistaking the image on it: a schematic of the palace. Strikland pointed at the screen and explained. "Dornmier and Veskarson were in their apartments near the Council Chambers, and Nvalheim took them first. She's got the other three councilors surrounded with Kristdokar in her suite. Those two Blacksword women managed to retrieve all the mission principles but Palmutter, and they're surrounded as well. Palmutter's in a large, ground-floor maintenance garage with Nvalheim. Now Aubrecht moves in, saves the world, and he's the hero of the day,"— Strikland gave Machtberg a sly look—"and the soon-to-be newly appointed member of the Executive Council."

Machtberg grinned like a young schoolboy about to receive a medal for winning a race. But then he frowned and put a hand to one ear. "What? What did you say?"

Machtberg's face clouded with anger. "No-fly zone?" His eyes darkened as his anger deepened. "Martial law? Operations Command?"

He pointed to a subordinate at another console. "Get me Vice Skalde Erdstadter at Operations Command on the double."

The subordinate sounded frightened as he responded. "Right away, maestra."

Machtberg took several deep breaths and calmed himself. Then he looked at Macus, Faith and Strikland. "Some idiot at Operations Command declared martial law and issued a no-fly order above Emkeldstadt, and they're enforcing it with armed gunboats in orbit and in the airspace above the city. It's nothing to worry about, because I'll damn well get this cleared up in short order."

••••

Once Carla got her armor sealed up, she ran it through a full pre-combat check. It highlighted a few maintenance issues, but nothing came up flagged for immediate attention. She quickly stripped her assault rifle and checked it carefully. She had been meticulous about her maintenance and encountered no surprises there.

John's voice came over the command circuit. "May, please send one of your squads up here. Tell them to set up a defensive perimeter around the entrance to the bridge. Until we've got this boat cleared of the assholes trying to take over, I don't want to take any chances that I missed something. If someone took over the bridge, we'd be fucked."

May responded in the Kelk fashion. "Yes, maestra. And I should probably send a squad to Engineering as well."

"Good idea. Do it."

Torguard had come up with the idea of augmenting May's dregkraag platoon with his own platoon mates, and May now had six fully functioning squads under her command, which gave them a lot more options.

John continued over the open combat channel. "Listen up people. I dug into the ship's log. I figure anything comp-locked before we changed the rules was probably crew under lockdown, so we don't have to worry about them. We'll leave them locked down until we know we have all the non-friendlies boxed up, then we'll free the crew. Any compartment not comp-locked before we took the bridge was wide open, so I might or might not have trapped a non-friendly in it when I locked everything down. You people are going to clear them one at a time. I've identified one location where someone keeps clearing comp-locks, and I keep resetting them to keep them trapped there. I'm assuming there's a non-friendly officer there."

In the process of checking her armor seals, May paused. "Just one officer? I would think there'd be more."

"Just one," John said. "But Neibouer, Torguard and I killed two taking the bridge, both females, a command superior and a command hawk."

May glanced Carla's way, and Carla looked at Leeze

Leeze grinned. "I'm guessing the one left alive is Command Superior Asshole."

Carla returned her grin.

Since John had trouble keeping the one officer contained because he kept clearing comp-locks, they started with him. John guided May and her remaining three squads down two decks, opening hatches in front of them as they went. Since each compartment they entered might contain trapped enemy combatants, they didn't take any chances and carefully cleared each before moving on. But even then, they moved quickly because they had the advantage of numbers and full combat armor, which allowed them to operate with a certain level of confidence. May kept reminding them that too much confidence could get them killed.

John stopped them a couple compartments short of where he had located the lone remaining officer. Carla asked May, "Mind if my squad takes point?"

Leeze flashed an evil grin.

May's eyes narrowed. "As long as you don't kill him unless you absolutely have to."

Carla shook her head. "Don't worry, I want him alive too."

Leeze's upper lip curled with distaste. "You take all the fun out of it, but okay." With a finger Leeze traced a big X over her left breast. "Cross my tits and hope to die."

John cleared one more hatch. Carla and her squad moved through it into an open compartment that looked like an electronics repair shop with several workstations. At the far end of it the telltale above another hatch flashed red. That hatch plus one more separated them from Command Superior Asshole.

They checked the compartment carefully, then Carla positioned the rest of her squad out of sight on the other side of the hatch they had just come through. She and Leeze split up; Carla went right and Leeze went left, with the locked hatch between them. Carla found an empty recess in the bulkhead intended for a parked maintenance bot. She slipped into it as Leeze's voice came through her implants, "I'm in position."

Carla's recess was deep enough that a casual glance in her direction wouldn't give her away. From it she had a slanting view of the compartment and some of the workstations, but she could duck back and be almost completely hidden; almost. She keyed her com. "We're in position."

John's voice came through her implants. "I just let him clear a comp-lock. He's got one more hatch to clear before he gets to you. It wouldn't look right if I let him get through it on one try, so I'm going to reset it a couple of times first, like I've done with all the rest."

Carla waited. She was an experienced combat veteran. She was supposed to be cool under fire, but her heart rate slowly increased as the seconds ticked by.

"There's one," John said.

She tried to calm her heart and her breathing.

"And another. I'm going to let him through on the next one."

Carla tried to stay relaxed as she waited. Then she heard a hatch pop open as John's voice reached her. "He's through. He's all yours."

Carla pressed herself a little deeper into the recess. She had a clear view of the hatch Asshole would head for, the hatch behind which the rest of her squad waited.

Command Superior Asshole came into view carrying a grav pistol. He marched toward the hatch on the far side of the compartment like he owned the place, didn't bother looking back. Behind him walked the two kriegers and the female non-com who had accompanied him the first time Carla had met him, also carrying grav pistols. But the non-com glanced to one side, saw Carla and froze. Carla raised the muzzle of her assault rifle, aimed it at the woman, and stepped fully out of the recess. On the other side of the room Leeze stepped out of her hiding place and did the same. She and Leeze had the four of them in a nice crossfire.

The female non-com wasn't stupid. Carla watched her consider the odds—four grav pistols against powered combat armor and heavy assault rifles. She slowly reversed her grav pistol, and holding it by the barrel, she carefully placed it on a workbench, then raised her hands above her head.

Asshole reached the hatch, looked up and said, "Wait a minute. This one's already cleared. There something wrong here—"

He turned, looked back and saw the non-com with her hands in the air, then saw Carla and Leeze. Behind him the hatch opened, and two of May's platoon members stuck the muzzles of their rifles through it.

Carla keyed her exterior speakers. "You can surrender and live, or not surrender, and not live. It's a digital choice. Take one or the other."

Asshole hesitated, but Leeze fucked it up. "Yah, asshole, and then we get to see if your balls bounce any more than our tits."

Asshole's eyes widened, he looked at Carla, then at Leeze, then at Carla, his eyes blinking rapidly. Then he shouted, "Fuck this," and raised his pistol.

Carla took a chance. The combined fire from four heavy grav pistols, if held on target for several seconds, could overwhelm her powered armor. But the non-com had already put her pistol down, and the two kriegers looked like they were about to provide a live demonstration of Sergeant Major Prescott's shit lecture, so Carla took a chance. In fact, she took a double chance by not going for a kill shot. She aimed for Asshole's knee, pulled the trigger, and shouted over the command circuit, "Hold fire. Hold fire."

As Asshole's knee exploded and he fell to the deck, May shouted the same thing. Leeze had the presence of mind to rush the two kriegers and hit them with a full body block. The three of them went down, but padded inside her combat armor Leeze wouldn't even have a bruise or two to show for the stunt. On the other hand, the two kriegers were probably going to limp rather badly for a while. Throughout the whole thing the female non-com hadn't moved, just stood there with her hands up and her eyes closed, trembling quite visibly.

Asshole lay on his side gripping his knee and screaming in pain. He had dropped his grav pistol on the deck nearby. May elbowed her way through the hatch and kicked it aside. The rest of Carla's squad followed her and collected the weapons from Asshole and his friends.

As Leeze picked up her assault rifle, May marched up to her and face-butted her visor-to-visor. Then May demonstrated that she had some of that DI gene in her DNA, demonstrated it with some serious attitude and a lot of volume. "I should bust your ass all the way back to buck private, you fucking moron. But I don't have the authority to do that, so I'm certainly going to recommend that to my boss, whoever the hell my fucking boss is when this is all said and done."

May spun away from her, took command of her platoon, and saw to it that the prisoners were manacled, but treated properly.

Leeze eased her way over to Carla, moving like a ballerina dancing on a floor covered with glass shards. She dilated her visor. "I fucked up, huh?"

Carla just shook her head.

32

A Trick Up the Sleeve

THE NON-COM told Anders to stay close to the cluster of offices. He sat down on the concrete floor of the garage with his back to a wall a few paces from the entrance and watched a lot of people come and go. He saw one common-face enter the office complex, a short, fat, balding fellow. Anders caught a few words of the fellow's speech as he stepped through the door, and he recognized a Sarkovie accent. But other than the Sarkovite and Palmutter, he hadn't seen any other common-faces.

After ten minutes of sitting on his butt, the door to the office complex opened and the officer stuck his head out. "Eindride, with me. She wants to talk to you again."

Anders pushed off the floor and rose to his feet, then followed the officer down the short hall and into the office. Palmutter still sat in his chair, visibly radiating anger and fear. Nvalheim stood in one corner huddled with the Sarkovite and a male command eagle, all looking over the shoulders of a tech sitting at some sort of console. The officer waved Anders to one side where a female Kelk in civilian clothing stood by herself. He didn't provide any introductions.

"Maestra Eindride," she said. "Tell me what happened to your team this morning."

Anders had thought carefully about the story he would tell if asked to go into detail. If they sent someone back to the doctor's office, his story needed to match up with what they found there.

He grimaced and shook his head. "I don't know what the plan was, because nobody really filled me in, but everything did seem to go to plan until we got to the doctor's office. Dagborne told me to cover the rear, so when we went in, I stayed at the door to the hallway. Dagborne, Kristensen, and Thoran swept the office, then converged on one examination room. That was when all hell broke loose, must have been twenty or thirty rounds fired in just a few seconds. Thoran tumbled out of the examination room, all shot up and clearly dead, then a bunch of people started shooting at me, so I took to my heels. It's not much, but that's all I got to tell."

He decided to add a little something for dramatic flair. "I don't think we got the Vreekande bitch."

The woman grimaced. "Yah, you're probably right there."

Anders hadn't realized Nvalheim was paying attention, but at that moment she looked up from the tech's console and focused on him. "Were there any Blackswords?"

Clutching the amulet suspended from her neck, she crossed the room and stopped a pace away from him. Earlier Anders hadn't realized the significance of the amulet, a medallion probably old enough to predate the first Blackswords. And the crude workmanship: probably the work of an amateur, an artifact possibly hand-made by an ancestor and inherited by Nvalheim. The Curse of the Blacksword. He couldn't believe anyone actually believed that crap, but apparently Nvalheim bought into it completely.

"No," he said, "I didn't see any."

Her eyes sharpened with fear. "But they could have been there, and you just didn't see them."

He didn't know what to say, but thankfully the tech seated at the console rescued him. "Mistress Nvalheim, Vice Skalde Erdstadter at Operations Command reports that Maestra Machtberg just contacted him and is demanding he rescind the no-fly order, at least for authorized military aircraft."

Nvalheim threw her head back and crowed with laughter. She shouted in Anders's face, "He fell for it. The fool fell for it. They all did."

She spun around to address the tech. "By all means, tell Maestra Erdstadter to lift the no-fly order. Let them send in their rescue teams. Let them send in their dregkraag with powered combat armor. They think they'll overwhelm us, but they have something to learn."

She turned back to Anders. "I need all of them to show their hands so there won't be any surprises. I don't know what they've got or how much they've got until they do, but when they do—"

She raised her hand with her fingers spread, then she slowly closed it into a fist. "When they do, I'll crush them."

She grinned. "Victory is close, Maestra Eindride, very close indeed."

••••

Once Carla and company apprehended the officer they referred to as Command Superior Asshole, May split up her squads so they could operate independently, with John directing them from *Drakan Helgis*'s bridge. It didn't take long to clear all the complocks where they might have trapped more of their captors, and they ended up with eleven prisoners.

"Maestra Mathius."

At the sound of a woman's voice, John looked up from the screen where he kept a map of the passageways they had cleared. A small, female Kelk non-com stood next to his console. Slight of stature, she wore the uniform of a seergentmeister, and stood there saluting him in the Kelk fashion, standing every bit as rigid as any DI. She gave him a sardonic look as she said, "Seergentmeister Kelbacher reporting for duty, Maestra Mathius."

John had trouble focusing, and it took him a moment to remember where he had heard that name before.

Torguard stood behind her, still clutching at his side. "Wasn't hard getting her here alive."

John returned her salute and struggled for a moment to remember all the Kelk forms of *at ease*. "Ease and relax."

She eased her rigid stance and smiled. "Maestra Torguard told me you want guidance on staffing the bridge."

"Um," John said, realizing he sounded like an idiot. "Yes. I was thinking Com, and Scan. We need to know what's going on outside this ship."

She nodded, a thoughtful frown on her face. "I know just the right people, Maestra. Well trained they are, and quite experienced."

"Excellent," John said, glancing at his screen and feeling the urgency of all the comp-locks that remained sealed.

Kelbacher saw him glance that way and looked there herself. "You have much more urgent things to worry about at the moment. Leave it to me. I'll get the right people here."

"Thank you," John said. "And make sure everyone understands they don't give up any information about what's going on inside this ship. We're going to just look around and find out what's going on. And hopefully we'll find Captain Taugrim and the rest of our officers."

The woman shook her head. "We know where Captain Taugrim and the officers are. They took them down to Hyvaldsborg to stand trial for treason."

John's nascent plans crashed. He had assumed that Taugrim and the other officers had been thrown in a cell on Heilbronn. In the back of his mind he'd harbored the idea that May and her platoon, in full combat armor, could break her out of jail.

Disappointed and struggling with what he would do next, he pointed an angry finger at Torguard. "And you go see a medic; get that wound taken care of. And I'll tell Mistress Forrester to assign a couple people to Mistress Kelbacher. We'll give priority to clearing the comp-locks on anyone she needs. But we need Com and Scan asap."

John turned back to the business of releasing the crew from lockdown. May had told him about Command Superior Asshole's harassment tactics, and he had to be prepared for the possibility that one or more of the shithead's friends had been harassing crew-members when he locked down the ship. If they got locked in with crewmembers, he could end up facing a hostage situation. He and May operated on that premise, and from each compartment they first took a few people out into a passageway to make sure they weren't under any form of coercion. They confirmed their identity, and if they got the all clear, then they swept through the compartment and checked each crewperson against the ship's roster. It didn't take long, and they didn't encounter any more hostiles.

As the ship came back to life and its operational stations were once again crewed, John leaned back and checked his implants for the time. Only an hour and a half had passed since the five MCs had come for him in the hospital sector. His arm had begun to hurt, just a nagging pain that he shoved into the background of his thoughts, but still something that worried him.

Birkvand stopped beside the command console. "Maestra, Oberkrieger Torguard told me you were wounded in the thigh."

John had forgotten about the thigh wound. He extended his leg, but it had stiff-ened while sitting there.

While Birkvand worked on John's leg, he glanced around the bridge. Com, Scan and a few other stations were occupied by techs, and the place now felt a little more like the bridge of a warship, with lights blinking, and people's eyes glinting with reflec-tions from their screens. Granted, they were all demon-red eyes, but if that had ever bothered John before, it certainly didn't now.

When Birkvand finished, John stood up, limped to the Com console and looked over the shoulders of the female tech seated there. "What have you got?"

She glanced up, fear in the look she gave him. "Someone's attacked the Hyvalds-borg Palace. Supremacy Operations Command has declared martial law and issued a no-fly order for the city of Emkeldstadt. I got that much from the news feeds. I sent a secure inquiry to Fleet Communications Central, and they confirmed the info from the news feeds, but didn't provide any additional details."

Martial law and the no-fly order were news to John, but that was a reasonable thing to do under the circumstances. On the other hand, Fleet Communications Cen-tral should have provided more details for a Kelk warship, even if nothing more than telling a damaged ship like *Drakan Helgis* to shelter in place.

John needed to get hold of Primatov so she could tell him what to do. "Can you communicate with the palace at all?"

The young woman shook her head. "I've tried, Maestra. Nothing. Someone's jamming signals in and out of the palace."

John eased his way around an instrument cluster and stepped up to the Scan con-sole. The fellow seated there had a few years on John, and looked none too happy. John repeated his question. "What have you got?"

The tech shook his head, as if he didn't believe the data coming his way. "There's almost nothing happening in-system, a few gunboats moving about here and there, but none of the usual traffic. Everything's real quiet, too quiet. But a little less than two lightyears out I count at least eighteen transition wakes that look like warships driving hard toward us from all directions."

"What's the makeup?" John asked. "Commonwealth, Kelk, what?"

"All Kelk, maestra."

John looked at the fellow's screens, but without interfacing his implants to the Scan console, he couldn't interpret them with the same precision. "What about the Commonwealth warships that came with the diplomatic mission, *Hellfire*, *Endurance*, *Lightspear*, and a couple of other hunter-killers?"

The fellow shook his head. "Nothing, maestra. They're just sitting there two lightyears out, not moving."

"Maestra."

At the sound of Seergentmeister Kelbacher's voice, John looked to where she stood behind the com tech. "There's a lot of transition com traffic between those Commonwealth warships and *Lady Victorious*, though it's all heavily encrypted."

Lady Victorious! John had completely forgotten about her. He crossed the short distance to the Com console. "I need to interface my implants to the Com."

The tech nodded. "I'll ping you. All you have to do is respond."

John got the ping, then engaged a secure channel and encryption key Primatov had given him. He got an immediate response. "This is Null-Echo. What do you need, Mr. Mathius?"

"I need to know what's going on. I've been on the run, trying to stay alive, exercising a lot of Plan Z discretion. I've been out of the loop for the last hour or more, so please fill me in."

John got a rapid-fire account from Null-Echo about a coordinated assault on the palace. Null-Echo was in contact with Primatov, and she now had a link to Kristdokar and several members of the Executive Council. They were quite certain Nvalheim had orchestrated the attack. The assault boats carrying combat armor had been hampered by Supremacy Operations Command's enforcement of the no-fly, but that order had just been lifted, and everything would be all right soon.

"Tell Colonel Primatov I'm on *Drakan Helgis* with the rest of her crew, except we have no officers."

"Will do, Mr. Mathius. Null-Echo out."

John carefully explained to Kelbacher and the bridge crew what he had learned. "Please spread the word to the rest of the crew that this should be over fairly soon."

John glanced around the bridge for a place to sit down, but Kelbacher had a crewmember at every station. He didn't recall telling her to find someone for all the stations. He had a little trouble ignoring the nagging pain in his arm, and recalled the medic's admonition that without proper treatment, the nerve-block's effectiveness would diminish. At that moment he just wanted to sit down and watch the drama at the palace play out to its conclusion. Then he could get treatment for the damn arm, and the thigh wound too.

"Maestra," the scan tech said. "I'm getting some sort of anomaly in orbit around Viktorkinde. I've patched the information over to your console. You should review it. It looks very unusual."

His console! Only one station remained unoccupied, and he stood right next to it: the command console.

He glanced down at the screens. Two assault boats descended from *Lady Victorious*. Two assault boats had lifted from a residence on the outskirts of Emkeldstadt. The residence had been assigned the designation MACHTBERG. Two more assault boats had ascended from a compound designated NYGAARD and located in a wealthy suburb.

John saw the reason for Primatov's confidence. With the nullheads working with Nygaard's people, and all in full combat armor, they would have a decided advantage. Machtberg was a wildcard, but all indications were he wouldn't side with Nvalheim, though John still wanted to know if the man had been complicit in Novalis III.

On John's screens the scan tech highlighted some sort of structure in close orbit around Viktorkinde. "Maestra, this is the anomaly that concerns me. It's listed as a transfer station for an export company, but its emission signature has just jumped off scale for anything of that nature. It's also slowing in its orbit, and it's not descending."

Now John saw it too. As he looked on the transfer station slowly killed its orbital velocity until it came to a stop four hundred kilometers above the planet's surface, and directly above the palace. It had entered into a forced synchronous orbit. But that required some serious grav-drive power, and no transfer station should have that kind of capability. Only a warship could—

"Shit!" John shouted as he sat down at the command console. "Com, reopen that channel to *Lady Victorious*. Get me—"

John's scan summary spiked, and one of the assault boats descending from *Lady Victorious* disintegrated in a flaming shower of plast and metal.

"Maestra," the scan tech said. "That was a transition battery. That transfer station has transition batteries."

"Com," John said, "get me that link to *Lady Victorious*."

"They're not responding, maestra."

Transition batteries were designed to range on targets at two hundred million kilometers, and a mere four hundred kilometers was little more than point-blank range. John and the crew of *Drakan Helgis* sat helpless as the fake transfer station destroyed the other assault boat descending from *Lady Victorious*. Then it obliterated the four coming from Machtberg's and Nygaard's residences, and following that targeted the residences themselves, as well as portions of the Hyvaldsborg Palace. Black columns of smoke rose from the palace, the two residences, and crash sites for the six assault boats. It reminded John of the early days of Novalis III when the factions had stopped trying to take territory from each other, and focused instead on destroying it.

An eerie silence settled over the bridge of *Drakan Helgis*. Like everyone else, John was too stunned to think, and he sat silently staring at his screens.

When Seergentmeister Kelbacher cleared her throat, he looked her way. She stood near the Com console. "Maestra, it appears we are at war, but not with the Commonwealth as certain fools had hoped. Help us make sure they don't succeed."

He had no idea how he would do that, and he was about to tell her so when she snapped to attention and saluted him in the Kelk fashion. Her eyes pinned him to his seat like the points of butcher's daggers. "Captain, what are your orders?"

33

Command

WHEN ANDERS STEPPED out of Nvalheim's makeshift office, he paused in the doorway as four kriegers escorted a group of manacled prisoners down the hallway. Just below their rank insignia, the prisoners wore the emblem of Naval Operations on their sleeve, and all were Kelk officers, more than a dozen of them. Anders had only been back on the planet for three days, but no one needed to tell him the identity of the female command hawk with spiky red hair. Even if her face hadn't been repeatedly splashed across the vids, Britta Taugrim had a reputation for brilliance and flamboyance. It was said of her that she could have gone higher in the ranks with less of the flashiness.

As the last of the prisoners walked by, followed by two kriegers, Anders stepped into the hallway behind them. "What's going on?" he asked.

One of the kriegers glanced over his shoulder. "Making room for more prisoners. Higher-ups want the rooms in the office complex for some bigshots."

Anders took note of the fact that the prisoners were cuffed only in hand irons, not leg irons, and a long plast tether tied them together. *More* prisoners; did that mean his employers had run into a shortage of manacles?

He didn't need to ask the next question, but hoping to learn something he did so anyway. "Who are they?"

The krieger answered as they stepped out into the garage proper. "Officers from *Drakan Helgis*. They fucked up some of the old woman's plans and she ain't happy with them. But she said we still gotta treat 'em nice. Ain't their fault they followed orders."

The kriegers led the prisoners out of the office complex and to one side, where they made them sit on the floor. Anders walked with them and said, "Yah, I guess we're going to need all types in the new Supremacy."

The krieger's eyes brightened. "Exactly."

The office complex protruded out from one wall of the garage, as if built as an afterthought. Anders noticed that once they got the prisoners settled, many of them were not visible from much of the garage floor. He stood there trying to think how he might use that to some advantage, when a gravity spike punched through the garage and the building shook. Anders's implants came to life. *All personnel should remain calm. Those are our batteries firing on our enemies in the building, and there is nothing to worry about. This is merely the final stage of ending their resistance.*

As the bombardment continued, a couple of the prisoners at one end of the group stood. The two kriegers near Anders moved quickly toward them, leaving Anders alone standing above Britta Taugrim, which was not a coincidence. He leaned down close to her, lowered his voice and hissed, "I'm a friend of Kristdokar. I don't know if or how I can help you, but if and when I do, don't be surprised and be ready to act."

He straightened just as one of the kriegers walked back toward him, and he knew he needed to give the fellow a reason for leaning close to the woman. He snarled, "Bitch."

She growled, "Fuck you, asshole," and he wasn't sure she'd gotten his message.

"Here, here," the krieger said, stepping between Anders and Taugrim. "The skalde said to treat them nice, so back away."

Anders snarled, "That woman's got a mouth on her." Then he shrugged, held up his hands and stepped back. He turned around and walked away, but he glanced over his shoulder for a brief instant.

Taugrim's eyes met his and she smiled pleasantly, then with the faintest bit of motion she gave him a single nod.

••••

A gravity wave slammed into Katrine and knocked her on her ass. The building shook with such violence she couldn't have stood, and was forced to sit there for a few seconds before getting up. She struggled to her feet as a cloud of dust rolled into the room.

She shouted at Ed Fleming. "That was a transition battery. There aren't any warships in this system."

She staggered out of the room, marched across the central sitting room to the entrance to Thealone's suite. Another gravity spike hit her, the wall in front of her exploded, and the hand of some great god slapped her down.

Pain. Horrific, terrible pain in her arm, and then the blessed peace of oblivion.

••••

"Captain, what are your orders?"

John didn't understand Kelbacher's question. It simply didn't make sense, just didn't compute. Taugrim and the ship's officers were all under arrest two hundred thousand kilometers away in the Hyvaldsborg Palace. Captain Taugrim was not present on the bridge to answer the woman's question, so to whom had she . . .

John carefully scanned the faces on the bridge, and all looked at him, waiting for him to respond. He didn't want to respond, but realized he had no choice. He returned Kelbacher's salute, and tried not to appear hesitant when doing so, tried to appear captainish, though he wasn't sure how to do that. Then he sat down at the command console.

The pain in his crushed left arm returned to the forefront of his thoughts. He looked at the hard casing the medic had wrapped around his forearm and hand, thought he should call the fellow up to the bridge again, see if he could do something about the pain. But before he did that he should answer Kelbacher.

He looked at her again. She didn't understand that he was not ready to captain a warship, and his mind raced as he came up with one hollow excuse after another for abdicating the position. But who would he abdicate it to? May was the only other officer on the ship, but she wasn't an operational line officer in *Drakan Helgis*'s chain of command. And among the Kelk, even the highest ranking NCO would never be allowed to command a ship.

He was too young. He was too inexperienced. All of that rocketed through his thoughts as he tried to think of a way to break the news to them that he wouldn't accept the position. And then he recalled the words of one of his instructors at O-School. "When an officer is *given* command of a ship,"—the instructor had placed particular emphasis on the word *given*—"more often than not Fleet assigns him or her to that position, usually under peaceful circumstances with a pleasant little ceremony accompanied by drinks for all. The other way you might come to command a ship is that circumstances put you in that position. When you suddenly become the ranking operational line officer on a ship, you are not *given* command. You do not *accept* command, nor do you *reject* it. At that moment you are already the captain. Period. And if you fail to carry out that duty, you are derelict."

The absolute silence on the bridge sounded wrong to John's ears. He looked carefully at the bridge crew, and they were all staring at him with expressions ranging from outright fear, to simple uncertainty. Somehow he needed to eliminate those concerns.

He broke the silence. "We need more accurate information. Can we launch the drones while docked?"

Kelbacher crossed the bridge to stand beside his console. If he had to be captain, she could damn well be XO. She looked at him with anticipation. "We'll have to launch them manually one at a time, and all out through the port launch bay, otherwise they'll slam into the docks. What do you have in mind?"

John nodded, bobbing his head up and down. He was certain he didn't look at all captain-like at that moment. "Do we have crews on station at our main batteries and our secondaries?"

She frowned at him as if to question his sanity. "Of course. All essential stations are operational with trained and qualified crew, maestra."

John forced himself to stop nodding like an idiot. "We don't need a full complement of drones. If we need to target, it's going to be in the neighborhood of that transfer station, and on and around Viktorkinde. And that's at most a couple hundred thousand kilometers. But we need pinpoint accuracy."

Her eyes widened and she grinned. "Yes, yes, I'll see to the drones right away."

Once they had some drones out feeding them high resolution data, they'd need to cast off. But for stability, plast and steel docking gantries tied *Drakan Helgis* rigidly to the station. Standard procedure would be to contact Heilbronn Port Operations and ask them to disengage the docking gantries.

"Yah, right," John said. "Like I'm really going to do that"

While giving instructions to a tech, Kelbacher broke off and looked at John. "What was that, maestra?"

"Nothing," John said. "Nothing."

He started to ping May through his implants, but then remembered that as captain, he should work through channels when possible. "Com, get me Lieutenant Forrester. I need to speak to her right away."

"Yes, maestra."

A few seconds later his implants chimed and May said, "Captain, this is Lieutenant Forrester."

"May," John said, "I need your help to cast off."

"John, is that you?"

"Yah, it's me."

"Com told me the . . . captain wanted to speak to me. Isn't that Taugrim?"

"Taugrim and all the officers are in a cell in the Hyvaldsborg Palace, so I guess right now it's me."

The long silence that followed was perhaps an indication that May had no more confidence in John than he had in himself, and when she spoke it startled him. "John, be the fucking captain. You don't get a choice. You have to go all-in and be the captain all the way. So be the fucking captain and don't look back."

John recalled that May hadn't been in that same class with him. But that course had probably been required for all cadets at O-School, and she probably had had the same fucking instructor.

"Yah, I kind of figured that out."

The tone of May's voice changed. "Very good, Captain, what do you need from me?"

John outlined his plan. "We need to cast off, but I'm not about to ask permission from Heilbronn Port Operations so they can decide they don't think we should cast off. I need you and your people to go EVA and plant charges to cut us loose from the docking gantries. And you gotta move fast."

"Yes, maestra."

She didn't say anything else, and they sat there for a few seconds in silence. He demanded, "What are you waiting for?"

"I'm waiting to be dismissed, maestra."

He could easily imagine the grin on her face. "Just go plant the fucking charges, god damn it."

"Yes, maestra."

••••

The muffled pop and crack of distant weapons fire came so faintly that for all intents and purposes the stairwell remained silent. That meant Nikaela could hear anyone moving about nearby and be prepared to defend herself. It also meant that if her enemies remained still, they could hear her moving about and possibly ambush her. But she couldn't just stand there frozen with fear, so she moved cautiously downward step by step.

When she reached the intermediate landing between the second and third floor, a gravity spike punched her in the gut, the building shook, and a shimmer of fine dust settled out of the structure. That had been the unmistakable signature of a transition shell passing nearby. There weren't supposed to be any warships in the system. The closest were at least a couple hours out, and she wondered how someone had snuck one undetected into the vicinity of Viktorkinde.

The building shook again and she gripped the handrail on the stairs to steady herself. She almost panicked, thinking she needed to get out of the building before it collapsed around her. But she forced herself to remain calm and think the situation through. Combatants from both sides of the conflict occupied portions of the palace. To destroy the entire building, whichever side had control of a transition battery would have to kill comrades as well as enemies, which meant the strikes were probably more surgical in nature. And the stairwell was a modern addition to the old structure. Constructed of plast girders and reinforced concrete, she was probably standing in one of the safest places to be during a bombardment, though the building shook with such violence she clutched at the handrail to stay on her feet.

When the shelling finally ended, complete silence settled over the building. She consulted her implants to check the time. For the last hour and a half there had been the occasional span of true silence, brief periods of up to five or ten seconds without the pop or crack of weapons fire, but such episodes had been unusual and rare. Nikaela listened and counted the seconds, and the complete lack of any sound at all bode ill for one side. But which side?

Nikaela continued down the stairs, taking them one at a time and moving with extreme caution. She needed more information, needed to know if the shelling had produced victory for one side or the other, and if so, which side. On the second floor landing she decided to reconnoiter before continuing down to the ground floor.

She turned the latch on the stairwell door with infinite slowness, fearing each little click and ping of the mechanism would advertise her presence to everyone on the floor. She opened the door a crack and peered out into the hallway. Dust filled the air like a light fog on a misty morning and she couldn't see very far down the corridor. She stepped out into the hallway, and stayed in a crouch close to the wall as she silently worked her way to an intersecting corridor. She peeked around the corner and saw three kriegers standing near a bank of elevators. Through the dust in the air she caught a faint glimpse of a blue armband, then another. The last time she had spotted a group of kriegers wearing blue armbands, stepping out and firing several rounds at them had not proven at all effective, so she thought she should try something different. Luckily, all three were male, none were officers, and she thought she could use both of those factors to her advantage.

She pulled the blue armband out of her pocket and slipped it onto her left wrist, then up to her upper arm. Carrying her pistol casually by her side and aimed at the floor, she stepped openly out into the corridor. She marched toward them, taking long confident strides and trying to adopt the attitude of a skalde who would expect nothing less than absolute obedience from three low-ranking kriegers.

She waited until one of them noticed her, then loudly called out, "Have you checked to make sure the lifts are secure and working properly after that bombardment? The skalde sent me to find out."

The three of them stiffened. An NCO and one other had slung their assault rifles casually over their shoulders, while the third held his resting in the crook of his arm. He could easily raise the muzzle and aim it at Nikaela.

The NCO shook his head. "No, mistress. We didn't know we were supposed to."

As she strode toward them she ratcheted her volume up a notch. "You didn't know? After a bombardment like that, you mean you're not smart enough to figure that out on your own?"

The NCO grimaced and nodded. "We'll take care of it right away, mistress." He turned toward the bank of elevators.

At that moment one of them had the presence of mind to ping her implants for an ID sequence. Her implants responded with a null sequence and the fellow with the rifle in the crook of his arm hesitated and frowned. Nikaela raised her pistol and shot him in the chest. He staggered but didn't go down, so she shot him in the face. She swung the pistol around and shot the NCO in the back, but the third krieger dove for her and tackled her, landing on top of her with his full weight and knocking the wind out of her.

He had managed to wrap both his hands around the wrist of her right arm, and held it immobilized above her head. He head-butted her in the cheek as she fired another round, but it zinged off the wall of the corridor. He swung her arm around to her side and slammed it against the floor. He had the advantage of upper body strength, and clearly knew it. Pinning her right hand to the floor with his left hand, he took his right hand off her wrist, raised it high and slammed his fist into her cheek, sending a shock of intense pain through her face. Then he pounded on her ribs once, twice, a third time, and pain sent her to the edge of consciousness.

Her vision narrowed to a hazy tunnel with his face at its center, his teeth gritted, his jaw clenched. But he had either forgotten her left hand or chose to ignore it, and until that moment she had forgotten about the butcher's dagger sheathed on her left hip.

Again he clamped both hands around her right wrist. As she struggled to find the handle of the dagger, she couldn't allow him to wrestle the pistol out of her hand. He bent her right wrist painfully, angling the weapon toward her hip. Then he jammed his finger over hers in the trigger guard. The gun fired and pain shot through her right thigh, but still she managed to maintain her grip on the weapon.

He again removed his right hand from her wrist. She found the hilt of the blade and pulled it from the sheath just as he raised his fist to hit her again. With his right hand raised high and cocked to strike her, she grunted as she jammed the blade into his armpit, burying it to the hilt. He screamed and sat up straight on top of her, releasing her right wrist and reaching across his chest for the dagger. She raised the pistol and shot him in the throat.

He froze, a look of surprise on his face, his mouth open, a trickle of blood drizzling from the entrance wound just below his larynx. He choked and coughed blood on her. She shot him under the chin and the top of his head exploded upward. A shower of blood and brains spattered down over them both as he slumped forward and lay on top of her like an exhausted lover.

Her ribs hurt. Her wrist hurt. Her face hurt. Her hip and thigh hurt.

It took every bit of strength she had to roll him off of her. She struggled to her feet and leaned against the wall to stay standing. Holstering her pistol, she retrieved the butcher's dagger from his armpit, wiped it off on his tunic and sheathed it. The bullet he had forced her to fire had grazed her right hip, and while it bled profusely, there were no major arteries near the wound so she applied pressure with her hand and trusted it would eventually stop.

At least she had answered the question about who had been victorious. Somehow she must find Nvalheim and kill the woman.

The doors of one of the lifts whooshed open. She staggered around to face it and found herself looking down the barrels of four heavy assault rifles carried by four kriegers wearing blue armbands.

34

Surrender

THE BUNKER BENEATH Machtberg's compound proved more than capable of protecting them from the orbital bombardment of the transition batteries, though the pounding of the shells did rattle their teeth quite a bit. Once the orbital transition batteries had obliterated Machtberg's assault boats, and his prized dregkraag with them, Faith noticed that his contingency plan seemed to be nothing more than shouting a lot of epithets, and swearing on various ancestor's graves that he would enact revenge on Marta Nvalheim, and that traitor Erdstadter at Operations Command. Faith decided it would not be politic to ask how he would do that without his assault boats and combat troops to carry out his orders.

When the bombardment finally ceased, Machtberg and three of his Kelk soldiers opened a locker of heavy assault rifles. Machtberg handed one to Macus. "You trained in ComSecCorps, you know how to use this."

Macus couldn't deny it. While he checked out the weapon, Faith leaned close to him and whispered, "Hold back and let them do the dying. Then we'll surrender and see if we can get out of this alive."

He gave her a pained smile. "My thoughts exactly."

"Good," she said. "Just aim the damn thing and don't pull the trigger."

He shook his head. "No aiming. People tend to shoot at anyone who aims a weapon at them. No, first sign of other people with guns, I'm weapon on the ground and hands up."

The bunker included a protected stairway up to a hardened plast and concrete door. Machtberg activated some sort of switch through his implants, and the door made an awful racket as it slowly swung open. He explained, "The door is opened by a hydraulic ram capable of pushing any amount of debris out of the way."

To Faith, it sounded like it was pushing a lot of debris out of the way.

Before the door had completed opening, Machtberg sent the three soldiers out through the widening crack of daylight it exposed. Faith heard the report of rifles and the crack of other weapons, then silence.

The silence lasted for several seconds, then a male voice outside shouted, "Maestra Machtberg. Mistress Nvalheim has ordered me to spare you and your guests if you surrender peacefully. Otherwise, we are to take no prisoners."

Machtberg was no martyr to any cause, so Faith was not surprised when he dropped his rifle and shouted, "Okay, we're coming out unarmed."

Macus dropped his weapon as well, then he, Faith, Strikland and Machtberg walked forward into the sunlight. At least thirty armed Kelk soldiers surrounded the entrance to the bunker, and a blunt and ugly boat bristling with weapons circled overhead.

They cuffed them. Faith had never been cuffed before, and it infuriated her that they would do so. She did not look at all good in manacles, and the loss of control particularly upset her.

••••

John considered contacting May to ask her what was taking so long. It shouldn't be that difficult to set charges on the docking gantries, just go out there and set the damn things. Trying to control his impatience, he keyed his implants to an exterior vid pickup. A half dozen of her people clung to the gantries, most in simple vac suits, while only one wore powered armor. May had had the presence of mind to make her people change into the simpler suits because a bunch of dregkraag in armor swarming over the gantries would have looked odd. That had taken a little time, and John didn't get to hound her about it precisely because he was the captain. At that moment he didn't like being captain.

It occurred to him to call that medic up to the bridge. The fellow could probably juice John up a bit and do something about the constant throb in his left arm, and the ache from the thigh wound.

"Captain, the readings I'm getting off that transfer station don't make any sense."

John focused on his screens. With three drones out they had a much clearer picture of the transfer station that John suspected was actually a warship. Even in the summaries pushed to him by the scan tech, John easily saw a number of discrepancies. Riding on its grav drive to maintain a stationary position four hundred kilometers above the Hyvaldsborg Palace, the emissions from the anomaly just didn't add up. John had assumed they would find a warship disguised as an orbital warehouse, but it was apparently neither.

The scan tech had a lot more experience than John and would spot details John might miss, especially with only summaries to look at. "Spell it out for me."

"Maestra, they're running their power plant hard, but its emissions profile is nothing close to what I would expect from a warship, even a small destroyer. They're putting out enough to maintain a forced synchronous orbit, and to power a bank or two of transition batteries, along with basic life support and other essential functions, but that's all."

Seergentmeister Kelbacher leaned on John's console, her eyes focused on his screens. "They must have built that thing in orbit, probably took a couple of years to sneak all the pieces up for a rudimentary grav drive and a bank of transition batteries."

John looked her in the eyes. "Nvalheim's planned this for years."

Kelbacher shook her head. "But she'd have to be prescient to know a Commonwealth diplomatic mission would come. That whole concept came together just a couple months ago."

John had first seen the complexity and depth of the planning characteristic of their enemy's thinking on Reisenar, and during its immediate aftermath. And he had witnessed it again during the last year and a half. Kelbacher didn't have the advantage of that perspective.

He shook his head and shrugged. "They were probably planning for just a straight-forward coup, and then the diplomatic mission came together as a pleasant surprise. I'd guess that galvanized their most fervent supporters, and they decided to take advantage of a situation that fell into their laps."

John needed the answer to one piece of the puzzle. "Scan, does it have powered shielding?"

The fellow shook his head. "No way of knowing until they power it up, and that'll only happen in response to incoming ordinance."

"Captain, Mistress Forrester wishes to speak with you."

The com tech pushed May's signal to John's implants and her face appeared in his vision. "We just got a call from a maintenance supervisor on Heilbronn, wants to know what we're doing. I had one of the Kelk non-coms answer because my accent is shit-of-bull."

John considered asking May where she had learned that expression, but decided he didn't want to know.

May continued. "We told him we detected a minor hull leak at one gantry coupling, and that we're repairing it and checking all the other couplings. He wants to talk to the captain, was pretty insistent about it."

John couldn't speak to the fellow. His accent was a lot better than May's, but it would still label him Commonwealth in an instant. "We need to buy time so you can finish. Is that non-com online?"

"I'm here, Blacksword." For some reason it pleased John that the dregkraag NCO didn't call him *captain*.

They needed time. "Tell him the captain is taking a shower, and will get back to him in a few minutes. And tell him she said he'd better have a god damn good reason for interrupting her."

"Will do, Blacksword."

"John," May said. "I have an idea. We've got charges set on the two gantries amidships. We still have to worry about the two remaining gantries, bow and stern, but I think our secondaries can target on them. If so, there's nothing more to do out here, and we're ready to go."

Kelbacher had listened in and her eyes widened. She turned without a word and edged around the scan console to Fire Control. She leaned over the tech there and pointed at the young woman's screens, the two of them speaking rapidly for several seconds. Then she spun toward John and pointed her thumb at him, aimed it at him like an awkward imitation of a pistol. It took him a moment to recall that she was giving him their equivalent of *thumbs up*.

"May," John said. "Great idea on the secondaries. Bring your people in. We're getting the hell out of here."

An afterthought hit him. "And get your people back in their armor. We're going to need them."

••••

Dust everywhere, a white-ish coating of fine powder covering everything and floating in the air between her eyes and the ceiling. A nullhead medic leaned into Katrine's field of view. "How are you feeling, Colonel?"

Katrine thought about that for a moment. She recalled reestablishing contact with Kristdokar and her comrades. She recalled Supremacy Operations Command lifting the no-fly order for military aircraft. She recalled agreeing to put herself and her nullheads under Kristdokar's command to create a combined force of nullheads and dregkraag. They had planned a counterattack, and working together, with the advantage of heavy combat armor, they had hoped they could end it quickly. And then she recalled the bombardment, a wall of heavy stone blocks collapsing, and horrific pain in her arm.

She lifted her right arm to look at it, but it was no longer there. Her arm ended just above the elbow in a bloody bandage.

"Crush wound," the medic said. She focused on him, had a little trouble doing so. "We couldn't save the arm. We'll have to grow you a new one when this is over."

She smacked her lips, needed something to wash the dust down her throat. "To answer your earlier question, I feel like shit."

The medic nodded. "That's how you should feel. You've also got hairline fractures in two ribs, but I've repaired them. Nothing else is broken, but you are going to feel sore all over. We've blocked the pain from your arm, but blocking pain from all over is problematic."

He opened a secure link between their implants. *You should know that we are prisoners of the attacking force, whoever the hell they are, though from what I've seen so far, they're all Kelk.* His eyes glanced sharply left. She looked that way and saw two Kelk guards in light combat armor carrying heavy assault rifles and standing at the entrance to the room. Both wore blue armbands.

Katrine concentrated hard to focus on her implants. *How did they do it? How did they conceal a warship in orbit?*

He carefully shook his head just the slightest amount. *It wasn't a warship. It was some sort of orbital warehouse with one bank of transition batteries, plus enough of a grav drive to kill its orbital velocity and hold it four hundred kilometers above us in a forced synchronous orbit. It's up there right now.*

He helped her sit up and held out a plast cup of water. She reached for it with her right arm, but her arm didn't go that far. She took the cup in her left hand and gulped at the water, drank the whole thing. She glanced around and saw other patients, all lying on cushioned pallets on the floor. "Please help me up."

The medic extended a hand, then hooked his elbow under her left armpit.

Once on her feet, she didn't feel too much like standing. She staggered and reached out with both arms, but again her right arm wasn't there. The medic caught her, kept her from falling and held on to her tightly. "It'll pass," he said. "I've juiced you up pretty good so you can function. Colonel Blacksword says you're going to need your wits about you."

Katrine felt a little better with each passing second. She took several slow breaths then carefully pushed the medic away. He hovered close by as she took one step, then another, walking cautiously between the pallets of injured people on the floor. She noticed a familiar face, stopped and looked down at Tarsik Obradour. The financier lay with his eyes closed, his flesh a paltry gray.

She looked at the medic. "How bad?"

He grimaced and shook his head. "Crush wound. Had to take his leg off at mid-thigh, but we're not done yet. If we don't get him to real medical facilities in the next hour or two, he's not going to make it."

Katrine was afraid to ask. "What about the rest of the mission principles?"

He gave her a pained grin. "At least there's some good news. Gascoigne and Catarvin have a few scratches and their feathers are pretty ruffled, but otherwise unhurt. Colonel Blacksword has a broken wrist and some broken ribs, and several cuts, but she's okay."

At that point Katrine was fairly certain she could cross the room without falling down. "Where is she?"

The pained grin disappeared. "When the dust settled they allowed me to treat anyone wounded. First thing, they hustled Catarvin and Gascoigne down to some sort of base of operations they've got on the ground floor. And when I finished patching up Colonel Blacksword she went next. You're to follow as soon as you can walk on your own. Can you walk on your own?"

Katrine almost snapped a sarcastic retort at him, but suppressed that impulse. "Yes, lead on."

She followed him out of the makeshift infirmary. The central sitting room acted as the crossroads to hallways that led to other rooms in Thealone's suite. And in it, the entrance to the palace proper had been completely obliterated, replaced by a hole in the floor where Katrine saw a sizeable pile of rubble one floor below, and a gaping hole in an exterior wall that showed clear, blue sky.

Two Kelk soldiers took charge of Katrine, and were actually quite careful in the way they treated her. They had parked a four-seat, open-frame grav skiff hovering just above the floor, and were quite considerate of her missing arm as they helped her sit down and strap in. No mistreatment, no angry looks, no epithet-filled retorts about Blackswords. They did have her sit in the seat next to the pilot, with an armed krieger in the seat behind her, his pistol unholstered. Their sympathetic attitude only went so far.

The pilot flew the skiff out through the hole in the exterior wall, then around to the side of the building where he descended slowly to ground level. Hovering a meter off the ground, he drove the skiff past two large assault boats parked on the lawn, then through the entrance to a spacious garage. Several sedans and trucks were parked neatly in a row, with plenty of room to spare for more. Only a few kriegers moved about, and they were mostly enlisted personnel, with a few non-coms and the occasional officer among them.

It appeared Nvalheim had taken the palace and the reins of the Supremacy with a fairly small force, and little or no powered combat armor. Suckering them into exposing their available combat armor had been brilliant. Katrine recalled an analysis in Nvalheim's dossier: as a young officer she had repeatedly proven herself to be a masterful tactician, but as she grew older her unreasoned fanaticism had limited her support among the Larscom.

The pilot drove the skiff to the far side of the garage and parked it in front of a cluster of offices. Her guard climbed out of the seat behind her, stepped a few paces away and held his grav pistol casually at his side. The pilot helped Katrine unstrap, then climbed out of the skiff, walked around the front of it and helped her step out of it.

The pilot said, "Please follow me."

He led her into the complex with the guard walking a few paces behind her. As he led her down a long hallway, she spotted Kristdokar in the distance stepping out of sight into a room. The skalde's hands had been manacled in front of her. It occurred to Katrine that if she had had more than just one hand, they probably would have manacled hers as well.

Long before they reached the room into which Kristdokar had disappeared, the pilot stopped, opened another door, and indicated with a nod of his head that Katrine should precede him through it. She turned and stepped into a small room that contained a utilitarian table and chairs, and three occupants. Fran Thealone sat in one of the chairs and looked like Katrine felt. An hour of rapid healing had closed a nasty gash on her cheek that extended from her ear to her chin, though it needed a lot more time to reduce the angry red inflammation. Mani Gascoigne sat beside her, his hair ruffled and sticking out in all directions. Next to him sat Jenine Catarvin, her hair spikey, her makeup smeared, her dress torn, exposing even more cleavage than usual. All three of them were covered with smears of white-ish brown dust. Katrine glanced down at her uniform and realized she probably didn't look much better.

Catarvin jumped out of her seat. "Oh you poor dear." She rushed across the room, pressing that little clutch purse of hers tightly against her breast. Emitting a constant stream of chatter, she took Katrine by her left arm and guided her to a chair, got her seated, then retrieved a glass of water for her.

Katrine didn't need any water, but she sipped at it anyway, wondering if their captors had bothered to search that little purse.

35

Wildcard

LIKE ALL WARSHIPS, *Drakan Helgis*'s systems operated differently on full alert. John had refrained from elevating the ship's combat status prior to that moment, fearing some exterior telemetry feed might alert Heilbronn that a new player had entered the game, but that no longer mattered.

John keyed him implants into the command channel. "Com, sound general quarters."

"Yes, maestra."

A horn burped with a grating noise no one could ignore, then the alert klaxon filled their ears with an unholy din. The com-tech's voice sounded over allship. "Battle stations, all hands, this is not a drill . . ."

John ignored the noise. "Engineering, we need full combat status soonest."

A female Kelk appeared in John's vision, a senior NCO he vaguely recognized. "We're pushing our ramp, but it'll still be five minutes."

In his virtual vision, John looked the woman in the eyes. "We're not going far. Just let me know when we can power our shields and a few of the secondaries. And for a few minutes following that we'll only need limited grav drive capability."

She smiled. "For that, maybe more like two minutes."

When Taugrim had ambushed the hunter-killers while swinging around the white-dwarf, *Drakan Helgis* had run silent, with a trickle-feed to its power plant keeping it hot, and they had ramped up in ten seconds. But in the dockyard, with their transition drive under repair, they had shut her down completely. From his training John knew a five minute ramp from cold stop was pushing it, though even two minutes might be an eternity for what they needed.

That also reminded him that they didn't have a transition drive. Their immediate future would likely be a shooting war inside the Viktorkinde system, so technically they didn't need one. But if they got into a bad situation, with a fully functional transition drive they could force up-transition and squirt a couple of astronomical units out of the way. Inside a gravity well they wouldn't have much control over direction, but it was a common maneuver warship captains had used time and again to get out of trouble, and John didn't have that option.

"Captain, this is Lieutenant Forrester. My team is clear."

To avoid cycling people two at a time through a personnel hatch, May and her people had exited the ship's hull through the hangar bay doors, and they returned the same way. John checked their status and saw that they were all back inside the hangar bay, with its doors sealed and pumps re-pressurizing the compartment.

When Engineering gave him the go, John wanted to be ready, so he keyed the command channel. "Stand by to cast off. Remember, we're going to explosively detach from Heilbronn. On my command, do the following."

He followed that with a series of instructions, but in the middle of that Kelbacher leaned close to him and whispered in his ear. "Maestra, might I recommend you rescind those orders."

John froze and looked her in the eyes, feeling like the greenest recruit standing before a DI. He keyed his implants. "Belay that."

In answer to the look he gave her, she said, "If your crew follows the orders you just gave them, we'll tear off about ten meters of our bow."

"We will?"

She nodded like a mother gently correcting a child. "Yes, maestra. You're giving too many orders. Just tell them to cast off. They'll make it happen the right way. And we get to keep the whole ship, rather than leaving a chunk of it behind."

To John's amazement, her voice did not carry even the slightest hint of sarcasm. "Thank you."

Her smile softened, and he understood the stress she had been under when correcting the captain of the ship. "You're welcome, maestra."

John sheepishly reissued simpler orders.

Standing beside him, Kelbacher said, "Captain, if I might make another suggestion, you should address the crew. These are unusual circumstances, and they need to know . . . what you intend to do."

John didn't know what he intended to do. He'd started out running from a bunch of military constables trying to kill him, then he'd crawled across the surface of Heilbronn, expecting to find friendly faces on *Drakan Helgis*, and a captain who could tell him what to do. And since then he'd simply reacted. In that moment he realized it was time to stop merely responding to the moves of a shadowy enemy, but he wasn't sure he knew enough to start dictating his own moves on the game board.

He recalled the way he had announced himself the first time he reported for duty on *Drakan Helgis*'s bridge. Remembering that, he keyed his implants into allship. "This is Lieutenant John Mathius, ComSecCorps, Blacksword Regiment. But none of that matters anymore, not here and now. Right now I am, above all else, a member of this crew, and my duty, and my responsibility to you, my comrades and friends, compels me to command this ship."

Standing beside him, Kelbacher smiled and nodded.

He continued. "Someone has attacked the Hyvaldsborg Palace in an attempt to illegally overthrow your government. I feel it is my duty—our duty—to place this ship under the lawful command of the rightful government of the Supremacy. And I intend to find whatever members of the Executive Council remain alive, and let them define our mission. But we'll probably have to kill a bunch of shit-of-bull assholes in the process."

Kelbacher's face shifted from a gentle, motherly smile to a broad, shit-eating grin.

"Captain, this is Engineering. You've got the power you need, but only just the bare minimum you wanted."

John was still keyed into allship. "It's show time, people." He sure hoped he had translated that properly into Kelk.

May had given control of the charges her team had planted to Fire Control, and John had one last thing he needed to do before they started blowing shit up. "Fire Control, it's your show, but hold off until I give the command. Com, connect me with that maintenance supervisor who contacted Lieutenant Forrester, the one who wants to speak to the captain."

Kelbacher gave John a look and raised an eyebrow.

John shrugged. "I want to kill as few innocent people as possible."

She raised the other eyebrow to join the first and nodded, telling him she approved of his decision.

The maintenance supervisor appeared in John's vision, a middle-aged Kelk fellow who'd gone to fat and had an extra chin or two. "Who are you? And don't tell me you're the captain. The MCs arrested her and took her down to Viktorkinde."

John said, "I am Lieutenant John Mathius, ComSecCorps, Blacksword Regiment." The fellow's eyes widened. "And I am the ranking operational line officer on this ship, which makes me her captain. I—"

The fellow interrupted him. "What kind of shit is this? You can't—"

John interrupted him. "We are about to explosively cast off from Heilbronn's docks."

The fellow frowned. "Explosively?"

"Yes," John said, "and I am concerned that there may be some damage to the compartments anchoring the docking gantries, which may result in a loss of pressure. You should evacuate them so there won't be any needless loss of life."

The fellow shook his head and his upper lip curled with anger. "You can't—"

John raised his voice to a shout. "You have ten seconds."

The fellow froze and John continued. "Fire Control, on my count. Ten . . . nine . . ."

Kelbacher leaned close to John. "They can't evacuate those compartments in ten seconds."

John grinned and met the supervisor's eyes. "Eight." He spaced each count about three to four seconds apart, so they'd really have more like thirty seconds. "Seven."

The supervisor disappeared from John's vision but didn't cut the audio feed. In the background John heard the scream of emergency sirens and the whoops of alarms echoing through the station's compartments. "Six."

John stopped wasting his time counting. On the station he heard shouting and panic, but after about thirty seconds the noise died down, leaving only the whine of the sirens and alarms. He asked Kelbacher, "Satisfied?"

She nodded. "Eminently, maestra."

"Engineering," John said. "Power priority to our shielding. Fire Control, execute."

The charges May's team had set detonated and at the same time Fire Control opened up with carefully selected secondaries. The docking gantries disintegrated, sending heavy splinters of torn plast and steel ricocheting off the hull, taxing their shields and pushing power demand to the limit since they were still in the middle of the ramp. The helmsman had the difficult job of holding the ship rock-steady relative to the station as the force of the explosions pushed on the hull of the ship. The secondaries continued to hammer at the fore and aft gantries until they too ruptured. John noticed that several rounds missed and punched holes in Heilbronn's hull, and was glad he'd given them the chance to evacuate those compartments.

In an instant the secondaries went silent, and the young woman at Fire Control said, "I believe we're free, maestra, if Helm confirms it."

The tech at Helm said, "I confirm we are free, maestra."

"Good," John said. "Back us away from Heilbronn slow and easy. Get some distance between us, then launch the rest of the drones; we need more eyes. And watch for any hostile action. I can't imagine what we might run into, but be prepared for anything."

"Captain," the com-tech said. At the alarm in the young woman's voice, John looked her way. Her eyes were wide with fear. "Vice Skalde Erdstadter at Supremacy Operations Command demands to speak with you immediately."

John looked Kelbacher's way, but all the seergentmeister did was grimace and shrug. "Please monitor this," he asked her, "but don't join in."

To the com-tech, John said. "Put him through."

The man that appeared in John's vision gave him the immediate impression of distinguished older gentleman, with quite a bit of salt in his hair. He smiled and spoke calmly. "Young man, I'm taking remote command of *Drakan Helgis*."

Kelbacher shook her head slowly from side to side and looked uncertain. John had never heard of remote command before, didn't know if it was possible or not. "I'm sorry, maestra, but I don't believe that's legal."

The older man frowned. "What do you know of our ways, Blacksword?"

John carefully avoided sounding impolite or insubordinate. "Probably not very much, maestra." It was time for one hell of a bluff. "But I know quite a bit about your navel regulations. I trained under Captain Taugrim, and she drummed them into me, made me study them quite extensively." That was true, and at the time John had quietly grumbled unhappily about more homework. But he'd never come across anything about *remote command* one way or another. The concept did not exist in the Commonwealth, and he would bet that it didn't exist in the Supremacy either.

Erdstadter's eyes hardened. "Very well, then I'm ordering you to stand down. Put that ship into a parking orbit, and take no action."

John didn't know what to do. He'd been trained to obey orders from a superior officer, and a flag-rank vice skalde was about as superior as they got. If he disobeyed those orders, he'd betray everything he'd learned, everything he'd trained for.

Kelbacher leaned down and whispered in his ear. "He is birth-contracted into the Nvalheim family, has several children and grandchildren that bear that name. His ties to Marta Nvalheim are extensive."

John started, and realized how Marta Nvalheim had always been one step ahead of them. But this one time, pure, dumb luck had made him the wildcard. Thinking again of that firing squad waiting for him, John said, "I'm sorry, maestra, but I can't follow those orders. I will take orders only from someone I know, or from a member of the Executive Council." It occurred to John he would have a lot of debriefing to do with Z-Dog when this was done. He decided to go for broke. "Tell that transfer station, or whatever it is, that if they stand down, return to a standard static orbit, and do not fire upon us, we will not fire upon them."

Erdstadter stared into John's eyes for the longest moment. John decided not to play the game of who blinked first, went ahead and blinked, but returned the man's stare, determined not to be intimidated.

Erdstadter finally nodded. "Very well, Lieutenant, I'll pass those instructions on to them."

John saw the lie in the man's eyes, but would gain nothing if he called him on it. He nodded and smiled politely. "Thank you, maestra."

John killed the circuit and tried not to sound desperate. "Fire Control, watch your defensive stations, we're about to take fire. Engineering, we need full combat status now, and power priority to the shields. Fire Control, target all main batteries on that—"

A gravity spike punched John in the gut. Alarms blared and damage control warnings flashed on John's screens. "Helm, get us moving, head straight for that transfer station."

With the shields taking priority, and still short of full power, they could only push the ship at about a hundred Gs, though that increased with every second the power ramp approached full combat status.

"Fire Control, target their main batteries and do not—I repeat—do not target their power plant or their drive."

In a forced synchronous orbit, sitting stationary four hundred kilometers above the surface of the planet, if they disabled the transfer station's power plant or their grav drive, it would drop like a rock onto the city of Emkeldstadt.

Like John, the tech at Fire Control sounded both frightened and excited. "We have a targeting solution, maestra. But we only have enough power for one bank of batteries."

John almost lost his breakfast as incoming transition shells slammed another gravity spike through the bridge. With their shields now fully powered, and the transfer station fielding only one bank of batteries, no damage alarms sounded, no whooping sirens warned of decompressed compartments.

John would like to concentrate fire from all four of *Drakan Helgis*'s banks of batteries, but until they had full combat status, he didn't have that luxury. One bank would have to do, but at least it would keep the enemy honest.

"Fire Control, on my command, all active batteries . . . fire."

Drakan Helgis's hull thrummed like a massive kettle drum, and the scan tech didn't need anyone to tell him to report. "Direct hit, maestra, but no signs of damage. And we have confirmation that they do have powered shielding."

Another gravity spike punched through the bridge, and John again gulped back his breakfast. It occurred to him that he had eaten that breakfast only a few hours earlier in the hospital.

The tech at Fire Control reported, "We now have power for two banks."

Her words made John realize his mistake. They were effectively firing at point-blank range and they didn't need to approach the enemy. And feeding power into the drive sucked it away from their transition batteries. "Helm, all stop. Fire Control, without the grav drive sucking power, how many active banks do we have now?"

"All four, maestra, and we have a targeting solution."

John wanted to kick himself. "All main batteries, on my command . . . fire."

Again, the boom of the batteries echoed through the hull.

The scan tech reported. "Direct hit and I'm getting a debris field. We damaged them, though I'm not sure how badly."

"Fire Control," John said, "once more, all main batteries, on my command . . . fire."

John ignored the boom in *Drakan Helgis*'s hull and willed the scan-tech to give him good news. The fellow stared at his screens for a long moment, then grinned and nodded. "Direct hit, serious damage this time. And . . . they're moving."

John focused on the scan summary on his screens. Moving slowly, the transfer station had shifted position. Were they changing location to target a different portion of the city? They were also shifting to a lower orbit. A hundred questions raced through his mind.

"Maestra," the scan-tech said, "their emissions profile just dropped off scale. I think we damaged their power plant and it shut down."

With that piece of information, John now understood what he saw on his screens. With their power plant dying, the transfer station had tried to accelerate to orbital velocity to maintain a static orbit, an act of pure desperation. But they had only moved a little before the power plant died, and were now falling at a steep angle into the planet's atmosphere.

"Helm," John demanded, "get us there."

The groan of *Drakan Helgis*'s grav drive vibrated through its decks and bulkheads. They started out limited to about eight hundred Gs, but as Engineering completed their power ramp that grew to ten thousand. They turned over half way there and decelerated. John ordered them to come to a stop two thousand kilometers above Viktorkinde and coast in slowly, all systems on alert and watching closely for danger.

Falling at one G the transfer station accelerated toward the surface of the planet. It didn't hit any serious atmosphere until it reached an altitude of about fifty kilometers, but by that time it had fallen for almost five minutes and was travelling at close to Mach eight. It hadn't been designed to operate in atmosphere and wasn't constructed with any aerodynamic considerations. As it hit thicker atmosphere, a large chunk of it tore away, and the drag produced by a Mach eight air flow ripped away small pieces of the station one after another. Then the station shuddered and it folded down the middle, like closing an old fashioned book. It split into two large pieces, and as drag forces ripped it apart, it rained down onto the city of Emkeldstadt in hundreds of fragments large and small.

36

Undeniable Message

LOOKING DOWN THE muzzles of four assault rifles Nikaela froze, and not for a nanosecond did she consider trying to draw her grav pistol. The four kriegers stepped out of the lift and surrounded her. Two of them disarmed her, removing the pistol and holster, along with the butcher's dagger and its harness, then handed them to their leader, a female oberseergent. They didn't cuff her, but two of them gripped her elbows and locked them painfully behind her back.

The oberseergent showed no expression on her face as she looked Nikaela in the eyes. "Bring her."

They hustled her into the lift, then down to the ground floor. They marched her down a long hallway, then into a large garage with several vehicles parked neatly in a row, but with room for many more. The wound in her hip slowed her down as they crossed the concrete floor of the garage, and by the time they reached a cluster of offices, they supported her by her armpits and dragged her feet across the floor. They dragged her down a corridor and into an office. When they finally stopped, she managed to get her feet beneath her, though without the two kriegers sandwiching her between them, she couldn't have stood on her own. They had stopped next to a table littered with the remnants of a couple of field-ration packs. In front of her stood an old woman, almost ancient in appearance.

Nikaela's face had begun to swell, partially closing one eye, but even then she had no trouble recognizing Marta Nvalheim. The matriarch of a wealthy family, in recent months the woman's reputation had mutated from famous to infamous.

The old woman grinned unpleasantly and looked Nikaela up and down. Nikaela expected her to rant and rave, but instead she spoke calmly, almost softly. "It's the breschkada-se! We finally meet, Mistress Vreekande."

Silas Palmutter stood behind the old woman, his eyes blinking as he looked at Nikaela, then at Nvalheim. He stepped forward to stand beside the old woman. "Just kill her. She and that breshakuda young man of hers know too much. Just kill her, dammit."

Nvalheim stared at Nikaela as she shook her head sadly and spoke. "It's too late for that, Silas. They've already connected the dots. They know you're as guilty as me when it comes to that Novalis III debacle. And given time they'll connect the dots to Machtberg and Strikland as well, though Aubrecht thinks if you and I die first, they won't learn the truth about him, but he's a fool."

Nikaela tried to process what she had just heard. Had it been an open admission by Nvalheim that she, Palmutter, Machtberg and Strikland were guilty when it came to that tragedy? But then she realized Nvalheim would not have spoken those words in front of Nikaela if she intended to let her live out the day, and her heart raced.

The female oberseergent tossed the pistol and butcher's dagger onto the table, both tightly wrapped in their harnesses. "She was wearing these."

Nvalheim's head slowly pivoted and her eyes settled on the butcher's dagger. She picked it up and carefully uncoiled the harness wrapped around it, then pulled the dagger from the sheath. Looking into Nikaela's eyes she smiled. "You, and this,"—she glanced at the dagger, then back to Nikaela—"have been a problem for some time now, and I have to think of a way to remove you from the equation. What were you thinking; breschkada with a common-face, a ComSecCorps soldier . . ." She hesitated for a long moment, gripped the amulet suspended from her neck and shook her head. ". . . a Blacksword?"

"Dammit," Palmutter said. "Just fucking kill the little slut."

Still holding the dagger, Nvalheim looked his way. "Interesting choice of words, Silas. I suppose to you all women are sluts. Was your own mother a slut, and is that why you view all woman so? Or perhaps you're the slut. I've noticed that flawed people frequently accuse everyone else of their own faults."

His upper lip curled into a snarl. "Fuck off, Marta."

She grinned at Nikaela. "I think I struck a nerve."

"God damn it," he snarled, "why don't you just kill her and be done with it?"

Nvalheim looked carefully at the butcher's dagger in her hand. "I can't kill her, Silas. The ramifications of a Kelk killing a Kelk breschkada . . ." She shook her head. "No, I can't kill her. On the other hand—"

She reversed the dagger, holding it by the hilt with the blade protruding from her fist, then she slammed it down point-first into the table top. She released it, and it stood upright on its own, the point buried in the table. She stepped back and looked at Palmutter. "Since you so desperately want to see her dead, why don't you just kill her and be done with it?"

Nvalheim had stepped out of the way, leaving an open path between Palmutter, the blade, and Nikaela. Palmutter's eyes widened, and he looked at Nikaela, then at the blade still quivering in the table top, then again at Nikaela. Anger clouded his features, and he radiated fear like heat from a hot brand.

"No," Nikaela shouted, struggling and frantically trying to pull free of the two kriegers, but they responded by tightening their grips on her elbows.

Palmutter extended a shaking hand toward the blade, but stopped inches short of it, as if he feared the thing might contaminate him in some way. A strange sound came out of his throat, a faint whine, almost a plea for help. Nikaela tried again to break free of the two kriegers. Palmutter looked at her and the anger fell away from his face, leaving only fear.

He lunged for the blade and pulled on it, but his first attempt failed to dislodge it. "Ah," he cried, grunting with effort, and pulled it free. In a single motion he stepped forward, crossing the short distance between them, and thrust out with the blade. A sharp lance of pain shot through Nikaela's gut and chest, but when she tried to cry out, the agony blossomed ten-fold, and all she could do was take short, choppy breaths. Palmutter stepped away from her, leaving the blade buried just below her rib cage, his eyes filled with fear and hate.

He looked at the blade buried in her chest, his eyes frantically darting about the room. He held up his hands as if to deny what he had just done, then stepped back several paces, emitting strange little whimpers.

Nikaela tried to breathe in rapid, shallow gasps as Nvalheim stepped forward, looked carefully at the blade protruding from her chest, and shook her head. "Silas, you can't even kill someone properly. You stabbed her in the diaphragm, didn't even angle the blade upward toward her heart, and quite possibly didn't hit anything vital. She may live for hours."

She reached out and put a finger beneath Nikaela's chin, then forced her gaze upward so their eyes met. "On the other hand, the medical people tell us we shouldn't remove a blade from a stab wound like that. The blade itself might be preventing arterial blood loss, and if I pulled it from the wound you might bleed to death. But if I were completely ignorant of those little medical facts and removed it to save your life, when you died I wouldn't be the one who killed you, would I?"

She wrapped her fingers around the hilt protruding from Nikaela's chest and smiled. "You sealed your own fate that night on Reisenar."

In that moment the unmistakable sound of a sonic boom rocked the building and the ground shook.

Nvalheim looked upward toward the ceiling; she released the hilt without pulling it, then closed her eyes, obviously listening to her implants. "What?" she shouted. "*Drakan Helgis*? That's not possible."

She turned to the NCO. "Bring her."

Nvalheim stormed out of the room, and as the two kriegers dragged Nikaela in her wake, she could not have stood on her feet even had she tried. Following Nvalheim, they half-carried Nikaela out of the office complex, then across the main floor of the garage, and out through the entrance into the sunlight outside.

Still sucking air in short choppy breaths, Nikaela looked out over the city. Another sonic boom hit her, and she watched a large piece of some sort of structure slice out of the sky and slam into some buildings about a kilometer away.

Nvalheim turned to face her. "It's him, him and *Drakan Helgis*. He's been a curse upon the entire Supremacy since that night you didn't kill him on Reisenar. And now it's time to end this once and for all."

She spun toward the NCO. "Bring them, bring all the prisoners. Bring them out here immediately."

She leaned down and put her nose a fraction of an inch from Nikaela's. "I know what'll get him down here. I know exactly what will bring him to me. And then I'll finish this."

••••

John tried to ignore the pain radiating from his arm. "Helm, put us in a forced synchronous orbit five hundred kilometers above the Hyvaldsborg Palace. We need to see what's going on down there."

Five minutes later, *Drakan Helgis* hovered in almost the same position the fake transfer station had occupied earlier.

"And we need to watch our backside too. I don't know what might come at us, but we have to be ready for anything. If one of those gunboats decides to make a suicide run, they could put a big warhead up our ass if we weren't ready for them."

The scan-tech came up with the idea of splitting their drones into two groups. They sent four of them to a point ten thousand kilometers off Viktorkinde, where they put them into a complex spherical orbit with a baseline of five thousand kilometers. That gave them fairly accurate eyes on all the space in and around the Viktorkinde system. They put the other two drones into a simple circular orbit around *Drakan Helgis*, which gave them extremely high resolution when looking at the planet's surface a mere five hundred kilometers beneath them. They could literally resolve the faces of people walking the streets, though with columns of black smoke rising from dozens of locations inside Emkeldstadt, the streets of the city were deserted.

Once again, the summaries on John's screens were just not enough. "Scan, what have we got down there?"

The scan-tech stared intently at his screens with the look of one who needed to integrate data from his implants with that in front of his eyes. "It's real quiet, maestra, two heavy assault boats circling the palace, a couple of gunboats in orbit, and eight of them patrolling the airspace above the city. No traffic on the streets within about ten kilometers of the palace, and for that matter only the occasional pedestrian. I've identified gun emplacements on the roof of the palace and scattered around its grounds."

John assumed the assault boats operated under orders from Nvalheim. The gunboats would be taking orders from Operations Command, which meant Erdstadter, but that didn't mean their crews were fanatics like those two maniacs. They could simply be obeying orders and were just as fearful and confused as the rest of them. And he wasn't about to blow them out of the sky based on an assumption. If he was wrong, he'd be killing innocent people. "Have you fed those coordinates to Fire Control?"

"Yes, maestra."

"Fire Control," John said, "do not act on that information, at least not yet."

John needed to be in contact with whoever had control of the palace, friend or foe. "Com, see if you can raise—"

"Captain," the scan-tech said. The urgency in his voice got John's immediate attention. "Two gunboats just appeared over the Viktorkinde horizon, and two more are dropping down from Viktorkinde Prime. All four are pushing thirty Gs, which is about the limit for those boats."

"Fire Control," John said, "if any of them fire upon us, return fire and target all four boats. Com, warn them off. Tell them if they cut drive and reverse course we will not—"

"Incoming," the scan tech shouted.

The secondaries and defensive stations responded immediately and opened fire. It didn't produce the kettle-drum sound of the main batteries, was more like a harsh grind echoing through the hull. A new sun appeared just above Viktorkinde, and John's implants said, "Extra atmospheric detonation. Estimated yield strength one megaton." Then the unmistakable sound of *Drakan Helgis*'s main batteries drowned out everything else. And where a moment earlier four gunboats had been driving hard toward them, now four debris fields coasted with inherited velocity, dispersing further with each second.

John waited so the people doing the real work could do their jobs: the scan-tech watching closely to identify anything more that came at them; Fire Control on edge, ready to respond if something did.

"Captain," the com-tech said, "Vice Skalde Erdstadter wishes to speak to you."

John took a breath and tried to calm his nerves. "Put him through."

This time the distinguished older gentleman appeared in John's vision as if seated across a table from him. Erdstadter smiled as if at some private joke. "Do you understand what you've done, young man?"

John shrugged. "So far I've delayed the illegal overthrow of the lawful government of the Kelk Supremacy. Next, I have to try to stop it all together."

Erdstadter shook his head and his eyes hardened. "This isn't your fight."

John wanted to shout at the man, but he forced himself to speak calmly. "You made it my fight."

Erdstadter leaned toward John and pointed a finger at him. "You murdered innocent Kelk citizens. You—"

John cut him off. "Innocent? I'm not so sure about that. Murder, I know a lot more about murder than you might think. I grew up on murder. I grew up on Novalis III."

By that time, that piece of information was common knowledge, but occasionally someone needed to be reminded of it. Erdstadter flinched, but quickly composed himself. "Before this day is out I'm going to stand you up in front of a firing squad."

John had learned long ago not to make threats, idle or otherwise. "Be that as it may, you have five minutes to ground all your gunboats, because after five minutes *Drakan Helgis* is going to open up with her main batteries on anything in the air above Emkeldstadt, and ground them the hard way."

Erdstadter hesitated and sat in silence for a moment staring at John. Then he seemed to come to a decision. "I have a message for you from Marta Nvalheim. Look closely at the east side of the Hyvaldsborg Palace. Look very closely."

Erdstadter cut the signal and he disappeared.

The fellow's message bothered John, and he suspected he was about to learn something unpleasant. "Scan, what's on the east side of the palace? Look closely, ultra-high resolution."

"Yes, maestra." John waited for several seconds, then the young man said, "Maestra, I don't know what this means. I'm transmitting an image to you now."

John closed his eyes to take in the image sent to his implants. He had parked *Drakan Helgis* directly above the palace, giving him a view straight down from above. It appeared that a large crowd had gathered on the east side of the building. About them stood a ring of armed guards, perhaps a dozen kriegers carrying assault rifles—no heavy combat armor.

John keyed his implants to zoom in closer and noted that the crowd was shaped like a donut, a ring of people surrounding an open area. He zoomed in closer, and in the ring he spotted Primatov, Catarvin, Gascoigne, Kristdokar, three members of the Executive Council, Taugrim and the officers of *Drakan Helgis*, Macus DeLeon, Machtberg, Strikland, just about everyone who mattered in this game, and some who didn't. They all stood in a circle with Marta Nvalheim standing in the middle of the open space. Nikaela lay on her back at Nvalheim's feet, much of her clothing soaked with blood. Nvalheim stood looking upward, shaking her fist at him, delivering a message he already knew: she would remain defiant to the end.

37

Hidden Allies

AS MARTA NVALHEIM stood over Nikaela and shook her fist at the sky, Anders desperately tried to think of some way to help the young woman. He considered killing Nvalheim in a suicidal assault, but she wore light combat armor, so he'd have to get close to make sure he didn't simply wound her. And two of her younger kinsmen hovered near her at all times, both reputed to be quite loyal to their clan, but not as fanatical as her. Anytime someone who was not a close confidant or lieutenant approached Nvalheim, both young men tensed and grew quite suspicious.

When Nvalheim finished her show and they hustled the prisoners back into the garage, from a quick head count Anders learned there were only a dozen guards herding the captives. With guards on the roof of the palace and dispersed around the grounds, her limited forces were clearly spread thin.

Taugrim and her officers were kept in hand irons at all times, but not leg irons, and a long plast tether looped through their arms kept them bunched. None of the other prisoners were guarded so closely, probably because Taugrim had thwarted Nvalheim's most recent attempt to disrupt the diplomatic mission. Anders held back and kept an eye on the guard overseeing them, and again he noticed that once they were settled, because of the way the office complex had been constructed, many of *Drakan Helgis*'s officers were not visible from much of the garage floor.

Hovering nearby with nothing to do could prove to be dangerous, so he turned about and walked away. He passed a krieger going in the opposite direction headed toward the *Drakan Helgis* prisoners. Anders continued walking but glanced over his shoulder. The fellow stopped and had a few words with the guard standing over Taugrim, then the guard handed him something—probably keys to the manacles. Then the krieger took over from the guard overseeing the prisoners while the old guard walked away. Anders had just witnessed one guard relieving another.

As Anders crossed the garage floor contemplating what he had seen, a female command hawk approached him with two female kriegers in tow. "Maestra Eindride, we need your help. The Vreekande woman killed three guards two floors up. Please take charge of these two and clean the mess up. They know what to do."

The two kriegers led Anders down a long hall to a bank of elevators, then up two floors where three bodies lay sprawled in the hall in front of the lifts. All three had been shot and were long dead.

One of Anders's two kriegers carried a duffel bag rolled up in a tight bundle. She opened it, they stripped the three bodies of their weapons, and stuffed them into the duffel. Then Anders helped drag the three bodies into a nearby office and dump them there. The two kriegers gave Anders the duffel full of weapons, then took up positions guarding the bank of elevators.

Anders asked them, "What do I do with this, hand it over to someone?"

Both kriegers looked confused as one of them said, "I don't know."

That response produced the seed of a plan. Anders took the lift down, but got off one floor below. He encountered a couple of guards there as well, but he outranked both of them by quite a bit and neither of them hindered or questioned him as he walked out of the lift carrying the duffel. Once out of sight he found a supply closet and hid the three sidearms high on a shelf, along with spare ammunition magazines and holsters. The assault rifles were too bulky for his purposes, so he carried them in the duffel down to the garage. He went to the office complex, found the command hawk, and asked her what to do with the weapons they had recovered. She pointed to a corner and said, "Just dump them there. We're too busy to worry about them now."

He did so, and as he stepped out of the office complex he thought he'd have to find another duffel. And it occurred to him he should slip away, make his way back to that doctor's office. He had dumped one functional pistol in a trash receptacle nearby, and that might come in handy.

••••

From the instant John saw Marta Nvalheim defiantly shaking her fist at him, he had no choice but to go down there and face her. His memory of his mother, father and sister demanded it of him, and twenty million dead countrymen demanded it of him as well. He knew he must face her, and Nvalheim knew it too. But there would be a lot of opposition from certain people.

"Com, send that image to Lieutenant Forrester, Sergeant Nigurski, and Corporal Caputto. And tell Lieutenant Forrester to get her platoon aboard our assault boats and stand by for a high G drop to the Hyvaldsborg Palace."

John scanned the faces on the bridge and saw a lot of uncertainty in the looks they gave him. "Helm, take us down to an altitude of two hundred kilometers, and hold forced synchronous orbit there."

Reducing the range to target increased Fire Control's accuracy. At two hundred kilometers they could target their opponents with surgical precision. "Fire Control, when I give the order, destroy those two assault boats circling the palace, and take out all the gun emplacements. I want you to be as surgical as possible: main batteries for the assault boats, and secondaries for everything else. And Mistress Forrester and her team will need close air support for their boats during that drop. Scan, what's the status of Operations Command's gunboats?"

"They all went to ground, maestra."

John had seen that on his scan summary, but needed confirmation. "Fire Control, going forward, if any of them lift off the ground, target them immediately with our main batteries and remove them from the equation."

"Yes, maestra."

John unstrapped from the command console and stood. "Seergentmeister Kelbacher, please come with me."

She frowned.

With her following, he walked the short distance to the entrance to the bridge, and stopped in a small recess at the entry hatch. He turned to face her and lowered his voice. "I have to go down there and face her in person."

A Commonwealth NCO or officer would have argued with him. She simply said, "I understand that."

"Then you have to help me."

"Of course."

There was no *of course* about it, because she didn't understand what he was about to ask of her. "I need you to be my XO. I need you to take the conn of this ship while I'm down there."

Her eyes widened and she sucked in a quick breath. "I can't do that. I'm not an officer."

He grinned without humor. "And I'm not Kelk, but I'm in command of a Kelk warship."

In the Commonwealth, senior NCOs were given the same command codes as any officer, which theoretically gave them the ability to command a warship. But the Kelk had a much more restrictive delineation between officers and NCOs.

John opened up a secure link between their implants.

Her eyes hardened with anger. "What are you doing?"

Another difference between the Commonwealth and the Supremacy was that, as an officer John had push access to limited portions of her implants. Without asking permission he uploaded the full catalog of *Drakan Helgis*'s command codes to her non-volatile memory cache.

"I've just given you the command codes of this ship. I don't have time to help you with it, so you'll have to sort it out on your own. Now come with me."

John walked back to the command console with her following. He stopped there and scanned the faces of the crewmembers on the bridge. "I've just promoted Seergentmeister Kelbacher to warrant command boss, and she is now the XO of this ship."

John knew for a certainty that such a promotion would not be legal in the Commonwealth, and was pretty certain it wasn't legal in the Supremacy either. But he only needed the crew to pretend for about an hour, and after that, fuck it all.

He turned to Kelbacher and saluted her in the Kelk fashion. "Command Boss Kelbacher, you have the conn."

He didn't wait for her response but immediately turned away from her and walked off the bridge. On the deck below he headed straight for the lift, called it and programmed it for Hangar Deck. When the lift doors opened May, Carla, and Leeze stood just outside the lift waiting for him, their visors dilated. A couple of Kelk non-com's stood behind them. The looks on their faces made it clear the com-tech had sent the images to all of them.

May stepped forward and shouted, "I know you. You think you're going to go down there and confront that raving bitch face to face. Well no, you're not going down there with us."

John kept his voice calm and even. "Kristdokar uncovered irrefutable evidence that Nvalheim and Palmutter were complicit in the fuck-up on Novalis III."

Leeze apparently agreed with May. "There's no fucking way you're going down there to face that maniac-bitch, Johnny-boy."

Carla shook her head and spoke a lot more calmly than the other two. "No. You're both wrong. There's no fucking way he can't go down there. He has to."

At that point everyone shouted at everyone else. John keyed his implants and contacted the com-tech on the bridge. "Can you sound the alert klaxon just here on Hangar Deck, and do it really loud?"

The klaxon screamed with such volume John thought they all might need to have their hearing repaired when this was done, if any of them lived to do so. When John's friends finally shut up and stood there staring at him, he told the com-tech, "Enough," and the klaxon went silent.

May and Leeze both stared daggers at him.

He hoped that somehow they would understand. "This is between Nvalheim and me. It's always been that way, and that's the way it has to be. It doesn't matter if I live or die. I have to go down there, and I have to finish this."

A female Kelk non-com nodded. "Vendetta requires it."

One of her comrades frowned at her. "He can't claim right of vendetta. He ain't Kelk. They'd just kill him."

She answered him with a shrug, though that didn't work well in full combat armor. "Not if he kills her first."

"I have to go down there and kill her," John said, "but there's no reason I can't clean up the playing field first. And no one said I couldn't bring along an entire platoon of dregkraag in full combat armor."

May and Leeze looked none too happy. Carla displayed a big flashy grin.

The seats on the assault boats could be adjusted to accommodate full combat armor, a small child, or anything in between. And with the boats packed full of dregkraag in armor, they simply didn't have a place for John. But unlike Commonwealth boats, the Kelk pilot and copilot were not dregkraag and did not wear armor, so for the drop John displaced the copilot in one boat.

As John buckled into his seat, his implants came to life with a message from Kelbacher. "Captain, we're stable in forced synchronous orbit at two hundred kilometers above the palace. Fire Control has mapped out all targets in the vicinity of the palace and is prepared to execute."

The boat had a feed from *Drakan Helgis*'s high resolution scan systems, and John keyed his implants into it. "Tell them to execute."

Drakan Helgis's main batteries roared once with that characteristic kettle-drum sound. Nvalheim's two assault boats literally disintegrated and rained down on the palace in pieces. Then the warship's secondaries opened up and one by one surgically eliminated the gun emplacements on and around the palace.

John didn't wait for them to finish the job. He looked at the pilot in the seat next to him. "Let's drop."

For a brief period of time John had nothing to do but be a passenger, and it was at moments like that that the pain in his arm and leg came to the forefront of his thoughts. It was getting worse, and it occurred to him that he should have given some priority to seeing that medic again. But it was too late for that now.

As the boat's docking boom ejected it from *Drakan Helgis*'s Hangar Deck, John reached across with his right hand to his left thigh and touched the hilt of the butcher's dagger. For some reason, that gave him comfort.

The pilots of *Drakan Helgis*'s two assault boats didn't push them to their maximum drive of thirty Gs, but held them at twenty where they could still compensate internally. But even at twenty it only took thirty seconds to cross half the distance to the ground, where they flipped over and decelerated. But at that point they were traveling close to orbital velocity, and they probably made a hell of a racket as they boomed through the atmosphere to the palace, leaving two ionization trails behind them.

As the Kelk pilot slowed the boat to hover a hundred meters off the ground, he looked at John and grinned. "I just love doing that."

Pilots were pretty much the same everywhere.

The other boat diverted to the roof of the palace and dropped off two squads with heavy gun emplacement teams. Then both boats settled to the lawn about a hundred meters from the garage entrance, opened the large hatches in their sides, and May's platoon spilled out of them, double-timing it to set up a closed perimeter around the palace.

John waited for everyone in bulky combat armor to exit the boat before making his way aft. When he stepped out of the hatch onto the lawn, May stood there waiting for him, her visor dilated. She held a holstered grav pistol in her right gauntlet and extended it toward him. "At least take this."

He shook his head. "They'll just take it away from me."

"Dammit," she said, "then let us go in and clean the place out."

Again he shook his head. "She'll kill the entire diplomatic mission before you can get to them, and then she'll have what she wants: interstellar war. No, we have to do this her way."

A funny thought occurred to him. "I guess it's my way too."

Another thought occurred to him, but not a funny one. "If the signal from my implants shuts down, you know I'm dead. Immediately execute a hard-target assault on the building, and try to save as many lives as possible. But do me one favor, make sure Nvalheim doesn't survive."

Leeze came online. "You better not fucking die on us, Johnny-boy."

He smiled at May. "I'll try not to."

He stepped around May and limped toward the gaping entrance of the garage.

●●●●

When *Drakan Helgis* changed the rules of Nvalheim's game, Anders had a couple of things working in his favor. While most of the old woman's people didn't know him by name, he had been seen in her presence a couple of times and had become a familiar face wearing a blue armband. And with the destroyer now controlling the airspace above the city, uncertainty had everyone concerned the *new* Supremacy they hoped to inaugurate might not come to pass.

Anders returned to the office complex. With Nvalheim's people hustling everyone out onto the main floor of the garage, it was basically deserted. As he had hoped, the duffel with the assault rifles remained where he had left it. With the situation rapidly developing, he decided to take the chance it had been completely forgotten in the confusion. He picked it up, slung it over his shoulder, and walked out of the office complex, moving briskly as if he had some assigned duty he must hurry to.

Everyone out on the garage floor was in motion, and no one questioned him as he crossed to the doors that led into the palace proper. He used the lift to return to the floor above, where the guard there had now been reduced to only one krieger.

The fellow demanded, "What's going on?"

Anders gave him a worried look. "The shit's hitting the fan. They've got me running errands, so I'm just doing what I'm told and trying to keep my head down."

Anders returned to the supply closet where he'd stashed the sidearms and shoved them back into the duffel. Then he made a side trip to the three guards Mistress Vreekande had killed at the bank of elevators and stripped them of their armbands. He made his way back to the doctor's office where he had killed Thoran, Kristensen and the command eagle. He retrieved the one sidearm he had tossed in the trash receptacle, but more importantly, he recovered two more blue armbands.

He left his own sidearm in its holster and did a quick check of one of the others. Then he slung the duffel over his shoulder, and gripping the grav pistol tightly he hid it between the duffel and his body. He headed back to the bank of elevators.

As he approached the lone guard there, he tried to sound frightened. "Anything happen while I was gone?"

The fellow glanced fearfully at the elevator doors, and Anders shot him in the side of his head. One more assault rifle, one more grav pistol, one more blue armband. The damn duffel was getting awfully heavy.

38

Confrontation

WHEN *DRAKAN HELGIS'S* guns went silent, a strange, anticipatory stillness settled over everyone in the garage. Of Nvalheim's forces only a dozen or so guards remained to support her grab for the reins of the Supremacy.

"I told you she'd want to gloat."

Katrine tried to focus on Haugrund's words, but couldn't, her mind awash in a sea of pain. It was imperative that she conserve her energy for the ordeal to come, because if Nvalheim failed and somehow John Mathius survived, Katrine had an important role to play. Someone must help John draw the line at where to stop the killing.

She watched as a couple of Nvalheim's flunkies placed Nikaela Vreekande's stretcher on the concrete floor about thirty paces inside the garage entrance, the hilt of the dagger still protruding from just below her rib cage, her breathing nothing more than short, staccato gasps.

Catarvin rushed out and sat down on the concrete floor next to Nikaela, still holding that little clutch purse gripped tightly against her breast. She took one of Nikaela's hands and caressed it gently. "Oh you poor girl. You poor girl." At least she had the presence of mind to leave the blade in the wound.

Nvalheim marched forward and stopped facing the garage entrance, standing triumphantly over the young woman like the victor in some gladiatorial contest. Apparently the old woman didn't object to Catarvin's actions, probably because a distraught woman fretting over a dying girl fulfilled some aspect of the twisted scene she wanted to play out. Or perhaps she felt even more victorious standing over a senator of the Commonwealth.

"Yes, Dortea, you did warn us about her."

Katrine glanced to her left where Haugrund and Tiegnordan stood discussing the tableau in front of them. Next to them, Nygaard sat in a chair, her color a little pale, even for a Kelk. And behind her stood Kristdokar, a nasty bruise on her cheek.

Nvalheim had grouped the surviving members of the Executive Council with those of the Commonwealth diplomatic mission, though Obradour and Palmutter were exceptions to that rule. Tarsik Obradour was still alive, but in no shape to join the festivities in the garage, and Silas Palmutter stood with Nvalheim's flunkies. As far as Katrine was concerned, that only confirmed the evidence of his guilt. Gascoigne and Thealone stood next to Katrine.

Aubrecht Machtberg, Lawrence Strikland, Macus DeLeon and Faith Carlton made up a third group standing not far away. Taugrim and her officers formed a fourth group, but they had been isolated on the other side of the garage, with many of them hidden behind a section of the office complex that jutted out from the wall of the garage. For a moment Katrine thought she saw Anders Eindride carrying a heavy duffel slung over one shoulder and crossing the floor toward them, but the pain clouded her thinking enough that she was probably mistaken about that.

"Colonel Primatov."

At the sound of Tiegnordan's voice, Katrine looked her way. The councilor seemed calmly detached from their situation. "Colonel, you know that young man better than anyone else. Will he come to confront Nvalheim?"

Katrine nodded. "Most certainly."

Haugrund closed her eyes and shook her head sadly. "She'll want him to beg."

Katrine shook her head. "He won't."

"She'll do everything she can to make him."

"He still won't."

Haugrund sighed. "Good. The longer he holds out, the longer it'll take her to get around to killing us."

It was then that Katrine realized the three councilors had surrendered to the situation. They assumed Nvalheim had won, but a catalyst wildcard named John Mathius was still in play on the game board, and Katrine had learned to never discount that young man.

Haugrund said, "She knows he's not going to let her out of here alive, but she's still won."

Tiegnordan frowned uncertainly. "How so?"

Haugrund looked quite sad. "She'll get what she wants. She doesn't care about her own life. She just wants interstellar war, because that will keep the Kelk bloodlines pure and unadulterated. At least that's what she believes."

Katrine focused on Catarvin who sat beside Nikaela, tears streaming down her cheeks. Since hearing of Catarvin's betrayal and possible complicity in the Novalis III mess, Katrine had struggled with that information, and she just couldn't believe it. She still wondered if anyone had bothered to search that little clutch purse, and she decided to go with her gut on the plump little woman.

Katrine happened to be looking at the entrance to the garage when the silhouette of a young man stepped into view, his features hidden by the glare of the bright sunshine behind him. He walked forward with a limp, one arm clutched tightly to his side.

••••

The interior of the garage was well lit, but the change in contrast from the bright sunlight outside momentarily blinded John. He stopped to give his eyes a few seconds to adjust, and then took in the tableau before him.

Nvalheim had carefully orchestrated the scene. About thirty paces directly in front of John she stood facing him, Nikaela and Catarvin at her feet. Behind her on the left stood a small group consisting of Machtberg, Strikland, DeLeon and the blonde whose name John couldn't remember. Behind Nvalheim and to the right stood some of the Executive Council and much of the diplomatic mission. When he saw that Primatov's left arm ended above the elbow in a blood-soaked bandage, he grimaced. She smiled at him, but she looked pale and drawn.

Directly behind Nvalheim, Palmutter stood with a couple of young kriegers. His eyes met John's for the briefest of instants, then darted away, casting about the room like prey in the presence of a large predator.

As John walked toward Nvalheim, he tried to keep his limp to a minimum because the room was full of predators, the kind who preyed on weakness. About twenty paces from them Nvalheim bent down and for the first time John noticed something protruding from Nikaela's chest just below the rib cage. Nvalheim gripped it, pulled and stood, revealing to John that she held a butcher's dagger, a blade she had just withdrawn from Nikaela's chest. That confirmed what John already knew: neither he nor Nikaela would live through the day.

Catarvin reacted by pressing her hands on the wound, and looking over her shoulder at John.

John needed to live long enough to accomplish one clear and well defined goal: kill Nvalheim and Palmutter.

He crossed the distance to the stretcher on which Nikaela lay. She looked up at him and smiled, her breaths coming in short, rapid gasps. Blood welled up freely from the wound in her chest, soaking Catarvin's hands. John sat down on the concrete floor next to the senator, lifted Nikaela's head and placed it in his lap.

"Dammit," Catarvin shouted, looking up at Nvalheim. "Do something for the poor girl."

John looked up at Nvalheim. "Please help her."

The old woman simply smiled.

As a young kid on Novalis III, John had learned to put pride aside. "I'll beg, if that's what you want."

Nvalheim's eyebrows rose and she grinned. "I would dearly like to see a Black-sword beg, so go ahead."

John saw her answer in her eyes. "But you won't help her?"

She shook her head. "No."

Nikaela coughed, spraying him with blood. "John."

She tried to speak, so he bent down and put his ear close to her lips. He could barely hear her words. "Nvalheim . . . Palmutter . . . Machtberg . . . Strikland . . . all guilty . . . Novalis . . . Old woman . . . admitted it."

He looked her in the eyes and she stuck her tongue out at him. "See . . . not . . . forked."

He smiled.

She smiled back at him, and for a few seconds she spoke clearly. "Fucked 'em, John. Fucked 'em all. Fucked 'em good." Then the life went out of her eyes, and the blood stopped welling from her chest. Her jaw muscles relaxed, her mouth opened, and her last breath escaped her chest with a gurgling wheeze. He leaned down, kissed her gently and tasted blood.

John looked up at Nvalheim and wanted to kill; start with her, then work his way up to Palmutter, Machtberg, and finish with Strikland. Just kill. Vendetta? Yah, he'd show them what vendetta meant. He'd show them all what it meant. He could probably get Nvalheim, and maybe even Palmutter, before they killed him. But his desire for vengeance must have shown on his face, because the two young kriegers behind Nvalheim tensed. He should have remained calm, not broadcast his intent that way, and in doing so he'd given up what little chance he might have had of getting that vengeance. He tried to calm his racing heart.

Catarvin looked up at Nvalheim and shouted, "Why did you do this to her?" She stood up to face the old woman, clutching a little purse to her breast as if it meant more to her than Nikaela's life.

Nvalheim looked at the butcher's dagger in her hand. "I didn't stab her. I'd be a fool to kill a Kelk breschkada. The populous would crucify me. No, it was Silas who stabbed her."

Behind her Palmutter took a step forward. "Why did you tell her that? You didn't have to tell her that."

Frowning, Catarvin shook her head. "Silas, you murdered that pretty, young girl? You murdered her? Why?"

He rushed forward and stopped an arm's length from Catarvin with Nikaela between them. "She was an animal."

Catarvin continued to shake her head as if to deny the reality in front of her. "You murdered her. Just like that you murdered her?"

She looked down at her hands. They were soaked with Nikaela's blood, as was the little purse and the front of her blouse. "Oh dear, I think I've smeared my makeup."

With her hands trembling, she opened the purse and reached into it. But she hesitated with her hand in the purse and looked at Palmutter. "Silas, I can't allow you to commit murder with impunity, not when you take the life of such an innocent."

The end of the purse exploded and Palmutter staggered back a step, a bright red stain blossoming in the middle of his chest. Nvalheim cringed away from Catarvin as the two kriegers next to her reached for their sidearms. The plump, little woman removed her hand from the purse, and in it she held a tiny pistol. She raised the pistol, aimed it at Palmutter's face, and a blast of smoke and fire erupted from the barrel. The back of Palmutter's head exploded, and he toppled to the concrete, landed with a crash, raising a small flurry of dust.

As the two kriegers cleared their weapons from their holsters, Catarvin raised her hands in surrender. One hand held the little purse, and the other the small gun. She tossed the pistol aside as the kriegers aimed their sidearms at her, but Nvalheim shouted, "Hold your fire."

Catarvin smiled at the old woman. "The little gun is only good for two bullets, then it's useless,"—she nodded toward Palmutter, lying lifeless on the floor—"much like him, though he never had more than one bullet in his weapon."

Still holding the butcher's dagger, Nvalheim pointed it at John. "Seize him."

••••

As John Mathius took his first steps into the garage, Anders walked toward Taugrim and her officers with the heavy duffel slung over his right shoulder. He held the trench knife gripped in his right hand and hidden in a fold of the duffel.

Seated on the floor, Taugrim's eyes flicked his way as he walked toward her, but she remained otherwise motionless. Standing over her, the guard nodded to Anders as he approached. "What they got you doing now?"

"Shit work," Anders said. He jiggled the duffel bag on his shoulder. "And this fucking thing weighs a ton."

At that moment Anders stood between the guard and Taugrim, which allowed him to give her a glimpse of the trench knife while keeping it hidden from the guard. She blinked her eyes once.

"Dump that thing on the floor," the guard said. "You can stand here with me and enjoy the show."

Anders took his time pulling the strap off his shoulder and lowering the duffel to the floor. He put it down just inside the blind spot created by the cluster of offices. He stood with the guard on his left, the trench knife hidden tightly against his right thigh.

He didn't think he'd have a problem killing the fellow, but doing so without being seen by others in the garage was a different matter. And then the loud report of a gun-shot echoed through the large space.

The guard next to him tensed and craned his neck, his focus on Nvalheim and the drama unfolding at the center of the garage.

Anders swung the trench knife low in front of him, bringing it up and stabbing it into the guard's solar plexus just beneath his ribs. The fellow grunted and fell, but Taugrim and one of her people had moved in the same instant as Anders and got to their feet in time to catch him. Anders barely managed to catch the man's assault rifle before it clattered to the concrete floor.

He hissed at Taugrim, "Get him out of sight while I take his place."

Anders stood up straight and casually rested the assault rifle in the crook of his arm. Then he tried to look like a bored guard as Taugrim and one of her people dragged the guard into the blind spot and finished him off.

Anders stood there pretending to watch the main show in the center of the garage, hoping that anyone who glanced his way would see a Kelk soldier in a uniform holding a rifle, and wouldn't look close enough to realize he wasn't the guard who was supposed to be there. While two of Taugrim's people searched the guard for the manacle keys, Anders hissed, "Take the guard's armband, and there's a half dozen more in the duffel, along with assault rifles and pistols. Use the armbands to get some people in better positions to take out the remaining guards. We don't open fire until I give the order."

Had he not been cashiered, Taugrim would certainly outrank him, and someone might think he shouldn't be giving the orders. But that was his past, and this was his show, so they could fuck off.

39

Vendetta

AT NVALHEIM'S ORDERS to seize him, two young kriegers stepped around Nikaela's stretcher, neither of them looking terribly confident at the moment. They gripped John by his elbows and armpits and hefted him to his feet. Then they hustled him around the stretcher and stood him up in front of Nvalheim. She held Nikaela's bloodied dagger in her right hand, but her left hand clutched at some sort of medallion suspended from her neck by a chain.

"Blacksword," she said. "It's an auspicious day, don't you think? In a short span of time I meet the breschkada-se, and then the breschkada-sa. Though, in fact, you're no longer breschkada." She glanced past John at Nikaela's body. "That ceased to be the moment she died. You're now just a common-face Blacksword."

John hoped to put a crack in her confidence, even if only a tiny one. "You said your people would crucify you if you killed a Kelk breschkada, but you did kill her." The fellow holding John's left elbow tensed.

Nvalheim sneered in disgust and shook her head. "No, Blacksword. Silas Palmutter killed her, and he as much as admitted it—" She looked past John to one of the young men holding him. "—didn't he?"

The fellow sounded tense as he said, "Yes, grand dame."

John had hoped to crack Nvalheim's confidence, but it appeared he had instead damaged that of the young man behind him holding his right arm. "No," John said. "He admitted to stabbing her, but she was alive and might have remained so had you not pulled that blade from her chest. When you did so, you killed her."

Clutching desperately at the medallion between her breasts, she leaned forward and spit in John's face, "No." But then she looked past him and spoke to one of the young men behind him. "He's a Blacksword. Don't let his lies fool you. He's probably already gotten into your head, and as he sucks the life out of you, he'll make you doubt everything you value. Don't listen to him."

She stepped back, and with her left hand still grasping the medallion, she looked at the bloodied butcher's dagger in her right hand, Nikaela's dagger. Her eyes widened with fear, but then she looked at John and that morphed into joy. She lunged forward, cried out and stabbed the blade into John's chest.

Pain blinded him and he tried to scream but he couldn't. His knees buckled and the two kriegers sandwiching him held him up. He couldn't speak. He couldn't move. But he found the strength to get his feet beneath him and stand on his own.

"Yes, Blacksword," Nvalheim shouted. "Silas had the right of it, a diaphragm stab, and angled so you don't die right away. It's impossible to breathe, isn't it? Well let me help you just like I helped the girl."

She reached out, grabbed the hilt of the dagger and yanked it out of John's chest.

John fought to stand on his own, and now with nothing to lose, he decided to play the card Nikaela had told him never to use. "I claim . . . right of vendetta."

With those words everything froze: the two kriegers holding him, Nvalheim clutching her medallion and the twice bloodied dagger, and everyone watching them.

"Vendetta," Nvalheim said. "You're not Kelk. You can't claim right of vendetta."

John now understood why Nikaela had struggled to breathe, but pulling the dagger from his chest had helped a little. "I claim right of vendetta . . . for my family who died on Novalis III."

The two men holding him tensed again.

"I claim right of vendetta . . . for my twenty million countrymen . . . who died on Novalis III."

The young man on his right released his arm and stepped back.

"I claim right of vendetta . . . for my breschkada-se."

The young man on his left released his arm and stepped back.

Still clutching the medallion, Nvalheim looked at the two young men. "He's in your heads, isn't he?"

She held up the dagger and looked at it carefully, turned it to the right, then to the left, as if she wanted to know and recognize every inch of the thing before she used it to finish John. "It's time to end this, Blacksword. And your breschkada-se gave me just the right weapon." She looked carefully at the point, turning the blade toward her. "And it has the perfect point to rightfully bring a criminal to justice."

At that moment she stood less than a step from John, looking straight down the blade, the point aimed at her face.

John dove for her, put every bit of strength he had into his right arm and slammed the heel of his palm into the base of her fist where the tip of the hilt was visible. The force of his blow jammed the blade up into her face. He aimed for her eye, the easiest point of entry into the brain. But he missed and it entered her left nostril. The blade came to a stop with about four inches of it buried up in the bone of her sinuses.

People screamed and gunshots rang out, but he ignored them, and so did she. She stood there, holding onto the hilt of the dagger jammed into her nose, her eyes wide, her mouth open. He swung his damaged left arm around her shoulders, hooking her neck in the crook of his elbow. Then he again slammed the heel of his right palm into her fist and the base of the dagger, grunting with the effort as he did so, driving the blade deeper into her skull. He repeated that again, and again, and each time he buried the blade deeper, until the point punched out through the back of her skull about two inches above her brain stem.

She dropped out of his arms like a rag doll, and he stood over her swaying from side to side like a drunk. He desperately tried to get air into his lungs, every shallow, little breath producing a sharp stab of pain.

Nvalheim's two young kinsmen lay dead at his feet. He spotted Taugrim near Primatov and the diplomatic mission. She wore a blue armband, held a grav pistol casually at her side, and another krieger wearing a blue armband lay dead at her feet. John glanced around the room, saw more of *Drakan Helgis*'s officers wearing blue armbands, all armed and standing over dead or captured kriegers.

Aubrecht Machtberg declared, "Well done people." He strode confidently across the floor and stopped standing over Nvalheim's corpse. "I'm taking command and we'll get this mess cleaned up."

The floor swayed beneath John and he staggered. Machtberg threw a fatherly arm around his shoulders to steady him. "We need to get this young man some medical attention."

He looked John in the eyes. "And I do believe vendetta has been served."

John shook his head. "Not quite."

Machtberg frowned. "What?"

With the last bit of strength he had, John reached across to his left hip and drew his own butcher's dagger. He thrust upward, buried it in Machtberg's solar plexus and the man grunted. Just as quickly John yanked the blade out, and using it the way it was meant to be used, he jammed it up under the man's chin into his brain.

Machtberg fell to the floor, gurgling and choking on his own blood. What seemed a century ago Kristdokar had told John that the butcher's skills did not translate well to the talents needed for a swift execution, and John now understood why. There was a lot of bone in the way when trying to get the damn blade into the brain from that angle.

He bent down over one of the dead kriegers and retrieved the fellow's grav pistol. He saw Primatov marching across the floor toward him as he pressed the muzzle of the pistol against the side of Machtberg's head, pulled the trigger and blew his brains out all over the floor.

One more to go, and then he could die. He turned, looking for Strikland, but found Primatov standing in his way. "No, John. It has to stop now."

Still struggling to breathe, he gasped, "He's . . . guilty. He has to . . . die."

Shaking her head, she leaned close to him and lowered her voice. "We have no proof. If you kill him here, in front of witnesses, the Commonwealth will hang you. Leave it to me. I made you a promise. I'll get the proof, and make sure vendetta is served correctly."

Taugrim stepped up beside her. "She's right, Blacksword. Let her worry about that, while we lay your breschkada-se to rest properly."

John engaged the safety on the grav pistol and dropped it. It clattered on the floor as he turned and looked down at Nikaela. He sat down on the concrete beside her and rested her head in his lap. When he closed her eyes, if he ignored all the blood she seemed rather peaceful.

He recalled sitting in his parents' small apartment on Novalis III, holding his mother's lifeless body in his arms. He had always thought his journey had begun the day his father had died, but he realized now that had only been a prelude. His real journey had begun that day holding his mother in his arms, and it ended now holding Nikaela in his arms.

••••

"You were lucky."

It took a moment for the surgeon's words to penetrate John's thoughts. "Lucky, how so?"

Baldness was quite rare among Kelk men, but the surgeon was an exception. "The blade did some nasty damage to your diaphragm, but it didn't hit anything vital, and didn't cut into anything that might cause you to bleed out. But it was close to a few critically important things, and if that old woman hadn't removed it, your exertions might have changed that outcome. In an odd way, I suppose she saved your life."

Nikaela had not been so lucky.

Two days after Nvalheim's failed coup attempt, speed healing and rapid regrowth had helped John recover sufficiently to stand on his own, though he walked with a noticeable limp. He put on his service dress blues with a coat that didn't include the special sheath for the butcher's dagger; he had decided he would not wear that again. He checked his uniform carefully, then made his way to the staging room for *Drakan Helgis*'s aft personnel hatch. Because of the circumstances, John had been allowed to dictate who would attend: Primatov, Catarvin, May, Karya, Carla, Leeze, Matsen, Taugrim, Kristdokar, and Brynjar. He would have included Thordahl, but the command superior had been on one of the boats the transfer station had blown out of the sky the day of the coup, and they had laid him to rest earlier along with Kolbeck.

Taugrim put *Drakan Helgis* on a collision course with Viktorkinde's sun, and that day they laid Nikaela to rest. Like so many before her, she would become the stuff of stars.

••••

Tarsik Obradour recovered from his injuries, though if medical care had been delayed by another hour or so, he might not have.

It was reported in the news feeds that Silas Palmutter died of a massive stroke while on Viktorkinde, though a different story circulated through the rumor mill on Trafalgar. Those in the know heard he had died during a tryst with a male Kelk prostitute in which some very dangerous drugs were involved.

Erdstadter committed suicide, probably fearing that John might claim the right of vendetta from him as well. It turned out that suicide before the claim was made was one way to protect his offspring from the right of vendetta, because one can't claim the right of vendetta against a dead person.

The Supremacy did not recognize Seergentmeister Kelbacher's warrant promotion to command boss. In fact, they simply pretended it never happened, and when John met her briefly before returning to the Commonwealth she seemed pleased with the status quo.

Kristdokar received a promotion to major skalde and was elevated to the Larscom General Secretariat. Rumor had it that she would eventually take a seat on the Executive Council, though not for some years to come.

Brynjar received a promotion and took command of First Liaison Company.

Anders Eindride was surprised to learn that he had never gone to Novalis III, never been cashiered, never lost his rank, never spent any time in SecureMax. In fact, according to his file he had served continuously as an officer with a spotless record, and recently distinguished himself working under cover for the Executive Council, though the details of that were all hush-hush. That was all news to Anders, but he could live with that. He did receive a nice promotion, and returned to Hyerdride, where he and Viktra happily entered into a birthing contract.

Interstellar war between the Commonwealth and the Supremacy never came to pass.

Epilogue:

A Promise

OUT ON THE street outside the hotel, rain slanted down at a sharp angle, adding to the gloom of a cloud-darkened night, and filling the gutters with a torrent of water. It was always the same on Norandyne. Katrine had heard that once or twice every tenday the clouds cleared to reveal a brilliant blue sky and verdant, green vegetation, but she wondered at the veracity of that information. She had been to the damn planet a dozen times, and not once had she experienced anything but rain and gloom, skies so dark that those from off-planet might easily mistake mid-day for early evening.

Her thoughts drifted back to that point in time two years ago standing in the Hyvaldsborg Palace and facing John Mathius. With her right arm missing because of a crush wound, pain had clouded her thoughts, but she distinctly remembered that moment with stark clarity. She had made him a promise then, and every day since, her failure to keep her word vexed her no end.

A grav car floated up to the pedestrian quay in front of the hotel, the dark shadow of a lone passenger barely visible in the back seat.

"Miss Fallon."

At the sound of the name of her assumed identity, Katrine turned to face the bell captain, a small man with typically dark, Norandynian features. He wore a tailcoat modeled after styles of a far distant past, and a black, broad-brimmed hat, all classic attire for a Norandynian.

He smiled pleasantly. "We're most pleased to see you again. What has it been, at least a couple of years since we last had the pleasure of your company?"

Katrine returned his smile, recalling that her last visit to that mud-ball had been shortly after Nvalheim's failed coup attempt. "Yes, it has been a couple of years."

His eyes brightened. "What brings you here this time?"

She shrugged. "A promise."

He extended his arm. "May I help you to your car?"

"Thank you," she said. "That's most kind of you."

He gave her a warm smile. "I'm pleased to be of service, madam."

He escorted her out to the car, shielding her from the rain with the gravity field of his greatcoat. When he opened the rear door of the vehicle, she bent down and stepped into it, sitting next to the car's only passenger.

As the car sped away, the man seated next to her said, "Colonel Blacksword, it's good to see you again."

She looked at him carefully. "Thank you, Major. Is everything ready?"

He nodded. "We have everything prepared as you instructed. It took a lot of time and work to entice him to come here personally, but he's here, and anxious to meet with us. Well, not actually us. He's anxious to meet with some criminals who he thinks will further his agenda. By the time we get there, he should be in custody."

She smiled and nodded. "Excellent."

He handed her a small pistol-shaped object. "You asked me to supply this. It's nonlethal, painless, and can be turned off in an instant with an antidote."

In her hand Katrine held a small gun that fired darts that immediately dissolved when in contact with human bodily fluids.

They rode in silence to the same warehouse where she had met with Thordahl and Brynjar a couple of times. The car pulled up to the pedestrian quay in front of it, they climbed out, then rushed the short distance through the rain and into the building. Ed Fleming and a few of his nullheads stood waiting for them outside a small, inner office.

Katrine noted four body-bags arranged in a neat row on the concrete floor. "His bodyguards?"

Fleming nodded. "They didn't want to listen to reason."

Inside the small office, Lawrence Strikland sat at a Spartan table with two of Fleming's nullheads standing nearby. He exuded confidence as Katrine removed her raincoat and tossed it over the back of a chair.

She sat down at the table opposite him and smiled politely. "Mr. Strikland."

He returned her smile. "Colonel Blacksword, to what do I owe the pleasure?"

She looked into his eyes. "I know you came here to meet with some very unpleasant people to set up some very illegal business operations."

He shrugged, displaying not the slightest bit of concern. "But the only people I've met with are your people, so you have no evidence against me."

"That is true," she said. "But I'm not concerned with the reason you came to Norandyne, only that you did."

He raised a curious eyebrow. "I'm intrigued."

Time to change the subject. "Were you aware that Skalde Kristdokar uncovered evidence that pointed to Jenine Catarvin as complicit in the tragedy on Novalis III?"

He frowned and shook his head. "No, I was not, though knowing Senator Catarvin, I'd be surprised if that were true. I really can't imagine she would get involved in something like that."

"Me too," Katrine said. "So I investigated, followed the money as it were, which ultimately led to laundered money deposited into the corporate accounts of a company owned by her husband."

He pursed his lips. "That alone isn't conclusive, but I'll bet you looked closer and found more."

"Yes," Katrine said, "I did, and we discovered that the bank records of her husband's company had been manipulated by external players, a small group that does a lot of cyber contract work for a company you own. Dots, Mr. Strikland. We identified a dot or two from them,"

He didn't react in the slightest, and she continued. "That dot led to another dot, and another, and eventually we connected the dots to you, Mr. Strikland."

He shook his head slowly. "You can prove nothing."

Now she grinned. "But we can. We have hard proof that you were as responsible for Novalis III as Marta Nvalheim, and at this point we even have hard data on your interactions with her leading up to that mess. We have a smoking gun, Mr. Strikland."

He continued to shake his head. "I'm confident I can prove my innocence, so let's go to court and have a magistrate decide how good your evidence is."

"No," she said. "We're not going to prosecute."

He frowned.

She stood and lifted her raincoat off the back of a chair, then shrugged into it. "You'll spend millions on lawyers and bribes, and it won't go to trial for years. And by then you'll have eliminated witnesses and contaminated evidence, and the picture that is so clear now will have turned murky gray."

She pulled out the small dart gun, aimed it at him and shot him in the chest. He frowned, stood, and touched his hand to the center of his chest. "What did you do?"

She didn't answer him.

"Dammit, what did you do? You can't . . . you . . ."

His voice trailed off and his eyes fluttered. He reached out and leaned on the table to steady himself. She nodded to the two nullheads; they stepped in and helped him sit in the chair. She didn't want him to fall and hurt himself.

Ed Fleming and his nullheads bundled Strikland up, then carried him and his dead bodyguards out to a grav truck. Katrine and the major followed them in the car out to a small airstrip, where they boarded an assault boat. Twenty minutes later the boat docked in the hangar bay of a Special Operations Blacksword destroyer. The destroyer's captain set the ship on a collision course with Norandyne's sun, and they ejected the body-bags containing the bodyguards.

Katrine had thought long and hard about what do to with Strikland if the day ever came when she could do something about him. She didn't want to simply put a bullet in his head. That seemed too quick and easy. And she didn't believe in torture, except as a means to get information, but there were usually much better ways to accomplish that. She wanted Strikland to have some time to contemplate his fate, and to understand that he could not escape paying for twenty million lives.

They had disabled all the systems in a lifeboat, everything but life support, and the receive function of its com. They placed Strikland in a bunk in the lifeboat, gave him the antidote to the dart, and as the major had promised, he awoke immediately.

"What are you doing?" he demanded. "I have a right to know."

Fleming's nullheads ignored him, and as he shouted orders at them, they sealed the lifeboat and ejected it.

Katrine opened a com channel to the lifeboat. "Mr. Strikland, this is Colonel Blacksword. You're in a lifeboat on a collision course with Norandyne's sun, and six hours from now you'll plunge into the surface of that star, though I don't think you'll live more than about five hours. By that time I'm sure you'll find the temperature in the lifeboat pretty extreme."

The destroyer changed course so they didn't collide with the star, and they tracked the lifeboat for the next six hours. It didn't actually plunge into the surface of the star because so much of it was vapor long before it got there.

••••

John awoke sitting in a chair in the shade on a beach and thinking of Carla. He had fallen asleep reading an article in one of the news feeds about the new supervisor of the forty-third precinct in Trafalgar City. Macus DeLeon had just declared his candidacy for a senate seat, a big step up for a rising young star in the political world. The polls favored him strongly because his fundraising efforts had proven quite successful. John didn't care to dig any deeper into the story, but he suspected that if he did, he'd find Lawrence Strikland had something to do with that. When little things like that brought Strikland to mind, John had to forcefully suppress his feelings and frustration regarding the man.

After the diplomatic mission returned to Trafalgar, Carla's and John's different assignments had sent them lightyears apart. But then two years later they both found themselves in the Miriteen system. She arranged for a little bungalow on a beach and he joined her there. And while lying on a beach was more her style, upon arrival the previous night, he had thoroughly enjoyed their reunion in the bungalow.

He spotted her crossing the beach and carrying a couple of fruity drinks. Fruity drinks were also not his style, but when Carla wore almost nothing on a beach, it was sexier than if she walked around just plain naked. He'd happily drink plenty of fruity drinks just to watch her carrying the damn things across the sand.

She sat down in the chair next to him, handed him a drink and grinned. "You do realize that when you look at me like that, it's pretty obvious what you're thinking."

He grinned back at her. "And as I recall, those thoughts frequently lead to you having a rather good time."

"Yes," she said, sipping her drink. "There is that. On second thought, you have my permission to keep having those thoughts."

A young bellman from the hotel that provided the bungalows stopped at the edge of their shade. "Lieutenant Mathius."

John looked the fellow's way. "That's me."

He held out a small, flat package. "This arrived for you. It's got a Blacksword priority stamp on it."

Carla's eyes widened as John took the package and thanked the young man. In it he found a small envelope. He opened the envelope and from it took out a small card.

Actual written messages sent over interstellar distances were extremely rare, and the message on the card had actually been hand-written.

> John
> I think Nikaela will now rest easier. I know I will,
> and I hope you will too.
> Vendetta has been served.
> > Katrine Primatov

Carla leaned forward and asked, "What is it?"

John couldn't stop smiling. "She kept her promise."

Acknowledgements

I'D LIKE TO thank Clyde, Tory and Dave for fixing all my dotted t's and crossed i's, and for their invaluable insight, criticism and advice, Karen for both supporting my dream and being my most valuable critic, and Steve Himes, and the whole team at Telemachus, for getting a quality product out the door.

Books by J. L. Doty

Series: The Treasons Cycle
Of Treasons Born
A Choice of Treasons

Stand Alone Novel
The Thirteenth Man

Series: The Gods Within
Child of the Sword
The SteelMaster of Indwallin
The Heart of the Sands
The Name of the Sword

Series: The Dead Among Us
When Dead Ain't Dead Enough
Still Not Dead Enough
Never Dead Enough

Series: The Blacksword Regiment
A Hymn for the Dying
A Dirge for the Damned
A Prayer for the Fallen
A Requiem for the Forsaken

Series: Commonwealth Re-contact Novellas
Tranquility Lost

About the Author

JIM IS A full-time SF&F writer, scientist and laser geek (Ph.D. Electrical Engineering, specialty laser physics), and former running-dog-lackey for the bourgeois capitalist establishment. He's been writing for over 30 years, with 15 published books. His first success came through self-publishing when his books went word-of-mouth viral, and sold enough that he was able to quit his day-job, start working for himself and write full time—his new boss is a real jerk. That led to contracts with traditional publishers like Open Road Media and Harper Collins Voyager, and his books are now a mix of traditional and self-published.

The four novels in his new hard science fiction series, *The Blacksword Regiment*, were released in July 2020. Right now he's fleshing out ideas for the next book in *The Dead Among Us*, he's writing another episode in *The Treasons Cycle*, and he's working on a new fantasy series *The Deck of Chaos*.

Jim was born in Seattle, but he's lived most of his life in California, though he did live on the east coast and in Europe for a while. He now resides in Arizona with his wife Karen and three little beings who claim to be cats: Tilda, Julia and Natasha. But Jim is certain they're really extra-terrestrial aliens in disguise.

Visit the author's website at http://www.jldoty.com
Contact the author at jld@jldoty.com